Horses and Heartbeats

Horses and Heartbeats

Polly Thompson

Copyright © 2010 by Polly Thompson.

Library of Congress Control Number: 2009912862
ISBN: Hardcover   978-1-4500-0814-3
                 Softcover   978-1-4500-0813-6

All rights reserved. No part of this book may be reproduced or transmitted in any form or by any means, electronic or mechanical, including photocopying, recording, or by any information storage and retrieval system, without permission in writing from the copyright owner.

This is a work of fiction. Names, characters, places and incidents either are the product of the author's imagination or are used fictitiously, and any resemblance to any actual persons, living or dead, events, or locales is entirely coincidental.

This book was printed in the United States of America.

To order additional copies of this book, contact:
Xlibris Corporation
1-888-795-4274
www.Xlibris.com
Orders@Xlibris.com
69279

Introducing, *in order of appearance:*

Brownie
Researcher
Smokey
Safe Flight
Quaker Lace
Corn Cob
Hickory Nut
Banner
Barrister
Escort
Spirit Lake
Dakota Clover
Tannenbaum
Copper Penny
Midnight

Dedicated to the wellbeing of our longstanding friends, the horses.

Chapters

1. Horse Country 11
2. A Horse Show 17
3. A Horse For Sale 32
4. Smokey 39
5. A Private Lesson 45
6. A Setback 51
7. Schemes 59
8. A Group Lesson 67
9. All Kinds, Her Kind 73
10. From the Stands 85
11. A Torn Jacket 95
12. Home for a Strawberry Roan 102
13. A Visit from Mrs. Knott 112
14. A Mare With a Mind of Her Own 121
15. No Experience Required? 128
16. Theo in the Center 135
17. A Visit from the Veterinarian 138
18. Primary Care 144
19. School Horses 153
20. A Fresh Horse 162
21. A Personal Best Cut Short 169
22. Down Time 176
23. An Initiation 182
24. A Visit from the Farrier 191
25. A Visit to One Oak 197
26. A Music Lesson 205
27. Bareback 214
28. Hasta la Vista 219
29. New Friends 222
30. A Visit from Andy 227
31. Theo in Charge 231
32. Another Visit From Andy 237
33. Homecoming 240
34. Neighborhood Upheaval 246
35. Strawberry Shortcake 255
36. Good Hands 263
37. Contact at Last 272
38. The Lucky Clovers On Their Way 281
39. Nerves 292
40. In the Race 299
41. Priorities 306
42. A Grand March 316

1

Horse Country

YOU GET A HORSE and you've got your hands full of excitement, could be even more than you're ready for. You'd be surprised by the instincts and intelligence ingrained in this marvelous creature. Horse-keeping takes up an awesome amount of tending and reckoning, and can make you worry and work so hard there'll be times you could plop down and bawl. Of course Bailey Mason hadn't thought of all that all the times she had thought of how wonderful it would be to have her own horse. She had let out a moan escalating to a shriek when she heard her family was to move. Take her a thousand miles east, from Parkwood, a congested Chicago suburb, to a town in Connecticut called *Grennam* but spelled *Greenham*. The British pronunciation just added to the strangeness of it all.

THE RUTTED GRAVEL LOOPS through clumps of stately conifers and shaggy shrubbery, on the approach to a big yellow house standing on enough land to fit six houses in Parkwood. Even more than her own state-of-the-art bathroom, it's the enormous backyard—some three acres of scrub and sparse grass and scattered trees—that intrigues Bailey Mason. There's an old shed out there. The tin roof has rust along the edges, the weathered walls cracks between the boards. Yet the relic has possibilities—once she gets her hands on the horse she's pleaded for ever since her first pony ride. The shed sure is airy, and looks roomier from the inside. She paces it off, figuring three feet for one giant stride—all of fifteen by thirty feet. The wide opening on the south wall suggests this shed was used for livestock. The mound of desiccated lumps in one corner proves it. No excuse for Daddy not to follow through. They were moving to *horse country,* he'd said, but it could have been just to humor her, to sweeten the prospect of an unfamiliar future. Bad enough to be uprooted; even worse for it to happen two months before she would have graduated with all her friends from Parkwood Junior High.

Light falls through the shed's wide doorway. Bailey lingers there in the sun. A beautiful, friendly horse stands beside her. She drapes an arm over its relaxed neck and strokes its broad cheek, and tries to think up the best way to make it all come true.

OUT FOR A RUN that first morning in Greenham, past Custer Lane's back-country mix of woodland, grassland, and fastidiously clipped grounds, Bailey was feeling like a tourist without a passport when, from across a split-rail fence, she spotted a horse.

"Hi, you big brownie!" She propelled herself across a gully and snatched a hank of ditch-grass. Duker jumped after her and sniffed around the underbrush. Framed by a little barn with black shutters, the horse was a magnificent statue, motionless except for the long black tail swaying in the breeze. Bailey waved her bouquet, and the horse lifted its head. The huge haunches shifted; both ears pointed. The early sun caught the glint of a halter, the plaid of a blue blanket. Her heart swelled as she imagined herself galloping astride that big broad back.

Six miles from town was not totally cut off from civilization. Here was big Brownie, after all. But she hadn't seen any humans, even though her brother Michael had reported that two boys lived in the house next door.

"There's Andrew, my age, and Theodore, fifteen," eight year old Michael informed her, wiggling his eyebrows as though expecting the news to excite her. Andrew and Theodore *North,* according to their mailbox. This would be exciting if Theodore was even halfway human. Easterners had always sounded aloof and proper. In four days, she should find out. Greenham's spring break would be over then, and she and Theodore could be riding the same bus.

The next day, Bailey found the big brown horse away from its barn, dozing near the fence. "Always alone, huh Brownie?" She spoke quietly, not to scare this wonderful creature. She itched to finger the black ruff running up that muscular neck. The horse stuck its head out for the feathery grass she offered, and she braced for enormous teeth streaked like old piano keys to yank it out of her hands.

"Just standing around with nothing to do, huh Brownie? Like me, these days." She wanted to stroke the wrinkly nose while the horse was occupied chewing, but couldn't reach that far. Instead, she reached out to Duker. The spaniel had been watering the fence posts, enjoying himself without seeming to bother the horse. She began telling Brownie about Parkwood and her friends in the *Lucky 13* club . . . hyper Sylvia Schermerhorn, arty Emily Ambrose . . . She wished Brownie could talk, and tell her all about Greenham. Her friends had promised to write, but other than one envelope from the State Bank of Greenham addressed, *Philip L. Mason*, the only ones in their mailbox came addressed, *Occupant.*

THE BUS WAS DUE at 7:30. Out the door at 7:20, Bailey inhaled New England's crisp April air while Duker paused to splash a bush. The bowl of oatmeal she'd forced down coated her nervous stomach; moving out with the scampering dog dispelled a little more of the anxiety. Now her feet slowed down and her heartbeat sped up. At the entrance to the driveway stood a boy.

"Yo," he called out before she was halfway there. "You just moved in, right?"

She pulled up hardly out of breath, but her heartbeat on high. With the sense of getting a guarded once-over, she flashed her lashes. She had lovely green eyes, according to her grandmother. Probably he'd notice her reddish-brown hair first, gelled tight to her scalp today. She hoped some bizarre curl hadn't sprouted while she was running. This might be a guy she could really like. No doubt he'd take her figure into account: average height, kind of stocky. All muscle, though. She'd been the strongest fourteen-year-old in the Parkwood School of Gymnastics.

"Theodore North, right? My little brother told me about you," was all she could think to say. "Mikey's the same age as your brother. Sounds like they've been all over the place together. Mikey says Andy showed him some old Indian trails."

"Yeah, just call me Theo." The boy looked off through the trees. "I used to play in the woods lots when I was a kid."

She tried to picture this guy as an eight-year-old. Cute, she bet. Tall and slim, now, with soft blue eyes and soft brown hair falling across his high forehead.

"I'm Bailey—" she'd started to say, just when a burst of brown and white came barking after a rattling gardener's truck, the only vehicle in sight. Custer Lane was mostly birds whistling and pine trees whispering in the wind. The spaniel ran up to Theodore as the truck disappeared over a rise.

"Duker, be good!" Bailey rolled her eyes. The freakin' clown had poked his nose into Theodore's crotch, right in front of her.

"Hey, pooch." Theodore swung his arms to catch the stubby muzzle, scratched the feathery chin. "Dogs are great," he said, glancing up. "My Mom's got allergies, so no pets at our house." Still fondling the elated dog, he added, "Mom's not about to miss Greenham's spring horse show, though.

A nurse at Dad's clinic's entering her new hunter and needs moral support, he says, so the whole family's going. You like horses?"

Bailey's hands flew up. "I love them! I was mad we had to move, but now with all these horses . . . People right up our road have one!"

"Yeah, that's Researcher, Marian Joyner's champion hunter."

"Well, I call him Brownie. I go see him every day. He likes me 'cause I feed him the long grass he can't reach. I almost got to pet his nose, but I'm too short. Boy, would I like to get on his back!"

"How come you didn't want to move? I grew up in this town. Greenham's cool." Sunshine flickering through the trees lit up Theodore's face. He'd cocked his head, as though waiting for her answer. He seemed really interested, which made it easier to explain.

"See, graduation from junior high is a big deal in Parkwood, but I won't be there. I'm missing parties, yearbook swapping and signings, a big dance with all the kids. Here is foreign country compared to where I grew up. To make up for all I'm missing," her eyes twinkling, "my father's getting me a horse. We're on as much land here as practically our whole neighborhood in Parkwood."

"Yeah, more than enough for a horse. And there's that shed out back."

"I hope it's still usable. Loose boards and peeling paint shouldn't matter that much. To a horse, anyways. Trouble is, my father's darn particular."

"There's the bus." Theodore slung his book bag over his shoulder. "Say, did your dad change jobs?"

"The same company, promoted to sales manager for all New England. His office used to be in Chicago." The bus rumbled to a stop, so noisily Theo probably didn't hear her mention they'd lived in a busy suburb near O'Hare airport. He'd have no idea how alien she felt. The doors flapped open, and she got a look at the dark-skinned woman perched behind the steering wheel, incredibly tiny to be handling a bus.

"New customer, Gussie!" Theodore stepped up after her. "Name of Bailey Mason." He edged past and headed to the rear.

She found an empty seat. Naturally he would want to sit with his friends. A burst of laughter from the back of the bus sounded like the guys in Parkwood.

2
A Horse Show

"HOW WAS SCHOOL, BEE?"

"Ummn," she hummed through a mouthful of graham crackers. Her mother looked so hopeful, she couldn't say how she really felt. A few kids had said "Hi," but she'd been left on her own to navigate, and it hadn't gotten any better once she'd found her assigned rooms. You couldn't expect Greenham's curriculum to be on the same page as Parkwood's, but the advanced math was totally out of sync.

She swallowed hard. "They've got me in Communications A-group," she said cheerily. This would please her mother. She wouldn't mention the class was a zoo, kids coming out with snide remarks while Miss Perolini held forth in a voice that grated like a drill.

"Well, that's nice."

"Uh huh. We've got a Wallace Stegner story to read tonight, which might be good." She slathered peanut butter over another cracker. This seemed like a good time to bring up the horse show. "It's this Saturday, Mom. I hung out with Theo before the bus, and he's going." She bit into the gooey, sweet graininess, her comfort food. At lunch, she'd been too wound up to eat much.

"Hm, the older brother. What's he like?"

17

"Nice, I guess. Doesn't particularly like girls, though."

Her mother laughed. "That may or may not be true, sweetie. At least he's someone to talk to."

"I guess. There's nobody else around. That's why I need a horse. Can we go to that show?"

Her mother's lips slipped sideways with regret. "Sorry, Bee. Too much here to do."

Slowly Bailey screwed the top back on the peanut butter jar, as her wits scurried for a solution. In Parkwood, they wouldn't have minded dropping her off to join up with her group. She couldn't ask the Norths to take her, she didn't even know them. But if she found someone at school—

"We could drop you off, Bee. It should be safe enough if you find someone to go with."

BAILEY WAS DEVOURING THE *Greenham Gazette's* write-up for *A Day in the Country,* when it struck her that the massive stone gates in the photo were the same ones she'd peered through from her bus. Wherever she went, she kept an eye out for horses. When at last she could step through those gates, she expected a view abounding with horses. But the field she found herself in that Saturday had row upon row of motor vehicles. She headed for the striped yellow and white tents spearing the horizon, and kept looking left and right down the rows of shiny metal. At last, horses: two, and two girls with cobblers' aprons over their breeches, busily sweeping imperceptible flecks of dust off hides that already glinted like they'd come through a car-wash. Right, *she* would be just as fussy. She took a little skip and scurried on. A raucous whinny split the air. Stamping and stomping came from a trailer bouncing on its wheels. A young couple in long jackets and tall boots pushed at the bar across the back door. This demanded a detour, to see how horses got transferred long distances. The trailer shook alarmingly. Suddenly the back door swung open. Bailey's hands flew to her throat as a humongous horse with its legs wrapped up to the knees backed out and banged down the ramp. Through all the clatter, the two palominos by the next trailer dozed on their drooping ties. "Hi, guys," she mouthed to those two. They looked so sweet—the kind of horse *she* wanted.

The sound of hoof beats grew louder as she approached the last tightly parked row. Her heart accelerated in anticipation, and then soared. Even more magnificent than she'd been counting on. Grays, browns, blacks, bright coppery-chestnuts, and spotted white horses filled the field of faded stubble on her right. Horses limbering up trotted the margins in a business-like manner; hides steamed from horses resting over their locked knees. Strains of leather on leather; gleaming hides rippling over powerful muscles—the reality of it all was awesome. Hoof beats reverberated through the soles of Bailey's feet as a big bay galloped by, rocking its long, shapely neck to the beat of its long, rhythmic stride. A surge of positive energy shot up her spine. She zoomed in on one horse after another, loath to miss a thing. A gangly black toward the middle of the field was getting sent back and forth over a flimsy pole set higher than its nose. Now a tall, skinny chestnut took off, racing for another jump. She gasped when the fence-poles burst into the air like toothpicks.

In the field across the lane, riders with serious expressions on their faces strutted about in groups, obviously pacing off distances between the widely-spaced jumps. No horses involved, so she turned back to the warm-up field. It was after nine before she tore herself away, suddenly remembering she'd arranged to meet Glenna Munro at eight-thirty. She hurried on, hopping to one side for a sweaty horse sauntering up the lane, then headed for the food stand, where Glenna Munro had suggested they meet.

"Magnum ice-tea with strawberry syrup, please." Bailey dug out cash from her Parkwood baby-sitting cache and, for the umpteenth time, peered through the mob of marching horses and mingling people for a telling mop of pale yellow hair. Nine-thirty already, and her new friend hadn't shown up.

She had asked every girl she knew at school Friday if they liked horses. By the time she got back to her locker, she still hadn't found anyone to meet her at the show. She had her hoodie off the hook and was staring blindly into the metal abyss when a pile of books came crashing out of the next locker over.

"Gawd, this isn't my day." A girl with shoulder length hair the color of corn silk had her peep toe oxford off and was massaging her foot.

"Here, let me help." Bailey stooped down. In the process of rearranging the mess into a sturdy pile, she discovered that all the books concerned horses. *Veterinary Notes for Horse Owners* in hand, she looked up with a toothy grin across her face. This girl was crazy about horses! Her name was Glenna Munro, and, of course she'd be going to Greenham's spring horse show.

"Just one person?" her mother had groaned. "You take my cell phone and leave it on, in case I need to reach you."

"Oh, sure!" In case *she* needed to call, her mother really meant.

Bailey gazed back down the lane for Glenna. What a crime to miss all this. Manes tidily tied into tiny braids; brightly colored ankle wraps; white rubber hoof-cups that flopped conspicuously with every footfall. A smooth-moving gray, unadorned except for a polished saddle, caught her eye, and then was blocked when a clone of the Black-Stallion swept by. The elderly gentleman in the saddle was wearing a bowler hat and carrying a bone-handled whip—right out of a hunting print! A few feet away, another man, wearing a feather in his Tyrolean hat, slapped a shimmering rump going by. The horse shied, and the rider jerked around, shooting the trespasser a fierce look. Lesson #1: Handling another person's property without permission is totally unacceptable. She could identify, though—horses horses everywhere, and not one for her to pet.

The sharp pop of a backfire gave her a start. She looked, then looked again. Theodore North was talking to some guys by an old pickup truck. Now he was climbing into the truck, which coughed, sputtered, and chugged off toward the gate. Obviously, Theodore had had his fill of horses.

Shouting from Ring B sent Bailey skirting the struts of a striped canopy casting shade on a group of tables and folding chairs. She had sidestepped a steaming hill of droppings and managed to worm herself up to the rail, when a cry of, "Heels down!" rang in her ears. A woman with her hair-clips coming loose was shaking her finger at a little girl on a little spotted pony. Ring B was full of ponies. Bailey tracked the spotted one's bobbing rump, her heart going out to the rider, whose pigtails kept hitting her shoulders. The pony pattered along the rail, but another one charged across the ring, sending the judge into a matador's twirl.

"Pull your left rein," a man leaning into the ring shouted.

"Johnny, sit up," directed at a chubby boy on a chubbier pony. "Kick him, kick him, hit him with your crop!"

Bailey's emotions wavered between envy and empathy. These kids were doing their best, they just needed practice. "The girth, the girth!" sounded in her ears, and her eyes darted up the rail for flopping pigtails. The little girl was at a tilt with both pigtails swinging toward the same side. The woman clutched the rail, her face flaming red. "Oh, sweetie, push that stirrup down hard!"

"Aaand, walk," the ringmaster intoned, raising a sigh of relief from everyone around. The red-faced woman squeezed through the rails and lumbered across the ring. Rescue in effect, Bailey looked around for Glenna Munro. A bunch of big, glossy horses had gathered at the gate. Some of the riders looked about *her* age. She'd never seen Brownie with his mane in braids, but one horse there did look familiar. A pretty gray at the edge of the group traveled in short, bouncy steps, tracking loopy circles with the rider's left leg hitched up on its shoulder. The rider's hand was under the saddle flap, tugging at a girth strap. It looked awkward, but must be better than stopping and getting off to fix something. Hopefully, before long *she* would get to do that.

She was imagining herself up on the pretty gray, when cold hands blanked her vision. She wriggled around, then melted with joy under Glenna Munro's pearly smile.

"You made it! Oh, you missed—"

"Me mater drove me insane. Forty minutes of her precious time from town here and back, and she keeps putting it off." Even in jeans, Glenna looked like she'd stepped right off a page of *Seventeen*. The stenciled sheepskin vest she wore made Bailey, in her old Parkwood sweatshirt, feel like she was wearing a tent. Glenna rested her water bottle on the rail next to Bailey's tall cup and struck a pose with her high-laced boot propped on its toe. "Sorry, Bailey, I kept thinking of you wandering around alone. Though," and she laughed, "I don't know anybody here either."

"I did see somebody. Theodore North, practically the only guy I know in Greenham. He lives next door to me."

Glenna's trendy boot toppled off its toe. "Oh, you lucky," she gasped. "He is so fine."

"Huh, horses bore him. Last I saw, he took off with some guys." Bailey cupped her hand over what was left of her tea and squinted into the dust drifting across the ring. The pony class had reversed and appeared quite orderly now. When she was as little as those kids, she didn't even know horse shows existed.

"What adorable ponies," Glenna crooned, stroking the shock of hair dropping from her tortoise-shell barrette. "Absolutely adorable." She consulted her program while the ribbons were being given out. "The next class is 'Green Hunter Under Saddle.'"

Bailey laughed. "There's lots of grays and browns and blacks here, even caramel colored, but I haven't seen any green ones. None being shown without a saddle on, either."

"I think *green* indicates horses that aren't seasoned, like in their first or second year. *Under saddle* means on the flat, no jumping. I've got my own rule book."

"Really? How'd you get that?"

"At a book sale. I've got a veterinary book, a couple on stable management, and the Pony Club manual."

"Wow." Bailey adjusted her jaw, which she'd caught hanging open. Her horse-reading consisted of stories; she'd never thought of doing research.

"I'll bring you the Pony Club manual. It's real easy to get through."

"Gee thanks." She wasn't sure she'd like to read a whole textbook. She liked to look at real horses and pet them and ride them.

The ponies paraded out. The judge stood up straight and adjusted her skirt. The group parading in included the pretty gray Bailey had noticed before, its coat shining like airy clouds tinted with sunshine. The horse came around swishing its tail back and forth, and the young woman in the saddle looked down at the gaping admirers.

"Hi girls," came a deep, cheery voice.

"That's Cappy Kaufmann," Glenna whispered as the horse traveled on. "I can't believe she'd remember me."

"You know her!?"

"She works at One Oak Stables, head trainer. My dad took me over there one day, back when he'd come see me on weekends. He's off in California now." Spurred by Bailey's fearsome look, Glenna declared, "Yeah, they're splitsville."

"And, trot!" the ringmaster barked. The pretty gray's hocks pumped vigorously, yet the gait appeared smooth, with Cappy Kaufmann barely rising from the saddle. "And, walk," leveled the group's flow, the pretty gray's shiny black toes pointing daintily. "And, canter," sent all together into a sedate rocking gait, except for a rangy bay bent on traveling sideways. Bailey cringed as the rogue advanced on the gray she liked, whose tail swished furiously now. Suddenly the steely gray rump swung out at the bay as though to kick. Bailey stole a look at the judge, who was frowning.

"That blew it," Glenna moaned as Cappy steered into the center. The ribbons were given out, but none to the pretty gray. "From what I've read,"

Glenna said, "it sounds like owning a horse lets you in for big-time trouble. I had to give up begging when it was just me and me mater in a condo."

"A bummer, Glen." Breaking up your family had to be even worse than breaking off from your friends. "When I get a horse, we'll share. It'd be a miracle, though, if we got one even half as pretty as that gray. I've never seen anything so beautiful in person."

"Absolutely. Hey, there's your horse again." The pretty gray marched down the lane beside the short and solid Cappy Kaufmann. The girls hung back, giving way to the eye-boggling parade of horseflesh. The temperature couldn't have been much more than sixty, yet many horses were sweating. Cappy's head barely reached the top of her gray's shoulder and, from time to time, she skipped a few steps to keep up. The girls followed along as if pulled by a magnet.

The parking lot, compared to the strain of competition, was positively tranquil. Cappy tethered her horse to a ringbolt on a big truck with a leafy oak tree painted on its side. She stretched to pull the saddle off the sweat-darkened back, and then propped it carefully against one of the truck's big tires.

"Like to tell her hello?" she said with a little swagger, and waved the girls over. "Meet Quaker Lace, four-year-old filly." The wet, steely hide glistened like a sheet of straight pins. Bailey tried to imagine herself up on the horse's back. She blinked.

Cappy was offering a towel. "How about rubbing Lacy for me?"

She stroked the sweaty neck reverently while Cappy tended to her tack. Glenna engrossed herself with the display of gear set out near the truck. Dreamily Bailey worked the nappy cotton down across the dripping chest, back to the heaving rib cage. This was her horse. She'd rub some more, then walk it around a bit. She'd pet it and tell it all about the little shed at her place, and the big pasture. Unh uh. Horses fine as Lacy needed a real barn, built as good as Brownie's.

"Cappy," Glenna said, "might I ask why you went and stood in the center? That eliminates you, right?"

The trainer winced and threw up her hands. "This sweet li'l ole Lacy was winding up for another one of her wingdings. The judge saw it, so no way could we make the ribbons, not even a pink. Hunters get rated on manners, you know. I figured this dingbat might just as well watch how the more experienced campaigners behaved." She slapped her charge's rump, setting the filly's big eyes at tilt. "Girl, you learned something today, right?" Then, retrieving her towel, she scrubbed out her handprint and smoothed the steely coat so every hair lay in the same direction. Bailey understood this horse. The slightest thing could go wrong when she was in a rebellious mood and make her explode, too.

The girls exchanged startled looks as Cappy hoisted Quaker Lace's tail.

"Just a rush job for now," she said while wiping away the froths of sweat. "I need to be somewhere else right now. I've got a client due on the field course. Novice Field Hunter has fairly low fences, so hopefully this will be a positive experience. For them both. That horse likes to get rolling out in the open."

The newest love of Bailey's life received a round of hasty pats before Cappy led it up the ramp. Once the horse was settled in its stall, the girls rushed off with their new friend to the course that Bailey had noticed before, with the widely-spaced jumps. A powerful looking carrot-colored horse with four white stockings broke from the starting line just when they got there. The long-legged rider looked elegant in her navy blue jacket. Hoof beats grew louder as the horse bounded up the field and headed for an enormous stack of brush. Bailey seized up at the tremendous leap, then let herself breathe as the strapping chestnut went on to negotiate two rustic panels effortlessly. "Hold him Sheri," Cappy muttered as the horse thundered up the course. "Steady, Safe Flight, steady . . . " Bailey shut her eyes against flying dirt clods as the horse barreled past. When she opened them, the chestnut was making a mad rush toward a massive spread of logs.

"Whoa, whoa," echoed across the field. Cappy's expression was grim. Sheri was leaning back and tugging. "Turn, you bastard," groaned Cappy. Instead of jumping, the brute had veered off and was lunging against the bit. Sheri pitched forward, smack against the upright neck. An anguished cry rose from the crowd. The horse was in charge now—head up, white legs flashing, it bounded along as if bent on jumping the moon. At the last minute before the last obstacle, it swerved and charged through a gap in the ropes. Cappy swore, and took off after them. Bailey's stomach had tightened into a hard nut. How awful to finally get a horse and have it turn out so stubborn.

A fresh round of cheers and whistles drew the girls over to the main ring, to a more complicated set-up than the hunt course. Not rustic, widely-spaced jumps here, but brightly painted and set closer together in different directions, adorned with extravagant pots of shrubbery. One element looked like a wide stream but had been concocted out of a stretch of blue plastic. To make it all the way over without even the tip on one hoof touching required a huge burst of speed.

"That fence right after the water causes the most faults," Glenna remarked after several horses crashed. Running flat out, one needed to quickly gather itself for the ladder of green striped poles higher than its ear-tips that came up next. One of the few that went clear stumbled upon landing and staggered to a halt.

Bailey groaned: something was wrong with its leg. The rider had jumped off, and was bent over the hoof when a big guy in jeans and sneakers ran out and picked up the reins. Bailey's chin quivered as the horse limped out of the ring.

"The worse kind of elimination," Glenna sighed. She stuck her nose back in the program. "Going off course and not completing a round in the specified time, or knocking a fence down, even leaving half a hoof print in the water, can incur faults. Nothing here about injuries, but that's obvious."

An ominous feeling fell over Bailey. She started walking to shake it off, skirting the crowd as one horse after another entered the ring to tackle the course. Stop thinking about injuries and learn something, she told herself, and began studying the approaches and landings from various angles. The crowd gasped and moaned and cheered. "Hey Theo, don't be such a stranger, son," she surprisingly heard, and turned around. One look and she trotted back for Glenna. Theodore North was here with his parents and a young woman with streaked, crinkly hair, wearing a navy blue riding jacket.

"We can't just go up to him, Bailey. He's with people. I don't know him that well."

"Come on, Glen, there's room on the fence. We can just happen to be standing there. I think the one in navy blue is Dr. North's nurse. Doesn't she look like Cappy's Sheri? Better not say anything about the hunt course."

Theo had seen them, and was coming their way.

"I saw you leave," Bailey teased slyly.

"Sssshh." He edged her and Glenna farther down the rail, muttering that his folks knew nothing about him going AWOL.

"I guess you got tired of looking at horses."

"Yeah, some guys I know from church were trying out their new wheels. A dinged-up pickup that cost a hundred-fifty bucks, but it runs."

Glenna stopped fiddling with her hair and asked for names. Theo glanced back at his parents. His mother was gushing about the "mind-boggling" fences in this class. The horse in the ring, even running all out, negotiated the tight turn to a broad spread of black and white rails flanked by evergreens. Then, with but one stride to gather itself, it took the rails diagonally. Bailey was amazed they stayed up. The jumper galloped on, looking as big and gorgeous as Brownie. Bailey tried to see the rider's face, wondering if it was Marian Joyner. She sent Theo a questioning look, but he wasn't looking.

"You girls wouldn't know those guys," he said as the horse headed out the gate. He grinned sheepishly, adding, "They've sort of got a reputation,' then went on in a drawl about the time the Calderone brothers brought a pot-belly pig to school. "Ha, Billy Calderone had to tie it up in the boiler room, and then they made him clean up after it."

Bailey giggled, and Glenna snickered, egging him on.

"And his brother Chuck is famous for the time he lit up a stogie in the high school rotunda."

"Stogie?" the girls hissed as one.

"You mean 'ganja,' Theo?" Glenna looked horror-struck.

"No, a cigar," he snickered. "Chuck Calderone puts on this cool Groucho act, waving it around in front of everybody. Kids thought it was funny, but he got put on detention."

"Do those guys have horses?" Bailey asked.

"Uh, no. But they work with horses. They're grooms at Ludlow Farms. That's how they saved up bread for that clunker. It's so rusted ten coats of paint wouldn't do it any good."

"It sure was noisy," Bailey said.

Theo let out a devilish laugh.

Bailey moved in, sniffing. "Beer?" she whispered. Not drinking beer and driving!

Theo gulped, shooting another look up the rail. Now his mother was talking about the Greenham Mounties. Once the ring was clear, the troop was due to perform.

"It was supposed to just be a little spin. I'm wedged in the narrow cab and all the sudden we're out the back gate. I almost lost it when this humongous van barrels down on us. Billy makes it to the shoulder just as the monster shudders past."

"While you shuddered, too?" Glenna squawked. Bailey rolled her eyes, then switched back to the excitement in the ring.

"Probably shoulda told somebody," Theo muttered. "No way would they let me take off in that old heap, though. The passenger door doesn't really shut. Ha, Billy's my age and doesn't even have a license."

"My mom would kill me," Glenna moaned.

"I didn't have that much to drink," he claimed, looking down his nose. "What could I do? Chuck keeps saying, 'On to Bepi's, on to Bepi's,' which turns out to be this crummy dive in Byrich. I've never even been to Byrich. The entire business district is one short block."

"Me mater's dragged me to more than a few of those dives," Glenna volunteered. "I get to sit there while she makes eyes at some guy she doesn't even know."

"Actually, it's my first for a place like that. Not the Calderones', though. Chuck high-fives everybody and tips his cap to the cook. They both know the guy behind the bar, and they sure know good pizza." The mention of pizza made Bailey's mouth water. She could almost smell a crisp, thin crust drowned in tomato sauce and goopy cheese. She hadn't eaten a thing; she was thirsty again, too.

"I s'pose you downed a whole pitcher, Theo," she said.

"Yeah, so what if we did."

Her mouth quirked in disgust. She wanted a ride on a horse, while he wanted a ride in a truck "So, you missed out on some gorgeous horseflesh," she said, and had begun to tell him about meeting Quaker Lace and Cappy Kaufmann, when a tangerine-colored convertible pulled up. The woman at the wheel flicked her long, flying hair at Glenna, then whisked her daughter away.

"Hot car," Theo said.

"Gee, she got here hours late, and now she has to leave already." Bailey sighed. "At least she got to see these beautiful horses and speak with a trainer. Horses are awesome when you get up close, Theo. You should have hung around."

"Yeah. But the whole thing seemed kinda cool, at the time." He shrugged. "I feel kinda guilty now though, getting away with it all."

"Be a lamb, Theo, run back for our cake?" His mother had tracked him down. He seemed fine with it: his face lit up and, with a quick salute was off—clearly happy for a chance to make up for not sticking around. Poles clattered to the ground as the fences were dismantled. A wave of exhaustion hit Bailey, and she flopped down. She leaned back on her elbows and watched old wooden flatbeds haul the standards, poles, and pots of greenery out of the ring. Her mind swirled with horses, and happiness over getting better acquainted with Theo. Curious rumblings rose through the ground, a steady thumping. The idea of hooves on the march brought her to her knees.

Sheared manes showed off the proudly arched necks. Ten rows, four abreast, every horse in the troop a gleaming brown. The trappings clinked and jingled as they swung around to the arena. Bailey was on her feet, admiring how smoothly they split off into single file, when Theo ran up.

"Hey, check out the Mounties," he exclaimed as he slid to a stop beside Bailey. He stood riveted with his feet firmly planted, and simply gaped. His mother relieved him of the cake-pan and cut out two large pieces. "Sure didn't expect to see the cavalry here today," Theo remarked out of the side of his cake-engorged mouth. Bailey bit into her creamily-frosted chunk. The horses had lined up nose to tail in front of the gate, gold braid glinting off the riders' horizontally-set hat brims. A sharp volley of trumpet notes punctured the air.

The troop moved out, and surged up the center line: yellow-checkered neckerchiefs fluttered at upright shoulders; striped red and white banners rippled high over glossy rumps. The ground shook as, one by one, horses peeled off left and right to stream back along opposite rails. Engulfed in a dusty rumble of drumbeats and squeaky leather, Bailey stopped chewing and simply stared. She was oblivious to crumbs, too engrossed to swallow.

But she hadn't forgotten Theo. She nudged him and sent him a quizzically happy look. His exuberant, wide-eyed response nearly made her burst.

The horses were traveling at a fast-paced trot when each column all at once pivoted ninety degrees, head on for the center line. Still trotting. Bailey clutched the rail, praying they wouldn't collide. At this pace, somebody'd get hurt. But incredible military precision passed the chargers in between each other to carry on to the opposite rail.

"Magnifico," Theo said, sounding as awestruck as she was.

The troop came around eight abreast in a splendid five-row formation. A series of complicated drills sent chargers swirling up and down and around the ring. In a breathtaking climax, they came pouring out of all four corners to cut the ring diagonally in a mighty crisscross.

"Magnifico," Bailey heard again. Theo was impressed, too, his heart maybe beating as hard as hers! Hers pounded so hard she could feel it against the fence.

3

A Horse For Sale

"THE TYPICAL BRUSH-OFF, THEO. Daddy came home in a good mood but then when I started talking horses, he blew up. Even after I promised to keep my grades up and never ask for anything else, if they'd let me have one!"

"Geez, practically signing your life away. I brought it up to my folks, but didn't go that far."

"You di-id?!" Big smile. It seemed everything Theo did and said made her like him even more. In the last four days since the horse show he'd sat in the second row behind Gussie, with *her*. They rarely ran into each other—she in eighth grade, he in ninth—except on the bus. Her finger-drumming math teacher was keeping her after school lately, okay with her. Mr. Lederle's catch-up sessions landed her on the same bus Theo took after running his miles for track. "Cool, Theo, if we both had horses. A gray's my first choice, like Quaker Lace—the one I told you about at the show? We should at least start to look, but my parents drag their feet. Dinner last night was a bummer." She cringed inside, recalling how her father had slapped his fist on the table.

"Bottom line, my plate is much too full, and that's the truth," he had bellowed. Then, glancing at the small mound of peas left on his plate, he had looked up with a little laugh.

"I'm serious, Daddy! Certainly I'm mature enough for the responsibility! You prahhh-missed . . . "

"Don't you put words in my mouth! I never said I'd get you a horse right away. Things are a helluva lot more expensive than I thought they'd be. A horse falls way down on my list, Miss Narcissist—that's all there is to it."

His *Miss Narcissist* set her off. "This place sucks if I can't have a horse," she cried, jumping up. "Kids here are weird! They make out in the hall in front of anybody and fool around in class. Even Miss Perolini's *A* group! I don't identify with anybody. All those girls in their cliques walking five abreast in everybody's way. The kids back home know how to have fun without being snotty."

"This is home now, get used to it."

"There's Theo," her mother said. "And you've made friends with Gle—"

"Don't mollify her, Beth. It's time Miss Bailey Elizabeth learned the universe does not revolve around her!"

The bus swerved past two bikers and rumbled along. Bailey stroked her stomach, still queasy from last night, and told herself not to think about it anymore.

"You can never find what you're looking for in here," Theo grumbled, thumbing through the Greenham Gazette's back pages. He spread out the paper and flipped the center fold inside. "What about this?" His hand smoothed over the want ads to the livestock columns. The bus picked up speed as Bailey looked where his index finger pointed. She snatched at the paper, but he was quicker.

"Give it here, come on!"

"Ask nicely." His self-satisfied smirk enraged her. But a horse auction, in Lakeville, Connecticut . . .

"Please?!"

No directions, or miles, included to Lakeville. "Can *you* go, Theo?"

He braced for a turn with one knee propped against the wobbly seat in front. "My dad only takes us anyplace during vacations," he said over the big tires' whine. "That horse show was an exception, politically correct, you know, for the sake of good rapport at work. All Sheri Dembinski talks about there is problems she's having with that new horse of hers. By the name of Safe Flight—ironical, huh?" Bailey started. The names clicked. She'd been right: Dr. North's nurse was the one who messed up on the field course. "There's no way he'd spend a whole day off at some sale for me," Theo went on. "But you might swing it!"

"Ri-ight." Last night's outburst had her on the blacklist. Next time, she'd remain perfectly rational. She scanned down the column. Amazing, how far people went to find horses: sales listed here in Pennsylvania, New Jersey, upstate New York. She'd better find out how far Lakeville was. "Maybe we could get our mothers to go, Theo, and take turns with the driving."

"I doubt it." He made a prune face. "Mom hates speed and never takes thruways if she can help it. I showed this to Dad. He puts his journal down and starts reeling off archaic adages: 'No foot, no horse,' he says, and 'Dasn't overlook the delicacy of equine legs.' Snide comments that tick me off. I swore I'd feed and water it every day and he goes and accuses me of making a horse sound like a friggin' houseplant." That *was* funny, but she wouldn't laugh. He slipped deeper into their seat and let his knees ride up. "Basically, Dad's negative about keeping large animals in captivity. He likes things left in a natural state. That's sorta obvious," with a snort, "when you see our front yard."

What little Bailey had seen behind that tall iron fence actually did look sort of jungly. She chuckled. Theo had a way of cheering her up. No more stomach ache.

"Dad claims if I want to learn something about horses, riding lessons are the ticket. Better than any auction, anyway."

"Well, at least you'd get to ride." But lessons would never do for *her*. She needed her horse home, with her. Being there whenever she needed a friend. She'd never thought of looking in the newspaper. Later, when she did, her finger jumped on "Gray."

15 h. Gray QH g. Easy keeper, quiet for trails and jumping. 123-869-7667.

Her heart raced. She read the ad again, puzzling over the abbreviations. Obviously "QH" meant Quarter Horse; what about "h" and "g"? This horse couldn't be awfully far away: the first six digits were identical to hers.

She punched in the number. Her parents were out testing the new car's GPS (*geo-positioning satellite*) system on Greenham's convoluted back roads. They could actually be driving past this horse right now. A woman answered on the second ring. Trying to sound mature, Bailey inquired whether the gray horse had been sold. No, it hadn't. Who was calling? They exchanged names and addresses. Mrs. Harvard Knott of Lavender Lane volunteered her son had grown up with this horse, whose name was Smokey. Most everyone in Greenham liked Smokey.

She sounded nice, Bailey thought. Something official, in print to show her parents, was good. She'd better find out what the "15 h" and "g" meant.

The "h" stood for "hands," which had her mystified, until the woman explained it was customary to measure horses from the bottoms of their hooves to the tops of their withers in four-inch hands. She got lost taking notes and had to start over during a lengthy explanation about the "g," which stood for gelding. Writing fast, she stumbled over "castrated." Smokey? What a cute name.

"Withers!" Mrs. Knott sounded amazed that anyone wouldn't know about withers, the bony prominence rising from the shoulder at the base of a horse's neck. "It's so much easier describing these things with the horse to look at," the woman went on. "Why don't you come over here and see for yourself?"

GUSSIE SWIVELED ON HER high seat and aimed a toothy, powdered sugar smile at Bailey. Then the white paper sack in her hand rattled at Theo, who jumped on with a whoop, and hair still wet from the shower.

"I was at Sheri's stable Saturday," he announced breathlessly as he dropped next to Bailey. Hnh, she'd thought his parents didn't like driving him around. *Her* parents didn't mind, but when she'd showed them Smokey's ad, they weren't about to go right out again. She'd held on to rationality, hadn't begged but deepened her voice to say that she understood. And that they could go the next weekend.

"The first barn was built ages ago," Theo said. He sounded impressed. "It's in town here, so Mom didn't mind going." Bailey stared at his shiny comb streaks while taking in accounts of watering systems and wash stalls. The place sounded like a spa. "The main barn's really quiet," he went on, "considering all the large animals. But kinda dark. I stumbled into this humongous wheelbarrow full of you know what. Geez, what a stink."

"Did you see a pretty gray horse, named Quaker Lace?" was all she could think to say. And probably he'd met Cappy Kaufmann.

"So many there, who knows? Sheri's horse, though. I didn't know it was Safe Flight until Mom spots the brass nameplate. We stop for a sec, and Safe Flight just shifts his haunches and stares out of the gloom."

Bailey's heart thumped. Safe Flight would be dying to get out and run.

"The trainer there showed us around to some champion hunters. Cappy's got an opening Saturday mornings, and I met Corn Cob, the horse I'll prob'ly ride."

"Corn Cob?" Bailey giggled. She started saying, "Hey, a gray—"

"No, sort of yellow. Corn Cob kinda brightens up the back lean-to, where school horses get exiled. Cappy wades right into the muck—hardly enough room in that stall for the horse and her, too, but then she signals me in." Theo stuck his leg out and braced his foot on the seat across the aisle as the bus took a curve, and their shoulders bumped together. "The thing is," he said in Bailey's ear, "horses have this reputation for kicking."

She sent him a dubious look. Surely One Oak didn't put customers on horses that kicked. "Smokey, this gray I found in the want-ads?" she blurted. "He's supposed to be really nice, everybody likes him. Smokey would never kick."

"Anyway," Theo shrugged, "Cappy waits for me to come in and tell the guy hello. I had to suck in to get past that rump." He straightened up. "I just realized that's the first horse I ever touched!"

"Sounds like progress," Bailey murmured to the window. More than she'd made, anyway. The other side of the glass had horses running, their short, spiky manes cutting the wind. Once they were lost from sight, she turned back to Theo. "Basically I'm still on square one," she said, trying to make light of it. "I thought the main objection would be costs, but just as bad is all the time it'll take. My father's in denial, nowhere near talking horses."

"Hey, that field down back of your house is a ready-made pasture. With the shelter, what's the problem?"

"I kno-ow . . . We can't seem to connect, though. That shed's an eyesore, he tells Mother, and's got to be torn down. Our whole place is going into grass and perennial gardens."

"Geez, what a waste!"

"I think I've got her on my side, though. She claims the shed has weathered beautifully and gives our place character. It's one of the things she wants to paint, when she finds time for her watercolors."

"That'll give you time, if she's anything like my mom."

Bailey slid down, remembering another thing her father had said: that she shouldn't believe everything she read in the newspapers. "Daddy keeps warning me off," she muttered. "This gray horse could be some sickly old nag standing knee-deep in muck."

"My dad's suspicious, too. He thinks I'm just going through a phase. No riding clothes, he—"

"Not boots and breeches!?"

"Huh, S.O.P. at One Oak. That place belongs in some film from the twenties. People strut around slapping riding crops at their boots. Mr. Sebastian wears this tweedy cap and long coat. And you should see this old dog he's got there, fattest Dalmatian in the world. You can tell when Mr. Sebastian's coming from Inky's toenails clinking up the aisle. This humongous oak tree towers over—"

"The aisles actually are paved?"

"The main barn's. And there's an entire room just for saddles and stuff. It smelled kinda nice, soap and leather in there, know what I mean?" She thought of her mother's leather purse. She liked Theo's Irish Spring, too. She breathed it in as he went on. "Some other old guy and Sebastian were riding around in the indoor arena, talking low, I bet horse-trading."

"Weren't any kids riding?" The place sounded awfully impersonal.

"Some girls only Andy's age, out in this little ring by the parking lot. Only too wild, how they raced over those jumps. A good thing One Oak's got so many rules."

"But if you can't get boo—"

"I called Cappy and explained. So I've gotta wear my good shoes, the only ones I've got with heels. You need a regulation helmet, too, so she's going to let me wear one of hers the first coupla times, until I get my own, which needs to be marked 'tested and certified.'" He made a face, adding, "Should anyone have the misfortune to fall on one's head."

Bailey's laugh was weak. One Oak sure sounded particular. Whatever. She would never settle for riding lessons.

4
Smokey

SHE HAD SMOKEY'S AD circled in red, stapled to Mrs. Knott's directions, and taped to her father's shaving mirror. Not too subtle. Nor confrontational. Yet made it clear that she'd simply die if she didn't get to see Smokey. She'd spent her Saturdays these days catching up on sleep and poking about with her stuff; on this one, however, she intended to see that horse. The sun was out, the weather perfect for her parents to go driving. And take her. She piled her books and papers together, stripped off last week's sheets with the peach scallops, tucked on the crisp white ones with crayon-print tulips, and plopped Ellie, her floppy elephant, on top of the pillows. If her campaign worked, when she crawled back into bed tonight, she'd have made friends with a horse.

"I was beginning to think you were going to sleep all day." Then, indicating the remains of last night's dessert, her mother asked, "Wanna share, Bee?" *Bee.* Her heart beat faster. *Bee* meant love and happiness. Certainly Mother wouldn't expect apple pie for breakfast to make up for not seeing Smokey.

Her mother set her fork down, her eyes dancing. "You nearly slept through your chance to see that horse! Your father'll be ready to leave in two minutes." Bailey's chin dropped; the sugary juice trickled. A last minute pee, map in hand, and she dashed to the car.

"Honey, don't get your hopes up."

39

"Better listen to your mother," her father added. "You won't find anything in the classifieds like the horses at that show." He sounded negative, but he had his cowboy hat on, usually a positive sign. And it was spring. The trees glided by, long willow branches draped in lacy green veils. Brownie cantered over his domain with his blanket flapping like Pegasus's wings. They turned west, past a grassy field dotted with white fleece, which materialized into a flock of sheep.

"Domestic animals everywhere," piped Bailey. "We need at least one."

Her father's hard eyes in the rear-view mirror squelched further remarks, and made her sorry she hadn't worn something more presentable than the old sweatshirt. Fourteen is beyond security blankets, she scoffed. But even with the frayed cuffs, the whitish gray, and the Purple-Demon logo practically indistinguishable, this Parkwood sweatshirt made her feel good. It was comfy, and hardly as ugly as Greenham High's bilious green hog. Considering all the horses around here, a handsome charger would make a better logo for Greenham than a hog.

The car veered, then corrected to the right. "How darling," her mother cried, as they passed a foal prancing at the haunch of a much larger horse ambling across a field. "The first of May today," she added wistfully. "Not like when your grandmothers found gift baskets on their doorsteps."

"Yeah, Gammie said May Day had everybody running around in the dark. By the time she'd get home there'd be neat stuff at her door."

Her father grunted. "That was a different era." She crossed her fingers and shot darts of hope into the nape of his sturdy neck. *A ti-isket, a ta-asket, a green and yellow ba-asket* . . . How about a humongous one on *her* patio, bulging with a real live horse!? "You let me do the talking, buttercup," her father flung over his shoulder. "Remember, we're only going to look. I mean that, literally."

"I know." *Literally* rankled. He always had to make things sound so important. She leaned out into the sweet spring air. A brilliant pheasant sauntered along the ditch, trailed by a tweedy brown hen. How come males always wanted the lead? Females had minds of their own, too.

A check on her map skipped her heartbeat.

There, a little red barn mailbox lettered *Harvard Knott*.

Tires crunched white gravel as the car crawled past a white brick house and on back to a big red barn. Bailey sat erect, her eyes fixed on the husky gray dozing at the hitching post.

A tall, strong-looking woman swung her stout braid and waved a brush at them.

"Come meet Smokey," she cried as they were getting out of the car. "He is what he is, winter coat and all." Smokey was a lighter shade of gray than Lacy. This horse had more freckles, too. No problem, Bailey told herself—with her freckles, they'd be a matched pair.

She stationed herself by the gelding's blocky head and gazed into its sleepy eyes. Her father was raving on to the woman about her magnificent white driveway, of all things, totally oblivious to the horse, even to the grayish froth wafting around his best sneakers. Her mother had on the puffy smile she normally wore in unfamiliar situations.

The horse stretched its stout neck and poked its nose into Bailey's chest.

"Don't worry, Smokey," she whispered as the devilish logo on her sweatshirt underwent snuffling. "That's not a real pitchfork." A saddle dangled from a hook on the barn by its silver stirrup. Suddenly she needed to pee again. That saddle didn't have a horn. There was a noticeable knee crack as Smokey's owner bent over to brush dirt off his hind leg. Bailey looked up to see what her father might be thinking, but he had gone off and begun wandering in and out of stalls. The barn looked so big—maybe a western saddle, too?

"How many horses you keep at your place?" her father hollered out.

"Enough," the woman replied, flipping her braid. "The rest of my brood's turned out, just Smokey here in case anybody came." She patted her hip pocket and retrieved a metal handle pointed on the end. "Glad you all could make it today," she said, waving the utensil. Now she aimed it at Smokey's near front hoof. Immediately the horse picked that hoof up.

"What all do they eat?" Philip Mason boomed. Bailey flinched. He hadn't even noticed how smart the horse was. Mrs. Knott was bent double over Smokey's hoof and hacking out gunk. Bailey wished her father wouldn't sound so hostile. After all, this woman was going out of her way for them to make her horse presentable.

"All depends." Once she'd set the hoof down, Mrs. Knott straightened up, her ruddy face even ruddier now. "Best hay available," she gasped; then, "plus vitamin-mineral supplements when my pasture dries up." Smokey lazily swished his tail. Bailey passed a finger over the tickly whiskers. Her hand traveled to a cheek that felt as big and flat as a pie plate. "Horses in light work take a quart or two of cracked corn a day," Mrs. Knott declared, waggling her hoof pick between father and daughter. "Boosted with a grain-mix on harder days. Good oats are hard to get, and commercial feed is spendy. Especially feeding a bunch like mine here," she huffed with a laugh.

Now she eyed Bailey up and down.

"So, young lady. Would you like to ride today?"

"Me?" Indicating the saddle, Bailey confessed she had only ridden western.

"No matter, our Smokey is a gentleman. You run along to the tack room and find yourself a hard hat."

THE DUST-CAKED WINDOW let in but a fraction of light. Her eyes adjusted gradually, and a virtual forest of gear emerged from the gloom. In the darkest corner crouched a monster: she let out a shaky laugh, making out a heap of toppled boots. No hats—maybe in one of those cupboards? On tiptoe, passing a sawhorse precariously piled with saddles—not one sprouting a horn, she made her way to the cupboard nearest the window.

Inside was what looked like a fully-stocked emergency room. She shut the door against the medicinal odors and mounds of rolled bandages, only to be enveloped by even sourer clouds when the next cupboard's clump of cumbersome horse blankets flopped to her feet. Gingerly, she lifted the least repugnant one by a fold. Certainly she was mature enough to put up with icky smells.

Holding one arm up to stem the flow of whatever was ready to spring, she unlatched the third cupboard door. Hard hats, mounded in dust. She lifted one by its beak, then stifled a shriek when a spider scurried over her hand. The dust cloud exploding when the bulky headgear got knocked against the shelf brought on a sneezing fit. She dabbed at her nose with a towel she found draped over a saddle, then wiped out the hard hat. The torn lining was actually silk.

The hat pinched, so she wiped another one out and then set that one on her head. She kept wiping out and trying on the old, neglected hunt caps until she found one that neither pinched nor bobbled. Part of the metal shell showed through this one's velvet nap, but it stayed on when she bent over, even when she wiggled. Her towel was completely soiled now. She brushed the scuffed velvet off on her pants, set the antique on her head, and stepped back into the sunlight.

Her hand flew to her stomach. The horse was parked next to a decayed stump, and had an English saddle on its back. A long line from the bridle slithered through grass and stubble as Mrs. Knott worked her arms to gather it up in large loops. Bailey took a deep breath, threw out her chest and jammed the hard hat down. Making straight for the stump, she stepped right up and stuck her foot in a stirrup. Trying not to think how insane it was to place her confidence in someone she hardly knew, she swung her leg over Smokey's broad back.

The pointy ears looked awfully far away. She fingered the bony prominence in front of the saddle, tracing Smokey's withers. Fifteen hands, the ad said, making her sixty inches off the ground, taller even than her father. She wouldn't look down, just focus on those swiveling ears. Unconsciously she let her fingers tour the beefy neck up to the mane's warmth. She patted the horse softly, only vaguely aware of her stirrups being adjusted and the excitement in her father's voice.

"Sit up tall, honey! Look how you're holding your reins."

Mrs. Knott stood back and let some line out. Her chipper cluck sent Smokey clip-clopping along. Bailey swayed from side to side, and threw her parents a triumphant smile.

"You happy now?" her father cried.

She leaned forward and smoothed the bushy mane. "Hi, guy," she whispered when one long ear flicked her way. She leaned back and twisted to pat the undulating rump. Wads of hair flew up. "That's okay, Smokey," she murmured, wiping her hand off on her pants. This horse sure was shedding.

"Ready for a little trot, young lady?" Mrs. Knott had her whip pointing straight up. "If it gets too bumpy, dear, just remember to post, if you know what I mean."

She was straining to hear over her father's never-ending comments when she got spanked. Every beat jarring her spine, she tried to catch the rhythm while Smokey trotted nice big circles. The saddle seemed too big; a few bounces later, it seemed too small. Horrified to think she might be hurting this nice horse, she anchored her fingers into the cramped space at the head of the saddle, which kept jabbing at her crotch. It struck her posting meant going up and down. Sitting was next to impossible, but it took courage to relinquish the saddle.

Posting was not as scary as she expected, but nearly as bouncy going up, even with a hank of mane in one hand, so she sat back down again.

"Get with him," Mrs. Knott implored. "One two, one two!"

Bailey stood, then immediately sat, sometimes with the beat, sometimes not. The reins, she discovered, offered no support at all.

5
A Private Lesson

ABOUT THE SAME TIME Julia Knott was exclaiming, "One two, one two!" to Bailey, Cappy Kaufmann was explaining the two-point position to Theo. He'd arrived at One Oak Stables to find five other people waiting in the front aisle, standing around a sturdy platform built up on one side with three tall steps. Something to mount from, he figured, making it easier for senior citizens. Sprawled in front of the office, an obese spotted dog thumped its tail. Theo's nose was adjusting to the muddle of smells when Cappy stuck her head out of the arena. She cast an approving look at his good black shoes and handed him a helmet. Mr. Sebastian wanted to see him, she said and then disappeared down an aisle. It was 8:45 a.m. Everybody dressed to ride and looking about as anxious as he felt, except for a mournful looking woman rummaging through a bag of carrots.

"Ginger's laid up," the woman told the group. "Nobody noticed he'd thrown a shoe, and now he's off in front."

A man with bushy gray eyebrows spoke up. "No matter how careful you try to be," he grumped, "sooner or later a horse will stick you with trouble."

"A fellow I know had it happen lots sooner," a petite woman wearing a canary-yellow vest said. "He brought a horse home from a sale, and it showed up lame the very next day." Sympathetic groans traveled through the group.

45

Theo knowingly shook his head. His father'd said even what started as a minor cut could knock a horse out of service.

The group fell back for what sounded like a small army. A heavy-set woman in heavy boots was clomping up the aisle with the sort of horse used to lug heavy artillery.

Time to take a leak? But now Inky lumbered to his feet, and Mr. Sebastian came out of the office. The director steadied the gentle giant while, teeth bared, breathing hard, the woman boosted herself to the top of the mounting block. To Theo's surprise, she placed her foot in the stirrup daintily and, making it look incredibly easy, swung herself up. The anxious expression on her face smoothed into bliss once her big bottom wriggled into position.

The monumental pair passed under the header-beam, with inches to spare.

One-by-one, the other riders mounted and headed out. Then the director's gaze fell on Theo.

"Doc North's son, heh? You go fetch Corn Cob."

The long aisle leading to the lean-to had three horses stationed on crossties. Theo gave them a wide pass, ducking the light-gauge chains cautiously. A foul whiff came through as he descended the annex ramp. A grisly old guy shuffled through the gloom, and Theo followed him down the aisle to a horse. He flinched when a crosstie clinked against a stall-post, and could only nod when handed the reins, tongue stuck to the roof of his mouth. Those big hooves would be clomping mighty close to his thin shoes.

The horse marched up the long aisle as though he had made the trip a hundred times blindfolded.

Climbing the three tall steps made Theo think of some innocent guy doomed to the gallows. Blindly he followed Cappy's cool commands, and found himself perched on a mountain—which moved. A drum roll sounded in his head as he was borne into the arena.

"We need your feet out of the stirrups, Theo." Cramped knees were awkward, but certainly he needed stirrups. His foot objected to the message from his brain until she gave it a nudge, and then went about unbuckling and rebuckling straps, all the while talking about joint angles and cushioning, and the importance of setting the stirrups just long enough to allow some give for support. It looked like nothing was going to be easy today. But at least this huge, murky space was all his, with only Cappy here to see his goofs. What with one leg after the other getting shoved out of her way, little of her tutorial sunk in. He did catch how to gauge the length for himself, before mounting up: simply set his finger tips at the buckle and pull the stirrup out as far as his armpit. He never would have thought that!

"Relax, Theo, old Corny's not going anywhere." Cappy had the balls of his feet square on the rubber treads. He was tense, yet complied when she hoisted his left leg even higher than before, leaving him on the edge of a sheer drop. He'd soon be hitching the girth like this, too, she said, but he couldn't see it. Buckling up with one hand while tending his reins with the other, all while staying on with one leg up?

Cappy crouched in front and inspected her work. Then, giving a little hop, she took a rein in each hand, allowing slack to the bit. Theo was pondering the girth situation when she started pulling.

"Take a firmer grip, Theo." He'd let the reins slide through his fingers. She drew back again, pulling his hands toward her, then forward, toward him, and back and forth to simulate the effect, she explained, of a horse's bobbing neck. "Educated hands make for effective communication. Horses swing their necks up and down at the walk, and a good rider's hands follow."

His hands jerked when she released her pull abruptly. Riding was unbelievably analytical. He was doing it all wrong and they weren't even going anywhere. Corn Cob stood like an old soldier, seemingly content to space out. Suddenly Theo found his hands hanging stupidly in the air.

"You're lost, because we're trotting now. Corny raises his head and holds it steady at the trot, so you need to shorten up."

He walked his fingers up the reins awkwardly until they met resistance.

"Now turn me to the right."

He knew his right from his left, anyway.

"Okay, but your left rein lost it. Stay in touch. A light touch keeps your horse attentive, that's all you need when things go well. But corrections or changes of direction require definite cues."

Unexpectedly his arms flew forward.

"We're walking again, pay attention."

He was getting the feel of the walking concept when she hauled on his arms hard.

"Cantering now, gotta stay with me." Geez, he'd heard of riding from the seat of your pants but not from your armpits.

He had begun to wonder if Cappy would ever be satisfied, when she delivered the horse's rump a slap that sent them off to the rail.

Fairly comfortable as Corn Cob clopped along the hollowed path, he rocked with the saddle. They'd managed a full circuit when, "Come over here," Cappy barked. "And halt!"

He thought he'd managed that quite well until she heaved a sigh, clearly dissatisfied. His hands were in gear, but a horse was not an easy chair. He sat up straight and threw back his shoulders. "Eyes up!" And he needed more seat and leg work. A correct position involved more than just shoulders, which at the walk should be aligned with one's ears, hips, and heels. Cappy hopped into a crouched stance to demonstrate: knees slightly bent, back erect, feet spread in a fulcrum.

"For you, Cap," somebody called.

"Walk around out here and practice," he was directed before his caretaker scampered off.

He hunched forward, aiming for the rail, and Corn Cob obliged. A few pointers filtered back, and he realized he was leaning too far, practically hugging the horse's neck. He straightened his spine, repositioned his legs. The saddle swayed, the yellowish mane wobbled. The rhythm came through and he swung his arms accordingly. Faint strains of a lively Latin tune wafted through the air. Without thinking, he gripped both reins in one hand and reached the other one out. The mane felt like straw. Hadn't seen a brush in days, maybe never. If *he* were in charge, the horse would come out spit-shined, fit for inspection.

A distant yammering came through—too high-pitched for Cappy. He relaxed a little more. A gruff voice—most likely Mr. Sebastian's. The boss sure was conservative with electricity. It was kind of spooky in here—the only light what little came through some tiny, high windows. Thin rays penetrating the shadows gave him a passing glimpse of himself in the mirror. The next time around, he headed straight down the center to see himself better. He'd sure have a lot to tell Bailey.

"You got those legs in gear?" The drill sergeant, back on duty. "Let's see you come up out of the saddle." He gave it a try, which Cappy protested put him up too high. Balancing in thin air with his knees slightly flexed was even harder than standing up. "Keep at it, Theo. Once you learn two-point, you won't need to rely on a pitching saddle for support, no matter which horse you're on.

"Try it leaning on Corny's neck.

"Push your heels down and keep those legs back under you . . . Good!"

Not good. Rebellious pangs from muscles he never knew existed shot through his thighs. He couldn't stay up for more than five seconds without a fistful of this shaggy mane. Two elderly women rode into the arena on high-steppers with outrageously long manes. They left the track clear for the novice, who fought the wobbles while his old soldier plodded on.

"That's a start, Theo. I know it's hard. Your thigh adductors only get worked when you ride or ski. Go ahead and sit." Then, "Chair seat," Cappy scoffed. He had collapsed without thinking. "What if your horse shied with you slumped in that easy chair?" She laughed. "Don't worry, Corny won't.

But if he did, you'd lose it, unless your legs were in gear." She turned to speak to the women, who were sitting way back with their knees out in front of them, like *he* had been chided for. He expected to hear "chair seat," but now she was discussing the weather report. Those horses looked elegant, not very athletic. Probably not bred for hunting, so no *huntseat*. Must be different breeds required different techniques.

He tried the two-point position again, pushing more weight into his heels as he came forward. Cappy's way made sense, even though the stretch in his calves had them hollering *uncle*. For a few moments, before his inner thighs seized up and he had to lean on Corn Cob's neck again, he felt balanced. His time was practically up, and he hadn't even trotted. Corn Cob had wandered off the rail, once the reins went slack. Focusing on one thing had blocked out everything else.

Cappy waved them back to the rail, and then asked for a trot.

"If you're doing things right, you'll feel it in your inner thighs." Really? Theo struggled to go up and down in time. These spasms were good? Inwardly he begged for mercy.

6
A Setback

TROTTING AND PETTING AND putting her horse to bed in their very own shed . . .

Daydreaming about Smokey nearly made Bailey late for the bus Monday. That would not have been good. Bad enough to miss her ride, worse to miss her chance to tell Theo what she'd been up to. Duker raced her to the road. He looked sad-eyed as she bounced up the high steps.

"Thanks for waiting, Gussie!" The sculpted afro swiveled, big eyes rolling to the third seat back, where Theo was pulling up from a sprawl. Bailey slid past him to the window.

"Good news," she exclaimed over the general din. Well, not all good. Her father had seemed interested until—

"Me too!" Then Theo went limp again and stretched his legs back into the aisle. "You go first."

"Oh. How was Corn Cob?"

"He was good," sounding surprised. "You wouldn't believe that horse has thirty years on him. What a trooper, just stands there half asleep while Cappy drills me on positions. The lesson was half over before I actually rode anywhere, with all she covered. I thought I'd never get to trot."

51

"Gosh, I was trotting immediately! Bailey's hand flew to her lips. "Okay, go on."

"You got to ride, too?"

"Uh huh. On a gray named Smokey, and is he ever nice. I have to figure out English, though. I nearly wet my pants when I saw what kind of saddle they had there." Theo's yelp punched the air. Bailey buried her head between her shoulders, imagining ears in every row of seats tuned in. Theo slid further down in his seat. When he spoke, his voice was lower.

"I know what you mean. I'm waiting up front, and when Mr. Sebastian finally recognizes me, suddenly I have to go, too."

Bailey laughed into her hands. "The owner had Smokey—"

"Kinda weird, having a huge animal practically on top of me. Old Corny went wide on the turns, though. My good shoes didn't get a mark."

"It takes humongous trust to climb up there, right?"

"I just did what Cappy said, and there we were."

"It felt totally unreal having this warm, live animal carrying me. I held on to the bushy mane." Theo was quiet, probably thinking how well *he* had done.

"I got a look in the mirror there," he said then.

"I bet you looked great." Mirror!? One Oak sounded awfully fancy. "So how did it go?"

"Some operation!" He straightened up, clearly anxious to go on. "First Cappy has to fix my stirrup treads 'a smidge below the ankle bone.' And she's real concerned about contact." He thrust out his arms and then drew them in. "'Let your hands follow,' she tells me, 'cause the neck goes up and down, see, except in trotting. Going from walk to trot, you shorten up. Also, when you come forward in three-point."

Bailey was trying to make sense of it all when Gussie winked at her in the mirror. She choked back a laugh as Theo went on.

"Posting," he groaned. "You wouldn't believe all she goes through to get posting across, sort of alternating between two-point and three-point.

You're supposed to go up every other step." He heaved a sigh. "It's damn hard putting it all together."

"I guess! What in the world are two-point and three-point?"

"It's kinda complicated." He ran his hand through his flopped-over hair. "Three-point shouldn't be, though. Basically, that's sitting with your seat and two legs distributing your weight. Kinda hard at a trot," he added, with a sideways look, "all while being attacked in a vulnerable spot, if you know what I mean." A chuck of recognition stuck in Bailey's throat. "I didn't do so well in two-point, either—even harder to get the hang of. Cappy's some mighty midget, way tougher than she looks."

"And technical, sounds like." *She* had just climbed on and started riding, no problem. Okay, maybe teeny problems at first. But once she caught the rhythm, posting was really fun, sort of like dancing. The problem now was getting her parents to take her back. Daddy had acted so nervous over there. And once they'd turned out of that white driveway, he had exploded.

"Do you know how much she wants for that horse?" She'd stayed quiet, picking at the gray hairs clinging to her jeans. All that concentrating on getting the hang of English had her collapsed in the back seat, numb.

"The horse sure knows how to jump," her mother had volunteered.

"Right on, Mom," she'd wanted to shout. Smokey was well-trained and willing—they'd never find anything better.

Mrs. Knott had tied up the stirrups after she rode, and let the line run out. Her boy used to ride the horse bareback, "nothing but rope and halter." Urgent clucking from her sent the speckled gray loping around on the line and, before long, she'd sidled him toward a blocky chicken coop, which he sailed right over.

Quite a performance, her father admitted later in the car, but they could all just forget about it. $2500 was out of their league.

BAILEY CHECKED THE NEWSPAPER every day, haunted by the notion that somebody else would discover the nice horse Mrs. Knott had for sale. The ad still ran on Saturday, but rain banished any chance of going back. The next Saturday was sunny. Bailey dove into her chores right away so her mother couldn't say there was too much to do. Today would be perfect for a nice little drive. She changed the sheets. She vacuumed up the week's accumulation of dog-hair. She pulled each one of her nine china horses out of line for a gentle wipe. She hugged Ellie as if the plush toy were real, then propped it on her pillows with its nose in the air. She could hear her mother in the kitchen, and Mikey and Andy outside yelling. No sound of her father. Probably deep in paper-work, not to be disturbed. She should be, too. She had put off Mr. Lederle's assignment till last.

School had not gone well this week. Food fights in the cafeteria, snickering during the reading of a poem. She found nothing in common with any of the kids she sat near, and each rude instance made her miss Parkwood even more. Thank goodness for Glenna Munro and Theodore North. And later, perhaps, that girl just up the road, who liked horses, too. Unless Marian Joyner proved to be the snooty type. No matter, she'd probably never meet the fabled Marian. Theo hardly ever saw the girl, just knew she'd been by with Researcher when Custer Lane showed up with horse poop.

She ran her hand over the forget-me-knot-embossed book cover on her desk. There'd been oohs and ahs at her going-away party when she peeled the shiny paper off the beautifully bound journal. Then tears, when she began reading what her friends had written inside.

A sudden roar rushed her to the window.

Her father had a fierce expression of glee on his face, as the new mower edged into the rough like a giant, droning beetle. He whipped a U-turn, and the blackbirds pecking behind it scattered to the trees.

Good, they're gone—black might be bad luck. Nothing better interfere with her parents' positive thoughts of Smokey. This mower had cost over

$7000; a few more thousand for a horse shouldn't be a problem. She dug into her math with one ear cocked to the mower: the problems with her father occupied more attention than those in her workbook. Only a fantastically sensible approach would get Daddy to take her back.

The moment the roaring noises stopped, Bailey ran down the stairs, out into the grass-fizzed air. Tiny green spears stuck to her slip-ons as she raced across the lawn. Her father was behind the shed, where he'd begun piling rubbish. He stood hunched over his gleaming new machine. She drew a tremulous breath, willing him to look up.

"Hi, Daddy. Cool lawn mower . . . " First she'd get him talking about what interested him. No response, he just went on scraping at the green clots clinging to his precious machine. Perky violets peeked out of heart-shaped leaves at the base of the shed. Years of exposure had turned the walls all the colors of gold. She hadn't noticed any violets blooming last week, when Glenna was out here with her. They'd slithered through the drenched weeds, investigating the possibilities for *horse-keeping*, as Glenna's book called it. According to Glenna, it was a foregone conclusion she'd be getting a horse.

"You're really turning this into a show place, Daddy." He was on his knees now, crawling around the mower. And sneezing. The fresh-cut grass smelled like onions. Calling on her meager reserve of patience, Bailey rolled a firm violet stem between her fingers. If only Glen knew what she was talking about.

"I know something to make things utterly perfect here, Daddy." He seemed to have recovered from sneezing; surely he was listening. "A horse," she piped, her voice up an octave. "Any estate needs a horse! And all this field here needs is a fence. Maybe even only part of a fence, with so many trees and bushes guarding each side. Glenna and I policed it for trash and potholes. When more grass comes up, Daddy, think of all we'll save on feed!" Abruptly she repositioned herself. An object strangely resembling a hubcap glinted from a clump of weeds. How could they have missed that? She kicked the offensive disc under a rhubarb-like leaf while her father stared into his mower's complex undercarriage.

At last, he pulled himself to his feet. Bailey squinted into the sun, trying to read his mind as he stretched his arms and looked out across the field. Knee-high weeds and scrub trees grew wild here. He'd be gauging how much like a wall the older trees and shrubbery around three of its sides might appear to a horse.

"Wouldn't it be great to see a horse galloping around here?"

"Such a dizzy-pus," he muttered. Then he sneezed again, and blew his nose into his blue handkerchief. It took him a long minute to speak. Then, "Let me tell you something, kiddo. Every living horse, be it work horse, race horse, show horse, trail horse, even one just standing idle, requires more than what this plot'll yield in the way of feed. Horses eat money, and I mean that literally. Furthermore," sounding mad now, spitting his words, "horses devour major blocks of time." The color drained from Bailey's cheeks, as he went on about the food, equipment, and vet bills horse-owners faced.

"People that lived here kept horses," she ventured when he paused for breath. She should have saved those dried out clumps to show him.

"Listen, Toots, do you know how much a barn costs?"

Her eyes sparked, and her hands sprung to life. "Really, Daddy, I've been thinking about all of that, too! We wouldn't need a new barn, we've got the shed. A fifteen by thirty-foot run-in shed works great, Glenna's manual says. And we've got this one all cleaned out. Just find one cobweb!"

"This thing?" He kicked at a sagging board, then looked surprised when it held. "This disgrace is coming down."

"Horses like Smokey really don't need barns anyhow, Daddy." She was trying to keep her voice steady. It wouldn't pay to argue. What a break Glen showed her those books. "Smokey's not a fancy show-horse. He's a tough, rugged guy who'll do just fine out here. He'll have these trees to get under when it rains. And on hot days, they'll be shade." She threw back her shoulders. "They'll be a wind-break, too!"

"Sounds like you've been doing some serious research, young lady."

"Sure have!" With a sense of his undivided attention, her words flew. "Glen's got tons of horse books. Her *Manual of Horsemanship* tells all about ponies living outdoors. Even overnight!" She flung her arms. "It'd have to be the same for horses as ponies, wouldn't it? One like Smokey, anyway. Smokey even looks like a pony. A giant pony," she added with a chuckle. "Isn't he cute?" Her mind clicked along. Her father stared at her with his mouth open. "And Daddy, we shouldn't," she paused, determined to pronounce this key word correctly, "have *veterinarian* bills. The manual says ponies kept outdoors have 'less risk of injury.' And don't require so much hay and grain."

"Now don't get carried away, kiddo."

"Can't we go see Smokey again?" Her hands chopped the air. "You might talk Mrs. Knott into a deal!" His head jerked back, then down. He nudged his toe into some matted scrapings. She raked her brain for something to take the frown off his face.

"You think you're pretty smart there. Huh, cookie?" His pointing finger nearly poked her in the nose. "Make a deal, my eye. What do you know about deals?" He paused, and she was about to say, "sweetheart deal," something she'd heard him say on the telephone, when he said, "I doubt Lady Knott would take anything like a thousand."

She clasped her hands together to keep them still.

His lips twitched, then puckered, sort of like Duker's did for a delicacy. Funny how lip-activity helped her father think. Now he was gazing off to the poplar trees with his lower lip scrunching grotesquely.

"You could call, I guess," he said. "See if that woman is home today."

Her fist smacked into her cupped hand. Elbows pumping, she raced up the hill. "Please be home, Mrs. Knott, you nice, nice lady, oh pul-ease!" Her wonderful father was taking her to ride Smokey again!

The chant continued while she dug out the number. There were four rings before a familiar musical tone came through.

"No one can come to the phone right now," poured through the receiver.

"Mrs. Knott, it's me, Bailey Elizabeth Mason! If you're there, please pick up!"

"—your name and number. And if you're calling about the horse we advertised, sorry, it's been sold."

7
Schemes

BAILEY STARED OUT THE window unseeingly as the bus droned along. Theo was sitting in back with his buddy from speech class to work up a skit. She didn't feel much like talking, anyway, certainly not laughing at the funny lines he'd come up with. There'd never be another horse as nice as Smokey.

Her classes that Monday went by in a dreary fog. She tried to concentrate for Mr. Lederle, whose surprisingly gruff comments made him seem out of sorts, too. "Smiles hiding in your pockets," Gammie would say. The hands on the clock hardly moved. At last, the big one pointed to twelve. She slung her heavy back-pack over one shoulder and trudged to the bus. Gussie was passing out Tootsie Rolls.

"Thank you," Bailey replied automatically before shuffling to her seat. She pressed her forehead against the cool glass but didn't see Theo. She'd be poor company, anyway. She slumped back, unconsciously let her thumb travel to an incisor for a furtive fingernail check. Slowly she unwrapped a piece of candy. What had got into Gussie, the woman was clairvoyant! The caramelly chocolate seeped over her tongue. Smokey would have been such a pal. It only made things worse when you counted chickens before they hatched.

Sunday she had read over letters from Sylvia Schermerhorn and Emily Ambrose, then lost herself in her journal. She missed Parkwood more than ever now. "To Bailey Elizabeth Mason, my truest friend, I'll never forget you," Emily had penned in plum-colored ink, then elaborated on her notoriously twitty dream, where she's terribly upset until resourceful Bailey comes through with life-saving advice: "Recovery from hysteria requires seven sips of lukewarm water." After that, there'd be calls for lukewarm water whenever any of their *Lucky 13* stressed out. And Gail Jacobs' hilarious account of how they used to play house with Duker for their baby. Good old Duker. Bailey slipped another Tootsie Roll out of its crinkly wrapper. Tiny Gussie had a tremendous heart; this was better than lukewarm water. Parents could be understanding, too, but not hers this time. True, Daddy had come up to her room for a little talk.

"Granted, things are different here," he'd said while rubbing her back. "But you can hack it, honey." He was trying to cheer her up, but she refused to show any enthusiasm she didn't honestly feel. He'd gone on despite her stony look about how an occasional disappointment "on this confounding freeway of life" was not out of order. How she chose to handle a setback was the main thing. "I know you had your heart set on Smokey, honey," he'd said, sounding incredibly sweet. "We'll look for another horse sometime, find one that's even better. The best thing for you now is to steer straight ahead. You hold up your end, hon, and nine times out of ten you'll find something good emerges from the bad. Just have faith, and keep on doing your best."

The bus hit a bump, clonking her forehead against the window. No way could she do her best when she didn't feel like doing anything at all.

THE NEXT MORNING, GUSSIE'S caring, "How's you today, honey?" turned Bailey's eyes misty.

"Thanks for the care package," she replied with a catch in her voice. "That was really nice, Gussie."

"Humph, I can see it's nothin' sugah's gonna help."

She made it to her seat before the bus gave a lurch. Theo swung off the corner handle of the next seat and plopped down beside her. She avoided eye contact, not sure if she could talk about Smokey without sounding like a crybaby. She brushed at her cheeks and fluffed up her hair. His face appeared blurry when she looked—tears must magnify things.

"Miss me yesterday?" he asked cheerily.

"Sure did."

"Mom picked me up from track. Ever been to The Saddlery?"

"Unh uh."

"Well, that's where we went. The Saddlery's cool, even smells good, with all that liniment and leather, and there's more books than I ever imagined on the subject of horses. Saddles like at One Oak, and western stuff, too. Andy tries on this fringed leather jacket, claiming it makes him look like a trapper. Then he has to go and spoil the whole trip, begging Mom—"

"What did you get?"

"Uh, the basic requirements, mostly. Breeches, when I finally found some that fit. A hunt cap, regulation certified. And boots. Everything's kinda expensive there, so we settled for PVCs. You know?" Looking down, Bailey shook her head. She had no idea what *PVC* stood for. "Plastic, but it looks like leather. Not too shabby, even waterproof. Mom had to shell out $74.95 for the hunt cap. You know Tammy, the girl who works there? A sharp one, says we'll be glad it's regulation the first time I get bucked off."

That got a short laugh.

"Reassuring, huh?" He leaned in, his eyes searching for hers. "You get to ride Smokey?" One quick look trapped her. He really cared. She turned aside so he wouldn't see the flood in her eyes.

"Daddy was going to take me, but somebody else bought him already." Theo lay his hand on her arm and began patting her shoulder. The bus rounded a curve with them bracing their legs to keep from sliding across the seat. "See," she said in a wee voice as they rocked in sync, on the straightaway again. "I'm trying not to think about it any more." She bounced forward, then swiveled to face him. "Keep talking, Theo, come on, you've gotta distract me!"

So he went on about the tack shop. He'd figured Tammy was going to make things easy for him. Mr. Sebastian had taught her how to ride and she knew all about One Oak. But finding a pair of pants that fit and didn't cost a fortune wore them all out.

"The first pair she—"

"Describe them."

"Uh, beige kinda. Leather knee patches. Mom said they cost more than she'd pay for a dress. Then I tried some white ones on that only came to my knees, totally *un-macho,* but Tammy says breeches are supposed to fit below your calf muscle, so I got out of that. She rummages around again and comes out with some kinda rust colored ones. Geez, I hate trying on clothes!" He sent Bailey a cock-eyed look. "Better now?"

"I guess. Rust is a nice color. Really nice if you're riding a gray horse."

"Glad you approve. Those fit okay and only cost sixty dollars."

She gasped, then giggled when he told her his mother, hearing the price had whimpered, "Only?"

"Her face gets red and it looks like she's going to flush the whole deal. Until I go, 'See Mom? I like horses like you like your garden.' *Comprende?*"

"Gee, smart."

"I guess she felt better about it all then, 'cause she sprung for a boot-jack, too. Then, while she's paying, Andy has to go and louse things up, whining about that leather jacket. It did look good on him. Mom says she's spent enough already, and he winds up in this blasted, stuttering tirade about her spending everything on me! Tammy's standing there, taking it all in, and I wanted to sink through the floor." On impulse Bailey brushed her cheek on Theo's shoulder. Whistles came from the rear of the bus. "Geez, you guys," he muttered. Bailey straightened up, and caught the glint of Gussie's bright eyes in the mirror.

"Here's a thought, though," Theo went on. "Their bulletin board's loaded with flyers, one for another auction in Lakeville. This Saturday, I think. You should check it out, Bailey."

PUMP YOUR ELBOWS, SHE chanted to herself, push off the balls of your feet and go faster, faster. She would have ducked out of home room but doubted The Saddlery was open at 8:30 a.m. For sure it was at 11:30. If she hurried, she'd have a flyer in her hands by the end of lunch break and be in time for Miss Perolini. Despite intruding notions about the auction, she'd managed to read the Eudora Welty story to the end. The Saddlery stood on the highway that led out of town—fortunately, only about two miles south of the high school. Her heart thumped rapidly and she was out of breath by the time she found the place, raced up and down the aisles, and then found the bulletin board right next to the door.

FORTY HORSES—ALL AGES—ALL STAGES—MANY PROFESSIONALLY TRAINED, in big red letters. She craned her neck to read all the information over carefully, then realized the flyer was stapled with some other ones, conveniently removable. Taking pains to be neat, she extracted three. She looked around at the mounds of boots and saddles. She would have been happy to stay all day.

During sixth period study hall, she consulted the map in the library. Lakeville lay way up in northern Connecticut, nearly in Massachusetts. From Greenham, could be a two hour trip.

"My mother wouldn't go without Daddy," Bailey groaned to Glenna. "And I expect he is not about to sacrifice an entire Saturday for a project he's been trying to avoid. I'd wait till he's had a good dinner to ask."

The direct approach seemed best. She'd be open and honest and not let him think he was being conned. And she couldn't pounce, or he'd feel pushed. Just to introduce the subject, at dinner she mentioned that Theo was taking lessons at One Oak Stables; he'd seen all kinds of horses there. This led to talk about different breeds. She restrained herself, keeping the discussion impersonal. No way should she press, not just yet.

"Say, Daddy, I've got something to show you," she said off-hand as he shuffled away from the table. At last, granted his undivided attention, she passed over the flyer. So many entries, if only he'd go, he'd be sure to like at least one.

"How about it?" she asked cheerily. "We might look see what's in our price range," she added, doing her best to sound rational. But, with one glance at the flyer, her father handed it off to her mother. Her mother wagged her fingers in dismissal. Her father buried his head in his briefcase.

At least he hadn't said no. She typed up the directions and set the printout in plain sight—that had worked with Smokey's ad. This was bigger, though, calling for a long drive and an entire day. She stuck one flyer to the refrigerator with bunny magnets, laid another under the remote in the den, and clipped a third to the news magazine by the toilet in the master bathroom. "Please, Please, Please," she'd written across the tops, taking the direct approach to the nth degree. It was Wednesday already, and the auction was on Saturday.

She went out of her way to be pleasant and helpful around the house. By Thursday night, no results, even though her hints had grown exorbitant. Why ever had she bothered to get out of bed that morning to yank weeds out of the patio? Be patient, she told herself—last minute decisions in this family were S.O.P. She called in reinforcements, appealing to Glenna to stay over Friday night.

"Sorry to say, but Bailey, the end of a work week bodes not well for requesting favors from fathers."

"But with the two of us, it'll seem more worth driving that far."

"There's hardly time to cultivate your dad. We can't sound the least bit whiny."

"I know, but we've got to give it a try." She snorted at a sudden thought. "I'm steering straight ahead, Glen, just like he says."

By Saturday morning, all they'd settled on was to allow the head of the household to enjoy his eggs. The temperature had dropped overnight, and a harsh wind hit the kitchen's bay window. Bailey sipped her apple juice, mentally prodding her father to finish up. Glenna had spooned up the last kernel of her nutty granola and sat tracing a finger around the botanical graphics on her placemat. Philip Mason dabbed a scrap of English muffin into a pool of yolk. As he wiped it across his plate, Bailey drew a cautious breath. Her mother shot her a questioning look. Then Glenna spoke up.

"I wonder how many horses there'll be," Glenna remarked to her marigolds. That wasn't the plan, but Bailey took the cue.

"Where?" she said, making her eyes big and innocent. She sat poised, waiting for her father to swallow. When he picked up his napkin, she exclaimed, "Oh, you mean at that auction!" Now he seemed to be hiding behind his coffee mug. "All kinds, I s'pose, Glen," she added pointedly, then sing-songily, "Wouldn't it be fun to see them all? Daddy?"

This had to work. If they were going, they had to leave very soon. Her eyes snagged his over the coffee mug.

"Please, Daddy?" The mug went down, spilling a small splash over the rim, which he ignored. A tiny quirk worked at the corner of his lower lip. It could be a positive sign—her hopes soared. Then plunged, when he mentioned putting up shelves in Michael's room.

"I better go round up Mike," he said, and pushed back his chair.

She reached under the table for Glenna's hand. She threw a desperate look to her mother, who suddenly volunteered that Michael's Cub Scout troop had a hike scheduled for today. The wind chimes out on the patio swung wildly. "There's no reason for you not to go," her mother added. "I'll stay home with my watercolors."

Glenna started to hum. Bailey's chin dropped. Thank you, Mom. And how brilliant of Glen, positively un-naggy. Oh, what next? This might be overkill, Glenna's outrageous trilling—*Driving through Connecticut's cah-unn-tri—si—ii—ide* . . .

"Alright already," her father growled. "But don't get any fancy ideas in your head about bringing a horse back here."

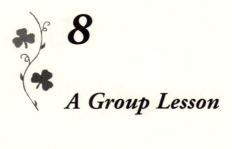

8
A Group Lesson

ALL WHILE BAILEY WAS traveling with Glenna and her father to Lakeville that Saturday, Theo was back in Greenham, performing calisthenics on a horse.

No sooner had he and Corn Cob joined the four other horses in line than Cappy boomed, "Spread out!"

He reined in to make room for the peppy little black in front of them. Its rider was the only other boy in class, who he figured went to Sage Hall. He'd never seen him or any of the girls here at Greenham High. Two wore sweatshirts discreetly displaying Sage Hall's crest, a tiny green wreath. Theo was as keyed as he'd been at his first track meet, determined to do well. He must be the least experienced here, his first time with a group, and the only rep from a public school. One of the girls had crinkled her dark Asian eyes at him, dispelling some of his nervousness. Being on the end of the line, where nobody could see what a rookie he was, helped, too. A silent litany ran through his head.

Heels down; shoulders back; hands steady; legs at the girth; eyes between the ears—

"Reins in the right hand, please," Cappy called out, no megaphone required. "Aaand, PROPELLERrrr." Five left arms shot up and started whirling. "Loosen those shoulders. Swing those arms. Faster. Harder. Other direction, now." Calisthenics on a horse felt weird; safe enough, though, with old Corny plodding along. The little black in front of them put more energy into bouncing up and down than moving forward.

"Reins in the left hand!" Five right arms propelled, until, "Pause in the air! Reach to your toe. Down, then up. Down. Up. Raise that toe to meet your hand. And keep your heels down. At the girth, remember, and keep your seat while bending over!"

Something pulled in the small of his back; something fierce was biting his calf; his shoulder sockets were hamburger. Ha, coach should see him now. Sitting on a moving horse was harder than running on your own two feet. Cappy marched at Corny's side, skipping ahead from time to time. Now she reversed her little squad and had them repeat the exercises in the opposite direction. He was getting the hang of it, reaching down without feeling about to fall off, when she called for everybody to drop their reins.

"Best to knot them up and lay them down, please."

"Now, arms out, like wings. And twist to the right." Without holding on? Hopefully, old Corny wouldn't notice he was on his own. "Stretch back to touch the opposite rump for three strides." Groans traveled back to Theo, a guffaw from Cappy. They'd be doing this at a canter soon, she boasted. No way!

"Drop your stirrups, please." She never failed to give him a toe-curling stretch without stirrups—to develop a good seat, she claimed. Stealthily he extracted one foot. Corny seemed oblivious so he extracted the other, then pulled in a cautious breath. "Raise your right leg to your horse's right shoulder!" Geez, more odd stuff. At this rate, he wouldn't be a beginner much longer. "Swing your leg back toward the loin—one dozen on the right side, one dozen the left." Corny cooperated, but the little black up ahead kept jigging up and down.

"Take your stirrups and . . . prepare to trot!" Theo's shoulders opened with confidence. "Remember, stay well enough back when the line moves out. If you can only see down to hocks in front, you're in the right spot. Hocks," she explained, shooting her eyes to Theo, "are the backward knees on horses' hind legs. If you can see all the way down to feet, better move up. But," she shouted, "if you can't see down to the hocks, you're inviting a kick. Do something about it quick."

Trotting at last, Theo squeezed his legs when Corny lagged behind, tapped his heels if more was needed. He'd be posting along, enjoying himself, and forget to mind his spacing. Finding his palomino too close to the black, he'd abruptly pull back, likely bringing Corny up short, and too far behind again. A few slip-ups like this taught him to run his eye up the line ahead.

"Very nice, Theo," Cappy remarked. Sinking weight into his heels, he had discovered, made it easier to sit deep. He pumped his hips, worked the small of his back. "That's the half-halt, pretty advanced," Cappy crowed, addressing *him*. He beamed. The horse was listening now: simply a nudged seat-bone or leg or tweaked rein adjusted the stride.

"Half-seat!"

The boy up front rose forward. Figuring Cappy wanted two-point, Theo came out of the saddle, too. Then her call for posting started a drill continuously switching them all from posting to sitting to half seat—calling on muscles Theo never even knew existed.

"Mind those rein lengths." He stole a glance at his two-toned sport watch. There was a crick in his side, and still twenty-five minutes to go.

"And, walk," collapsed him into a banana. Absently, he patted Corny's neck. Five more horses had entered the arena. They kept to the far end, two riders performing calisthenics on their own. Bailey would probably love all this, Theo was thinking, when Cappy began talking about cantering. One of the new riders halted close enough to hear her explanations about correct leads.

"First, make sure your horse is up on the bridle. That puts him on the alert."

So far so good; he knew that. The same with trotting.

"Sit tall and talk with your legs to prepare for the actual cue. It's easier for your horse to take the correct lead when you tweak his head a bit inside while pressing your inside leg into the girth." Theo strained for every word, trying to picture it all. "And then touch your outside heel back into his flank." Coordinate all that at once? *Muy complicado*. Maybe Cappy would talk so long, everybody wouldn't get to canter today. "You might need more than a touch. You know your horse's sensitivity, right?"

Hands on her hips, Cappy ran her eyes down the line. "Catch up, Theo," she said quietly as he and Corny came past. They'd fallen so far behind, he could see all four of the little black's hooves.

A gentle squeeze moved Corny up.

"The canter has a three-beat sequence," Cappy said, voice on high again. "Your outside heel behind the girth activates his outside hind leg, which gives you the first beat. Then the inside hind strikes along with the outside fore. Then the inside fore reaches out. That's three beats. If the inside fore strikes on the third beat, like it should, you'll be on the correct lead." She spun around, scanned down the line, and shouted, "I cannot overemphasize the importance of initiating the transition from that rear push. Hold him in until you feel the lift, then let him pull your hands forward. Don't check the lift, or you'll get a rapid trot, a rough, fast one you definitely will not appreciate." Cappy strutted like a drum-majorette, head carried at right angles to the line. "Any questions?" she barked.

Theo could have used a review, but no way was asking questions. His voice couldn't be trusted lately not to squeak. They were only walking, but beads of perspiration prickled his forehead.

The first girl in line was mounted on a flashy Arabian. "Last week," she wailed, "when I put my hands forward, Banner started racing like mad and I couldn't hold him."

"Put your arms forward when you feel Banner lift. Then, Roseanne, when his hind foot strikes again, and he brings his head down, you bring your arms back. If he's going too fast, each time you pull back, tug! Stay on the case and hold him longer, stronger, before you release for the next stride."

Cappy swung around and scrutinized the line. All five horses marched sedately.

"Anything else?"

"Am I going to canter?" He couldn't help the crack in his voice. The crucial thing to remember if he did get the go ahead, was to at all costs prevent a rough trot.

"Yes, everybody is going to canter. When their turn comes." Hands on her hips, Cappy stamped her foot. "What do you think I've been going over all of this for? One at a time, you pick up a trot, get balanced, then cue. That means you, too, Theo. On your turn you'll canter along the rail until you're back to the end of the line."

Banner glided off with Roseanne, picked his feet up into a canter and then picked up speed. Roseanne worked her reins, taking back more than giving. Halfway around the arena, she had Banner going like a carousel horse.

"Very nice, Roseanne!"

Jenny Han's troubles with Escort began with her first cue. She took back, then tried again, but the long-framed chestnut only trotted faster.

"Hold him," Cappy roared. Jenny's shiny braids kept slapping her shoulders. "Lean back and pull, make Escort lift!" Jenny's face twisted with determination. She dug in her heels and leaned back so far her braids brushed the horse's rump. Theo just about felt the jolts himself as Escort carried his petite passenger the whole way around in a running trot. The third girl was a real tub who looked strong enough for her stocky bay. But she could barely get the horse to move.

"Kick him, Barbie!" A series of whole-hearted kicks produced a half-hearted trot. "Hold Barrister in while you kick. At the next corner, hold him and stick your outside heel into his ribs, hard. If that wise-ass can't go forward, he goes up." Cappy closed in and waved her whip as they rounded the corner, exclaiming, "And can-TER!"

"He won't do it," Barbie wailed. The old bay knew his strength.

When the little black took off, Corny quickened his step. Theo's heart jumped wildly in his chest.

"Nice job with Hickory Nut, Joshua," Cappy called out when they'd pulled up at the end of the line. Sweat dribbled down Theo's neck. He braced for the go-ahead, heels set at Corny's ribs.

The willing trot had him bouncing like a beginner, ram-rod rigid, but he managed to shift his outer heel to Corny's flank. The horse lifted, and then rolled into a rocking gait giving the sensation of floating. In a state of wonderment, Theo floated all the way around to the end of the line.

Walking again, he stroked Corny's relaxed neck.

"Thank you, sir, thank you sir, you're the man."

9

All Kinds, Her Kind

THEY FOUND A PLACE to park half a mile past the sales barn. The hike back through the crisp morning air heightened Bailey's senses. There could be a horse here meant just for *her*. Exuberantly she hugged Glenna and, arms linked, they wove their way through the maze of steaming horse transports, staying close to her father. A low-slung stock-trailer shook and rattled as it backed up to a makeshift chute. It reeked of sourness, and was allowed a wide berth as they aimed for the pole-building's people-door.

A high-pitched hubbub met them inside. People scurrying and shouting, horses stomping and neighing, and row-upon-row of metal stall doors that clanged. Even with this vast barn's high ceilings, the air was sharp with nose-wrinkling odors. A "Heads Up!" flattened Bailey against a stall, just as five terrified colts scrambled past her. The accompanying ammonia and dung smells made her think of that polluted stock trailer. These colts must have come in through the chute—so wild, they had been sent in loose!

A hastily swung door herded the entire pack into one box stall. All five began milling anxiously, rubbing their mud-caked coats against the metal panels and against each other. The burly guy who'd closed them in was outside, sagged against the bars. He looked worried—probably his bunch wouldn't bring much. Who wanted a scruffy horse too little to ride?

A shoulder-tap sent her trailing after Glenna and her father through the din of slamming doors and piercing whinnies ricocheting through the aisles. She was here, now what? Everything was so confusing. And if even half of these people were serious about buying, she didn't stand a chance. Thunderous banging raised her eyes to behold fiery wild eyes staring over the top of a stall panel at least eight feet high.

"Quit it," a man there hollered; his shirt was soaked with sweat. The horse tossed its head in defiance and went on hammering its hooves. A woman with her hair swept up hovered near the bars. "Please be good, baby," she cooed. Now a "Heads up!" for a horse built broad as a boat being led through the congestion. A guy near Bailey with a Stetson like her father's remarked on this one's "hay belly." "Nah," his buddy drawled as the rotund beast trudged by, "That mare's in foal. Very." Glenna snickered. Shot a look, Bailey choked back a laugh. The abundance of horseflesh had her giddy.

The next aisle appeared comparatively sane. Soft, anxious snorting noises brought the girls up short. A raw-boned palomino stood nuzzling the straw. Tiny golden ears and large dark eyes emerged from the bedding. Then wondrously, four spindly legs unfolded. A petite, perfectly formed horse, its mane but a riff of white fringe, tentatively made it to its feet. Bailey crouched down. She'd nearly missed this little treasure, its fuzzy, golden coat a perfect camouflage in straw.

"Bye, bye, baby," she crooned, straightening up.

The large yellow head jerked up and down as if saying, "Get lost and leave us alone."

"Bye, bye, lady, I hope you and your baby find a good home."

She moved along with Glenna. Her father had run out of patience and gone on.

A virtual obstacle course confronted the girls on the next aisle. Saddles; bridles; buckets; trunks; sawhorses heaped with blankets. People leading horses past protruding gear cautiously picked their way. A cowboy reached out from his elaborately tooled saddle to slide a long pink comb through his coal-black horse's long silky mane. The well-built horse stood quietly amid the clutter. Bailey didn't particularly want a black horse. So far, she'd found only one gray, and that one bared its teeth at her. She might have searched the Internet, but photos and descriptions could be iffy. Anyway, Daddy wasn't up for intensive planning. He'd only agreed to this trip at the last minute. Oh, surely, a gray—one the right size, color, and price-range—was here today. Surely a certain horse was waiting for her to take it home.

Where are you, oh where are you, my friend?

"Does that dun go good?" A plump woman in overalls spoke to a big kid whistling a tune while wielding a stiff brush. His horse had zebra-striped legs and a black stripe up its back. The tan hide didn't look at all dusty.

"This guy?" whistling interrupted, but not the brushing, "Quiet as a lamb, m'am, do anathin' ya want." Glenna's eyebrows shot up; Bailey stifled a giggle.

Safely past the dun, they came upon a big white horse with big black splotches giving a kid no bigger than Mikey trouble.

"Hold his head, damnit," snapped a man wearing a fancy western shirt. The horse furiously pumped its head to avoid some menacingly buzzing clippers. "Hold it still, or I'll cut it off."

"Hey you, skewbald," the kid wailed, plainly tired of having his arm wrenched, "your name oughta be 'Screwbald'!"

Bailey's quizzical look had Glenna whispering, "Black and whites are 'skewbalds'. He's just being funny."

"Oh." Gosh, so much she didn't know. She'd study up, if only for her horse's sake. She turned the corner, and caught sight of some prettily pointing ears. Large, knowing eyes gazed back over the crowd. Not black, not brown—was that horse gray? She grabbed Glenna's sleeve and threaded her way up the long, clogged aisle. This horse was looking at *her*.

A stout woman wearing a man's overcoat turned the horse front to back for an elderly couple, who stared with their mouths open. Up close, these ears appeared more like a dark rose than really gray. The black mane was long and full with glints of red and silver. Bailey could almost feel the horse's eyes on her. Maybe saying, "You like my fancy halter?" Nothing like Mrs. Knott's mellowed leather, this one was nylon, bright fuchsia. Suspended ceiling fixtures illuminated the extraordinary coat, nearly charcoal along the neck, with rose flecks shading into a mottled rose-gray down the chest and along the barrel. The different shades didn't really amount to gray. What color was this horse? The flank's pearly gray darkened to a rich plum over the high rump. A sticker plastered there read #71.

Bailey gazed at the startlingly framed face for a long minute. A star on the forehead and markings down the nose made it even more interesting. She clasped her hands over her heart, taken with the horse's composure even more than its distinctive coloring. She listened for the horse's name but caught just the woman's name: Patsy Hemptfling.

"Three months in work," the woman was telling the elderly couple. Her weathered hands twiddled with the fine length of leather snapped to the outlandish halter. "Really," a lilt in her voice, "this filly's come along quite nicely."

Bailey tensed. Five more people had stopped to look.

"Does she take the bit?" came from a slender woman staring as if this was the first horse she'd ever seen.

"My yes, she's a natural." The hefty owner beamed. "My girl's about to saddle up, you'll see." She ran her eyes over the meager crowd gathered around her horse. "Anybody here partial to color?" she asked brightly, waving an arm at the hind legs. "Those fancy socks come from her sire, a chestnut Thoroughbred that'd knock your eyes out, white stockings clear up to his knees and hocks." Bailey edged closer. These hind legs were white around the pasterns, like they had on neatly turned-down anklets.

"This here's a jewel," Patsy Hemptfling crowed. "A healthy four-year-old, straight off a ranch in South Dakota." Bailey sucked air. The horse seemed focused on her, taking her measure. Her heart leapt with recognition. This was all she ever wanted. Out of all the horses here, this one was *her* kind. Hey, this horse had traveled more miles to Connecticut than she had traveled from Illinois. They'd be starting over in fresh territory together. "—some gray in places, but not officially gray," she heard, but that didn't matter now. "Roan. A strawberry roan—chestnut hair scattered in with white." Bailey's skin prickled. Some of that hair matched hers.

They found her father carrying on a one-sided conversation with a sturdy little horse prancing around the edges of its stall. A path was worn in the shavings.

"What kind of place is this to end up in, huh, fellow?" He pressed his shoulder against the bars to send home some advice. "Things look grim now, but don't you worry. A handsome buckskin like you'll be snapped right up. You're going somewhere where you'll get fed properly, be allowed to run."

The girls stood to one side. Bailey was about to burst with her news. The buckskin had stopped pacing to eye its talky visitor.

"Daddy, I found—"

"See how much happier he looks now?"

She fell silent, then laughed at the trick the little buckskin showed them, using its nose like a jailbird's spoon to strum the bars. The way it cocked its head then, quite pleased with itself, made them all laugh. She held her breath, willing the entertainer to allow a friendly pat. Her father had reached in. He was enjoying himself—in a positive frame of mind now. But the horse backed off. Bailey exhaled furiously. If Daddy didn't find something interesting soon, he would leave.

A long banner touting Riverview Quarter Horse Farms adorned the next aisle. A small knot of people there listened to what a guy in a sheepskin jacket had to say about the horse he had out of its stall. The horse was all muscle.

"She's by Four-eyed Jack," went the high-pitched spiel, "out of Jilly's Surprise by Conquistador, an own son of Red Dock Cody. That's fool-proof breeding, folks. Sons of Red Dock Cody, ya know, pass on the dang prettiest heads." All those names, Bailey thought—as if ancestry were the main thing. That wouldn't matter to her so much, if a horse wanted to be friendly. #71 had looked right at her, virtually saying, "Hi." And #71 was prettier than this one, even more athletic looking. This one's bulging muscles had it looking top-heavy.

The wrangler moved around his mare in a stoop, taking pains to set each of the fine legs to stand square. Then, evidently satisfied with the pose, he motioned his helper to bring another horse out, and bragged up this one. "By Diamond Dan out of Sugar Philly . . . another beauty by Conquistador, own son of Red Dock Cody . . . ain't she got refinement?" Bailey glanced at her father. His lips had compressed to a thin line.

"No mention back there of performance," he grumbled as soon as they were out of range. "Seasoned salesmen never tell the whole story," he added, with a jaded laugh. "Much better to bite one's tongue than burst a prospective buyer's bubble. Those buyers just better watch themselves."

"Really," Glenna said, and laughed like she knew all about it.

"We'll know more when we see how they ride, Daddy. Let's go over to the arena. There's a straw—"

"Sweetie, you can't tell much by looking. Anyone nuts enough to buy at an auction needs riches of hands-on experience. Or needs his head examined." Her heart sank. Daddy had been enjoying himself with that cute buckskin and now he'd turned negative. Once she got him into the arena, though, he should be fine. She sighed. Progress with Daddy always took two steps back for every step forward. But one look at #71 and he'd be sold.

There was a large pen at the end of this aisle, just thrown together out of rusty, old siding. The horses here hung their heads in silence—a dismal looking lot, some awfully bony. It took a minute to sink in when her father remarked this looked like the last stop. He had heard about killer pens but had never actually seen one. The muscles in her chest tightened. It hurt to look, but she forced herself to take in the swollen legs, the scabby hides, the glazed eyes. Her mounting self-pity shifted to these poor, doomed creatures. She was staring at a sickeningly scrawny gray when the image blurred into an angel-horse, with wings.

They'd been up and down every aisle. But instead of heading to the arena now, her father back-tracked to the first aisle. Bailey trailed along like a tired puppy. #71 could be cantering around with everybody looking. She choked back a whimper.

"Here's where we almost got run over," Glenna remarked.

"Huh? Oh, those idiotic colts." The aisle was nearly blocked, and she craned her neck. The colts were dashing about, careening off their walls. The heavy-set handler was in there with them, attempting to hook a halter over whatever bobbing head came within range. The colts dodged and swerved out of reach. Then one backed into a corner and stopped.

The handler lumbered over, tentatively advancing the halter. Bailey nearly laughed out loud when the wily rascal ducked under his arm and darted behind another colt. One look at Glenna and she would have dissolved completely. The crowd shifted restlessly, then gasped when a desperate lurch landed the handler in a corner. He slumped there like a comical oaf, rolling his eyes sheepishly.

"This bunch should have been started sooner," he grumbled to no one in particular. "Pickup met up with a grain truck, back Christmas-time, and knocked me out of commission." He made it back to his feet, adding, sounding almost ashamed, "Nothing for it but to leave them out all winter."

Bailey's chest hurt. Her heart went out for the guy.

"Hey, check it out," Glenna whispered. An old-timer as wrinkled as a walnut came elbowing through the crowd. The threadbare jacket he had on looked about as neglected as these colts' matted hides. Acting like he owned the place, the old-timer let himself into the stall, then motioned the stunned handler aside and took the halter. He hobbled into the center of the stall, holding the network of straps up in plain sight as if politely offering a glass of water. He stood very still while the colts pranced around him. Bailey could see his pant-legs quivering. He didn't look very strong.

A curious, rhythmical crooning started up, sounding like a sleepy owl. The hoo-hoo, hoo-hoo, hoo-hooing seemed to soothe the colts, and they traveled less frantically now. This guy was a wizard. As the crooning carried on, two of those rascals slowed to a walk. Then three came to a tentative stop. Five pairs of ears pointed at the halter dangling off one gnarled finger.

The old-timer took one imperceptible step closer. And another, until he stood less than two feet away from one colt that had stopped with its neck arched toward him. Calmly, he slipped the halter under its wary nose. And up. The captive, every bit as spellbound as the audience, accepted a gnarly brown hand kneading its scruffy brown back. When the hand lifted away, the colt appeared to be hypnotized.

"Cool," Glenna said. A happy look passed between Bailey and her father.

THE RUSTLE OF WOOD shavings; a horse's snort; a handler's shout. Compared to the noisy pole-barn, the atmosphere in here was tranquil. Serious, too—as people spoke in lowered voices. Bailey peered through the haze churned up by the hooves. Hugging herself, cozy in her new fleece hoodie, she followed #71's progress around the ring—taking in the other horses being worked but invariably homing in on the uniquely colored roan. A high hum of tension traveled through the air as the horses got called on to produce their best performance. A chunky black decked out in a silver bridle was running sprints, and kicking up blasts of wood shavings. A man in a maroon sweatshirt revolved like a maypole while a chestnut on a line circled him at a trot. A tall, mahogany bay performed an elegant side-pass to detour past the chestnut. A dozen or so horses tracked the rail; half as many strolled far enough off of it for the movers to get by. Now #71 trotted up the rail and, two feet away from the girls, quietly lifted into a rolling canter. Bailey sipped her magnum-sized hot-chocolate in hushed reverence. Her father needed to see this.

"Aren't you girls cold?" She pulled her hood up, his hand on the back of her neck sending shivers up her spine. His shoulders were hunched, his collar turned up to his hat brim. She hadn't noticed any breeze flowing till now.

"Here, Daddy, you take what's left of my cocoa." The mug shook a little, and he wrapped both hands around as if to warm them. She waited while he drank. A quick look caught the strawberry roan part way down the long side, still traveling nicely. "Check out number seventy-one, Daddy," she cooed, when the mug no longer blocked his view. "Most awesome, ever as pretty as Lacy. Actually a roan, though, not really gray. Look how beautifully she's trained. This horse is the most totally perfect one for me."

He stamped his feet, looking here and there. She might have hit him with too much for now. But if she could get him interested, he would forget he was cold. She threw Glenna a look. He would want facts. Glenna obliged.

"A stand-out, Mr. Mason, incredibly impressive. That reddish cast is rare, you know, qualifying this one as a *strawberry* roan." Glenna pointed with her elbow as #71 came on with its head carried at a cocky angle. Then the horse picked up a canter and came rolling past with the stirring force of combing waves—so close Bailey wanted to skim a finger into the light sheen of sweat. The girl rocking in the saddle didn't look any older than she was. She glanced at her father, and her heart fell. He wasn't even looking, but had his eye on a speckled pony trotting by. The kid in the saddle took the jolts straight-legged in his stirrups.

"Lacy?" Philip Mason retrieved his western-style handkerchief and noisily wiped his nose. "You mean Smokey?"

"Oh no, Daddy." She could have kicked herself for mentioning the other horse. "I just meant the gray I liked at the horse show. Quaker Lace was my ideal until I saw number seventy-one, whatever her name is, I've got to find out. Please watch her." She herself had lost sight of the horse. The silver-bridled black was running sprints again. All this time the chestnut on the line had kept on trotting, but now it suddenly shied.

"Did you see that?" her father exclaimed. The black had avoided a collision by diving into a deep slide. "What a mob scene."

Bailey seized up, recalling Lacy's blow-up. Young mares could be touchy. Her eyes scurried along the crowded rail for #71. The mare was walking now, swinging along with her head low, nearly plowing through the shavings. Nice and calm, even in traffic. This all must seem crazy after South Dakota.

"They're coming this way again, Mr. Mason. Just walking now, so you can get a good look."

But his focus was on the other side of the ring. Bailey drew in her lips. She'd have to wait out his contemplations of Lacy and Smokey and that speckled pony he had his eye on. It seemed like any involvement with horses required more than the normal amount of patience. She sighed, recalling the hypnotizer. Could she ever be so patient? It wasn't exactly a strong suit, either for her or Daddy.

"I thought it would be totally impossible," she said, trying to sound like her mother, "to find any horse I liked as well as that one at the horse show." He'd certainly had enough time to look around now. His curious gaze at her implied attention: she allowed more enthusiasm to show. "The incredible thing is, Daddy, my dream horse is here. Right here at this sale. Today!" More horses had come into the arena, blocking their view of #71. But here came that speckled pony again.

"When I was about nine, girls, a pal of mine had a little pinto. Not quite so spunky as this one, however." He coughed into his handkerchief and took some time to clear his throat. "Hard to tell much here. A horse could literally be lame, even mean, without giving anything away."

"Lameness," Glenna volunteered, "as a rule is detected at the trot."

"That's the one, Daddy, trotting now? See number seventy-one?"

"What happened to the tail?"

"Oh, that'll grow. Isn't this a cool color though?"

"Looks sound," Glenna pronounced with confidence as the roan came on in a resolute trot.

"Is that a scientific evaluation, young lady?"

Glenna drew a deep breath, then explained that a lame horse usually nodded its head up and down to keep the weight off the leg that hurt. If a right front leg was the problem, the head went down when the left front hit the ground. "On the next step, see, the head goes up."

"Is that a fact, Ms. Munro. Did you get that out of a book?"

Glenna's lower lip slid sideways. "Well, some," she conceded. "But I learned even more today, eavesdropping."

His explosive laugh turned people's heads. "Quite shrewd, young lady. And I'm not just whistling Dixie."

"She's coming around again now, Daddy."

They all agreed the strawberry roan's head did not bob once. The left foreleg swung out a little before it hit, but Bailey doubted any significance there. Her father readjusted his cowboy hat as the horse smoothly rounded the corner.

"Well, you picked a pretty one. Nice big eyes, refined head."

"I thought you'd like her, Daddy. See the cute anklets she's got on behind?"

"And see how well this mare moves, Mr. Mason? How economically, I mean. Economy is desirable in hunters, you know. A fox can keep the pack running all day. Hunters shouldn't be wasting energy on fancy, high steps. They're bred to be long-muscled, able to cover ground for hours, effortlessly.

"Economy, huh?" He fingered his lower lip. A big-barreled sorrel labored by in a lope, doing its best for its heavyset rider. Close behind came a gaunt, ungainly black in a white cape of lather.

"So you're set on a hunter, Bailey?"

She could only nod. It wasn't often he used her real name.

"That black's an accident waiting to happen," announced Glenna. Coming on fast, the horse already had side-swiped the sorrel. Bailey's throat closed up. The beast was closing in on #71. The same thing had happened to Quaker Lace, and that mare had kicked. She stared in horror as the dappled rump bounded inches in front of the troublemaker's nose. Her father would never buy any horse that kicked.

His eye was on #71 now. The scanty tail switched furiously. Clearly he expected fireworks. But the mare did something so incredibly sane here, Bailey's heart nearly exploded. Horse sense, combined with good riding, prompted the mare to veer out of line, and then simply circle back to an open spot.

"Wow. Nice manners, huh?" Glenna grinned up into her host's astonished face. "Pretty incredible for a horse used to running loose on the range."

Philip Mason pulled out his big blue handkerchief and held it up, as if expecting to sneeze. A light-footed bay cantered by, softly blowing through its nostrils. Bailey's eyes caromed like billiard balls for #71, then penetrated the haze just as a white anklet stepped through the out-gate.

10

From the Stands

"THREE-HUNNERT-DOLLAH-BID-will-you-give-me-four?" The fierce staccato rose deep from the auctioneer's throat and swooped and soared to the top tiers of the stands. A skinny two-year-old pawed furiously in the oval, peppering wood shavings into the front row. "Three-hunnert-dollah gimme four?" came again, with more insistence. The oval's deep shavings framed horse #14 in a golden backdrop. No saddle, Bailey noted, yet the program claimed #14 was broke to ride. Tucked under the hip roof of an archaic, clapboard amphitheater, she, her father, and Glenna gazed down from their hardwood perch. The air was close up here, but the good view made it worth it. The thickset old guy running the show and two secretaries on folding chairs worked from a small wooden platform just back from the oval. His beady eyes darted between #14 and the three men stationed down front to spot the crowd.

Now a whoop, and a spotter's arm shot up. The auctioneer slapped the podium. His jowly cheeks jiggled as his fervent appeal poured through the mike, pouring so fast Bailey couldn't catch a price. The horse's tired-looking handler was all dressed up in a western-style suit. Bailey winced. He'd smacked the horse's scrawny neck. The poor thing had soiled its tail. Now it reared, and got dealt a whack to the chest, and then three sharp yanks before its front hooves dropped into the hollow they'd dug. Bailey swallowed with difficulty; the sour-sweet aftertaste of the sloppy joe she'd eaten for lunch was stuck in her throat. Her heart went out to these horses coming through the oval. Some cowered there in confusion; others valiantly posed. The spotters kept alert for the renegades. They pushed and pulled one balking at the entrance, jumped and windmilled their arms to ward off another's desperate charge.

The gavel came down for #14 at $775. Bailey checked for her father's reaction: a blank expression. Less than $1000 for a riding horse was good news to her. #71 was a princess, so much finer than #14. Back in the stall, the mare was being primped and polished, waiting to come in. If only she'd live up to her looks and not act up when she found herself surrounded by this chaos, then Daddy might be swayed. Bailey stroked her sleeve where #71 had wiped her nose. Now the snuffled hoodie was more sacred than the purple-demon sweatshirt.

"Four now, four now," bellowed the auctioneer as his staff busily shuffled papers for #18, a wide-eyed, liver-chestnut yearling. "Three-fifty, four—four, now—four, now—three-fifty, four!" A spotter whooped. Bailey spied a stealthily raised blue card half-way up the other side of the stands. You needed a blue card to bid? She hadn't seen her father register. She hadn't seen any card. The cry sailed in crescendo, too fast to follow. Spotters pointed here, now there, and there, as a rash of blue spread through the crowd. Then minutes later, the excitement thinned, the bids dwindling. Anxiety about the blue card had Bailey in a state of shock. She lost track of the action, vaguely aware of the caller's tuneful tweaking. "Five-fifty, five, gimme five-fifty," eked another raise.

The pounding gavel brought her to her senses, down on $650. The liver-chestnut yearling strode out the door like a good soldier sent into the wilderness.

Glenna thumbed ahead in her program. "At this rate," she moaned, "it'll be hours before we get to seventy-one." Plenty of time to register,

Bailey assured herself. She shifted on her plank. If it wasn't so important to every horse here, she'd find the process tedious. What a letdown after all the excitement of meeting the horse of her dreams. Really, better than any horse she'd ever dreamed of. When those white anklets disappeared out the arena gate, she had run right over.

"Nice job, Steph, you worked her beautifully today," Patsy Hemptfling was telling the rider. Bailey motioned to her father and Glenna, and the three of them followed along as the horse got led back to its stall. Patsy Hemptfling concentrated on her father, while Stephanie Twomey carried on a conversation with her and Glenna.

"You can pet Dakota Clover, if you like," Stephanie offered. "Lay your hand on the neck, first." *Dakota Clover.* Bailey rolled it over her tongue as Stephanie went on about a horse's unique way of seeing. "They have eyes like flies, meaning they see miles on either side, but not so well right in front or behind. Just remember to think before you approach. An unexpected hand in the face can make one pull back, might break something and scare himself even more, and then take off."

"Did that ever happen to you?" Glenna asked.

"I'm not telling," Stephanie said off-hand, her cheeks suddenly red.

"Dakota Clover," Bailey murmured, and laid her hand on the horse's shoulder. Softly, she marched her fingers up the living shelf that sloped off the base of the slim neck, and found a cozy place underneath the smoothly combed mane.

"Steady, deliberate moves are best," Stephanie cautioned. Bailey used her whole hand to stroke the neck, applying more pressure. The mare swung her face around, and her hand switched to the swirl of white centered on the broad forehead. She ran her palm down the center stripe, and the pinkish snip on the upper lip crinkled, like a blown kiss.

Coming out of her reverie, she checked on her father. He was slumped on their hard board seat with his eyes closed. The unending chanting combined with the heat high in the stands was making him drowsy. Blinking dust motes sifted down through the light from a dormer window. Two horses occupied the oval. A mare planted her mottled-brown legs for the scruffy foal leaning into her. The auctioneer rattled on to a lackluster response, the words washing over Bailey. Did those two come as a package? Otherwise, it was the last time this foal got to nurse. Scary. A horse could slip through your fingers if you didn't stay sharp. Entire lives were at stake here, and her father was half asleep.

There was a scuffle at the entrance, as a pack of colts spilled into the oval. The spotters jumped to close in on the milling herd, all five hair-coats gleaming like sealskin. An appreciative hum ran through the stands. Something about the handler, a heavy-set guy . . .

"Look at this, Daddy." The guy with the jumpy colts! The auctioneer sprung into his spiel, and she nudged her father again. "Look Daddy, what happened to all the burrs and mud?"

Philip Mason blinked. "Incredible," he muttered.

The first colt went for $500. One right after the other, the others got snatched up—the fifth colt, the biggest, drawing even more than the first. "Incredible," Mason muttered again, as the bunch was ushered out. Bailey ventured a tentative smile, not sure if he meant that in a positive way. But he was awake now, and watching as a kid wearing rowelled spurs on his boots rode in on #45. Three quick galloping strides would have landed the horse in somebody's lap if it hadn't been rocked back on its hocks.

"For those of you looking for a showy stock horse," barked the auctioneer, "here's one handsome package of horsepower! Outfitted with brakes, too," he added as the front row brushed shavings away. He sung out the pedigree, extolled the conformation and the showy white markings. Four stockings and a big white star square on the forehead qualified this Quarter Horse for western pleasure. "He'll do it all, folks," as the kid sent the horse into a dizzying spin. "Why, he'll canter in the high-noon shade of an apple tree, one-thousand—one-thousand one-hunnert—two-hunnert—two-fifty!"

A head bobbed across the way, a finger pointed. Bailey sat tight. Her father's eyes darted like the spotters' eyes. "I've got!" one yelled, echoed by another spotter while his greedy hands snatched at air. A feverish cry ran the price up the scales without one pause to $1475.

The auctioneer took a moment to catch his breath, then spelled out the pedigree and the show record again. "Stockings guaranteed to catch even a blind judge's eye," he gushed coaxingly into the mike. "Take off that fancy saddle, kid."

A few quick moves had the ring-ties open, and a spotter bore the cumbersome apparatus away. The kid ducked under the belly and came up on the other side. He hopped behind the horse and leaned his weight on the abundant tail. "He sure knows his job," Bailey heard her father mutter. The price hit $1500 when the kid hung off the massive neck and swung like an orangutan.

"He's hooked now," whispered Glenna. Leaning forward with his hands jammed into the pockets of his scuffed leather jacket, Bailey's father pursed and pressed his lips. Then, when the bidding stalled at $1775, he assumed the appearance of an impervious block of wood.

"A buyer's market," he muttered, persistent sweet-talk having boosted the price to $1875, "not too shabby." He nudged Bailey in the ribs. "This one sure beats Smokey, and your Lady Knott wanted twenty-five hundred?" Then, grumbling about the hard boards management provided its customers, he squeezed himself between two people sitting in the next row.

Stepping this way and that, her father clomped down to the bottom of the stands while Bailey looked on helplessly. "He would pick now to tap a kidney," she moaned to Glenna, who immediately thumbed ahead in her program. Twenty-six more to go before #71.

A string of aged saddle horses came through before the crowd grew lively again. Then, "Yip!" "Here!" "I've got!" came all at once for #51, a handsome mahogany bay trained in dressage. A high hum of tension held during the time it took to sort out the three $2350 bids. Posed as majestically as any portrait model, the horse surveyed the crowd. She preferred a flowing mane, Bailey decided, to one done up in tiny, neat knots. A fresh eruption soared the price to $2600, the day's high. The crowd was hot, but Bailey felt as though she'd been plunged under a cold waterfall. At this rate, no way would her father participate. She bowed her forehead over her fingertips. Her butt was totally numb. Sell the horse already, please?

The gavel dropped on $4200, launching a barrage of cheers and stomps sending tremors through the old wooden stands. At last, the champ filed out with his entourage. Exhausted by now, Bailey spaced out, propped up by Glenna. "Daddy's sure taking his sweet time," she moaned twenty-five minutes later, as #55 went out. Maybe he had run into Mrs. Hemptfling. She sat erect. Those two could be working up a deal. He had sounded quite serious when he'd asked the woman why she wanted to sell.

"Too many to look after," Patsy Hemptfling had replied. "Even after I traded off two for this one. Pretty fillies that've weathered range life are a real prize, practically guaranteed to stay sound."

Oh, yes! Dakota Clover was all she ever wanted. Her father might be back there talking to Patsy Hemptfling right now. No, he already spoke to her; now he's signing his registration. She searched through the stands for a certain wide-brimmed hat. Fourteen more to go before her future, and Dakota Clover's future, went up for grabs.

Eight more horses through, nothing extraordinary. It wouldn't be long now, before a strawberry roan occupied the oval. Her heart skipped a beat. A black cowboy hat had appeared next to the auctioneer's platform.

"Cross your fingers, Glen, here he comes."

Slowly, laboriously, her father threaded his way up.

"Welcome back, Mr. Mason," crooned Glenna. "You've been sorely missed," she added as he lowered himself with a faint groan.

"We better leave soon, girls. Don't forget there's a two hour drive ahead of us."

Glenna unzipped her zebra-striped backpack. "Who'd like a Heath bar?" she asked cheerily, extracting three glittery packets. Bailey gratefully took two and passed one over to her father. Something blue she hadn't noticed before stuck out of his chest pocket.

"What's that card?"

"Oh, the secretary had me register, don't ask me why."

"So our number is two-fifty-three?"

He turned away waving her off with a hand.

She bent forward as though in prayer and stared blindly at the cover of her program. Did he actually intend to bid? He must be thinking about it. Maybe he registered because somebody asked him to, simply to oblige. Anyway, he'd picked up a number with no pushing from her. She must be very careful now.

She gave herself a little shake and straightened up. "Dakota Clover will be coming in soon," she said loudly enough for everyone around them to hear. "Did you see her again, Daddy?"

"Not in the stall," he answered, carefully unwrapping his candy bar. "I caught a glimpse in the aisle."

"You did?" He'd actually gone back. To see if the horse was as beautiful as he remembered? To get the horse talking to him, like the other one he liked? She bit into her candy bar.

"The girl had her in line already. The mare just stood there with her forehead pressed into the girl's shoulder."

"Oh, Daddy . . ." On impulse she leaned into her father's shoulder, her tongue washed in chocolate.

He frowned and crossed his arms over his chest. "Listen, kiddo. People don't just go and buy horses out of the blue."

LONG STRETCHES OF SHINY wood lay exposed in the stands by the time #70 left the oval. Bailey caught a glimpse of richly-hued gray, and then Stephanie Twomey trotted in on #71. Bailey clutched her stomach and strained forward. Under lights, the distinctively colored hide appeared even more dazzling. Here at last—so close, but so far away. She snuck a look at her father, who seemed cast in stone. His face had turned as white as granite.

The bidding started at $500, which seemed to be the standard opener for riding horses. #71 traveled easily with her neck flexed, and $500 for this clearly trained horse got snapped up immediately. Then a raise to $550, before the bidding stalled. #71 went on trotting, taking the confines of the oval smoothly. "Will you give me six?" the auctioneer croaked in desperation to his sparse assembly. Three hours of touting livestock had strained his voice. An interminable pitch for $600 hit a wall. He paused for breath, only the oval's swishing sounds during this heady silence. #71 flowed in one direction, then turned on her haunches and flowed in the other direction. The auctioneer pleaded for six again, carrying on with his arms raking, raking in mounds of missing bids. "Six now six now five hunnert fifty gimme six!?"

At last a whoop, indicating six took. Bailey pulled her eyes away from the radiant horse to locate the bidder. It couldn't be anybody as desperate as she was. A covert check on her father discovered him holding himself ramrod straight. "A classical stunner, folks, every bit as easy to ride as to look at," proclaimed the auctioneer valiantly. A spotter's hand shot up. Bailey hadn't noticed a signal. That older couple seemed to have gone home; too long a day for them. Her father held his arms crossed, hands hidden in his armpits. She loved him more than ever for sticking this out. At least they'd get to see where the horse was going.

"Buyer's market," he muttered. Her hopes fired. This was a plus, if they were buyers. He'd seen how sensible the horse acted, and how beautiful—ten times more gorgeous than anything in her horse scrapbook. She clutched his arm, raised her lips to his ear, and started promising anything she could think of. To help him in the yard, to try extra hard to be good. And she meant it. She couldn't even remember her last scolding, though. Oh, for biting her nails. She would even let her nails grow.

He shook her hand off. Wow, touchy today. But of course he'd be nervous, if he wanted the horse. His bicep felt hard; his jaw looked clenched. He looked so stern, she was afraid it would only botch things if she uttered one more word of encouragement.

Mrs. Hemptfling had stationed herself at the edge of the oval and was standing with her hands braced on her hips. The auctioneer sent her a peculiar look. Then he took another deep breath and, upgrading his spiel, begged what remained of his flock to reconsider on this one.

"Eight now eight now—seven-hunnert-fifty—will you gimme eight?"

"Dakota Clover, Dakota Clover," Bailey chanted under her breath. She and Glenna hunched forward with their eyes locked on the mare, whose ears pointed straight back up to where they sat. Bailey heard the horse give a quizzical snort. *She's looking at me.* Saying, "Buy me, buy me." Concentrate on the big guy right next to me, she was beaming back when a flash of blue glanced off her eye. Her father had the card in his hand. A spotter whooped. For us? Let it be true! She was squeezing Glenna's hand, hard, when a sharp yip buried that bid. The urge to scream *cease fire!* and set the price back to $800 had her out of her skin.

"Nine-twenty-five now, nine-twenty-five nine-hunnert gimme nine-twenty-five?" The jumped price put a fresh bounce in the cry. The stands hummed with a rustle of activity. The mare stood valiantly poised. Bailey's heart called out—what could she say to Daddy, what should she do? Even if he had put a bid in, it didn't count now. Now it would take $925. He looked eager; clearly wanted the horse. Pretty, pretty please, before the price goes higher. His face had turned even redder than his hair. The hand holding the blue card clutched his knee. His arm brushed hers as he pulled his blue handkerchief out. He steadied his hat with the card tight in his hand while he wiped his forehead. Bailey's big hopes spun like the little ball racing around the wheel of fortune. Directly down from where they sat, the spotter stretched to aim up a fixed expression, the crucial question plain on his face. Tints of color glinted off #71's rump, undulating under the lights. The left fore swung with the right hind, the right fore with the left hind as the coveted horse trotted on. For a few moments you could hear the swish of shavings.

"I've got!"

Bailey pinched herself. This was real!

"That's nine-twenty-five do I hear nine-fifty nine-twenty-five give me nine-fifty!" Her entire world went on hold while the auctioneer scanned the crowd.

"Sold," a voice from out of the clouds proclaimed. "Number two-fifty-three!"

11

A Torn Jacket

THEY CARRIED ON A delirious discussion driving home about all they'd need to get done before the horse arrived. Two young guys at the sale had brought horses up from Greenham, and agreed to haul Dakota Clover back in their trailer. There was a free stall at Ludlow Farms, where they worked, and they had no problem putting the mare up there for the night. Once they'd finished their chores on Sunday, they could haul her over to Custer Lane. Bailey had recognized Chuck and Billy Calderone as the same guys who abducted Theo at the horse show. They must know horses if they worked for the Ludlows. And, they had brought Theo back in one piece. Still, she wouldn't even begin to relax until the horse was safe at home, with her.

"Can't I stay, at least until the horse gets here?" Glenna whimpered into her cell phone. But Ms. Sondra Munro insisted her only child had been gone long enough. So Bailey and her father dropped Glenna off Sunday morning on their way to Fred's Farm & Home store.

The proprietor himself came to wait on them. He seemed a tidy, trim person, except for the stains on his teeth, and the noticeable bulge in his cheek.

"What's the problem?" Fred Depinna bypassed the usual preliminaries. His cheek bounced on *problem*. Bailey knew about chewing tobacco, but hardly expected to see it in New England.

"We're short on time," her father said, and passed the proprietor a sketch she had drawn of their back field, showing how the three sides were closed in naturally. A line of poplar trees ran between their land and the North's; a stone wall backed by a wooded area bordered the low end; locust trees and a huge mass of bushes blocked off what lay to the south. Their main concern was the west, open side, near their house. "What's the easiest, quickest, and cheapest way to secure this place for a horse?" Her father jabbed at the paper. "I'm not up for putting all this in posts and rails."

The protuberance in Fred Depinna's cheek shifted. "Well, barbed wire is easiest, quickest, and cheapest," he replied. "Just fools use that on horses, though." He swiped his chin with his sleeve before volunteering that they might do with hot wire. "Problem is, hot wire makes trouble for horses, and people. Course, you can tie on little streamers, if you want your place to look like a used car lot." A brown line of spit hit the floor. Bailey let out a nervous giggle. Daddy would never go for the car lot look.

"Those trees might work." Depinna ran his finger around the south, east, and north sides. "String heavy-gauged wire here, run posts and rails across the open end. Two-by-eights on top should do it, reinforced by a line of wire half-way down." He spit again, then added, "So the horse don't get under, ya know."

It sounded like a lot of work. Her father's wrinkled brow indicated he thought so, too. They'd never get everything done before the horse arrived.

"I reckon that'll look fine," the proprietor said, in a more encouraging tone. "Make a decent barrier."

Besides the lumber, they needed a gate, an electric fencer, ten dozen insulators, and thirty dollars worth of Fred Depinna's best wire. "I'll throw in the insulated wire for your fencer," he added magnanimously, then tucked a fresh pinch into his cheek. "This winds up the easy part," he said, turning to run his eyes over a rack displaying every tool imaginable, taking up the whole length of the aisle. He went straight to some shiny, long-handled spades coupled like giant pincers. "This'll give you something to dig with," he said after hauling them down. Bailey gawked at the contraption. Her father threw up his hands.

"Isn't there a better way?"

A furtive tongue retrieved a drop of saliva. "You could rent a post-hole digger. Son-in-law Clarence has one. Tractor-mounted."

BY 10:30, THEY WERE back and laying out plans for the fence. Bailey pinched the end of the tape-measure while her father puzzled out the spacing. Once they'd decided where the posts should go, they worked their way down into the field and marked the trees they wanted to use. Bailey kept track of the ceramic insulators and ten-penny nails while her father wielded the hammer. She squelched her usual chatter—he hated interruptions when he was trying to focus. A miss made him cuss, and she pretended not to notice. Any sign of sympathy'd only draw attention to the slip-up and make it worse. She gazed up to the shed. The way the sun hit those weathered boards turned it virtually celestial. Shiny little birds darted about. She'd discovered a bowl of mud inside, plastered to a high rafter. Just built, as it hadn't been there when she and Glenna cleared things out. Fortunately the precious shed had been left standing. She needed to thank Daddy for that on top of everything else. Not now though, not when he was aiming at the tiny head of a shiny nail.

They had the insulators set halfway around when Clarence Gould arrived with his noisy machinery. Bailey followed along as her father pointed out where he wanted the postholes. When Clarence's powerful drill sent up its terrific screech, Bailey went back to her trees.

Soon she was driving four-inch spikes straight through the doughnut-shaped insulators and into bark with three strikes. One time she did it in two. "Sorry, trees," she muttered, hoping one nail wouldn't hurt.

Michael had been commissioned to round up the North boys. Home from church, Theo came shouldering shovels, an iron ramming-rod, and a carpenter's level. He seemed nearly as happy about the horse as she was, crying, "Fantastico!" He'd just slapped her a high-five when Andy North roared up on his yellow dirt-bike. His mom had given in, Bailey guessed when she saw his fringed leather jacket. It had to be the one Andy made a fuss over at the tack shop. It looked too fancy for hauling lumber.

Clarence's deep holes got set with the flat sides of the posts facing the pasture. Theo tamped in the fill, pumping his weighty rod with steely determination. Several rounds of foot-stomping insured a tight set. Before long, Theo had peeled off two layers and was working in his tee-shirt; Andy had taken off his jacket. They had three sturdy posts standing straight as goal-posts when Clarence loaded up his tractor and went clack-clacking out the driveway. Bailey pulled her eyes away from Theo's bulging arm muscles and went back to her trees. By the time she'd hammered up insulators two-thirds of the way around, her arm muscles ached.

The horse would be coming any time now. Her mother called everybody up to the patio for a break.

The boys were guzzling cans of Dr Pepper. Bailey flung the heavy hammer aside, and then sat down next to Theo on the low flagstone wall. Everything was going according to schedule. She rubbed her sore arm and breathed a happy sigh.

She was examining the intriguing effects of bubbles in the carpenter's level when Andy came out with a yelp. He stood wailing like he was in agony, stuttering something unintelligible. The fancy jacket lay in his arms. The heavy hammer lay at his feet. His angrily contorted face was aimed at *her*.

"You w-went and t-t-tore it, Bailey!" Andy held up a sleeve showing a three-inch gash.

"He just got that for his birthday," Theo muttered. "Geez."

"I did that?" Contemplating the boy curled around his precious bundle of suede, Bailey warily set the carpenter's level down. Everything was going fine, until stupid Andy had to show up in that jacket. She rose to her feet and forced one, then the other, to provide transportation. Before she could get anything halfway apologetic out, Andy's hand shot up with its middle finger out.

"I'll g-get you for this!" Fighting tears, Andy tossed the torn jacket over his shoulder, then ran to his dirt-bike. As a high-pitched wail followed him out the driveway, Bailey shot Theo a helpless look. It wasn't like she'd torn the kid's new jacket on purpose.

Her parents had long faces.

"That was really stupid," she moaned, trying to sound just as grief-stricken as Andy. These fence posts marching across her yard signified the biggest day of her life, and no freakin' twerp was going to spoil it. He could still wear his precious jacket, couldn't he?

"If you knew the correct way to handle tools," her father suggested, "that never would have happened."

Theo bubbled down a long chug-a-lug. Bailey rolled her unopened, icy pop-can over her burning forehead. She would be pretty upset, too, she supposed, if something happened to her Purple Demon sweatshirt. A daunting premonition of her new responsibilities fell over her. She needed to be more careful handling tools. The same for handling her horse.

Theo cupped his chin, squelching a belch. "So Bailey," he said, leaning back on one elbow. "Fill me in on the new horse. A gray one, right?"

"Uh huh," she answered faintly. Still, his lopsided grin helped lift the weight off her chest. She could have kissed him for changing the subject.

"Are you going to let anybody else ride her?"

She examined her stinging palms for blisters. She hadn't thought about that.

"Anyone helping with the fence," her father said, "gets to ride the horse. That makes sense to me. And we'll have to see about Andy's nice new jacket," he added with a grimace of disgust at Bailey. A chunk of ice clunked inside her chest. Suddenly she was tired. She longed to rest against Theo's shoulder. She maybe would have, if her mother hadn't spoken up.

"How are the riding lessons going, Theo?" Bailey forced herself to sit up. It'd be okay for Theo to ride, but that freakin' brother of his wasn't coming anywhere near her horse.

Theo's pop-can met a flagstone with a sharp click. Hands braced on his knees, he courteously replied that he had progressed to the cantering stage.

Beth Mason's fingernails tap-danced over her pop-can. "Can't you be more specific?" she asked cheerily. "For instance, how does your instructor explain things? It can't be easy teaching a bunch of kids, all on different horses."

"Uh," and a short laugh. "She gets kinda detailed when we start something new. Mostly, though, Cappy stands there barking stuff like, 'Heels down, shoulders back, hands steady, legs at the girth, eyes between the ears!'" Rising to the occasion, he told how Cappy kept on about technique, especially to the kids assigned the worst horses.

"This Asian girl had this nasty chestnut, Escort?" The three Masons nodded encouragement, Bailey radiating approval. Wasn't Theo good at holding center stage! "Escort just gets trotting faster when he's supposed to canter. Geez, I'm lucky my old guy lopes along like a trooper. Probably last week's the last time I get old Corny, though, according to Josh Shapiro, a guy there who goes to Sage Hall." Theo made a face. "Just so I don't get One Oak's infamous express train, Escort, or that wily old tank, Barrister. The girl on Barrister never got to canter at all."

"Oh dear. Bailey, it sounds like you might need some lessons. Maybe Mike should take, too." Beth Mason looked around for her son.

"I think Mike went to take our shovels back." Theo fiddled with the can. It made a dreadful noise as he crushed it—so viciously, Bailey realized his brother's outburst still rankled. Her mother seemed aware, too, trying to smooth things over. Theo was surreptitiously tucking his lump of scrap metal behind his foot when she asked what else went on in his riding class. He thought a minute. Then, "Everybody's supposed to stay far enough back to see the next horse's hocks."

"Hocks?" the Masons chorused.

"Yeah, the backward knees they've got on their hind legs. You're too far back if you can see all the way down to feet."

"That makes sense to me," Philip Mason said. "A horse might kick if it gets run up on."

"Affirmative. No rear-end collisions. Corn Cob's good enough about spacing. He'll lengthen or shorten his stride, and halt, if I cue him right."

"So, who's the best rider in your class?" Philip Mason asked.

"Well, definitely not me." Chin sunk to his chest, Theo laughed a little. "Shapiro gets this spunky little black they call Hickory Nut to do everything, so I guess he is."

Bailey threw back a last swig. "I'll be happy riding just one horse," she announced. "One really good one, you know." One good one was best. They would belong to each other. They would get to know each other. She would read her horse's mind like she read Theo's mind, sometimes. She and her horse would have ESP.

12

Home for a Strawberry Roan

THE HORSE ARRIVED IN a rickety stock-trailer, towed by a rusty pickup truck. "Hey, I know these guys," Theo exclaimed through the volley of back-fires rolling it to a stop. The Calderone brothers piled out, both from the driver's side. A thin growth of hair covered Chuck's chin, a grimy engineer's cap the back of his head. Billy was shorter, huskier, crowned with the shiniest, darkest, curliest hair Bailey had ever seen on a boy.

"Where'd that heap come from?" Her father was not happy.

"It's okay, Daddy. They made it, didn't they?" This wasn't the classy trailer the guys took to the sale. Still, it had come through with hay and shavings and panels for the stall, and the most beautiful horse on earth, all in one piece. She peered through the slats. A long, loud whinny resounded. The fuchsia halter swung. The horse's upper lip curled, like into a smile.

"She likes me, Mom!" The nose was snuffling her arm. Awesome.

"What a cute way of testing our essence. I see what you meant now by strawberry. Here, Bee, let's see if she'll eat a carrot." Her mother poked a peeled carrot through the slats. One whiff, then the giant front teeth bit it in half. Enormous jaws were chomping away when Billy Calderone's ruddy face popped up right next to the horse's face.

One yank, and he'd untied the rope. The rear door screeched. The trailer quaked and thundered. Bailey rushed back in time to see a skimpy tail appear, then two white anklets, and the entire lengths of two mottled legs. With surprising daintiness, all four feet landed on solid ground. Bailey hugged herself. Truly, this most special horse had materialized in her yard as if by magic.

"Oh, oh," Michael said, indicating the raised tail.

"Ah ha-aah," Philip Mason drawled, "a contribution for the garden."

The rope Billy pushed into her hand felt electric. Around and around, over the same ground, was the way to go, to give a fixed point for the mare to get her bearings. Bailey felt a rush as the horse moved out. The animal radiated heat. The big eyes spun as though searching for something to recognize. A sense of the tremendous power in her hands had Bailey praying *Please stay calm!* For both their sakes. She aimed for a circular path, struggling to keep up without getting trampled, while her father crowed with delight over the "excellent muscling on those rolling hips."

Five rounds between the patio and the fence posts settled the mare into an easier stride. Chuck pulled off his grimy cap and contentedly fingered the brim. "That yellow on the off-hind's just salve," he remarked. "She banged her ankle going in the trailer. Best to keep an eye on her water," he added.

"Hasn't she been drinking?" Beth Mason asked.

"Some, like they go off sometimes when it tastes dif'rent. She's some tucked up. You can figure, like, as long as they're eatin' and drinkin' and shittin', they're okay."

Bailey caught a slapstick look from Theo. Her parents looked blank—that sort of talk bothered them, though. The horse seemed fine but was moving fast again. She stretched to keep up. Her right arm got wrenched, practically pulled out of its socket. She rubbed it while the horse clipped through a patch of dandelions. Oops, hoof marks in the new grass. That wouldn't be a problem, once all the posts and rails were up. A sharp clank from the trailer shot the head up, and Bailey's arm got yanked the other way. The horse froze, half-eaten stems and yellow fluff protruding between the lips, all through the stanchions' and stall panels' terrifying clanging as they got lugged away.

The work-effort shifted to the shed. The walking resumed, the horse's elongated shadow cast by the lowering sun walking along. Bailey rested her hand on the bobbing neck and let it ride. She was deep in concentration, gauging her stride in time with the horse's stride, when she heard an immense sigh. A bird trilled its evening song, clearly pleased with its day.

"Everything's ready," her father hollered.

A post loomed as they abandoned the circle. The horse shied, and Bailey stumbled to her knees. She scrambled to her feet with her head whirling, wondering if she should have expected that. There was so much to think about when you needed to think for two. She looked toward the shed, which looked like a long way to lead a jumpy horse. Stealing time, she pressed her forehead into the arched neck and prayed for strength.

"That was close," Theo exclaimed, running up. "Want me to take her?"

"Are you kidding? We're fine!" Straightening up, Bailey drilled her eyes into the waiting shed. The fading light had mellowed the battered walls. Her confidence grew as the horse followed along. The terrain was fairly level here, would only begin its gradual decline beyond the shed. Pointy-winged birds swooped back and forth, chittering irately. The horse seemed okay with the dive-bombers: she made up her mind not to let them bother her. What were they mad about, anyway? They'd still have their own nest.

"C'mon," Michael shouted from the shed. "You gotta see this!" Her parents and the Calderone brothers looked on expectantly from the far side of the doorway. The mingled hay and pine smells made the old shed seem more like a real barn.

"Out of the way, Mike," her father shouted.

The stall had been set up across from the doorway. The last rays of sunshine lit up the bars. Bailey let the rope fall as Dakota Clover stepped to the fresh bed of shavings. Then she stepped in, humming softly so the horse would know she was in there, too. One swing of those powerful hips could ruin everything. She stood to one side as the horse turned around and then dropped its head to the heap of hay in one corner. She leaned over this strange, wonderful creature, on her guard as she reached for the halter snap. Up close, the smell was intoxicating. Her fingers slipped in tentatively, and were fumbling with the unfamiliar device when a slice of hay burst in her face. She spit it away from her lips and focused on the halter.

The mare was surprisingly obliging when the crownpiece slid over her ears, and raised her head to let the halter drop. Bailey's fulfilled humming went running up the scales.

Six faces gazed in, Michael's half-hidden by the four-foot panel.

"There she is," her mother said in a tone of wonder. The shed looked bigger now. The stall took up ten feet of the north wall, leaving five feet on its west side for closet space and fifteen to its east for hay storage. The back panel blocked off the old wall's major gaps, and there was plenty of room for the horse to lie down. Bailey reached her free hand to cup the bony withers, then ranged up to the mane's coziness. The warmth and rich earthy smell were awesome.

The stall door clanged shut when she went out, and Dakota Clover's neck snapped straight up. Chewing no longer, the mare swung herself this way and that. With her nose pointed over the bars, she delivered a mighty whinny.

"She called last night, too," Billy Calderone said. "Prob'ly wishing she was home."

"You are home, Dakota Clover," Bailey sang through the bars. "You wouldn't be more family than if you were my sister." A long-distance move could be as painful for a horse as it was for a human. Still, if they both hadn't come so far, they never would have ended up in Connecticut. Together!

The mare snuffled restlessly, scattering shavings through the hay. Theo curled his hands around the bars. Bailey reached through from time to time, trailing her fingers across whatever section of the animal came close. After a while, the high hips shifted and the hind legs extended, for the release of a steaming, pungent stream. A bird called softly. More quietly now, Dakota Clover went back to nosing for tasty fragments of hay.

"OH GUSSIE, I GOT a horse!"

"Looking gooood, girrrl," hoisting her coffee mug.

"And she's right in my own back yard," Bailey called over her shoulder as she skipped up the aisle. Theo's grin widened as she shared how she had snuck along the side of the shed this morning and peeked. "Those ears were up, like saluting," she said in amazement. "She listened for me!"

"Yeah, she'd want breakfast."

"She says 'Hi' with a deep, gurgly rumble. I guess she slept lying down, shavings were stuck to her hip."

"The first night in a new place? She musta really been tired. How about that cut?"

"I think it's okay. I've gotta get a flashlight. Those guys are bringing buckets and a rake and stuff, and Chuck's gonna put more salve on. He has shop this aft and's going to leave early."

"So he says, anyhow. If he cuts, probably Billy will, too. They need bread to insure that truck. Once you get wheels, expenses sure add up."

"Daddy's already spent a ton." Bailey gave a hollow laugh. "And I don't even have a saddle yet."

Theo pillowed his head on his gym bag and shut his eyes. "Don't worry," he intoned sleepily. "Your father won't have you riding that Porsche bareback."

THE PERKED-EAR SALUTE AGAIN. "I love you very much," Bailey whispered with her arms around the vibrant neck. She gazed into the deep brown eyes. Whatever did this horse think of *her?* Two tough-looking buckets hung from large hooks snapped to the bars, flat-backed and snug against the front panel. The twenty-quarter red one was empty, the twenty-two-quarter gray one full of water. She splashed her fingers, suggesting a drink. "Good for your complexion," she chirped, sounding like her mother.

"I already topped her bucket," Billy Calderone told her. "Don't worry, your horse is drinking." She'd found him and Chuck stringing wire from a large spool they wheeled from tree to tree. A sturdy rail connected the fence-posts, entered through a smooth-swinging pipe-gate colored green.

"I'll be turning this on now," announced Chuck, with a final twist to his wire. "You can get the horse."

Her heart raced as she fumbled with the floppy halter. Billy checked how she'd fastened the rope.

"Just stay calm," he told her in a tone as gentle as his soft brown eyes. "She needs plenty of time to explore, Red, so keep a good hold. She might want to stop and stare, and some's okay. But mostly, keep moving and keep her mind on you. And if she acts up, Red, talk her out of it with a few jerks on that leadshank." The rope, he must mean. A whole new language. He adjusted her right hand higher. "Your right shoulder stays by her left shoulder, Red. Take her around the fence-line. She needs to see her bounds before we turn her loose." Nobody had called her "Red" since kindergarten. Anyhow, her hair was more like liver-chestnut.

"If she gets excited," Billy went on, "stay up close to the shoulder. Keep a short hold and tighten your circle so she don't explode."

There was a rush out the door, tempered by her shoulder jammed back into the horse's shoulder. *Keep moving*, she remembered, and, *Needs plenty of time to explore.* She was doing her best when a flock of black birds as big as shoeboxes flew up. The sudden shy gave her a lurch. Then suddenly the horse was moving fast and she was running. And here came some ears flopping, and a tail wildly wagging.

"Whoa," she cried. "No! No, Duker!" Both she and the horse froze. The dense stand of honeysuckle they'd stopped near was halfway into the field—Billy and Chuck too far away to be any help. The spaniel was permitted to sniff the horse's hooves, until, "Here Duker, boy!" rang out. While the dog dashed back up the hill, the horse strained against the rope with her tail in the air.

"Hey, not so hyper!" Thank goodness her mother had charge of the dog. "Easy, sis. Please, don't do this to me!"

"Take it easy there, Red," came from far away.

An abrupt dive for a dandelion had the trees swirling. Bailey fought for equilibrium while the horse began a voracious passage through a yellow patch. She looked back to gauge their distance from the shed. Her mother and the Calderone boys were leaning over the fence, gazing back at her. She coughed an exasperated grunt as the insatiable animal strained for more. "You're supposed to be exploring, not pulling me all over the place! Some sister you make, big and bossy." A squawk, practically under their feet, sent the neck straight up again. "A pheasant, you idiot. You saw pheasants in South Dakota, didn't you?"

The mare stood poised for flight. Bailey massaged her arm, the soreness from yesterday on fire. Maybe they should head back.

One flick of the leadshank got them moving again. They were well away from the honeysuckle when a sharp report made Bailey jump. The horse went right on walking, clearly accustomed to having dry sticks snap underfoot. Bailey was being tugged one way, then the other way, her white sneakers collecting scuffs. The field seemed bigger every minute—terribly far to lead around a horse you hardly know. A distant whine provoked another shy. The rope burned, spun Bailey around, and nearly got away from her.

How nice of Andy to let Mikey try his bike—Not! They sure picked the wrong time to start it up.

They had traveled to the far end of the field. The horse shuffled about in the tall weeds growing along the stone fence. Bailey was determined to get away from these rocks, and yanked harder than she meant to. There was a sudden flash of white, then scrambling hooves that left her hand empty.

"Get out of there," Billy shouted. Bailey took off after the dappled rump, but lost ground as the horse went rumbling up the slope. Both boys vaulted the fence. Dakota Clover was headed for the green gate, picking up speed as though meaning to jump, and run all the way back to South Dakota.

"Whoooa," came from the other side of the fence. Bailey was running for all she was worth. If only this mare had sense enough to . . .

A sudden prop on the forehand with inches to spare averted a crash. Gazing longingly over her pipe-gate, Dakota Clover bellowed out a long loud whinny.

"A smart one, there," Chuck said.

"Good mover, pretty as she looks," Billy added. The leadshank dangled from the halter. If only she could get there in time. Bailey edged along the rail. Her mother was crouched over Duker with a tight hold on the collar. "Easy, Red," cautioned Billy. But this mare wouldn't kick. Would she?

The question hung in the air as the horse pushed off again. Dakota Clover hurtled across the field blowing back heart-rending neighs to their chorus of *whoa's*. Bailey heard a sharp clang, and a silver disc shot out of the weeds. She cringed—that old hubcap could have made trouble. The loose rope flung up woody stems, whipped the whirling legs. Hard cracking noises carried back from the downed branches, and the horse came roaring over the rise like an empty semi with its horn stuck, seeming to grow in size.

"Don't step on your rope!" Bailey flinched as the hooves flew past, terribly close to the fence. She ducked stinging dirt-clods. Her horse was headed for the treacherous southwest corner, where the sturdy boards met the hot wire.

"Turn, turn," she pleaded desperately. Dakota Clover would hate it here if she got stung. "Go hoe-ommm," she hollered with all her might. "Hay and water in your staw-alll!"

The runaway handily negotiated the corner and, as if possessed, took off again. Desperate whinnies echoed back from the poplar trees. Treasured memories of home in South Dakota must be driving her on. Would she ever see her old herd again? They were running without her, and she was alone.

"Whoa, whoa," Billy yelled at the top of his lungs as Dakota Clover came barreling over the rise with a long weed trailing from her mouth. He had the southwest corner covered now, his arms spread wide. Chuck manned the northwest corner, waving his engineer's cap. Bailey gritted her teeth. Waving a hat was no help.

A deep slide pulled the lathered mare up directly in front of Chuck. Righting herself, Dakota Clover flipped the astonished guy's cap with her nose and wheeled as it sailed through the air. Neighing her 9-1-1 call, she pushed off again.

Bailey whimpered helplessly. Despite her fears, she was laughing.

"Man, what a mare," Chuck exclaimed. Cautiously he avoided the wire while slithering through the fence for his cap.

"Lovely, girl, lovely," Beth Mason called out as the strawberry roan bridged the rise in a buoyant canter.

"It looks like a race horse," hollered Mike, back home with his buddy, but no infuriating dirt bike. "This one," Mike told Andy, "looks big-time too fast for me to ride."

"Huh, my big brother c-could."

"So? My sister could, too. Wanna bet?"

"Hey, big girl," wheedled Bailey, "will you please settle down?"

"Come on, babe . . . easy, now."

"Time for dinner, Dakota Clover!"

"No, Red," countered Billy. "You can't feed now." At her startled look, he explained that horses need time to cool down after a workout like this one. "If you let her eat now, you're in for colic."

Chuck massaged his new chin-hairs, nodding sagely. "Mainly, blood's all up in the muscles," he said. "You gotta let a horse, like, stabilize."

13

A Visit from Mrs. Knott

THE SUN WAS PEEKING through the window Tuesday when Bailey opened her eyes. She lay in bed listening to the birds singing in the new day. No horse sounds—all must be well in the barn. She took a few more minutes under the covers to revel in her good fortune. Only a few because she couldn't wait to see her horse again.

The mare was on her feet, profiled cross-wise against the far wall, and seemed asleep. Then, even though Bailey had come up quietly, one eyelid flicked. Moments later, the ears pricked; then the horse swung front and center. *See, just like me, she takes a moment to pull herself together when she wakes up.* She'd be tired from her chaotic weekend. She wouldn't be jumpy now, not alarmed if something human came in there. At this moment, Dakota Clover appeared perfectly trustworthy.

She doled out three cushy flakes and then went back for fresh water. She tidied the bedding with an eye on the potentially dangerous hooves. Rain was in the forecast, a decent excuse to leave the horse standing in. She'd never be able to concentrate in school worrying about what was going on at home. *Good decision.* The rain was coming down in big splats that afternoon when she headed back out. A path had begun to show in the new grass. The sparkling white pail weighed against her arm as she hobbled over the slipperiness, feeling ridiculous lugging water out with so much falling from the sky. Tin roofs amplified noise, she discovered in the shed. Dakota Clover shifted from one foot to the other, acting just as jittery as *she* felt. Tentatively she raised the latch, slid it back.

"Relax, big girl." She was trying to sound calm. The thought of opening this door, even a few inches, had her rigid with anxiety. The scraping noise might set the horse off again. "Please try, aren't you tired from your busy weekend?" Raindrops pelting the roof was bad enough, it better not thunder. She opened the door a bit more and leaned in with her heavy pail. Her arms protested as, with one foot anchored back in the aisle, she boosted her quivering load over to the waiting bucket. She laughed. All this work, and that bucket was still half full.

WEDNESDAY MORNING, SHE SLID into the gate and struck her hip against a post. Hard, and it hurt. The slipperiness made an excuse to leave her horse standing in again—no way did she want Dakota Clover slamming into the fence. Mr. Lederle cancelled their math session and she caught the early bus home. The sun had appeared and, toting the prudently half-full plastic pail, she did not slip once.

A cheery whinny rang out as she stretched to slide the fuchsia halter off its hook. Clearly, the horse wanted out. Chattering away about what she was getting ready to do and what they might both get to do after she did that, she led Dakota Clover into the aisle. The Calderones had set up a crosstie station to make it easier for her to work around the horse. Getting into position so both chains reached to the halter required an awkward bout of backing and turning.

She launched into a makeover with an old hair brush her mother had donated to the cause. She smoothed down the long neck and broad chest, then went after the mane's stickered wood-chips. She switched from the brush to her fingers and, making happy, fussy sounds, freed the tangled ends before working into the matted clumps. These snarls made her think how, "What a rat's nest!" Gammie'd say while combing *her* hair. Pointy-winged birds flew trips to their nest. Duker came in and sniffed about, swirling his feathered tail. Bailey leaned an arm across the nice level back she couldn't wait to sit on. "Ah, touchy today," she softly observed when it flinched. "I know, sweetheart, what you need is exercise. Wait till I finish your tail, okay?" She hadn't decided whether to try another tour around the fence line, or simply turn the horse loose. She moved back to the tail with no thought of kicking. "You character, you," she murmured while extricating the woody flakes carefully, loath to lose even one precious hair. That funny bit with Chuck's cap revealed an amazing sense of humor. Aside from this skimpy tail, Dakota Clover was beyond ideal.

A better diet might help it. She had consulted Mrs. Knott, who sounded happy to explain about feeding. Brome grass laced with alfalfa suited four-year-olds. Timothy was good, too. Next year, when the horse matured, a less costly hay of mostly grass would do. She had the phone numbers of some dealers Mrs. Knott relied on for bales cut and raked clean with no rain damage.

Finished with the tail, Bailey stood back for a look. Pleased with her efforts, she collected the manure fork and the heavy plastic tub. The bulk of it sliding under Dakota Clover's nose made her jerk the crossties.

"Whoa there, girl," somebody yelled.

The manure fork dropped. Smokey's mother stood in the doorway, looking like she wanted to scoop this horse into her arms. Bailey moved up and shielded the withers with her arm. Dakota Clover stepped up, restoring slack to the crossties. She'd never expected company. At least the horse was clean.

"Don't let me interrupt, dear, get on with your chores while I feast on this delicious creature." Mrs. Knott dropped a floppy duffle bag by the door. Humming under her breath, casting occasional, approving smiles Bailey's way, she stepped here and there to view Dakota Clover from various angles. "Very nice," she cooed. "Rather rare coloring. The skimpy tail indicates Appaloosa genes."

"Really? But the father was a Thoroughbred. Won't her tail grow out?"

"Don't be silly, App-tails are quite respectable. The Nez Perce bred short tails into their spotted mustangs on purpose. They wouldn't get caught up in ropes or bushes, weighed down with mud. You see hunters' tails tied up for the same reason. Carriage horses' tails were bobbed, before it was outlawed." The horsewoman stood back from Dakota Clover and gazed appraisingly. "You've got a good combination here—Appaloosa power, hardiness, and fortitude. Thoroughbred heart, speed, and endurance. What more can you ask?" Bailey was reveling in the praise when, "Heeh!" the woman squeaked. "As it happens, both those breeds are notorious for winding up with an occasional wild notion. Still, your filly here *could* be an exception. Our Smokey's app genes didn't preclude his being perfectly reliable."

The visitor dragged over her duffle bag and dumped its contents into a square of light. "Could you use any of these odds and ends, dear?"

Bailey stared in astonishment, and tried to think. The motley collection of brushes and curry-combs looked still usable—better than anything she had, anyway. Nicked handles wouldn't matter. One curry-comb with rubber teeth was just like Cappy's, and it fit her hand exactly. There was a small brush with stiff, tawny bristles worn around the edges; a larger one with soft, longer bristles, which looked new. Fingers exploring, she wondered which got used for what.

"How about this?" Mrs. Knott held up a slightly corroded hoof-pick.

Bailey pulled the hoof-pick Billy Calderone had given to her out of her hip pocket. A pink plastic one. "Grooming-wise, this is as far as it goes here, except for a recycled hairbrush. This stuff is fantastic!" On impulse she threw her arms around the busty woman, who huffed and chuckled while extricating herself.

"Here, let me show you how I groom a horse." Mrs. Knott began applying the rubber curry-comb with authority. Even though the horse had already been brushed, loops of scurf rose to the surface. Chittering birds swooped in and out the door. Bailey began telling the busy groomer about the horse sale. She told about Monday's wild run, and confessed that now she was afraid to turn her horse loose. "She's an angel sometimes, Mrs. Knott, even when my little brother held her while I rubbed her down. But what if she goes bonkers again?"

"Uh hmm. See how this loosens the dirt, dear?"

"Oh, sure, wonderful." She drew another deep breath. The elation of having someone who really appreciated horses here kept her talking. Until her father had time to rig up a hose, she'd be hauling water from the house. And she'd feed outside, weather permitting, of course, and then shut the stall door to keep it clean inside. This aisle made a convenient shelter if it rained—

"She'll probably only want to come in on the hottest, humid days, when flies are atrocious. Horses actually like rain. Your two-by-four barrier over there—"

"Oh, Chuck and Billy did that so when she's loose she can't get into the feed."

"Right, you don't want a horse down with colic. Stomach trouble gives the number-one caregiver pains, too." The curry-comb paused. "The Calderone boys set all this up?"

"Uh huh, they brought Dakota Clover home for us."

"In that old stock trailer of theirs, I'll bet. Those boys work on a shoestring, but they know their business." Mrs. Knott knocked the hair-clogged curry-comb against the doorpost and then passed it to Bailey. "How 'bout you doing the other side, dear? Rub continuous circles. Pour on the elbow grease over muscle and go softly over bone."

Bailey clamped her mouth shut, moved to the horse's other side, and started behind an ear. She liked how the mare leaned her neck into the pressure. She circled softly over the backbone, alert to touchy undulating.

Flaky ridges appeared wherever she curried: the horse looked dirtier now than before.

Mrs. Knott passed over the stiff-bristled brush. "Industrious flicks of the wrist will get that grit out, and you'll soon have this coat glistening." A bird entered and made a full circuit of the shed. "Lucky you've got barn swallows, dear. They feed on insects, you know. This one probably wants the hair from that brush for her nest, just can't wait for us to leave." Bailey giggled with relief, thinking they were nearly done. "I imagine you're as eager as your horse to get outside," Mrs. Knott said, as if she'd read her mind. It seemed horse people understood each other.

"Two whole days without exercise isn't good, is it?"

"No grooming job is complete till you do the feet. How 'bout we use your hoof-pick? It's nice and sharp."

Uttering an "Ummph," the large woman bent over. Dakota Clover willingly offered a hoof. The woman was puffing by the time she straightened up again. "How 'bout you do the others, dear, while I supervise?"

Bailey stifled a groan. It would be dinner time before they got outside. She should be grateful, though. Not only for the brushes and stuff, for all the time the woman was spending to show her what to do with them. Holding the hoof bottom-up, she experienced the demands of supporting a huge leg with one hand. Even with cooperation, this was hard. Mrs. Knott leaned down and watched closely.

"I'll bet these feet haven't been looked at since the sale." Neither the plastic pick, nor the metal one, made a dent in the packed crud. Bailey shoved her knee under the hoof and hacked away.

"It sure takes time to do it right," she said after her struggle.

"You said it, sweetie." Mrs. Knott wiped her hands off on her faded jeans, then checked her turquoise-studded watch. "I've got a few more minutes," she said, "The mare seems content here. How 'bout a little trip up to my wagon?"

The tailgate swung open to even more horse stuff. Bailey could hardly believe her eyes. Or her ears when Mrs. Knott assured her the issue had already been discussed with her mother. "My children are grown, on their own now," she explained. "They can't spend much time home, much less with the horses. So, if you'll be riding English, dear, you can have this saddle, your mother says. We'll need to see how it fits, of course. Your mother wants to buy it, and I'm throwing in the snaffle-bit bridle. That hard hat you wore at my place fit alright, so you might as well take that along, too."

The astounding offer had Bailey speechless. Clearly, the woman had lost her mind. Those silvery wisps sticking out of her braid were a halo. "How'll I ever thank you?" she gasped. "It's just what I need!" She stroked the buttery leather. The idea of a tooled leather saddle featuring a horn ceased to exist. This old one was beautifully broken in. Her heart raced at the prospect of mounting up. Mounting up today! She gazed into the woman's gleaming eyes. "Mrs. Knott, you must be my guardian angel."

The old saddle fit perfectly. Fortunately, it had been padded to accommodate prominent withers. Mrs. Knott ran the stirrups up and tied the straps in knots, explaining the irons wouldn't kick this nice mare in the ribs now. "Do you have a piece of twine for me, dear?" What for, Bailey wanted to ask but squeezed her lips tight. Too many questions, and this big-hearted woman might back off.

The issue of time seemed to have been forgotten. Mrs. Knott painstakingly ran the long piece of baling-twine under a flap, across the pommel, and then down under the other flap. Bailey couldn't imagine why. Besides, this made the saddle look even older, as though you had to tie it together to keep it from falling apart. She repressed a nervous urge to pee. At least the twine wouldn't get in the way when she was riding. Any minute now.

The bridle was way too large. Mrs. Knott sunk to a bale and, muttering about everlasting harness grime, began poking the pink hoof-pick into a corroded buckle. Neglect had hardened the leather. The straps resisted, but she prodded and pushed at each one until its buckle's little prong found its new hole.

"Persistence pays off," she said with satisfaction when the bridle was buckled on, and it fit. Then her lunge line's brass-plated chain got strung through a bit ring, run along a convenient groove under the horse's jaw, and snapped to the other ring. Surely they were ready now, Bailey thought. But apparently the reins needed rearranging. "Just a precaution," Mrs. Knott explained as she buckled them through her twine hanger. They wouldn't drag now, not snag a leg if the horse acted up.

Bailey winced. If? The stirrups were tied up; the reins held out of the way—this woman must have some idea what she was in for.

Mrs. Knott slipped off her wrist-watch and pushed it into her front pants-pocket. She loosened her shoulders and drew a deep breath. "Righto, my girl," reaching for her whip. "Let's see if we know anything about lungeing."

Dakota Clover got led out to the level area near the post-and-rail fence. She endured having the whip graze her neck. She endured having it tap the saddle, rub her rump, even hoist her tail. As it slid over her legs, her eyeballs spun like pinballs. Seemingly unfazed, Mrs. Knott stood back and let out a few loops of her line.

"Righto, Clover, walk on." Nothing happened. "Walk on," again. "Walk ah-on, Cloverrr," more sweetly, with a little wrist action, which gained a wary look at the menacing whip. The mare stood with her long legs askew, clearly unclear about what to do. "Walk on, walk on," Mrs. Knott urged while wiggling her whip. Not until she clucked did the horse shift into gear, and then saunter over to her.

"This simply will not do! Come on, Bailey, you walk along and lead from the off side."

That got the horse moving, as long as Bailey's left hand was on the right rein to enforce the verbal cues. Whenever she let go, the horse veered in again, braving the brandished whip like a toddler wanting its mommy. Perspiration glazed Mrs. Knott's forehead. Her plaid, previously neatly tucked, shirt-tail flapped with every move. "Back off, dear," she hollered to Bailey. "This gal needs getting after!"

A sharp crack sent the startled mare up on her hind legs. A broadside of dirt shot up. Bailey's hand flew to her throat as Dakota Clover dove into a run. The line streamed out. Then it caught and jerked the horse straight toward Mrs. Knott, who turned into a toreador to swirl both herself and a straggling loop out of the way.

"Righto, we're getting somewhere, my girl!" Mrs. Knott arched her spine and worked her arms as the horse galloped around her. Bailey looked on from the side-line, marveling at the woman's dexterity, the horse's beauty. The long mane rippled in the wind; the long legs went on reaching and folding, reaching and folding. Why, this could go on all day. She'd never get to ride.

"Easy, now, Clover." Mrs. Knott tweaked the line and dropped her voice an octave for an elongated "TRR-aaht"—again and yet again, before the buoyant canter converted to an extended pumping gait, which sent reverberations through the soles of Bailey's feet. She was about to run off for a hasty pee, when she spotted her mother coming with Duker on the leash.

"Please stay for dinner, Julia!?"

"Heavens, what time is it?" Mrs. Knott patted her pants pockets. "My bunch must be at the gate right now," she cried on retrieving her wrist-watch. "I must dash."

14

A Mare With a Mind of Her Own

A HARD LOOK FROM the gate detected nothing roan like. The gentle knolls lay in sunlight; the shed glowed invitingly; but the horse wouldn't be in there. Horses liked to wander, and eat along the way. They were large animals, but their stomachs were small, and designed to process small meals. The vegetation here was hardly nutritious but, after Daddy mowed, a healthy spread of grass would grow. Mrs. Knott claimed what they had now was enough to keep a horse nosing around all day.

Bailey had put out some hay that morning, just to be safe. Roughly one and a half pounds of feed went into each hundred pounds of horseflesh, even more once a horse got into training. At fifteen hands, Dakota Clover weighed some one thousand pounds. So at three pounds a slice, she would need five slices a day. Or maybe six, Bailey decided. And when she started riding, they could up the grain. But one flake plus the pasture should have been enough to hold Dakota Clover till dinner time today.

"You be good, now," she had cautioned, and then unsnapped the leadshank before she could change her mind. That workout on the lunge line was supposed to have left the mare calmer. Even so, Bailey had been haunted all day by visions of busted wires and chaos all over the neighborhood. It'd be horrible if the horse got hurt.

Some movement now, near a brownish clump. Her anxious grip on the pipe-gate eased. There, the level top line gleaming in the sun. She began her advance through the expanse of bleached stalks and brown grass, taking soft, regulated steps. No way would she startle the horse.

Up popped the finely chiseled head. Bailey moved in, and the muzzle swung over. Experiencing her leg being nuzzled delivered waves of happiness. She wound her arms around Clover's neck and, leaning in, soaked up the warmth and heady aroma. Just to be here with her horse was pure heaven. Clover went back to poking around in the leafy litter at their feet, and found a dandelion. Bailey raked her fingers over the sun-baked back. Clover was used to her now—no flinching, no ripples scurrying through the hide, even when she pressed down with her forearms.

Dakota Clover gravitated to a greener patch, with Bailey's arm riding the backbone. Daddy's mandate against getting on without his presence was ridiculous. Mom sure didn't need to pass along Mrs. Knott's, "A wee too much horse for your daughter, I'm afraid." Clover was walking and her arm was riding—what about that! She tested for touchiness, rubbing here and there as they ambled along. When the horse got delayed by some minty weeds, she leaned on both arms, and pushed down harder. Dakota Clover lifted her head, flicked an ear, and then dipped her nose back into the weeds. The birds fluttered back and forth between the branches of two trees. Bailey wove her fingers into strands of the mane and pressed her upper body against the ribcage. A bird chirped sharply and hopped farther out on its branch. Resting, with her cheek on the horse's back, Bailey became consumed with a longing to sit up there.

Absently she swatted at the cluster of hairs clinging to her shirt, and they wafted away. She grinned, thinking, Dakota Clover won't mind if anyone sits on her while she chews. She's used to carrying weight, and she certainly knows me. Just sitting quietly won't count. The horse had found another dandelion and seemed focused on rooting up the greens. "What say, sis?" Bailey patted her hand up and down the backbone. "It'll be okay."

Her knees went into a taut crouch. The mane cut into her fingers when she sprung.

The ample back was firm and wonderfully warm against her stomach. And now it was moving. She clung to her handful of mane and squirmed. "Whooooaaa." They weren't going that fast, but she was sliding. Her head bobbed as if a wire spring had it attached. Giving her all, she hooked her right leg over the rocking stern. She braced both hands against the rolling withers and tried to sit up. The hooves pounded, picking up speed. She'd got herself hunched over the mane before she could raise her head. The renegade was on a bee-line for the fence.

The universe spun. A thump sounded in her chest. Her arm stung from slamming into an imbedded football-size rock. She pulled herself up gingerly, reeling from the thrill of it all. But Daddy might have the right idea about waiting. A good thing Memorial Day weekend was coming up, and he'd be home for three days in a row.

In the meantime she surreptitiously avoided hard chairs. And she set about familiarizing herself with the tack.

Getting the bridle on wasn't as simple as Mrs. Knott made it look. Whenever the floppy headpiece went as high as the horse's eyes, the head went up. "Does she take the bit?" rang in Bailey's ears. That woman at the sale must have had the same problem. Clover shifted her feet as Bailey strained from her tiptoes, trying to work fast. She had the long brown reins looped over the neck and the glitzy halter back over her arm. Those reins were hardly a restraint this way. She should have paid closer attention to Mrs. Knott's system. It'd been easier for her of course, being tall.

Muttering, "Whoa, whoa, whoa . . . ," she offered the bridle again. The jointed snaffle swung loosely from the cheek straps. Was that supposed to go in first? It seemed God actually intended for horses to hold bits—whatever else would these gaps at each side of the bottom row of teeth be for? She braced the leather crownpiece against her horse's flat forehead, which nodded unpredictably while she tried to make up her mind about the safest way to get the mouth open. She certainly didn't want any fingers bitten. Mrs. Knott knew just where to stick her thumb. It took timing, which *she* had been pretty good at as a kid jumping a swinging rope. This stupid bit was swinging, except not in time. "Come on, sis," she implored, as the towering head bobbed anxiously. "Dakota Clover, will you please cooperate!?"

The crownpiece slipped behind the near ear on a down-stroke, and squashed the other ear.

"Whoa!" The towering head had advanced with the jointed snaffle jiggling and swinging. She anchored the crownpiece with her right hand and forced her feet to keep pace as the horse sauntered out the door and over to the fence.

Her hastily hiked knee thwarted a swipe at a greenish stalk. She'd done it without thinking, the idea of sticking her thumb into a horse's mouth on her mind. With her tongue protruding from between *her* lips, she probed between Dakota Clover's surprisingly malleable lips. She'd lose ground if this bit didn't get in that gap—like now! She was staring at huge incisors ten times whiter than Brownie's streaked piano-keys. Painstakingly, she extricated the ear trapped by the crownpiece, then experienced a joyous rush as the bulky pink tongue mouthed up the bit.

The bridle sat crooked, but it was on. She rested her tired arms against the horse. "It'll go better, next time," she mumbled into the big roll of muscling along the neck.

FRIDAY, HER FATHER WAS out in his new work clothes when she stepped off the bus. He had the horse out there, too. Gussie and the kids cheered, and Dakota Clover did a little jig. Her father's new boots looked horribly scuffed.

"Just a little advice, hon," he said as he exchanged the leadshank for her book bag. "Look sharp, now. This nag nearly got loose a minute ago, gods-honest truth." All he'd done to set her off, he grumbled, was lean over to retrieve a dead branch.

"She could have taken that for a snake." Bailey was on the defensive.

"Huh, she could have avoided my feet, too, when she took after Duker. Had me hopping, that's the truth. Suddenly she's whirling and snorting at that evil branch, even though I'd tossed it back under a tree. What's so funny?"

"Oh, Daddy, new places always turn her on. You should have seen the first time she got loose."

"Well, she better not get loose out here. The Thoroughbred in her makes her a runner."

Bailey kept her shoulder even with the horse's shoulder and checked with the leadshank. Her heart rate soared whenever she handled the horse, and having her father here made it beat even faster. They made it through the green pipe gate with inches to spare. With the horse safely cross-tied, she selected her hard-rubber curry-comb. Her father leaned against the door-post and pulled off a boot.

"She's partial to dandelions," he remarked as he stretched out a sock, and got awarded a knowing look. Convincing an animal that weighed five times more than he did to cooperate must have totaled his patience. "I just said, 'Move along, toots,' and it worked. That time, anyway. Not silly, talking to a horse. You'd think basic psychology would work. When it didn't, I'd tug and talk, use the rope, voice, the flat of my hand—"

"You struck her?" The curry-comb hovered in the air.

"Ah, just once. You get this nag's attention and she's a trained poodle." He gave a hollow laugh. "Except when she crushed my foot going out the gate. Remarkable, how people handle beasts ten times their size."

She would never hit. Oh, maybe a light reprimand on the neck, but never a real slap. Not smart to take Clover to the road, either. And her horse was not a nag.

"She's got a mind of her own, you keep this side of the fence."

Duh. The big question now was this confounding bridle. She'd better not screw up. First the saddle, though, set Mrs. Knott's way over a clean towel. She peeked under the floppy skirts to see if the girth lay flat—Clover didn't need any rough edges digging in. She reached under the belly to catch the buckle-end.

"I'd pull that up a few more holes, if I were you."

"Mrs. Knott showed me this way. I'll make it snug just before I get on."

"Hmmn, I guess you know what you're doing."

The unexpected note of respect stirred her to mention the trouble she'd had with the bridle. *He* had practically been outsmarted, too. His lips held still, his face creased with concern while she described how the horse nearly got away.

"Lemme see that!" reaching for the complex network of straps. One look, and he handed it back. She waited while he tugged at his ear, weighing the situation with his feet planted as if the hard-packed ground under him might shift. A light breeze wafted through the door. Suddenly he threw his hands in the air. "We'll try it with me playing road block!"

One crosstie pinged against the stall; the other struck the south wall, and Clover moved out. Right in step, Bailey held the crownpiece high.

"Whoa!" her father shouted, waving his arms.

Her thumb found the gap. The bit went in. She stretched to her toes and hastily tucked an ear under the crownpiece. After she'd pulled the other ear through, Clover stopped her fidgeting. Bailey straightened the noseband and buckled the throat latch—all quite business-like she thought, then stole a look at her father. He looked as though his old mower had started with just one pull.

"I see the problem. Next time, leave those crossties hooked and drape the halter across her chest. That should stop her long enough. We'll put a chain up across the exit."

Her heart raced ahead of her as he led Dakota Clover out. They stopped well short of the fence. The girth was quite loose and Bailey carefully adjusted it. Mrs. Knott had stressed this, and she'd remembered, even so set on mounting. Clover stood quietly while, with every one of her muscles tuned, Bailey stuck her foot in the stirrup and climbed up.

She focused on the horse's long, flowing mane, not about to gauge her distance from the ground. This horse was even taller than Smokey, not as round, and ever so lovely to sit on. Her legs dropped to the stirrups naturally, and both toes went in. She rested a hand on the warm flank. Indulging in a comfy slouch, she heaved a sigh. On her horse at last, the hard part was over.

Her father heaved an even deeper sigh. His new boots squeaked as he hustled to keep up with the free-wheeling walk, lots livelier than Smokey's walk. "Some different horse under saddle," he muttered—limping, she noticed, and pulled back on the reins. He pulled his rein, too, and Clover swerved, heading him off.

"Hold everything," he barked. "I'll get the rope." She wished she'd thought of that. There'd been no trouble on Smokey with Mrs. Knott holding a line.

Having the rope attached to the bit-ring improved matters, walking. When they started trotting, her father had trouble keeping up. When he wouldn't let go, the horse traveled in rowdy side-passes harder to sit than riding the Tilta-Whirl.

"Let's walk!" she cried. The cantle was spanking her. The helmet was loose.

"You said it, honey. And mark down some of that long webbing on our list."

15

No Experience Required?

IT HAD BEEN A long day. Her father was tired, but he had kept his promise to work with her, even after they'd waited all morning for the hay to arrive. Then he wouldn't be satisfied until all fifty bales were stacked in the shed. After a hasty wash-up, they'd jumped in the car, and come out of Fred's Farm and Home with a length of chain. Then they fought Greenham's stream of holiday traffic to get to The Saddlery.

"Look Daddy, saddle pads on sale for only ten dollars. And sweat-scrapers! Billy Calderone says we should have a sweat-scraper."

"You don't save money by spending it, Bailey." Yet, along with the lunge line and whip, he threw in those, too.

It was after four by the time everything was ready. The chain across the exit and the halter across Clover's chest took care of the problematical bridle. But then her father marched the mare right out to the middle of the field and swirled the whip. The line streamed out of his hand as an innate wildness sent the horse into a frenzy.

"Your friend took a powder, honey! Run check the gate!"

"Good thing that gets out of her system," Bailey called over her shoulder. Clover would be nice and calm by the time she got on. The horse galloped up and down the pasture, jumped the downed branches, charged the gate then abruptly whirled away. It was the first her father'd seen of their horse's speed and power; from the look on his face, he was awestruck.

Up to the gate for the umpteenth time, Clover broke into a trot and disappeared behind the shed.

Bailey found her waiting in her stall with thirty feet of white webbing tangled between her legs. Clever footwork, she hadn't tripped. Bailey was pushing against the shoulder to convince a hoof to lift when her father hobbled in. He had picked out the stall while she tacked up, and the lunge line wasn't even dirty. He tried to be helpful, but should have listened to her. She had wanted to start by tending Clover's off side, like Mrs. Knott had her do. She had explained all this quite tactfully—sorry, but Daddy hated being told what to do. He stood rubbing his sore hand at the moment, studying the horse.

"If we rush things now," he said gloomily, "we'll end up paying later, I kid you not. Look how she's sweating, Bee. This horse has had it. You'll not be riding today."

"I will too! Oh, Daddy, she'll be okay." Clover wouldn't be half as worn out as he was. But . . . "Really, she's too tired now to make any more trouble."

He shot his fist, and Clover shied right there in the stall. Even Bailey jumped. "Watch out," he huffed. The mare's nostrils were flared, but he was breathing even harder. "Neither of us have any idea what we are doing here!" The box-stall felt crowded with his finger pointing at her. She averted her eyes, and noticed a fresh scuff on his boot. He didn't need that on top of everything else. "Get your scraper in here! It's nearly dinner time. At least I know enough not to leave this nag standing hot."

"I'll take her out and walk her." The sweat-scraper was still in the sack, back in the house. "She'll be fine in a few minutes, Daddy." They couldn't stay here arguing, someone might get hurt. His steely gaze had her squinting back, lips pressed in a thin line. Certainly she could ride, she told herself, determined to stare him down. Everything would be fine now, with the lunge line.

"Give her a break, Bailey Elizabeth! She's had a traumatic week. That crowded sale, shaky trailer, strange people, new schedule, new house . . ." He tugged at his earlobe and ranted on about mental exhaustion. Bailey's lower lip quivered; she had backed into her horse's solid, warm shoulder, away from the jabbing finger. "Isn't that a fair statement? She's all worked up. This sort of situation breeds mistakes. Might set you back months." His eyes softened. "The same thing happens to overtired people, Bee. Gotta admit, today's agenda has me bushed." He ran a hand through his frizzled hair. "Let's quit while we're halfway ahead. You could get hurt, honey. Hear?"

Clover did look tired. Her knees were trembling. Still . . .

"C'mon, Bee, we've all had enough."

"But if she's tired, Daddy, she'll be good and I—"

"You're not listening to me! You get that saddle off or this nag goes down the road!"

ALL THE CHEERY DANDELIONS had gone to seed. Bailey picked one, blew listlessly and watched the downy tufts waft away. Clover grazed nearby, her forelock fluffed by the breeze. It was Memorial Day Monday, the last day before Daddy'd have to go back to work. The conspiratorial looks they'd swapped during breakfast this morning had Bailey thinking they'd come out here right away. Then a long distance call came from Chicago, and he was still in the house. She flicked an orange speck off her jeans, then another, and another. Clover had demolished her carrot in two bites. Daddy better come soon. She had flipped through her math workbook while waiting for his conversation to end, then impulsively slammed it shut. Final exams were coming up, but she couldn't study with her mind on the solo flight. If she did well today, she'd graduate from lungeing.

On Sunday, after some initial tension, they had put in a good session. Clover behaved on the line and then trotted decent circles after Bailey stepped away. Mr. Grim-Face had taken her advice. And, when the time came to mount up, his cautious tone revealed she wasn't the only one with jitters. She'd reached forward from the saddle to rearrange the mane, all to one side, and discovered stretching actually helps ease tension. She'd soon located the saddle's sweet spot, and was ready to go faster when her father told her to get ready to give a little squeeze.

"Wait till I say, 'T-R-O-T,'" he added with a studied air of nonchalance, and let out a few loops. Quietly he pointed the whip, spoke the cue, and, as the horse moved out, the mechanics of riding began to fall into place. Posting, Bailey figured out as she caught the rhythm, worked beautifully if you waited for a boost. Clover's trot was stronger than Smokey's; they were merely circling yet it felt as though they were really going someplace.

Her hands dropped to her sides, fingers twiddling with the grass instead of the reins. Her eyelids drooped as she listened to her horse chew. An ant sent tickling sensations up her arm. Off in the distance, some birds cawed discordantly. Faint rustlings overhead, and a little bird started up a song. She got a glimpse of brown-striped feathers flitting through the branches. The bird flew off to another tree, and she imagined Clover with wings. She was Thumbelina poised between the broad-swept wings, soaring over sparkling oceans, swooping to rolling waves. She squeezed her eyes shut, seeing herself cantering Clover over sandy beaches, skipping through frothy waves. Why ever had she been so particular about color? She would love this horse no matter what it looked like, even if it were purple.

She sensed her feet being sniffed, now all over, and erupted in giggles as the flabby lips checked her hair. Her eyes popped open to find the horse looming over her like an imperious gargoyle.

She was brushing the hindquarters when her father came out. Wearing his sneakers, she noticed. Her heart pinged at the thought of blisters; he was enduring pain on her account. She made a vow not to contribute anything more to his grief.

They were in tune for the bridle switch and it went without a hitch. Then the horse put in a decent stretch of trotting. "She understands English, honey!" Daddy was happy today. Their mare had moved out on the line as soon as he said "trot," and was behaving just as well now with *her* up. All he needed to do was pivot, while *she* practiced slowing down when they got going too fast. He remarked on the head carriage, higher than he'd noticed before. "Try pulling her head down," he said. But, under saddle, Clover persisted in trotting with her nose up.

A scent of lilacs came through on the breeze. Cloud buttes rolled in from the south, racing their shadows across the field. The fresh spring day, the heat and power of her own horse carrying her, was awesome.

"I don't know why I'm standing here, Bee." Her father moved in to unsnap the line. Wow, this year's Memorial Day was totally memorable.

She tried to continue circling and found out her steering needed improvement. Clover worked her ears and shook her head. The pace was springier now, showing an eagerness to move out. Before Bailey could do anything about it, Clover had pushed into a brisk trot and veered off toward the fence.

Her father hiked over to retrieve them from the corner.

"Thanks, Daddy," shrinking into herself. His poor blisters. She needed deep, gaspy breaths to get herself going again.

"Keep it to a walk, big girl." He backed off again, speaking to Clover as though she were human. Bailey's butt was snug in the saddle, yet her heart pounded in the hard hat. I'll be super strict, she told herself as she rearranged the reins. He doesn't need to babysit. From up by the house, Duker barked. Now crackling gravel noises, some commotion on the driveway. Her head snapped; propelled backwards, she threw her hands up. They'd traveled as far back as the shed before the horse stopped.

Theo's funny little bike with the banana seat bumped off the end of the driveway. Clover planted her feet and snorted. Theo stood up and set the bike down, and Clover stood up on her hind legs.

"Geez," Theo moaned with his hands up. "*Que estupidez!*" Clover stood down, once the two-wheeled monster had transformed into a human being. "You okay, Bailey?"

"Stop it!" In her scramble to recenter herself she had lost a rein. "Not you, Theo," she added, seeing his dismay. Her father gave a happy shout and launched into the virtues of this spirited mare he had bought. Bailey cringed. He sounded horribly self-congratulatory. Besides, he might show some consideration for what she was going through.

"Whoever says horses are dumb doesn't know diddly squat! Ever seen bigger, brighter eyes? That's intelligence. Fact of the matter, Theo,"—loud enough for the whole neighborhood to hear—"this horse knows more than I do, that's the truth!" Theo was wide-eyed, nodding agreeably to every boast—meant for the horse's sake, Bailey supposed. If Daddy only knew how braggy—

Duker barked again and suddenly they were trotting again, taking the corner with nothing to hold on to but swinging vines. "Who-o-oa," someone wailed as they emerged from behind the shed. Here came Andy on his whiny, yellow dirt-bike. Her father flailed his arms. She was fighting for stability when a wheelie launched her into space.

"Don't move her!" Theo vaulted the fence. "Get out of here, Andy!"

Grotesquely shaped clouds reeled before her eyes. She could not speak or breathe and lay very still, wondering if she was paralyzed. A familiar face swam into focus. Daddy. Then Theo, both hovering over her like two anxious nannies.

"Bailey?" they said at the same time.

What started as a giggle came out as a whimper. Breaths—hesitant at first, then determined—restored her quaky lungs with precious oxygen. She lifted one arm, then the other; wiggled each finger, then the toes. She sat up. That juvenile delinquent of hers needed a talking to. Her right leg hurt from banging into the fence, and she had lost her hard hat.

"Where's Clover?"

"God, what a spill you took," her father croaked. "You all right, honey?"

When he'd helped her to her feet, she snatched her hunt cap away from Theo and jammed it on her head. One look sent him running after the horse. Supported by her father's arm, she limped over the weirdly wavery ground.

Clover faced her people with her head lowered.

"You bad girl," Bailey growled, hoping to instill remorse. A scolding like that would send Duker moping under the bed.

"The reins were dangling, but she didn't step on them," Theo said wonderingly.

"I'm getting back on."

"Oh, no. You've had enough." Her father had her by the arm and was brushing her off.

"I'm getting on! You're supposed to. It's good for the horse."

"That's right," Theo said. "Well, kinda," he backtracked, upon a seething look from her father. "That is, if you're okay."

She pulled away and seized the reins. She kicked her foot to the stirrup.

"Wait!" A vice-grip had her shoulder. "I'm getting the lunge line, or she goes down the road today!"

16

Theo in the Center

"LOOKING GOOD UP THERE, *muy simpatico!*" Theo followed with his eyes as Bailey posted and the horse trotted around him. He had been on the sidelines, rubbing Duker's wiggly stomach and idly dreaming about riding a horse as nice as this one, when Mr. Mason called him over. Bailey had looked surprised, and then relieved, when *he* got handed the line.

"Thank you Daddy, for making all this possible. And thanks, Theo. I need all the practice I can get. He goes back to work tomorrow, I bone up for exam week, and it's gonna be days before I get to ride again."

Theo revolved like a radar detector. The breeze plastered Bailey's shirt in front and rippled it out in back. Clover's head seemed unnaturally high. Bailey's leg was shaky—the effort to hold it still must make it hurt more. Her hands were all over the place, but the horse's edgy head carriage could be causing that. What did he know? He had never been thrown by a horse and, before today, had never seen anybody else thrown. Other than in movies, he'd never seen a horse rear. *Que bravada muchacha*, climbing right back on.

Now she was wriggling her butt into the deepest part of her saddle—oh, reining in.

"Hey Theo, let's just walk and talk. One fall's enough for today, don't you think? My legs are wet spaghetti." She anchored one hand in the mane and swung one leg over to sit sideways.

Fine with him. Most times together, she'd be sitting next to him and he'd be craning his neck for a look. This view was *excelente*. She was smiling at him, swaying in the saddle as the horse marched along on a loose rein—the head lower now, the long neck bobbing, the hips swinging freely. All he heard for a while were the softened track's muted hoof beats and the gently creaking leather. And then Bailey started telling about the horse's wild runs. Given this placid walk, those antics sounded fantastic. Bailey was *muy bonita*, wickedly cute telling her stories. Kinda weird, he admitted to himself, how Spanish helped express the weightiest thoughts. He had his own style. "*Muy interesante, amiga*," he commented in his macho voice.

Mrs. Mason was watching from the patio, and he suddenly remembered he was supposed to be studying. He'd already gone over algebra, but still had an entire spiral notebook to get through for civics, if he could read his own writing. As if she could read his mind, Bailey mentioned her exams.

"Mine start Wednesday," she said. "Communications—spelling, grammar, short stories. There's still plenty of time." She took up the reins in her left hand, seeming about to dismount, so he moved in and started gathering up the line.

"Too bad I can't take notes on a laptop," he said, thinking of his scribbled notebook. He hated to leave but duty called.

"Ha, too bad Greenham doesn't hand out computers. Glenna says private schools do."

"In your dreams, not overtaxed Gre . . . " He couldn't breathe suddenly, catching her in his arms as her knees buckled. His head was spinning. Before he had a chance to follow through, she had righted herself and was talking as though nothing had happened, with her cheeks blushing all the way into her hunt cap. She babbled on breathlessly about her Math and

Social Studies exams on Friday, and Life Sciences, her biggest problem, on Thursday. She was horrible at memorizing, she said, sounding surprisingly husky. He didn't think she had a cold. He wondered what she'd do with his arms around her again. This time was easy. Just wondering . . . and at the next opportunity . . .

17

A Visit from the Veterinarian

BAILEY SET HER HEAVY water pail down inside the gate and looked around. Full of yesterday's excitement, she'd had to force herself to concentrate in school. Gauzy ribbons of clouds streaked the late afternoon sky. Clover was somewhere out here, but where? She experienced a ripple of uneasiness. The rectangle of leafy thatch left out for Clover that morning lay in the same spot, intact. She set out into the field, peeking into the tree line, peering into the woodland. Those trees on the other side of the stone wall blocked the sun, and hardly anything worth grazing grew there. Clover wouldn't have gone that far. And she wouldn't be in the barn. She must be hiding. Such a clever girl.

"You okay, Clover?" The cheery tone roused one ear to half-mast. She'd found the horse dozing half in and half out of the narrow block of shade behind the barn. "Thanks for the nice ride yesterday. Isn't Theo nice? Here, take a bite." She offered the yellow delicious apple she'd saved from lunch. "All that exercise this weekend, and you're not hungry?" The appetizing fruit had received a feeble nip. Of course, the horse had just woken up. Bailey cupped her hand over the normally velvety nose, which felt stiff and hot. That happened occasionally, it wouldn't mean anything.

She went around to unhook the chain, and the horse followed her into the barn. She topped off the water bucket, poured out a generous measure of grain, passed the rake over the scarcely soiled bedding. The familiar motions helped to disperse her forebodings. Clover would be fine. The Communications exam was tomorrow. *She* would be fine, too, if she hit the books tonight.

UNRELATED THOUGHTS WAFTED UP from every page she turned, bothersome notions concerning abnormal loss of appetite. Clover had cleaned up most of her supper's grain but left her hay untouched. Don't worry until you have to, Bailey told herself, and kept up the struggle to stuff syntax and semantics and story plots into her brain.

Think positively, she prompted next morning, when the gate-click failed to rouse a welcoming whinny. A heavy haze hovered over the land, the barn silent. She paused in the shadowed doorway to give her eyes time to adjust. She could just make out the horse's top line. She peered through the bars. Clover's ears leaned off at angles; her chin hovered inches above a neat mound of hay.

This was not happening!

She slipped into the stall and laid her hand on the drooping neck. The normally supple hide felt as stiff as a rough board. She curled her fingers under the impassive jaw and pulled up. The cumbersome head rose as high as the shoulder but dropped when she let go. A block of ice cracked in her chest. This was so not right.

Up with her pail at the patio faucet, she stuck her head inside the back door. "Mother? Clover looks sort of weird."

One look and Beth Mason ran to call Julia Knott. Bailey slugged down her orange juice, then headed back with Clover's water. The horse had not moved. She ran her hands over the oddly unyielding hide, and tried hard to think what to do. Ten minutes till Gussie. Miss Perolini had promised a "B" if she aced this exam. Miss Perolini would never understand staying home for a sick horse. Nor the few kids she'd met who boarded horses out. They'd be as helpless facing illness as she was.

Her mother was adamant about school. She would watch over the mare and be there when Julia Knott's veterinarian arrived. Bailey trudged down the driveway clinging to these reassurances, and pulled herself up the bus's steep steps. Theo jumped on and, waving a book, muttered about needing to cram. He slid into the seat behind her. Just as well. She'd need to sort things out.

She stared through the layers of grime shrouding her window, registering none of what passed by outside. Probably she should have eaten something solid. These worry-pins were too jumpy to be psychosomatic.

"How's it going?" Theo hailed as they got off the bus. His face clouded over when he heard that Clover was sick.

"It's like she's really tired, Theo, and hardly eats anything."

"Geez, she seemed fine Monday. And you didn't work her that hard."

"I thought of that, too. We're getting the vet. I wish I was home."

"I hope she's all right. When I get back, we can work with her again."

"Get back?" The first she'd heard he was going anywhere. "Cabin in Maine," she caught as they dodged the mob trudging up the broad sidewalk. "—a few weeks up there every June," came through clearly. The six steps leading to the double-doors blurred as though under water. "I'll get in a few more rides before we leave," he went on eagerly. "Mom's friends the Chazens keep horses at the lake. I might get to ride there, too."

A SMALL DIESEL PICK-UP stood ticking in the driveway. Bailey dropped her book bag and broke into a run. A tall, thin man in green coveralls was in with Clover, frowning at the listening box he had positioned behind her elbow. Bailey slipped to her horse's head, which hung listlessly.

"Dr. Goozeman," her mother told her quietly, as the veterinarian fiddled with the black tubes dangling from his ears. Solemnly he unplugged them and then, looking off into space, he began probing Clover's abdomen. At last, he stood back.

"You've got a case of *Equine Infectious Arteritis* here," he announced bleakly. "Commonly called influenza, or shipping fever." He patted the broad hump of muscle bridging the mare's hips. Clover never moved when he slid a thermometer under her tail. "You'll see it in horses that've been through sales . . . no fault of yours, Mrs. Mason."

Bailey and her mother exchanged a woeful look. The barn was dreadfully quiet, even the birds subdued. Clover seemed oblivious to the thermometer.

"Temperature one hundred and three," announced Dr. Goozeman. Horses normally registered 100.5. This mare was feverish, typically off her feed. They should keep her in, out of the light. "See," he gravely pointed out, "her eyes are starting to tear." He braced his thumb over the crest of Clover's nose and flicked some yellow matter out of the corner of her eye. "She'll probably get worse before we see any improvement. You can expect a nasal discharge, stocked up legs. I see they're filling already, so we'd better wrap."

"Oh, dear," Beth Mason said, hands clasped over her heart.

Bailey hustled to keep up with the doctor as he strode to his truck. He pushed the button that released the side panel, and she gasped. In this little truck, a fully-stocked emergency room. Dr. Goozeman extracted a hose, squirted water into a basin, and proceeded to thoroughly wash his hands, way up to the elbows. Then he swiftly gathered up sheets of cotton, boxes of bandages, and another thermometer.

Clover was in the same position. Bailey could see that the legs were hideously swollen. "I'll leave this one with you," Dr. Goozeman said, tearing open the narrow thermometer box. "It'll give you an idea of progress. You might tie a string through the tiny hole on the end," he added with a grim smile. "Thermometers have a way of traveling. Some people tie a button to the end of the string." Bailey half-choked. This would be funny if it weren't so serious. "Dab the silver tip in Vaseline before inserting," the doctor went on, "and insert it slowly to avoid puncturing the thin rectal lining."

Her heart was in it but her mind quailed at the responsibility.

Her mother, sounding hopeful, suggested medication.

"No antibiotics now," Dr. Goozeman snapped. Then, more agreeably, he explained that the mare would be more apt to build immunity if she could fight this off herself. But if the fever spiked, or lasted too many days, they would need to act. "The chest sounds fairly clear," he said. His emphasis on "fairly" sent chills through Bailey. "Most important now is stall rest and TLC," he went on with a weary smile. Tender loving care was highly regarded in medicine. He asked for a soft brush, and Bailey eagerly handed him the black body brush. "Easy, lass," he muttered, with his hand on Clover's inert shoulder. The inflamed arteries in this disease caused edema, he explained while gently swiping grit and shavings away from the bloated legs.

No wonder she won't move, Bailey thought. It hurts.

The veterinarian tore open a bandage box and peered inside. "How would plum-color look on this nice mare?"

The image of her horse in bandages made her eyes smart. Plum would look nice, though. The veterinarian squatted to the right fore. Through her threatening tears Bailey followed every move. While he smoothed a length of sheet-cotton over his thigh, she held more of the fluffy white sheets and the plum-colored rib-knits ready. He pressed a soft white length around the lower half of a stocked-up leg and fit it over the hoof before applying the tail of a plum strip. His movements were careful and steady. The vivid bandage got unrolled down from the fetlock and wound tight over the sheeting's lower edge; then back and around and up to the top, just below the knee—each overlapping plum turn covering up more of the pristine sheeting. This neat casing got fastened with a tidy bow, its ends tucked into the top. "Going up," Dr. Goozeman said, "make it evenly tight. A decent job offers support."

"Might that not cut off circulation?" Beth Mason asked.

"Right, Mrs. Mason, we sure don't want any strangled tendons. But the sheet-cotton's thickness distributes pressure. In just a sec, here, you can do a leg."

Bailey exchanged an anxious look with her mother.

When her turn came, her fingers turned to thumbs. The white sheeting came alive when she started unrolling. She ended up with appallingly lumpy wraps, which were supposed to last for two days.

Dr. Goozeman guardedly surveyed the surroundings.

"Does this mare like carrots?" he asked.

"Oh yes!"

"Definitely!"

"Salt sprinkled on a carrot-penny sometimes'll start drinking. See if she'll accept grain from your hand. Don't leave out more than a handful, though, until she's back on her hay. If the temp spikes past hundred-four, or doesn't read hundred-one by this Saturday, call the office. Best to keep her in till it's normal for twenty-four hours."

18
Primary Care

THURSDAY, THE ALARM WENT off at six. The science terms and horse concerns still buzzed through Bailey's head. She had endured her mother's quizzing until eleven, and finally fallen into bed—not to sleep without running her nursing duties through what was left of her mind: principally, the problems to avoid while taking Clover's temperature.

She stepped outside into a thin margin of light filtering through the tree tops. Fortified with a hefty scoop of oatmeal, she hurried over a path worn as firm now as her dedication to her horse. Her torchlight flickered into the barn's early stillness, and a bird cocked its head. Through the soft fluttering of wings, strange noises came from the stall. Clover's breaths were shallow, panting wheezes. She was standing with her head down so far, the thick mucus streaming out of her nose had her muzzle glued into her hay. A worry-pin stole through Bailey's stomach reinforcements. She pulled a deep breath and slid back the door.

The sickly head stirred. She's glad I'm here, Bailey told herself. She was trying to think positively, wearing her happy-face sweatshirt, but her eyes were filling with tears. The sight of Clover's nostrils, dark wells of mustardish gunk, was making *her* feel sick. She ran her hand over the drooping neck, which felt strangely stiff, and the hair-coat fuzzy. "Poor girl," she murmured. "You don't feel well, do you? Hang in there, sweetie, while I clean you up."

An empty grain-sack collected her mass of soggy paper towels, like the wastebasket in her bedroom collected tissues whenever she had a bad cold. *Infectious Arteritis* sounded far worse than a cold. "Blow, sweetie," she pleaded, holding a fresh paper towel to the nose. "Please blow." Gently she drew the forelock away from the mattery eyes. Her fingers traced the curve of the jaw. She raised the weighty head and pressed her palms against its flat planes. Holding on, she gazed at the most important thing in her life. "Keep healing," she said prayerfully. Surely the dynamic spirit behind those blurry eyes would hear.

She worked carefully, as quickly as she dared. She'd had no idea of the suffering mothers went through with sick children. She drew the thermometer box out of her hip pocket and carefully extracted the glass rod. In keeping with Dr. Goozeman's warning, she'd attached a button-equipped string. Her dreams of owning a horse certainly hadn't included nursing one. But here she was, even though the training had happened when her mind was numb from exams.

The torchlight's glow slid off a mess of snot on the wall, then pinpointed the thin line, still 103. She pinched the tiny rod between her pointer and her thumb, made her hand fall limp, and shook. 102. She shook again, vigorously. There must be a certain technique—this was taking too long.

When at last the column of mercury climbed back down the little red ladder, she set the torch at the base of a wall stud, next to the Vaseline jar, and remembered to dab Vaseline on the thermometer's tip.

"This shouldn't hurt, sweetie." She hoisted Clover's tail, conjuring an image of Dr. Goozeman. She wasn't sure what she was looking at and went back out for the torch, which cast a weaker light now. She had no idea what time it was. A second warning pat to Clover's backside; another deep breath; tail up again. The torchlight wavered, but the target was unmistakable.

Holding fast to the button, willing the horse not to move, Bailey slid the rod in. The tail swished just once during her count to 180. Then she twirled the elusive instrument slowly under her weakened light. Even though she'd wiped it super-clean, the line was indistinguishable. Ranging farther up the ladder, she found it up to *103.6*.

THE LIFE SCIENCES TEST went by in a blur. If she passed, it would only be due to her mother's painstaking grilling. She had boosted herself to the concrete wall fronting the campus to wait for her bus, when Glenna Munro found her.

"Gad, Bailey, you look terrible. Take a break and come home with me. C'mon," delivering a playful shove, "we'll eat ice-cream and look up *Equine Infectious Arteritis*. Me mater can drive you home in time for dinner."

This earned Glenna a look of disbelief. They sometimes went off together after school, but not since Clover had arrived. Certainly not now. "I couldn't, Glen! You just don't know how sick she is."

Even worse, Bailey was to discover. The mercury line haunted the danger zone, *104*. The bucket's water line had not changed. Bailey dashed back to the house and sliced up a carrot. Her heart raced as she flew her appetizers back to the barn. One by one, the salted pennies slipped between dry, flabby lips, and got the patient chewing again, and laboriously swallowing. Her heart in her throat, Bailey transmitted encouragement. Whatever went on inside that huge, rigid body was a total mystery. Stroking, then kneading the unyielding muscles, she began to calculate how long she could stay out here and still have time for review. The Social Studies exam would cover an entire year's current events. Normally she found the wide world interesting, but this box-stall was her world now.

Friday's alarm went off at 5:45. Bailey lay in a stupor with an ominous sense, something seriously out of sync. It seemed terribly dark outside . . . Rain? A peculiar lump . . . oh, elephant. The lining of her cheek was on fire. She'd consumed an obscene amount of caramel corn while plowing through her math and poring over her maps, and now she had a canker sore. Mr. Lederle's exponent problems swam into consciousness; Supreme Court justices; tin in Bolivia; coffee, Columbia. Clover! She pushed up and stumbled into the things she'd thrown off before falling into bed. Forget the shower, Clover needed her.

A lonely bird called through the mauve vale of mist. Bailey rounded the corner of the shed—to gurgling noises, and a dreadful smell. She peered in, hoping to see Clover's head. But the horse was stretched out flat. Her own throat constricted, Bailey rested her eyes on the huge hulk. She felt unbearably helpless. Clover's swollen eyes had the lids stretched tight. Rattly gurgles came from her vaulted rib-cage as it rose and fell in spasms. A fleeting image of the horse racing around the pasture had Bailey praying, *please come back.* She allowed the plum wraps a wide berth and, nattering sympathies, crept in close. The words meant to reassure her horse came out in little chokes. She crouched down and lay the flat of her hand across the forehead, the way her mother tested for fever. The thermometer would really tell. She flicked wood-chips away from the engorged eyes, smoothed back the matted forelock—stealing time before dealing with the nostrils' appalling amount of gunk. Thank goodness she had time, a whole hour and a half before Gussie.

The scary gurgling stopped. Then it started again. Bailey froze, her heart as heavy as lead. All she could think to do was clasp a floppy ear in each fist and work in her own strength. She forgot about the smells and concentrated on kneading Clover's ears. "She's sick," she wailed to Duker, who had his head in the door, his tail at half-mast. The dog's sad-looking eyes looked even sadder.

Clover gave a sharp cough. Bailey's eyes widened as the shuttered eyes quivered into narrow slits. The weighty head wobbled upward. One moment, and Clover folded her knees and rolled to her chest. Duker scooted as, in one mighty heave, which sent Bailey scrambling into a corner with a wildly beating heart, the mare made it to her feet.

"Thatta girl! You're gonna be fine!" The debris-stuccoed face swung widely. "Eeu! Snot. I do not appreciate being dripped on." A check on her plaid-strapped wrist watch showed ten minutes had passed. She'd clean up here and then jump in the shower.

"I should have stayed with her," she groaned, as she plunged her towel into the water bucket. She began by sponging the weepy eyes. "You must have been miserable, trying to breathe. At least I could have wiped your nose." Dark yellow mucus rimmed the buckets and spackled the walls. Bailey worked fast and attacked that mess, then the sour mass of bedding. These bandages couldn't be changed near so many germs. There was a surprising amount of poop, considering how little the horse ate.

A low bank of clouds had gathered by the time she dumped the polluted bucket, away from the path. She was scrubbing it out in the laundry room when her father came in. The kitchen clock read 6:46; forty-four minutes left, and she was a wreck. Under a roll of thunder, she scrubbed harder.

"You're up early," he said approvingly. "How's our mare?"

"Oh Daddy, she is really sick," got past the log jam in her throat.

"I'm sorry, hon." He whisked a shoe-brush across his black wing-tips briskly. "She has a good nurse, that's a plus factor."

Bailey stared into the depths of her bucket while it filled. "I hate seeing her suffer so." She grew aware of judgmental eyes on her messy sweatshirt.

"You wearing that to school?"

Her cheeks ballooned as she struggled to exit without spilling. A gust of wind caught the screen door. "Too bad," she shot back over her shoulder as it slammed shut, "if my choice of apparel does not meet with your approval!"

The bucket weighed her down. The rain was coming down in sheets, the wind whirling like the worries in her head. Inside the barn, the din on the tin roof set her teeth on edge. The patient appeared oblivious, the eyes closed again. More mucus dangled, and a fresh plug of snot was pinned to the chest. Tears of frustration stung Bailey's eyes—she needed to be here today. She snatched some hay and held it out to the grotesque creature before her. What had happened to her lovely filly? How could she think about clothes or stupid exams with her horse sick? She waited, holding out the feathery tips, and stared helplessly, willing the inert being to stir. The wind cried through the old loose wallboards. It'd been two minutes to seven when she left the house. Today, of all days, she needed to be on that bus.

One eye blinked. The mucus encrusted snip dimpled, and the muzzle brushed her hand. Bailey's heart beat as if she was racing for the finish line. She dug her fingers into the grain. The lips wrinkled, and the bit of white that showed made her heart soar. She let her tongue caress her canker sore; exorbitant amounts of sugar had caused one just like it before. It'd been gone by the end of the day, but Clover's inflamed arteries were in their fourth day. She sprinkled water over the grain to enhance the sweetness. Outside, rain roared a torrent against the roof. The horse had been in pain for so long . . .

During the long minute holding her hand steady, Bailey's heart slid into despair. She flung the sticky fragments down and went back to basic care.

She was up to the point of unwinding a foreleg when her mother stamped into the barn and threw off her jacket, casting raindrops everywhere, and then immediately tore into the tangle of unwound strips. After picking at the grit and chips stuck to the rib-knit fabric for awhile, she remarked she'd brought out a clean sweatshirt.

"Your black one, Bee."

"Huh. Suits my mood." Clover's leg was swollen straight as a stovepipe. Slight indentations showed from the bandage.

"That's just what your father said, young lady." Bailey smoothed out the used sheeting. Her father understood her, only too well.

"I hate using this dirty old thing again."

"At least no open wounds to contaminate. Get going, now. It's late."

She was trying to be neat. Her hands fought to steady the tube of sheeting, which kept falling apart. She had to hurry to unroll enough of the plum to hold it in place. Her mother was talking, but the heavy rain drowned out anything chastising, or encouraging.

"That'll have to do, Bee." At last, one leg was done. "You've got a few more minutes, so do a hind."

Down on her knees, assailed by sour fumes, Bailey began unwinding the off-hind. Her fingers were learning to work faster. Hastily, tenderly, she brushed the grit away, then managed to control the layered sheeting long enough to start with the binding. She was spiraling up when the leg shifted, and stretched straight out.

"Watch it, Bee, she could run you over!" There was a roll of thunder. A gust of rain spattered against the roof, and the partly unrolled binding popped out of Bailey's hands. She hobbled to her feet. "Try to relax, Bee," her mother said caringly as she handed over another roll. "And relax in those exams. The facts will ooze out of your brain, and you'll do just fine!"

It was 7:25. *Please, Gussie, wait.* Squatting, trying to ignore her throbbing knees, Bailey started over. A sudden clap of thunder, and Clover swung her leg, as she plodded after it like a stray duckling. The old shed shuddered in the storm. Her fingers spiraled faster.

"Run," her mother cried, and thrust a hunk of crushed foil into her hand. It was 7:29. The off-hind bandage's ends had been tied tight and tucked into the top. "You run, Bee, I can finish up."

THE BUS WHINED ALONG, the wheels throwing out sheets of water. Bailey had found Theo sprawled across their seat, apparently only half awake, so had collapsed into the next one back. A beaded curtain of raindrops slid down her window. She huddled into her grubby sweatshirt, relying on the droning motor to drown her hiccupy sounds. She'd done everything right, she guessed, except for the other two legs. So what if she forgot to change her sweatshirt. The bus splashed through a puddle, swerved, then groaned to a halt, bumping her head against Theo's seat. Cold metal. Bummer! She'd forgotten all about taking the temperature.

She hunched forward with her arms wrapped across her chest, and quietly wept herself limp.

They were in town now, passing houses set close together on neat, little landscaped yards. Lights in the windows blinked through the rain. She blew her nose on the paper towel her mother had included with the lumpy packet. She uncrinkled a corner of the foil and pinched off a hunk of fried-egg sandwich. Good, Mom had remembered the catsup—tartness was good for stupid tears.

SATURDAY CAME AT LAST. Clover craned her neck toward the thin glass rod protruding from her rump. Her eyes were runny today but less puffy, her nostrils still miserably clogged. Last night's handful of grain was gone, and Bailey was hopeful. The legs would tell even more. The bandages hung loose—no surprise, after that clumsy wrap-job. She flashed the thermometer into a dim slice of light, and the tightness in her chest lifted. *101.9*. She hooked the chain across the doorway and let her patient wander while she tidied up. Chuck Calderone's *Eatin' and drinkin' and shittin'* rang encouragingly as she kept finding more clumps. Clover rested her nose on the chain and somberly regarded her murky world. Bailey thought back to her exams: simply sitting and putting down answers had been easy compared to what she'd gone through *before* school. She might have maxed out math but had her doubts about social studies. Whatever, eighth grade was history, and she was free!

Ready at last to unwrap, she hooked up a crosstie. This flimsy halter was due for a pre-soak and a hard wash—another job for Nurse Bailey. She began unwinding: when the sheeting fell away she squealed with joy. A faint line, a barely perceptible groove, set the tendon off from the cannon bone. She began patting bits of debris away, humming . . . *Morning has broKEN*—. One hand helping the other, spiraling away. The fresh bandages, with the new wraps her mother had fashioned out of an old crib pad, looked as good as Dr. Goozeman's.

19

School Horses

"LET'S SEE WHAT YOU do with our new horse, Theo"—a note of pride in Cappy's voice. "You tell Bino to get you Spirit Lake."

The new horse was small like Hickory Nut—not black, but basically white with black points—the lower legs and mane and tail—and marked with big reddish-brown patches. The chest patch was a war-horse's shield: Theo imagined Indians galloping across the plains. Grisly old Bino unsnapped the crossties in his usual uncommunicative way. Bino wasted no words, displayed no affection for his back-aisle charges. Still, before handing over the reins for this little paint, he awarded its neck a hearty slap.

"Watch it," he called out as Spirit Lake bounded up the annex ramp.

The moment Theo's leg swung over, the horse jerked away from Cappy. There was a struggle at the door to the arena, the horse bent on the outdoors. Spirit Lake was a horse of a different color, and not just because of the extraordinary hide. Theo's determination fired to maintain control. Cappy'd given him a test: he'd need everything she'd taught, and more, to meet the challenge. Foul weather this morning had the weekenders riding indoors. A few, obviously more interested in socializing than riding, dawdled along, which left the ones trotting or cantering to weave in and out. Some of these people had no more idea of arena etiquette than this new school horse. Spirit

153

Lake swerved past a nonchalant group riding four abreast, knocking Theo's boot against another rider's.

"Sorry about that," he called over his shoulder, then set a stabilizing hand on Spirit Lake's shoulder. "Steady man, steady."

For a change, all three rows of ceiling fixtures shone brightly today. The glittering mirror put Spirit Lake into a fast scissors dance. A white slick of lather bathed the tri-tone hide. Theo was trying to rein in, conscious of someone moving up on the inside, when he recognized Sheri Dembinski on Safe Flight. Sheri shot a thumbs-up as she passed him. Now Theo was as pumped as his horse. He could have used some help, but Cappy was busy. She must be blind—

"Theodore North, you walk that horse for a while!" He cringed, grappling with the reins. Spirit Lake chomped the bit, humped his back, and boosted his front. Theo aimed for the center pool of light, where the two horses walking sedately might serve as role models.

The excited paint did soften some, but constant tests against the bit convinced Theo to gravitate back to the rail. Tapping this keg of nerves required at least a brief canter.

His cautious, muted cue resulted in an abrupt lift into a lively gait surprisingly easy to rate, and as easy to sit as a toy rocking-horse. Theo followed with his hands and quietly pumped his hips. Now he understood what Cappy meant by *collection*, positively worth working for. A look in the mirror showed dappled white foam on both him and the horse. On their third trip around, Cappy motioned them over. How come? The horse was behaving. Moving out had helped a lot, and got them communicating.

"That's using good judgment, Theo. Dealing with the goers takes finesse, what? A different story from pushing the lazies." He glowed with self esteem, while she swept foamy globs off the vein-engorged neck. "The hyperactivity is only natural, this little guy's first trip to the city." Cappy ran her hand through the glaze, then shook her wrist. "You can see he's out of condition. All this sweat would be running clear if he was in shape."

Theo learned a lot from Spirit Lake, and couldn't wait to ride the spunky little "goer" again. The family wouldn't be leaving for Maine for another week and, now with school out, he could get in extra lessons. He needed all the experience he could get if he'd be riding through Maine's forests.

Tuesday he went off to One Oak with high hopes, only to be assigned the complacent Corn Cob. On Wednesday, Mr. Sebastian's, "You come back with that new paint," twisted his heart with relief. The director had a glint in his eye. "Your group will be riding outside," he added.

Theo was excited. His first chance for the outdoor arena, on that little pistol! He had a sneaking suspicion it would be Spirit Lake's first time out there, too.

No sooner had his pants brushed the saddle, when the horse moved off. Theo ducked automatically, even though the tall entryway would accommodate percherons. Spirit Lake's rapid hoof beats across the pavement echoed into the morning fog.

"Whoa, take it easy, man!" He focused on the grand old oak tree standing guard over the trail.

A hasty descent down the sharp bank shook his legs loose, his first experience on uneven terrain. He shoved a low branch out of his face and got splashed by its dewy leaves. The arena came in view. Spirit Lake broke into a half-trot, half-canter, and danced all the way down to the fence.

Curious phantoms emerged from the mist. Theo rubbed his stinging knee that had been knocked against the gate post, and made out Barbie and Joshua. Spirit Lake trotted over to them on a light rein. Scuttling hoof beats from the trail heralded more horses, and then Cappy came out, wearing a navy striped tee and a brand new cap. She sorted the class into pairs, Theo's and Joshua's small horses together, and started calling out maneuvers.

The eager paint and the peppy black were wellmatched temperamentally. Mustering tact, between judiciously doling rein and drawing back, Theo tucked Spirit Lake into a tight canter, which persisted, alongside Hickory

Nut, who insisted on cantering, too, through Cappy's progressive calls for turns, circles, crossovers, and reverses. Theo was charged. *Que magnifico,* a mounted troop.

"BARRISTER," MR. SEBASTIAN BARKED on Thursday. Theo was counting on Spirit Lake. Never Barrister. What made it worse was knowing how hard Barbie had worked to get that Abrams tank to canter. His last chance to ride before leaving for Maine, and he gets to ride outside but on that clunker! Barbie had Escort today, Joshua Hickory Nut again, and Jenny, who had missed a few lessons, beamed from atop Corn Cob. The small group kept to a walk while they waited for Cappy. Hickory Nut marched in front, followed by the swaggering Escort, then the compliant Corny, with Barrister tramping along behind the pale yellow rump in granny gear. The horse's broad, comfortable back and rhythmically creaking saddle lulled Theo into loafing. Silently he cursed his mouse-colored rogue, who wouldn't be so bad if only he could move. What a comedown from the eager paint. Cappy must be saving her top school horse for one of her many devoted adults.

He choked back a yelp, jabbed in a vulnerable spot by the pommel. The tall grass growing through the fence had sprung Barrister to life—but rather than quick steps, an abrupt stop, in order to snip off the feathery, green tips. Theo braced his shoulders. He leaned way back to heave the mulish head up. This horse sucked, as sneaky as Andy, who'd yell, "Think quick!" after throwing a pass.

"Hey!" Now the beast had his head on the other side of the fence, snatching at every blade in reach.

A hard pull, plus a swift kick got them moving again.

"How goes it, Theo?" His instructor was grinning. Barrister's neck craned back for more.

"Huh! Did you see that?"

"Well, you're paying to ride. You get your money's worth with Barrister. That horse makes you ride all the time." Cappy had a new baseball cap on, with *Blah, Blah, Blah* across the front. Ho, that fit. She turned toward some people looking on from the fence. He could hear them discussing some "particularly bred" horse as he edged Barrister past. Maybe the new one he'd seen her on, a rich chocolate, wickedly handsome gelding. No way would she reveal the horse's age, its owner, or its name to him—only, "Yes, big, all of seventeen hands." Jenny Han had mentioned a German Warmblood had come in. Her parents boarded hunters at One Oak, so they'd know. Sheri Dembinski was in the market for a new horse, according to Dad. One readymade and reliable, this time. Her Safe Flight might be good when Cappy was there to coach her, but was apt to pull wingdings in public.

He nudged Barrister along, wondering if Sheri was up to handling a Warmblood. Cappy would have to work with her. You'd need to really know horseflesh to match a student with something suitable for showing. Bailey sure had been lucky, coming home from that sale with a sure winner. Sale horses probably went cheap, so lucky for Mr. Mason, too. *His* father would never buy animals at an auction. "They could have bought trouble," his father'd said, hearing their neighbors had suddenly become horse owners. "Lots worse trouble than one bout of shipping sickness. Sheri was appalled when I told her about it. Some guy she knows brought a horse home from that sale, and it limped whenever he went to saddle up."

Sheri, of course, had the sense to ask her trainer to conduct a search. Cappy'd get clued in by her network of pros and come up with something with training behind it, might just need a tune-up. *Mucho mileage, mucho dinero*, went into making a show horse.

"Everybody warmed up?" He snapped to attention. "Circles today. Get those hind feet tracking up to the fronts. No swinging haunches. No dropping the inside shoulder, or sidling! I consider that cheating."

Once the mouse-colored bay, the little black, the liver-chestnut, and the pale palomino were positioned well away from each other, Cappy called for circles. Twelve-foot-diameter-circles didn't sound complicated, but none of them turned out round. "Back to the rail, good people," Cappy bellowed after Hickory Nut collided with Escort. "Awaken your handsome steeds! Can't you feel that side-to-side sway as you walk? Get with him, and when he sways to the right, energize the motion with your left leg! Then visa versa!" The four handsome steeds came to life. "Now come into your circle." She paused while they got started. Then, "Position the head inside. Think of your horse bending around your inside leg. Emphasize that leg to activate his inside hind, which is the hardest working leg here. The smaller your arc, the more the inside hind needs to pivot." She allowed a few moments for the class to digest this—all new to Theo. Circles were like riding corners, except for no straight track leading in to help build momentum.

"Your outside leg behind the girth keeps his hind end on track. And trr-OTT!"

"Joshua, don't steer with your arm hanging out like a crippled wing! Your horse is happier with your hands as far apart as the width of its mouth. Sit up, Barb, and throw back that inside shoulder. Human shoulders parallel to equine shoulders!" Cappy paced her own little circles, on the move as usual. Fortunately, she had the kind of voice that carried. "Wake up, Theo, Barrister's falling asleep! Be tough with that guy." Geez, he'd been working on steering. He enforced his legs, squeezing the breath out of the old bugger. "Barrister needs a swift kick! Awaken that old blunderbuss! Shorten your reins! Keep after him! But be sure to reward any positive response by easing up."

Oh, on and off squeezes?

"Jenny, your circle is way too small. You're letting Corn Cob lead with his shoulder. No cheating! Push him out with your inside leg. Now, everybod-dee, re-VERSE! Don't look at the ground! Circles, not eggs, if you please. Back on the rail, to the very same spot you came off the rail. Please, people, look where you are going!"

It shouldn't be so darn hard to make a circle. Theo steered with his eyes and squeezed his thighs to Barrister's big stride. The clunky trot had developed a spring, power he'd never experienced with Corn Cob. And this trot was easier to sit than Spirit Lake's choppy trot. Barrister chugged along gamely, Theo in the groove. He wondered if Bailey had begun riding again. A lousy deal, her horse down sick.

"Canter, Joshua," Cappy boomed. "Take it all the way around the ring."

Theo pressed his inside leg, and his circle widened, Barrister edging away from the rail to make room for Hickory Nut. "Now you, Barbie," Cappy shouted after Hickory Nut loped by. "Keep Escort bent for the cue. He's got to push from behind!" The arena turned into a four-ring circus under the direction of a mighty-midget-ringmaster. "Circle again, Barb!" Escort was headed straight up the rail, still trotting. "Rebalance that freight train, then ask again. Sit up! Lean back! Hold him hard—hold him until you feel him lift!" Theo's heart went out to the chubby girl, whose back was rigid as she tugged with all her might. She'd had a job getting this lazy tank to canter, and now she was stuck with that long-framed brute that insisted on leaning on the forehand.

"Circle again, Barb, take your time. Now, ask again. If he doesn't lift, pull him right back into your trotting circle, push him into the bit, and hold while you kick!"

Barbie and Escort were lost from sight until all at once they whizzed by.

"Good, go around again! Push him, push him up to the bit and work your arms." Escort pounded his canter out in stiff-legged beats. "You think about what you just did, Barb," Cappy crowed, after granting permission to walk. "Next?!"

Theo tapped his heels into Barrister's broad barrel. The hard-core slacker had cantered for Barbie once, so there was hope. He legged fiercely, legged again and hissed, "Canter, you turkey!"

Barrister granted a half-hearted lift.

"Good man," Theo muttered after being ponderously rocked around the ring. He delivered a congratulatory cuff to the beefy neck, just as Jenny took off for a pleasant round on One Oak's old faithful.

"All right, good people, will you please sit-trot a ten-foot-radius around me. Space into separate quadrants. Pin one eye on my hat to gauge your distance." Having something to focus on made it easier. Theo zeroed in on *Blah, Blah, Blah*.

"Open your circles," Cappy warbled cheerily. "Your inside leg will drive him into the outside rein." The circles opened like flowers to the sun. Exploding puffs of dust muffled the sprightly cadence. Barrister actually felt springy now. "Stay bent to the inside and weight your outside seat bone for lateral expansion. And keep those heels down! It's the whole inside of your calf and your thigh, on and off, every step." For sure that comment was aimed at *him*. But how was he supposed to emphasize one leg and, at the same time, weight the opposite seat bone?

"Look here, at me!" Cappy shouted over the hubbub. "Sit up now, and can-TER! Shoulders level. Torso turning with the equine turns!"

He legged Barrister tight to the bit and vibrated the inside rein to keep him attentive. Up ahead, Hickory Nut took off. Escort simply accelerated his trot. Barrister offered one false start after another, lifting and dropping as the group revolved. Theo braced his back, forced his inside leg at the girth, and coiled the heavyset creature into a tight spring. Up ahead, Escort lifted. Then Barrister, thundering mightily on. Theo pushed to catch up to Escort, who was gaining on Hickory Nut. He could hear Corn Cob bringing up the rear, cantering as if he belonged on a carousel.

"Looking nice, everybody," carried over the sixteen drumbeats.

Barrister's newfound impulsion put Theo on automatic pilot.

"And, walk!"

He pulled back, and they hit a speed bump.

"Looks like we need a lesson on down transitions," his instructor groaned. "Basically, though, you're all starting to look like riders. Walk 'em out, good people!"

They traveled four abreast. Barrister inched into the rail. Joshua brushed the dust off his pants. Barbie's red face beamed. Jenny remarked that the boys' blue shirts and rust-colored breeches had them looking like twins. "Ha, more like Mutt and Jeff," Joshua quipped, with a self-deprecating laugh. "Right, North?"

"Say what?" Theo called back, having fallen behind for Barrister to help himself to a welldeserved reward.

20

A Fresh Horse

BY MID-JUNE THE HONEYSUCKLE was blooming and Dakota Clover's convalescence had advanced to the turnout stage. She flashed her tail, stomped her feet, swung her neck to snap flies off her back. A heat wave with soaring humidity had sent the fiends into a frenzy, and the harassed horse craved for shelter. One particularly horrid afternoon, Bailey discovered her darting frantic zigzags between the fence and her barn.

She raced out in her thongs and hurled back the chain. Clover was wild-eyed but had the sense to home in on the familiar clink. The harried horse plunged through the doorway and straight into her stall. The radiating heat, the wheezing and pouring sweat, rushed Bailey for her sweat-scraper.

"You poor thing, how could I have left you out so long?" This was not the sort of weather to be running around in, especially for someone who had just been sick.

The aisle was hardly cooler, positively no air today, anywhere. Mounds of lather piled onto the steel blade. Bailey scooped down one side and then the other, and around and around again. Evaporation cooled a healthy, overheated horse. This wasn't happening here. Distended veins in Clover's nostrils glistened red. Bright red rivers ran down her legs. Bailey reached and arced, over and over reached and arced her widespread arms, all the while murmuring prayers for forgiveness. After this, no chain.

Her thongs squished through puddled lather, and she hit the steaming hot back with a dripping cold sponge. No matter she herself was burning up; Clover wasn't hardened to stress, and this could bring on a relapse. A vigorous shake delivered a hot, salty shower, and sent Bailey over to the archaic filing cabinet donated by Glenna's mother. She plucked a fresh towel out of a squeaky drawer and went to work on herself. Lucky Glen wasn't here for this mess. Glen only came when her mother saved enough time for the twelve-mile round trip. Ms. Sondra Munro liked laying her sleepy head on her lacy pillow until the last minute, before starting her day at Greenham's Spa and Travel. Even so, during Clover's rehab she'd made the effort to taxi Glenna every day.

Bailey rubbed towels all over the steaming hide; rubbed hard, but hot spots rose to the surface. In less than a minute a towel was saturated. Maybe a leisurely walk outside? Maddening buzzes in the sun-baked doorway squelched that idea. Considering the roof's shade and the walls' missing boards, outside was no cooler than inside. The savages were after her too, and she slapped one off her neck. She slapped her stinging, bare leg. She swirled her arms in defense while counting Clover's inhalations. Dr. Goozeman had warned about labored breathing.

Fifty-five per minute. Not good, the norm was sixteen.

The insects hadn't been so mean during the rehab's walking phase. The girls had traded off ushering the horse from one restorative vitamin patch to another. Whenever they stopped, Clover dropped her head to graze; when they walked, she walked; when they talked, she pricked her ears to listen in. Two weeks of hand-walking had seemed like enough. "By the time a brisk walking pace is sustained for an exercise period of at least fifteen minutes," Glenna read from her book, "the patient may be allowed a brief taste of freedom."

Brief, alright. Instead of running off when she got turned out, the convalescent sniffed straight to her rolling spot. There she hovered, pawing and snuffling the ground. Then, quite daintily, she dropped to her knees and lowered her massive haunches. She flopped on her side and swept her neck through the dust. Relishing the freedom, Clover rolled her impressive hulk back and forth with exuberant thrusts, scrunching her back to work up the dirt. Poking up to paw at air those delicate legs appeared incredibly staunch.

Bailey grinned, recalling how Clover rolled up to her chest to rise effortlessly, and shake up a cloud of dust.

"If a horse doesn't shake after rolling," Glenna had warned, "it might be on count of a stomachache. Their long train of intestines raises the odds for cramps."

Colic. Just the thought now made Bailey drop her towel. Clover did look more relaxed, though, after her big shake on the crossties. She stood at ease, seemingly oblivious of her mid-section. No rolling eyes, like the book said colicky horses showed. And she'd certainly shook enough, from the looks of this teeshirt. When you hardly expected it, she remained calm. Like when the mouse scooted between her feet.

Bailey laughed out loud. Both she and Glen had gone bananas over one tiny mouse. Glen had screamed. *She* had grabbed the broom. Their patient had stood quietly with her head cocked.

"Some patient," Bailey muttered as she wiped a hind leg down hard. The left fore had acquired a sizeable notch, which needed attention. She'd never thought horses involved so much work. She'd seen herself petting and riding, not sweating and striving like this. "Some patient," she muttered again, going for a fresh towel. Of course, this particular creature was worth it all. "Ouch! Keep your crummy tail still. That's the thanks I get?"

She rubbed her arm and then went back to rubbing Clover's chest. "Looks like you're totally well, sweetie. I can't wait to ride again. You will be good, won't you? You were so very smart to remember what to do on the lunge line." The mare had been a lamb for Glenna, who, complaining she "couldn't do zilch," had needed to snap her wrist over and over to make the whip pop.

The hide was nearly dry, the respirations nearly down to normal, twenty-two per minute. Soon Clover would be at peace in her stall. During her confinement Daddy had removed some bars, and now she could stick her head out the shaded north side and look around. Bailey planted a kiss on the fuzzy muzzle, then peered around for the kittens.

"They'll be purr-fect here," Glenna had brayed when she presented the two darling fluff balls. "Company for Clover. And they can catch the mice!"

Huh, it would be months before Hasty Pudding, an orange tabby, and Heather, a bright, patchy calico, which Glenna figured was female, because only female felines came in more than two colors, would fulfill any destiny for mousing. All they did lately was cool their bellies with their paws in the air.

"Kitty, kitty, kitty?" Bailey raised Heather to the horse's warm back. The calico crouched in apprehension. Clover swiveled one eye, and did not move when her crossties swung away.

COOLER TEMPERATURES AND SOFT breezes came in overnight. Except for the chipped hooves, Clover seemed no worse from her run. She had regained her strength, and proven fit to give her nurse a ride. Yes, ride before another muggy spell set off those beastly flies. A little worry nagged Bailey about starting, after such a long layoff, without anyone here on the lunge line. If they got going too fast, she could tip off balance and get her arms flopping. Her hands didn't know what they were doing half the time as it was. But Daddy was off to a meeting in Boston, and Glenna was off to look into bed-and-breakfasts. Still, they shouldn't waste such a fine day.

She had waited, and worked so hard for this. Besides, yesterday's turmoil would have Clover all worn out.

She stuck to her old routine and closed the mare in, in case she needed to urinate. No excuse, then, for restlessness. She made certain to hook up the chain. Without Glen here, she needed to think of everything. She waited for Clover to pee. An angle of sunlight illuminated the stall. A barn-swallow darted through the rear entrance and hovered over a rafter like a Lilliputian helicopter. Bailey's heart was as fluttery as those wings. She'd be climbing up by herself, without anyone to hold Clover and slide her offside stirrup home.

The mare fanned her tail, and dropped steaming balls of dung on her tidied bedding. Before long, she swung her haunches, braced her legs, and let loose a golden stream. The musty ammonia pungency cleared Bailey's head. Clover's withers still weren't as high as her rump, she noticed. Taller haunches indicated room for growth, Mrs. Knott said, and that apps usually mature later than most other breeds. Still, Clover wasn't totally appaloosa, so who knew? For now, she was simply an adolescent. Like *me,* Bailey acknowledged with a self-deprecating grunt. Fortunately, both past the rebellious stage.

She set to grooming, a chore she enjoyed far more than hectic sweat-scraping. She needed to ask Lady Knott about a blacksmith, her father had said. Cool, how he kept tabs on Clover but didn't interfere. "How's that horse of ours today?" he'd call out when he got home. He had provided a sawhorse for the saddle and mounted a shelf for the brushes. After a whole breakfast's worth of hay blew away, he had arranged for the delivery of a humongous tractor tire. Bailey snickered, recalling how the tire man and her father and Mikey fought that monster through the gate. The tire had a mind of its own until it got plopped in a good spot for their manger.

Oops, pay attention. No guardian angel here. Hah, nor even Glen nor Daddy.

Feet clean, girth tight? Forget anything? Info on blacksmiths could wait till later. Just getting this horse ready was wearing her out. She lifted her shirt to the wafting cross-ventilation. Her father had turned this old shed into a barn, with a box stall, two sturdy buckets, a grain can, a handy shelf, the cross-ties, even a security-chain. He had set all this up for her. The fence, the high stack of hay bales, the humongous tire to keep the hay from blowing away, and, of course, her horse—all because of Daddy. She'd give her best to measure up for him.

Ready. A quick look confirmed the chain was up. It was mind-boggling to think of everything by herself. Her fingers trembled, releasing one crosstie, then the other. Her body-block into Clover's advancing shoulder granted barely enough time to change from the trusty halter to the tricky bridle.

Yay, good to go.

She positioned Clover close to the big tire, then stepped up on the rim, which felt strong enough to hold her but rather wobbly. Tottering on her right leg next to the horse's shoulder, she aimed her left at the stirrup, which jerked away.

"Whoa!" That surprised her. The horse had never ducked before. The hindquarters swung farther away as she clung to the reins. With her right foot hopping over wobbly rubber, her left strained to anchor the stirrup. Where was Glen when she needed her?

"C'mon, you gorgeous thing!" She held the cagey horse in a fiery stare. "Pretty is as pretty does, you know!" If she got her act together and handled this right, Clover would act as beautiful as she looked. "Hey!" Again, she'd gathered her reins tight to the pummel, only to be left tottering on the rim. What good was "gorgeous" if a horse didn't cooperate? "No!" she shrieked as her feet hit the ground. "You ugly thing!"

Had anybody seen, or heard? She wouldn't mind if Theo happened by. No chance, still at the lake. She let the reins hang slack and slumped beside the tire, stabbing her toe at a ragged weed. After all they'd been through, the horse didn't trust her! As if Clover didn't even know her. She hadn't carried weight for nearly a month, but that was no excuse.

Bailey inhaled deeply, restoring oxygen. Fluffy clouds drifted across the sky. She brushed a fly off Clover's nose.

"Dakota Clover!" her voice stern. "Meet Bailey Elizabeth Mason, who loves you even if you are a brat!" She raised an image of the slender legs rooted into the ground like saplings. She gathered up her reins and stepped back into the well of the tire. "Whoa!" she snapped with a burst of air, as her right foot hit the rim and her left the stirrup. Her right leg was well on its way up when the horse swung away, leaving her perched on one stirrup with a desperate grip on the saddle.

21

A Personal Best Cut Short

SHE HUMMED A HAPPY tune Sunday morning while waiting for Mrs. Knott to pick up the phone. Mrs. Knott would know who to call for Clover's feet. The first time up, after nearly a month off, had gone quite well. Once she was up in the saddle. She still knew how to post, anyway. But now to solve the mounting issue. She had put her mind to it and come up with an idea that should make it easier for both of them.

The answering machine beeped. With all those horses, naturally the woman would be outdoors. Bailey left a message about finding a blacksmith and said she would call back later.

While she cleaned out the stall, and Clover cleaned out the tire, she reviewed her strategy. "I bet that hay tastes pretty good," she called out, and Clover raised her head, as if to say, "You've got that right!" This horse was in for a surprise. Naturally she'd be eager to stretch her legs. Today she'd get to do just that before being asked, no, allowed, to stand still.

They swung along smartly, Bailey administering playful pats as they tramped a wide arc around the tractor tire. Dew on the few weeds that hadn't been trampled in the feeding area clung to the scuffed toes of her work boots and shined up Clover's hooves. "Just let go of all that tension, sis," she cooed, and kept her eyes away from the tire. She wouldn't think about using its stout rim, Clover might read her mind. This horse needed to relax.

The sun bounced off the healthy hide. By gradual increments, their radius decreased. Five times around ought to work as well as a mini-lunge session. A sixth circuit, then a seventh for luck, for help calming her own nerves, too. Then she positioned Clover up close to the tire.

Even this small amount of exercise had affected the girth by two holes, and she hitched it up. Then she traveled back and forth, both sides, alert for the slightest move. "Patience!" she barked, when a front leg shifted. "Please, just whoa!" Of course *she* also needed patience. But once her leg started up, she needed willpower.

More walkabouts, interrupted with practice halts to get the concept down pat. Then she transferred the reins back over the head, gathered them tight to the cantle, and formed a mental image of Clover's frame growing out of deeply rooted trees, planted four square.

"Whoa!" Quick as a cat she sprang.

"Whoooaa . . ." Ever so softly, she settled in.

"Good girrrl," she purred, as her boot caught the off stirrup.

Clover meandered off in a jog the moment Bailey's hands edged forward. Considering all the fussiness the horse had put up with, only fair for her to lead for a while. Soon Bailey needed to post. She strained to maintain straight lines over the uneven terrain. Downhill into the sun and up again with the sun on their backs until, gaining confidence, she eased up on the reins and pressed her legs. They were communicating, ready to canter.

The merry loping stride, the sense of power; the air blowing in her face and billowing out her shirt were sheer exhilaration. She came forward, stretched into her heels, fixing her legs like a fulcrum, and found the ground whooshing faster. When the course stayed tolerably straight, she felt tolerably secure. Cantering the down-slopes got tricky, Clover apt to lean into the bit. Bailey had never expected so much effort to be required of *her*. She was breathing hard; her arms and legs were tired. Besides, these sudden leaps might not be so good for ragged feet.

"You need a blacksmith, sweetie," she declared while toweling off. "You deserve the greatest care in the universe."

Few horseshoers were called blacksmiths any more, she learned from Mrs. Knott, who returned her call Monday at seven 'o clock in the morning. "They're known as 'farriers,' dear, because they work with iron, *ferrum* being the Latin word for iron. Shoes come readymade these days, and most farriers work cold shod. I'll give you three numbers of locals with courses in equine science under their belts. Elmer Klachner's always done my work, but he's getting on. 'No new clients,' Elmer says."

Breakfast time went into phone calls resulting in exasperating busy signals and answering machines. Quietly knitting in the back of Bailey's mind all that time were ideas for getting her way with Clover. The horse's behavior fascinated her; their progress would be like putting a puzzle together.

Clover's legs remained planted barely long enough today for Bailey to climb up. A keen, swaggering walk along the fence line gained energy as they came away to pass behind the barn. Birds twittered through the trees. A broom whisked back and forth on the patio.

"Lovely, Bee, to see Clover looking so well!" So, her mother was okay with her riding alone. The prospect of having the horse to herself this whole summer was awesome. She piloted toward the fence as her mother walked over.

"Mom, I like it here now. This is the greatest."

"Honey, I am happy you are happy. Just remember to be careful."

"I will. Oh, I am! Don't worry, Clover is being so good!"

She trotted off through the stubble, steering broad circles and posting smartly while her mother watched from the fence. To put on a show, she signaled a canter. The horse was traveling as sweetly for her as she had at the sale for Stephanie Twomey, when her mother waved and headed back to the house. The big sky, and this generous amount of land to ride on was all hers. She ventured farther out, with the idea of cantering down to the property line. The target was a long way off, the rough mounds of stone barely visible through the scattered scrub and trees. Clover picked up speed as they approached the honeysuckle bushes, and Bailey sensed tension. Suddenly Clover dropped her head and kicked a buck. Bailey jerked back, and the horse wrenched and tugged as though cross-tied over a bed of hot coals. The next desperate jerk triggered a high-headed rear. Bailey threw herself forward. Teetering up in her stirrups, she swatted the upright neck. "You stop that!" she shouted just as Clover plunged into a hard gallop.

"No! Slow down, Clover, go slow . . . " A low branch knocked her hard hat; leathery leaves lashed her face. True grit sent her weight and legs into action and, well past those bushes, Clover stepped into a strong trot and tracked an agreeable circle. The thrusts charged Bailey with power. She'd keep a firm hold now and make it down to the wall. They'd escaped those trolls lurking in the honeysuckle. That rear had been *her* fault. She needed to consider her horse's mindset. She needed to steady the horse instead of jerk. Thank goodness, Mom wasn't out here to see that!

They sailed along in a breezy trot, until a huge limb appeared directly in their path, scarcely fifteen feet ahead. Bailey wanted to pull up, already enough trouble today. But Clover had the bit in her teeth. Her rounded, tight back muscles indicated resolve. The limb's scraggly branches reached out like a witch's greedy fingers. Bailey came forward and clutched a fistful of mane. *Don't fall, don't fall,* she prayed. The scary snare loomed larger. If she tried to stop, even to turn, they would both wipe out. She had to trust—

It was a mighty lift, as if they'd grown wings. For one heavenly moment, they soared through the air. The branches snatched at Clover's legs, but she managed a straight landing. Then she threw in a lighthearted buck and went skipping and hopping over the uneven ground, with Bailey clinging like the giddy toddler Grandpoppy used to bounce on his knee. "This Is

The Way the Old Farmer Rides," Grandpoppy would sing while Bailey squealed with glee.

She was down, rear end first. Her head clanged, but the old hunt cap stuck. No gleefulness now. Her pinkie smarted, minus a strip of skin. Big deal. She should have dropped the reins. It wasn't as if Clover would run away—she'd just run back up the hill. But those hooves . . .

She stole a look to the poplar trees. Too bad Theo wasn't around. He would give her a hand and help her up. He would tell her it wasn't her fault, that she was an excellent rider. He would kiss—

Right, you goof. Anyway, poor riding isn't the only problem. Thing is, Clover does not respect me. Now she has her strength back, she has no use for people. Doesn't she know she needs me to get her a farrier? And right now she needs this spill erased.

No blood on the legs, the hooves looked no worse; the horse wasn't even breathing hard. Bailey climbed back up and headed off in the same direction. As if the bucking and rearing had never happened, they made it to the stone wall. A new personal best!

But, as she dismounted, the biggest horse fly on the planet zoomed in and buzzed Clover's head. Then it chose the humped, tense rump from which to test the air. Just one thing after another! The sticky-looking cellophane wings vibrated ominously. Bailey wanted to hide. Large insects made her skin crawl. Flies got hungry. Flies craved blood. If only this one would find a tempting current of air and vanish!

Clover had not moved, except for an explicit ear, pointed right at *her*.

She edged toward the imperiled rump. The horse's faith in her was awesome. She tried to still the trembling in her arm. Even if she aimed right, there could be trouble. The world stood still while she gathered courage. Clover could resent the whack, and then explode and knock her over.

Right on target, and Clover never flinched! She just dropped her head to eye the crippled wings flailing in the dust. Giddy with success, Bailey finished the job with the heel of her boot. She gripped the relaxed crest and waggled it passionately back and forth. "You understand, girl! We're a team!"

WEDNESDAY HAD RAIN IN the forecast. Yet the idea of another exciting ride was irresistible. That nasty bug experience proved Clover trusted her. And she trusted Clover. Everything would be fine, even if it did rain.

A few spots showed up on the saddle when she led the horse out. Clover stood quietly planted until Bailey, up and stirrups set, let her hands go forward. They walked around the tire and then disappeared down into the pasture, together in their own misty world. She let the mare pick her own way. When Clover shoved at the bit near the back bushes, she let her trot. The reins were sort of slippery but she hardly needed them now. Clover pushed into the heavy mist. And, coming up past the shed, granted a walk over the squishy, bare places. Bailey noticed a glob of mud on her boot. She bent over to clear the stirrup, and saw mud on the girth. It was loose, too.

She groaned. This meant getting off, and getting the watery payback she deserved for omitting last-minute details. The sprinkles had advanced to a hard drizzle. The birds were quiet, hiding under leaves. Beads of water ran off the tips of Clover's ears, and she stuck out her nose as if she would like to have it washed. The girth had priority, even if it meant sitting in a puddle. The rain poured down while Bailey tried to picture herself hitching it up without getting off. How would Clover react to a leg hanging over her shoulder? Well, she had cooperated with the bug.

A discombobulating shake dislodged the propped leg, and the horse took a notion to move along. Bailey fished for the dangling stirrup. One girth-strap dangled, too; if it hadn't been for the other one, the whole saddle, with her in it, would have ended up on the ground. "Whoa, now!" She clutched her knees and worked at doubling up enough of the slippery reins for a decent tug. One stirrup, loose girth, a clammy windbreaker clinging to her shoulders, and now her hard hat was loose. "Clover! Please be good while I fix this saddle!"

By the time the horse stopped, they had traveled half way down to the stone wall. "Okay, sister, we shall try again!" Bailey shouted over the rain, and pushed her hard hat down tighter. "You can't go anywhere on just one buckle!"

This time, her groping fingers zeroed in. The clouds opened just as she snugged the second strap into its buckle. Clover pushed into the roaring wind. Bailey hunched her shoulders against the rain streaming off her hard hat. The saddle was secure, but her jeans were so soaked her legs were sliding. Yet even this was fun, worth it all for the sense of accomplishment.

She was glorying in the latest personal best, too preoccupied with the wet conditions to see they had ranged within ten feet of the trolls' lair. The massed branches thrashed wildly in the wind. Clover had a big trot going, until a noisy horde of blackbirds exploded in her face. The startling shy knocked Bailey loose. Then a quick buck into a hard gallop left her hanging by the crook of her clutched right knee. Leafy stems and pointy stalks whirled perilously close to her head. She gasped for breath and got a mouthful of wet mane. She made a desperate grab for the mane. They were going too fast for a soft landing. But if she pulled hand over hand on her rope ladder . . .

Her eyes opened, then narrowed to slits assailed by pelting rain. Stricken leaves shivered against the dreary sky. The hard hat lay at her side, her left arm propped against it. She thought of Clover—all that jumping around better not have made those feet any worse. Then herself. She'd be fine as soon as she could breathe. A wave of disgust engulfed her. You'd think by this time she'd be able to cope with a shy. The breaths were coming easier, and she tried to move, then screamed as a searing pain shot up her left arm.

22

Down Time

SHE CALLED GLENNA MUNRO as soon as they got home from the emergency room. The X-rays had revealed a simple fracture of the radius, three inches up from the wrist. She attempted to make light of it, and laughed giddily when Glenna described the inn where she and her mom stayed, the whole thing painted a bilious green. The receiver dug into Bailey's cheek. Words caught in her throat when Glenna mentioned she and her mom would be taking off for another two weeks.

"C-call as soon as you're back," she got out. "With this stupid arm in plaster I can't be with Clover unless there's somebody with me."

"Oh, Bailey . . . ." Glenna was sympathetic; for Clover, too, observing that just when the mare had come around to her peppy, healthy self, she would be abandoned.

Odd joggles to the weighty cast shot pains up the arm, but Bailey tagged along at feeding time—feeling useless while, usually, her mother or Michael, on rare occasions, her father, measured out the grain and doled out the hay. She stood by inhaling familiar odors while Michael wielded the manure fork. The rich smells brought Clover closer, even though the horse would be roaming around outside, seemingly content off by herself. The kittens loitered in the sunny doorway, using their paws for washcloths. Once Bailey'd sunk to a bale, they came clambering over her cast. Duker nosed around, then parked against her itchy feet. At least she was allowed to pet the small animals. Another thing to do, and soon, she knew, was round up a farrier. Even horses out of service needed their feet looked after.

The memory redial got a workout as she tried to reach Mrs. Knott's recommendations, only to hear they were booked up months ahead.

Elmer Klachner was her last resort. She'd hound that old guy until he said, "Yes!"

ON SATURDAY, HER THIRD boring day, Bailey was wandering back to the house when a sporty Mazda tore up the driveway. Glenna jumped out, ducked back in, and reappeared with her arms full of a gigantic paper sack and books stacked to her chin. The sack contained Bailey's most craved indulgence from the mall. The books contained information on horses. So thoughtful of Glenna—there sure was enough time to read now.

"Remember, twenty minutes," the conspicuously made up Sondra Munro hollered through her sunroof.

"Understood," Glenna shot back, and rushed to dump her offerings on the patio. The diaphanous top she wore over her cammy got draped on the pile. "Mater's in a tizzy, 'fraid I'll soil my new outfit out here," she confided, as Duker escorted them to the gate. "I just couldn't go without saying goodbye." Clover pulled her head out of the tire and peeked through her tousled forelock. Glenna glanced back toward her mother. "There might be time to at least brush," she said.

"Gosh, would you?" No one had laid a hand on the horse since the accident. With Glenna here, she could brush, too.

She strained from her toes, once Clover was stationed on crossties, and wrapped the strapping neck in a huge, one-armed hug. Heather bounced up to claw the cuffs of her jeans as Glenna began rearranging the tangled mane to fall to one side.

"Does it hurt much?"

"Not really." Bailey made a face indicating otherwise. "Just kinda throbs at the worst times." Glenna pushed the curry-comb around, raising crescents of grit and buried scurf. On the other side, Bailey's cheek pressed into the horse's warm neck. A bit immobilized by the closeness, she managed a few mournful strokes, while the hug-hungry kitten hung on. Such a short time allowed—

"Undoubtedly," Glenna chirped, "Theo will come and kiss it and make it all well."

"In my dreams, you mean." Bailey coughed out a laugh. "I hear they're all back but he hasn't come over. Either he doesn't know I fell off or he doesn't really care."

"So? Maybe he's waiting for an invitation. You can share the caramel corn with him."

"That's stupid, he knows he doesn't need an invitation!" Her voice rising, "A lot of help your idiotic comments are. And now you're taking off again!" came out in a grief-stricken shriek.

Glenna threw down the curry-comb. Clover jerked back when it bounced off the doorframe. Hasty Pudding pounced on the spiraling missile. Hastily Bailey stepped back and narrowly missed Heather. "That's appreciation for you," snorted Glenna. Then, gazing over Clover's backbone with melancholy eyes, "Don't take it all out on me, just a brainless attempt to be cheerful."

"I guess this sweetie's trying to cheer me up, too." Bailey scooped Heather into her free hand, and smiled uncertainly at her distraught friend. Clover took a colossal shake, flopping her mane back to the way it had been. Duker wagged his tail. The kitten pawed at Bailey's hair. She felt calmer now. She didn't understand why, but animals had a way of instilling peace.

"Have a great Fourth of July," she called out as, spitting gravel, the Mazda roared down the driveway.

She lugged the stack of books upstairs, the hard edges digging into her chest. She slid them all into a jumble on her desk chair, then peeked into the center drawer. Her journal lived there, close at hand for shaky moments like this. Quickly she slid the drawer shut—she didn't want to cry. It'd be impossible to read those precious notes right now.

After a while, she began composing a letter to Emily Ambrose. She needed to talk, she needed to express herself. All about Dakota Clover's illness, and the lengthy recovery, emerged in neatly rounded script. "Then, the healthier Clover got, the harder she got to handle." Bailey drew a sad face. "Riding was awesome until she got so strong. Then it got kind of scary." She paused with her green felt-tipped pen in the air. It'd be tough to admit she had fallen off.

Well, cowgirls got thrown.

"The first time didn't do any damage, except to my ego. The second time, she got scared by a noisy dirt-bike and dumped me, but I was okay. The third time, after she jumped me over a huge branch, was mostly fun. Three strikes and out, they say, but I was safe. Until I fell off *again*, and broke my arm. Totally pathetic of me. Now I'm grounded from handling the love of my life by myself." She paused—she wouldn't dwell on that. Think positively. New paragraph.

"I'm going to try to think ahead, and be more careful—an ounce of precaution, you know. But how was I supposed to know my stupid hard hat would come off and land under my radius bone? I wish you were here, Em, to give me seven sips of lukewarm water."

Another pause, gazing longingly out the window. She could see Clover with her head down, feeding. Mike and Andy had come to the rescue. She'd needed to tell them how to catch the horse, and then what to do once they had. Clover couldn't be left running around with a saddle on. If she got it into her head to roll, it'd break the tree. She sighed, recalling how politely her horse bowed for Mikey to get the halter on—almost like saying she was sorry. If only those stupid blackbirds hadn't charged out of the bushes. If only the hard hat hadn't come loose.

I'm sorry, Clover, she mouthed to the window.

She dropped her pen and tramped down the stairs for more aspirin. Her endorphins were depleted, the cast about to burst. Nobody else in the den, she commandeered the remote. On the screen, a group of bizarre looking females in string bikinis struggled with barbells. Watching people work out when *she* couldn't was exasperating—no objections when her father came in and switched to golf. The announcer's boring commentary was hardly diverting. She dragged herself back up the stairs. She kicked through the clothes scattered across the floor and threw herself into her armchair. Curled up like a snail with steadfast Ellie clutched to her breast, she reviewed the "If Onlies." She was furious at herself for falling, furious at her parents for appropriating her horse. Now *they* were doing the chores. Now somebody else would get extra duty when the farrier came. Next week, Elmer Klachner at last had agreed.

By Sunday, the pain had condensed to a dull ache. Bailey spent the afternoon reading and dipping into the jumbo sack of caramel corn, while trying not to get Glenna's pages sticky. Duker propped his head on her shoe, alert for an errant kernel. She usually read stories about girls she could identify with, and daydream about horses in her own life. Now a chapter on training in *Horsemastership* took priority. It told how drawing on logic and finesse was more effective—brawn, evidently, not a factor handling horses. The thought of some weightlifter trying to out-muscle Clover made her eyes roll.

She flipped through the glossy pages of *Veterinary Notes for Horse Owners* to the section on "Equine Infectious Arteritis." The appalling pictures she came across made her shudder. Sections on colic, blindness, founder, bowed tendons, poisoning, fracture—now she was colicky, too. This caramel corn had sprouted worry-pins. What if it had been Clover's arm?

She crumpled the half-empty sack and stowed it in her bottom drawer. She flopped on her back and rocked furry Ellie to heavy metal's dreary beat.

She was grooving vacantly when a peculiar glint caught her eye. The loud, rhythmic pounding was pushing a delicate, sunlit bottle across the top of her dresser.

Ellie tumbled to the floor. It was a curious little bottle, one she had never seen before. The tiny label's lopsided letters read *Morning in the Stable*.

She yanked out the stopper. That instant she jammed it back in. Her head was on fire. "I'll get you for this, Michael Mason!" Still reeling, and shrieking at her little brother, she stormed into his room. He wasn't there. "Michael!?" she yelled, stomping down the stairs. "That wasn't funny!"

Her mother was scowling. "Turn off that horrible racket, you're not even listening to it! I've had just about all I can stand."

"Do you know what that Michael did?"

"Well, as a matter of fact, Bailey Elizabeth, I do know. Michael has a notion his *pee-fume* will cure gloominess. You've got a case of homesickness, kiddo. Both for Parkwood and your horse."

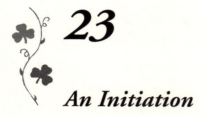

23
An Initiation

HE WAS SLOUCHED AGAINST the door jamb with his thumbs anchored into the belt loops of his jeans, looking even taller than she remembered. She had slept in, and her mother was back already from the barn. Seeing Theo here fluttered some hope for a moment's diversion. Probably he'd brought radishes over, something fresh from his mother's garden. She drew a shaky breath as he stared at her cast.

"Sorry about your arm, Bailey." Her aching heart melted; she had missed him so. His gaze shifted to her mother. "I thought you could use some help in the barn, Mrs. Mason. Like now? I don't have to be anywhere for awhile." He looked at Bailey again.

She had her workboots on in a minute.

Clover was in her favorite spot, head down and grazing. Bailey bounced along on the balls of her feet, flinging her good hand as she filled Theo in on their routine. She introduced him to the kittens, and had begun pointing out things in the barn, when he reached for the apple-picker.

All too quickly, he had the stall tidy and topped with fresh shavings. The little barn smelled like a dewy stand of pines. Bailey looked around for something else to say, or do.

"Um, smells good," she ventured. She really didn't mind the smell of manure, but this was so much nicer. Talking about horses while he did her chores had come easy. Searching for anything else, she fastened on the swallows' nest.

"Five babies up there," indicating the nest. "You'll see, when food appears." As if on cue, a parent swooped in. The iridescent wing-flashes prompted wide open yellow beaks to screech for attention. The kittens broke from their wrestling hold to look up. Bailey crouched to little Heather, the spotted one. Theo picked Hasty Pudding up by the scruff of the neck and settled this one on his shoulder. The orange tabby sat contentedly, and he was rubbing his head into the luxuriant fur when what sounded like a squeaky toy swooped very close.

"Geez," he said, backing up. "What's the story?"

"Little birdie is totally ticked! At the little beastie on your shoulder, I bet."

"Yeah?" He took the kitten up in both hands and held it nose to nose. "Don't let those birds scare you," he whispered. "And don't you bother them. They help control our insect population." His gentle advice was met with a resonant purr. Bailey was close to purring, too. She had forgotten about the ache in her arm. Theo swung his arms up and planted his hands on the door header. Leaning in, he asked, "How much longer, you think? For your wrist." His steely blue eyes seemed to drill through the solid casing.

"Just sitting home healing is a total bore," she answered with an indifferent shrug. No way would he get the idea she was a crybaby. She pointed to her scuffed hard hat, on its peg above her saddle. "There's the culprit," she declared. "It fell off when I hit." His eyes rolled in disbelief. "No chin strap," she heard him mutter.

"How was Maine?"

"Okay, I guess. We had a lot of company and I had to sleep with Andy. What a goof-off."

"Didn't you get to ride?"

"Oh yeah, in a little dressage ring. A waste, with all those trails." He'd lowered his head, and seemed to have found something interesting on the packed dirt floor. "I'd kinda like a chance to work around horses," he said now, questioning her with a look. "At One Oak, nothing starts till I step off the mounting block. In Maine, I'd muck out while Mrs. Chazen got the horse ready. A nice Morgan with a mane even longer than Clover's, which she spends a preposterous amount of time on." He gazed out towards Clover. "Could you, like, show me what else there is to do?"

"Honest?" Her heart swelled. He would be staying longer. And her horse would get some attention, too. "Do you mind brushing?"

The mare had the rubber serving dish clenched in her teeth. Theo stood back a few feet while she made a game of flopping the shallow dish up and down. A few overlooked pieces of grain popped out. Bailey tried not to laugh, willing the dish to drop. At last Theo reached out and, to her amazement, it did. Clover could be so cooperative. His first pass with the halter had it facing backwards. He turned it the other way and reached out again. Clover was moving now, Theo trailing along with the halter dangling under her nose.

"That's a first for me," he said when he had the halter in place.

Obviously. Bailey could barely manage a straight face.

When he'd secured the crossties, she got busy with the curry-comb, explaining how it loosened the dirt and dead skin.

"Let me try it." He circled the rubber prongs over the undulating back gingerly.

"You can press harder, Theo, where there's muscle. Lean in and rub. Don't worry, she'll let you know if you rub too hard or hit anything sensitive." She giggled to herself, then confided that she called those the *tickle spots*. He gave a sharp laugh, then applied the curry-comb industriously. Ridges of scurf rose to the surface. She handed over the tawny, stiff-bristled brush.

"Shorter, harder strokes, Theo. Flick your wrist!" He got the knack by the time that side was done, exclaiming at the amount of brushing required.

"It's good she's not any bigger!"

"Really, by the time I get her cleaned up and saddled, I'm totally pooped!" She offered him the hoof-pick.

"What's this?"

"To clean her feet."

"You have to clean feet?"

"Uh huh. It's gross. They're not so bad when she's turned out a lot, but in the stall they wad up with yuck. Bacteria multiplies, and you get thrush. I was just reading about it all. Thrush is the pits. Horses go lame. So," with a sly grin that plainly had him baffled, "check this out, Theo." Eyes widening, she uttered in a squeaky hush, "You need to open her soles to the air." He stared back at her, then down at the hooves. Her heart fell. He was going to back out. No way, this needed to be a positive experience.

"Really, Theo, it's not so bad when you get the hang of it. Come on, just stand by the shoulder, face the other way, and reach down."

He did as he was told. His hands worked awkwardly, yet both front hooves ended up reasonably clean. He faltered when it came to the hind hooves.

"She could kick!"

"No way! She's used to this."

"Yeah, right! This horse doesn't know me very well."

"Kicking hasn't even entered her mind, honest!"

He folded his arms across his chest.

She pointed to the near hind, on their side. "Look, she's standing on this foot. The other one's up on the toe. If she had kicking in mind, wouldn't this one be cocked?"

A swallow flew in from the north, circled around, and flew out to the south. Theo uncrossed his arms. He pulled in a deep breath, then edged closer to Clover's rear. She shifted her weight when he reached down, and presented her hoof. Bailey held perfectly still, dumbfounded by the shaking hoof-pick.

"That's another first," he said, plainly relieved. "First time that close to a horse's hind end."

"Aaah, would you like to ride her?"

"No joke?" He glanced at his two-toned sport watch. "Affirmative, but I have to leave in half an hour." Their eyes met, and one expressive eyebrow shot up. "Next time I'll get here earlier. So, what else is there to do?"

Next time? It took a moment to think. Clover needed steady work, if all her training wouldn't go to waste.

"Would you like to lunge her?" she asked, as though simply offering a cookie. She'd act nonchalant in case he didn't want to. His startled eyebrows demanded clarification. "She's getting soft, Theo, spending too much time just standing around here." His tentative smile indicated *maybe*. "Check the time, though," and she gave his woven leather wristband an encouraging tap. 10:30 now, and he needed to be home by 11:00. What if Clover went ballistic and needed rubbing down? Still, even twenty minutes would help.

Lungeing was another first. Six precious minutes passed before Bailey had Theo set up. Then Clover moved off in an easy-going walk, with one eye on the upright whip as she widened her circle. Stationed on the sidelines, Bailey hardly dared breathe. "Please be good," she transmitted when Theo called for a trot.

The polished coat shimmered, the mane rippled like silk, as Clover put in seven orderly circles. Then she gave a loud snort and powered into a gallop. Bailey gasped and reached out helplessly. Theo dropped the whip and went to working the taut length of tape with both hands.

"Whooa . . . " Clover pulled against the line while pounding her hooves exuberantly. "Easy, girl, whooooa," Theo kept saying while working his arms in an attempt to haul in. The flat, continuous chant proved effective, and tempered the thrashing stride into a lofty, much steadier lope. Bailey's heart soared. Clover rolled along making rhythmical puffing sounds, acting as though she could go on like this all day.

AT 8:30 THE NEXT morning Theo shoved a rigid poplar branch out of his face and began making his way across the field. Just as he'd hoped, Bailey was already outside. Clover had her head in the tire, and Bailey was perched on the rim, fussing with her shoelaces. He didn't think he was late. The horse would need time to digest her breakfast before any exercise.

She waved, squinting into the sun. She waited, hugging her knees. The PVC boots slapped against his calves, not the greatest things to walk in. She shouted something about a super day, no bugs—not yet, anyway. He paused, nearly there. Leaning back on one leg and flipping his hunt cap from one hand to the other, he glanced from her to the horse. It was up to Bailey to lead the way.

Her good hand smoothed the elaborate pompadour arranged in her hair. She stood up, and his eyes shifted to the appliqué on her teeshirt: gold and silver snaffle bits—like Clover's, but shinier. She'd had jeans and an old sweatshirt on the other day. These tight green shorts and flashy tee were cool—sort of dressy, except for the sneakers. Boots would have been okay, too. She knew bettter than to wear sandals out here.

"Hey, cool shirt, double-jointed snaffles!" It surprised him to see her blush. She seemed unusually self-conscious. Clover swung around and pushed her nose into the seat of his pants. Whatever brought that on? Half-patting the mare's neck, he pushed her away. Could be, it was time to wash these breeches. "Hey, Dakota Clover," he teased, "I bet you detect Barrister."

"I think this horse likes you, Theo. Who's Barrister?"

"Just an obnoxious friend of mine." He might tell her later. Right now he had better things in mind. She had handed him the halter and, this time, he knew what to do.

When he'd finished brushing, she fed him the hoof-pick. When he'd finished grooming, she fed him the towel, and helped straighten it with her one able hand. Mucho particular, he noticed.

"You probably ought to lunge her first, Theo." Geez, he had expected to mount right up.

It was twenty minutes before he put his helmet on.

Clover lurched as he pulled himself up—sure different from stepping off a mounting block. He tried again, and found himself perched on a much narrower back than Barrister's. His sharp knees poked up like some jockey's.

He jumped off and undid a stirrup buckle. With the tips of his fingers pressing it against the catch, he slid the iron as far out as his armpit. Down three notches, he figured. Then he checked the girth and set it up one. Blocking a fleeting notion of risk, he climbed back on.

It went easier this time. His position felt fairly natural, but the horse felt like a coiled spring. Barely a hint of give to the reins had Clover stepping out. He tussled with a few minutes of exuberance before she swung into a flat-footed walk. He sensed Bailey's eyes on him, spokes of encouragement radiating from the hub of the tire. She was sitting on the rim with her hands planted on her legs as if they needed to be held down.

He raised his arm, sitting into the flightiness he'd figured on. Bailey's screwy expression showed she thought he was nuts to wave his arm around. But he'd play it safe, proceed according to Cappy. The little dance incited by his surprising arm flattened out, and he resumed propellering as if it was the most natural thing to do on a horse. He swiveled to the left; he swiveled to the right; he dove ten times touching the toes of each boot—fully aware all the while of the horse's wild eyes and Bailey's look of disbelief. Still, Clover kept on landing all four of her feet flat. He picked up the reins, and the horse picked up a trot, even before he asked.

He hadn't mastered One Oak's steep path yet, and even this gradual incline flopped him over the horse's arched crest. It made a problem, without leverage, of reining in, until a familiar voice in his head urged him to arch his back and jam weight into his heels.

It worked. He surged with elation.

He was treating the field like one huge arena, finding navigating the natural terrain wickedly cool, when Clover suddenly dropped her shoulder and shied. Theo handled it well and tacked away from that line of bushes. They took the long grade back up in a working trot. Fastening his eyes on Bailey, he reined in.

"Do you like her, Theo?"

"Aaah," out of breath. Convincing the horse to walk again was a challenge. "Affirmative. She sure is willing!"

"Are you going to canter now?"

He thought a few moments. He didn't want to louse up her horse, or the good impression he might be making. What would she think if he begged off? Clover's trot was fantastic, but didn't guarantee an easy canter. Spirit Lake had an easy canter, and a trot that bounced you all over the place. Barrister's trot was comfortable, the canter horrible. It'd be nice to know in advance. The brisk walk told him Clover was primed.

A hesitant cue launched them into a stiff-backed trot. He was planning on a short one, just here by the tire. Hastily he cued again, and got a faster trot. Any attempt to check back only made the mare point her head higher and refuse to turn. He dug in his seat, despite the hectic trot, and pulled one rein harder.

Whew, a lift.

Their fast pace barreling down the field occupied only a corner of his mind. He couldn't believe the effort it took to stay with a galloping horse. Crouched over the churning with his leather-patched knees firmly clenched, he pumped his arms like piston rods. No way could he crap out. If Bailey could do it, he could, too.

She was on her feet when they came over the rise, the glossy hairdo radiating sunshine. The long grade back up hadn't made a dent in this definitely-no-school-horse's pace. He locked his eyes on the tire, determined to circle that tire or die trying.

"That was so great, Theo!" Five lively circles later, the horse had been cajoled into a fairly decent walk. Bailey sent an affectionate smack to the hot glazed neck, then stood back for him to release the sweaty girth. Now she moved in, slapped the girth over the saddle and hoisted the whole kit—girth, saddle, pad, and towel. She shut her eyes and, hugging the steaming heap close, breathed in deeply.

24

A Visit from the Farrier

ELMER KLACHNER BACKED DOWN from the high seat of his truck, then took a minute to steady himself before moving toward the gate. The wizened old guy looked much too frail for hoof work. His dark, sunken eyes darted in and out of the little barn's corners, then rested on Dakota Clover, standing like a queen about to address her subjects.

"Inside of that near fore's broke off good," Klachner said with a sour look. Meaning "bad," Bailey realized. At least the guy could see from under that furrowed brow. "She's toein' in," Klachner observed. "Shoes?"

Bailey raised a dubious eyebrow to Theo.

"You call it, sir. We kinda just ride in the pasture here."

"We want her hooves trimmed, I guess, like they were. Will that be okay?"

"Humpfh. Might be." The tool-caddy clunked down next to Clover's left fore. She remained still, a curve of slack in her crossties. The damaged hoof got turned bottom-up and propped against the farrier's stained leather apron. As if by magic a hooked drawing knife appeared in his hand. Bailey winced as putrid portions of the sole dropped to the packed-dirt floor, smelling worse than a nail parlor. Without looking, Klachner dropped his drawing knife back into its holster. Clover had tolerated having the sole of her hoof carved, but she flinched when the weighty caddy scraped to a new place. All while gigantic, treacherous pincers manicured the hoof, she sniffed the lean back bent directly under her nose. The crescent-shaped parings flipped as they fell. Bailey's fists were clenched. Clover was holding herself erect, straight enough to drop a plumb line from the point of her shoulder to the center of the supporting off-fore. But any minute she might bite the apron ties or jerk her foot away. Her big eyes followed Duker, busily poking his nose into the mounting, smelly pile of scraps.

Theo and Bailey jumped, and the spaniel scooted, when the cumbersome pincers clanged back into Klachner's store of tools. Charged looks of pride were exchanged—all that noise and the horse had not moved! Theo winked, the corner of his mouth going crooked, just as Elmer Klachner unbent—awkwardly, with a deep groan. Bailey covered her mouth. How awful if this old guy suspected she was laughing at him.

The farrier's kick skidded the caddy to Clover's near-hind. Theo guardedly swept the rank litter of scraps out from under her nose. Her hide rippled visibly: despite having been drenched with repellent, there were two flies parked on her back.

"Flies get mean when rain's in the air," remarked Klachner from the horse's rear. Bailey turned her rope into a pest-deflecting pendulum. Her hair was frizzy with perspiration, the waistband of her jeans wet and clingy. She doubted the horse could take much more of this.

"Quit it!" The hoof dropped. "Get that tail out of my face!"

Theo gathered the meager skein of strands off to the side. Tails stung, but Bailey hated seeing the horse defenseless. She kept her pendulum moving. This little barn had never been so busy. Or smelly. Klachner had finished trimming the near-hind and was contorted into an awkward crouch under the massive belly. He had it braced against his thigh, and looked like a little gnome under there, buzzing away with his rasp.

Bailey swung the rope and Theo guarded the tail as Clover's off-side got methodically trimmed.

"Done!" The farrier grunted to a stooped stand. "Good mare."

"Really?" Bailey and Theo replied as one. The film of tension peeled away from Bailey's shoulders.

"Tough hooves. Round feet. Shoun't be no trouble." While painstakingly rejuggling his tools, Klachner mentioned an insecticide he liked. "Just spray it where the wee buggers light," he said affably. His smile had a missing front tooth. "Like over the stink-basket. You ain't got 'em like the big barns, but these wee buggers breed."

Bailey accompanied him to the truck and handed over the check. She raced back through the first splats of rain. On top of old hoof smells, the barn had a sharp smell of ammonia. Theo had begun scraping up the wet spot. What a stinky day, she couldn't wait to get back to normal. She drew shallow breaths with one hand over her nose while the spade clinked away. "You sure know how to handle a shovel, Theo," she said through her fingers. She would, too, he claimed, if her mother was as nutty about gardening as his was.

The hoof-scraps went out with the morning's normal amount of sour soddenness, to get even more soaked in the rain.

"You sure were smart to bring in clean dirt before all this rain, Theo."

"*Clean* dirt?" He stopped tamping his refilled hollow to throw her a silly look. Then he swung a forty-pound shavings bag over his head so effortlessly it might have been empty. One lusty kick produced a gusher of golden confetti. Rain pattered against the roof, and a faint muskiness hung in the air.

"Everything fit for a queen," trilled Bailey. He'd even banked the bedding a ways up the walls.

"Yeah, nothing too good for Her Royal Highness."

She edged her boot into the curly slips of pine, contemplating. She could've at least made him cookies.

"TELL HER TO BEHAVE, dang it all. You know how to talk to this witch." Clover had resisted the bridle as if she knew something was up. Chairs dragged from the patio had been stationed close to the fence. Mrs. North's visits to One Oak had interested her in equitation, and she had come over to see how her number-one son would manage a young mare.

"Don't worry about *my* mother, Theo. She thinks Clover walks on water, even wants to paint her."

They emerged from the barn with Theo leading and Bailey on the off side. How cool, she suddenly thought, if Mom painted this scene. Especially if she left out the dorky cast. She perched on the fence after Theo mounted up. A second row of boards nailed to the posts had made it quite sturdy. Mrs. North was wearing shorts, and seemed to have lost a few pounds. Wiry strands stuck out of the fat rubber band anchoring her hair. Bailey preferred *her* mother's neat, boyish trim—the natural look. She'd opted for it, too, and let her mother's stylist chop off her curls, at least for the summer. She smiled to herself, thinking of the chestnut ringlet secured in Theo's wallet.

Now he wants roughout chaps, Mrs. North was saying. "Leather on leather, you know, for a better grip. They'd be good for working around your barn, certainly more comfortable than those breeches and heavy boots." Bailey exchanged a knowing look with her mother. With horses, it was just one thing after another.

"I wish I had chaps," she blurted. "They might help me deal with Clover's shenanigans. Like that," she added, pointing. The horse was traveling sideways along the line of honeysuckle.

Mrs. North chuckled. "Theo seems to have things well in hand. You taking Dakota Clover to Playday?"

"Playday? A show?"

"Oh, no. Fun and games. The Joyners, right up our lane here, are hosting this year. Their daughter shows a hunter, but the family is quite active in Greenham's Pony Club."

That didn't sound so snotty. Really, you couldn't stereotype easterners. Theo was looking her way. Clover was swishing around as though a burr got stuck under her saddle.

"She's all bugged-up," he called out, making for the tire.

"When that horse gets tense," Bailey offered, "you can't make her do anything. She totally ignores you." The idea of playing games on anything so hyperactive was totally insane.

"That field does get buggy," Beth Mason observed. "But Theo handles her nicely."

Bailey half-groaned an assent. Her own legs should be hugging the horse. "He's so good with Clover," she said wistfully. "I wish I could ride like that." They were circling back now, Clover settled in a docile lope. "Maybe I should watch a lesson."

Mrs. North startled. She squinted up, saying, "Well, maybe you could, sweetie. Why don't you ask Theo? It's certainly all right with me."

A triumphant look to her mother, and Bailey flew off her perch.

Clover was moving out now. Theo had his reins shorter and was testing her reaction to having his weight forward, over her center of gravity. But whenever his weight shifted over the withers, she'd lean on her forehand and want to go faster. Bailey crept into the tire's protective hub and waited, poised as a cat intent on a mouse. Theo wrestled with his position, and she wrestled with her question.

It took him over ten minutes of patient, repetitive work. At last Clover bore his change of position without changing her pace. She loaded her haunches, rounded her back, and cantered beautifully with him up in the half-seat. Bailey rode every stride in her mind. So fine to have their mothers get a good show. But a little worm of envy had wriggled into her pride. Before the summer was over, she resolved, she would be as good a rider as Theo. Maybe better.

She drew a deep breath as Clover settled into a walk. The question was on the tip of her tongue when her little brother came scrambling through the fence.

"Can I ride?" Michael called out.

Her mother jumped up. "Do you mind, Theo?"

She choked back from asking. Only fair to give Mikey a turn. The kid had never even sat on the horse.

Both hunt caps hung over Michael's brow, but Theo's fit well enough with the safety harness tightened. He hitched up the stirrups and boosted the eager boy aboard. Bailey retreated to the tire, her hopes temporarily on hold. The kittens came running and jumped in after her. With their plump softness snuggled into her lap, she watched Clover move along as if carrying a feather. The horse's ears had never appeared so expressive. One, sometimes both, pointed at Theo. The ear on her side would swivel her way. The kittens soon adopted the well of the tire for their boxing ring, and sent up fierce growls that commandeered both ears. Clearly Clover was paying attention. Michael, too, following Theo's instructions for how to give and take with the reins. Bailey listened closely. If she'd understood this concept of *continuous contact*, she might not have fallen off. She needed the horse's attention on her, not on some scary bushes. It struck her how much she had missed. Other than tips from Mrs. Knott and Daddy, she'd been left to figure things out for herself. She slumped against the tire. What a yutz, she didn't even know about following the head motion with your hands.

25

A Visit to One Oak

MRS. NORTH TOOK A shortcut through a residential section, turned up a narrow dirt road, then shifted into low for the steep grade. The springs groaned as the van swerved from the crest of one rut to another. One last bump at the top, and a rambling red barn came into view. Bailey was flying as high as the horse on the cupola when she followed Theo through the tall wide door.

"I'll give you a tour later," he told her before heading off down a dimly lit passageway. She stationed herself at the mounting block and gazed around. A horse partway down the aisle remained quiet on its crossties while refuse from its stall got forked into a wheelbarrow. She heard faint music, distant voices, scraping, a thump. The smell sure was familiar. A stern-faced man in breeches and tall boots slammed out of a door labeled, *Office*. Resounding clip-clops pulled her gaze back to the murky aisle. The man, surely Mr. Sebastian, gruffly warned her to stand back.

A perky Asian girl leading a palomino paused at the mounting block to skip up three stairs and climb into the saddle. More horses were led up, and paused at the platform. Bailey's eyes lit up when Theo returned leading a tall, dark chestnut. *Tall, dark, and handsome*, she thought. And then, what her mother would say, *Handsome is as handsome does*. Right. Theo looked so serious, she wondered if there were problems.

She found a grassy spot on the bank with a good view of the riding ring. Three rails lay parallel to each other in the center. And here came Cappy Kaufmann, striding into the ring with her ponytail swinging from her cap.

"You'll be training your horse today, people, as well as yourself," Cappy called out. She surveyed her group, tapping the toe of her dusty boot against a ground rail. "Trotting through cavalletti is a teaching exercise—requires the horse to gauge distances and pay attention to where he puts his feet." Bailey was all eyes and ears. There hadn't been anything like this at the horse show.

"Sound simple?" Cappy asked impishly. "Come in straight, allow time for calculation, and it will be, if your horse steps smack between these poles. I don't want to hear one tick."

Or two or three, Bailey added under her breath. She craned forward as a chunky little black picked up a trot.

"Don't fuss," Cappy boomed, as the horse headed for the grid. "Joshua, let *him* do it!"

The black planted each of its black hooves precisely, prancing straight through. Bailey "oohed" in admiration. Then she tensed. Theo's turn was up.

The gorgeous chestnut proved to be tall, dark, and gruesome—turning off to leave its shadow darkening a rail.

"Get with that rebel! Be definite. Show Escort what you want!" Bailey chuckled in spite of herself, at the "Blah's" on Cappy's cap. You'd need one healthy ego to wear something like that. The sand flew when the next horse went through, a beefy brown knocking a rail askew. Cappy kicked it straight. The line moved around. Cappy set down another rail. Bailey studied the horses. The palomino managed all four nicely. The big bay lumbered through. The little black lifted its knees high. Theo was moving up.

"Don't hesitate to employ a strong leg," Cappy yelled in Theo's direction. "Escort tends to lean on his front and get all strung out!" The horse overshot the turn again—what a bummer for Theo. Bailey sat very still as they came around again. That horse had a mind of its own; a tough mouth, too. Theo's face was red and he looked furious.

A sharp turn on the approach this time gave Escort a chance to veer inside. No way was the brute stepping in that bear trap. Theo delivered a swift kick, and Bailey cheered under her breath. One Oak's equitation had opened up a whole new world. There was so much to think about, it took her awhile to notice there were acorns under her, pinching.

"Hold him when you leg, Theo!" He was coming around again. "Balance Escort back, make him use himself! Theo, trace the arc with your eyes!"

Bailey sat tight, rooting for success. Reins taut, legs fixed, Theo seemed to be zeroing in. "Now bring him in square," Cappy encouraged. "Then raise your eyes to a point straight ahead." He seemed focused, until he looked down, and the handsome liver-chestnut clicked a rail while turning off. A snort of disappointment escaped Bailey's throat. But Theo wasn't the only one having trouble. There were a number of clicks when the clunky brown shuffled through. That horse couldn't, or wouldn't, pick his feet up. Bailey shifted positions on her lumpy mound. She was wide awake, even though she'd gotten up at 6:00 a.m. to shave her legs and wash her hair. She had her new tee on, blades of grass hand-screened across its front in luscious shades of green. This one had cost twice as much as her other tees. Fingering the soft fabric, her mother had admired the bold brush strokes, and caved. "Better watch out, Bee," she'd quipped, "Clover might want a bite."

Bailey snickered. Clover might snuffle and dribble, but she would never bite.

Most of the horses had caught on to the concept of cavalletti and the grid had been extended. Five solid thumps sounded between the six rails, as the chunky little black popped through like a pro. Here came Theo again. Cappy, from a few feet off, urged him to insist with his legs. "Don't look down going across. Escort needs to think where to put his feet by himself!"

The approach looked good; they both seemed focused.

Yes! At last, they had their act together. Theo shot Bailey a thumbs-up as he came around. Hugging her knees, she imagined herself braving cavalletti. With Theo along, on a handsome brown that behaved. They'd find some trail with a series of little trees lying across it.

"Bailey Mason?"

She tilted her head toward the lilting voice. Small button nose, streaked big-hair. A creamy polo shirt and curvy riding breeches. She had seen this person before. Yes, at the horse show, with Theo and his parents. It had to be Dr. North's nurse, Sheri Dembinski.

"I bet you came with the Norths." A crisp floral fragrance wafted up as Sheri lowered herself to the jacket she'd spread on the ground. "Isn't Theo doing good? He's learning so fast, he'll be jumping before you know it."

"Really?!"

The class had taken the rail, and was cantering now. Again and again, Cappy directed each of her pupils to start on the correct lead.

"What's that mean, Sheri, 'right lead'?"

"Oh, don't worry about leads. They're only important if you're into showing. It's just in the canter," Sheri went on, "where one front leg reaches farther out. It helps balance on the turns if it's the inside leg leading." Bailey tried to see which leg was which as the horses went around. "Now look at Hickory Nut, Bailey, that cute little black? Can you tell if he's on the right lead, I mean, the correct one?"

Hickory Nut loped counter-clockwise. Bailey stared hard at the black legs silhouetted against the sand. It took a few moments to see that the left front hit farther out than the right.

"Yes, correct. Isn't it? But how can you tell when you're riding?"

"Just glance down. And try not to be conspicuous about it. I'm learning to tell by feel. Do you ride, Bailey?"

She lit up, and launched into her tale about buying Clover and learning to ride, "Not all that well, yet." She went on about her broken arm, blaming it on her stupid hard hat. Confiding in someone who knew horses came easy.

"The new ones have straps, Bailey, and hi-tech padding. One Oak insists on regulation helmets."

"Oh." Sunlight filtering through the branches flickered camouflage patterns across the grassy bank. Sheri fiddled with a handful of acorns. Bailey twiddled with a spear of grass. The class was practicing figure-eights now, attempting to change leads right at the cross.

"Theo's lucky to ride so many different horses," Sheri remarked. "That sinks in the fundamentals, one reason he's learning so fast. Every horse teaches you something."

"I guess."

"Mr. Sebastian has a new horse in, that Cappy wants me to try. I got the morning off to have the arena all to myself." Sounding awed, Sheri added, "They found me a Warmblood."

"Oh. What's that?" Theo had Escort cantering, and seemed to be doing alright. Bailey nibbled on the sugary tip of her grass.

"The cream of the crop, you might say. Warmbloods are sport horses with European blood lines. They're out of cold-blooded draft mares crossed with hot-bloods, like Arabians or Thoroughbreds." Sheri gave a little laugh. "Hot and cold equals warm, right? Countries like Germany, Sweden, Belgium, and the Netherlands have bred Warmbloods for centuries, to serve in their cavalries. These days, though, they're mostly used for competition—cross-country, jumping, dressage. The big-time gorgeous one I'm meeting today is trained for all three. I might take up three-day eventing."

Bailey plucked a tender spear and poked it between her teeth. If all it took was a cold-blooded dam and a hot-blooded sire, then Clover would be a Warmblood. The horse could jump. Look how she'd sailed over that huge branch.

"HE'LL FLEX LOTS BETTER than that!" Hands on her hips, Cappy paced little circles in the center of a pool of light, while a majestic mocha-brown horse trotted around her. The cushy footing muffled the hoof beats. Birds twittered in the rafters. Deep in concentration, Bailey's grip on the old wooden bench she was sitting on tightened.

"That's a new horse Cappy's been working with," Theo whispered.

"A Warmblood, right?" Bailey whispered back. "Sheri might buy that horse." His startled look made her giggle—still pleasantly rattled from their hand-holding trip up the dimly lit staircase. Joshua Shapiro had come up to the balcony, too, and was sitting on the other side of Theo. Without his hunt cap, Joshua's hair had erupted into a mass of kinky wire. Theo's hair was plastered flat, and her fingers itched to fix it. She took a sip of the orange soda he'd bought for her. Despite the railing's collection of dust, she leaned her arms against it and peered into the shadows. The horse's bobbing rump mirrored light like a blinking semaphore. As it cruised under her nose, Bailey took in the long frame and floating stride. Tall Sheri looked like a little kid on this horse.

"Nice and fluid," broke the silence. "Demand more impulsion, Sher. Squeeze and release your inside hand and drive him with your legs. Try a little see-sawing on the bit." Cappy hugged herself while revolving with her prize in sight. "Good, now," she chirped. "He's chewing on the bit, accepting your hand. Feel that power through the back?" Cappy performed a little pirouette. "Ask for a halt now—clean, right from the trot. Brace your back and push him into your hand." Delicious shivers traveled up Bailey's spine. Straightaway, the horse stopped square. Bailey could almost feel it.

"And, baa-ack."

Sheri held her position and tapped her legs, and the horse stepped back and went right on backing until she let up on the reins. Then the horse stepped forward, and Bailey relaxed.

"Big time responsive," exclaimed Sheri. "So willing!"

"Oh, I knew you'd like Tannenbaum." Cappy was practically singing. She yanked off her smart-aleck cap and stuck her fingers into her spiky hair. Sheri cued and the horse rose into a trot. "You look great on him, Sher," cried Cappy. "Whadda you kids think?" she called up to the balcony.

The birds were quiet; the hooves' gliding swish enhanced the silence. Then, "An elegant combination," Joshua replied. "Really springy!" Theo volunteered. "Awesome," Bailey added. Tannenbaum was cantering now, rolling along with the efficiency of well-oiled machinery.

"He's to die for," Sheri cried. "So light on his feet!" The Warmblood cantered a circle at one end of the arena, collected, then straight across the long diagonal, extended.

"I think we've found one," sang Cappy. "What's your schedule this morning?" She gestured toward the corner, where a squad of white jump-standards stood at attention. "Is there time for a wee bit of jumping?"

"Oh, I hope so, I don't want to get off!"

Theo and Joshua hopped off the bench. Tannenbaum's head shot up as their boots clattered down the old staircase.

"Sit chilly," Cappy cautioned the grinning Sheri. Bailey grinned, too, imagining Clover's reaction. A few flighty steps wouldn't be unjustified with all that noise. But Tannenbaum held tough; still again as Cappy manhandled an unwieldy standard out of the corner. The horse towered over the crew, the wide-set eyes taking in the scene. Cappy's short legs goose-stepped off the distances, and the boys arranged the jumps accordingly. She had turned on all the lights, and the mirror glittered with hustling figures.

Bailey drummed her fingers on her knee. Cappy sure was finicky. Get this show on the road . . . and Theo back up next to me.

He came tramping up at last, clawing open a sack of pretzels. Venting a happy groan, he stuffed a handful into his mouth, and then held the wiggly sack out to Bailey.

"No, thanks." Her eyelashes flashed. She was too keyed up to eat. The cellophane crinkled as he leaned closer to pass the sack over to Joshua. His hand brushed her back just as Tannenbaum sprung into a canter. She held perfectly still, not sure if it was the horse or Theo making her spine tingle.

Sheri rode a circle and then enlarged the arc to approach a large set of crossrails. Smoothly, she was lifted up, and over. Soaring herself, Bailey impulsively squeezed Theo's arm. His hand found hers as the horse steadied and then cantered smartly on to the next jump and sailed even higher.

26

A Music Lesson

THE BUCKETS WERE OUTSIDE and the cats' sleeping hollow in the hay covered with an empty shavings bag. Wielding the broom had been awkward but, by bracing the stick-end in her armpit, Bailey had demolished the worst of the cobwebs.

"Ye witch's brew, cast thy hex on the archenemies of the universe!" She passed her arms over the lethal potion. "Death to evil flies. Be gone!"

Theo sniffed, then made a face. "This'll get 'em," he said, and poured carefully into the old garden sprayer his mother had volunteered. Plainly familiar with the canister, he clamped it between his feet and began pumping up pressure. When he aimed the slim wand arm's length, Bailey squinted her eyes against the pungent plume of mist.

"Watch out for the nest, Theo, in case our birds come back." She clamped her mouth against the fumes. Just yesterday, the fledglings had tried their wings. She had watched in dread when a brave one flung itself into the air and then plunged into a breathtaking loop. It'd sat in that nest all its life and the wings couldn't be strong yet. There was a desperate amount of flapping before the beginner made it back up.

She moved outside and peeked back through the door. Theo's wide bony shoulders tapered to hips so narrow, it was a wonder his pants stayed up.

She waited, patience draining, while the heavy mist wet down each beam. Imagine spraying like this at One Oak, it would take all summer. Lessons there sure had paid off for Theo. Now if only *she* rode better. Maybe he could give her some pointers . . . She'd ask. She needed a plan for when the stupid cast came off.

Theo let out a groan and shut the sprayer down. "Geez, this is hard on your arms!"

"Hey, take a break. It doesn't all have to get done in one day. 'Inch by inch is just a cinch, and yard by yard is very hard,' my mother always says. With horses, a legit philosophy." He sniggered at her simple rhyme and then went back to polluting the air. The sprayer hissed until every beam shone and the barn smelled like a chemistry lab.

"Hey, they're still alive." He began slinging his hands back-and-forth and flapping his fingers like rubber gloves. "What we don't do for this horse! I sacrificed a day of sailing to be a janitor here."

"Sailing! You could have gone sailing today?" She had been to the beach a few times with Glenna, just to swim and lie in the sun. Sailing would be so cool.

"Yeah, Josh needed a crew. He gave up on me when I told him I was coming over here." With a teasing smile, he added, "Her Royal Highness deserves the very best, of course." The implications of his choice spun in her head. She was about to mention riding lessons for *her*, but he started pumping again. Conversation would be drowned out. Anyway, their mouths needed to be shut against the fumes. After the beams, then the walls. She looked around for something to keep her from feeling useless. The birds chittered in the trees, calling anxiously to the ones on the ground. I'll groom, she decided. The cast was so much a part of her now, she'd completely forget it was there. Clover had her head in the tire, munching contentedly, even though the birds were unusually noisy. Bailey curried, brushed, picked out all four feet, and had the horse ready when Theo was ready.

"Good work," he said, with a punch to her cast-arm's big bicep. "Let's get that saddle on. After all, riding is what it's all about."

He rode off, and she watched the flying lessons. If only she would catch on to riding as fast as these birds learned to fly. Clover was circling tree trunks in evenly spaced patterns—repetition important in training, Bailey knew. Once she was riding again, they'd practice every day for hours. Idly, she hummed a tune, and in a little while had come up with a bright idea.

They were crossing the field in an energetic trot when she punched *play*. The volume was up, but she heard it when Theo shouted, and looked up to find her horse locked in a fierce stance.

"Turn it off!"

She did.

"Whaddaya think you're doing!"

"Just playing music, Theo!" After all the trouble she'd gone to digging out this old tape player and finding new batteries—

"Well, geez, you don't have to scare her!"

"I didn't mean to scare her," she shot back. "Do you think I'm brainless?"

"Yeah, right. You coulda warned me. Think about it!" The space dividing them was charged. He was as mad at her as he'd been yesterday at Escort.

"Well, I'm sorrrry. Com'ere, you gooney mare, nothing to fear."

The horse did not move.

"Her Royal Highness objects," Theo called back, sounding defensive. "She's had a sheltered life, you know. She's not used to alien noises. You've got to start at square one introducing stuff to a horse. 'Inch by inch,' don't forget."

Chastened, Bailey retreated to the other side of the fence, fifty feet away. Theo took the long way around the shed and, by the time they were back in the safety zone, Clover was landing all four feet flat, plainly relieved to be rid of alien noises. Funny, the birds' noise hadn't bothered her at all. She swung along sharply, alert for a cue. But this might do for now. Theo must be wrung out from spraying, and then this not-so-brilliant idea. She was about to call it quits when he surprisingly gave her a nod.

She turned the player on low.

"A slower one, you she-devil!" The raucous Elton John song had the horse rigid. Her face red with chagrin, Bailey fast-forwarded to catch a slower beat. Clover stretched her neck toward the discernible hum, and edged closer. But when the mournful tones of "Blue Eyes" wafted up, she fled to the far side of her tire.

Bailey set the noise-maker on top of a post and crouched down behind it. The horse wouldn't connect *her* with anything scary. Music again, volume even lower. She could tell when it registered by Theo's look of exasperation. Still, he had Clover in hand: his earnest, patient cajoling succeeded in widening the circles. Bailey could only watch. She might not have handled those jitters as well as Theo, but she longed for the chance to try. The music played softly. Clover walked and trotted, and came as close as five feet from the post before she hunched up and threatened to bolt.

"Enough!" Bailey stood up and stabbed the stop button. Even her own attention span was shot.

"YOU MUST BE TOTALLY tan, Glen!" She was trying to sound envious. Traveling might appeal to the Munros, but *she* was perfectly content to stay home. Even the prospect of a visit to Illinois didn't excite her. "When can you come, Glen? Get out here as much as you can this week, 'cuz next week we're going to Chicago. My grandmother's not very well."

"Oh, no! Who's taking care of Clover?"

"Well, maybe Theo. Neat, huh? He's totally into her routine, now. I'm not exactly jealous, but Clover is the main attraction here."

"Yeah, right. He's human, isn't he? Did he kiss you yet?"

"Huh?!" she laughed. "Don't I wish, you dork."

She wanted to see Gammie, but it hurt to think of not having Clover to hug and hang out with, even for only eight days. Lately, in the evenings her father joined her in the barn. He would fluff up the bedding while she topped off the buckets—a simple chore now with the hose he had run down from the patio faucet. One starry night, he paused on their way back to the house, and laid his hand on her shoulder.

"I was just standing by her door," he said in the tone of amazement he often took when speaking of their horse. "She came and put her head right next to mine, Bee. She let me clean her eyes. Then she goes nodding up and down to show her appreciation."

"I know, Daddy, she is so fine." Bailey twirled with her arms to the sky. "And you're the greatest, doing all this work while I'm out of commission."

"It's kind of a privilege, for *this* horse." A whoosh as he swung the screen door. "You kids pick up branches, and I'll take my mower out there. Should make riding easier. Not so buggy, either, with the weeds down. It'll sure look better."

"Wonderful!" She threw her arms around him. "I know what you mean about it being a privilege. As if she's a queen."

He headed to the washbowl. "Yep, best horse ever seen, bar none!"

"Really! To Theo, she's 'Her Royal Highness.'"

"He's not so dumb. We're lucky to have someone like him to look after things while we're gone, and I'm not just whistling Dixie."

"He'll do a good job, too. He's really getting into animals. Isn't Theo sweet, Daddy?"

Water dripped from her father's hands. His eyes swept from her head to her feet, back up and again. "Has your mother talked to you? About . . . you know . . ."

"Oh, Daddy, honestly! I'm not a baby." She and her mother discussed sex even before she got her first period. And the gross movies in health class showed more than she thought she'd ever want to see.

"Huh, however that may be, young lady," reaching for the towel, "our neighbor boy hangs around here a lot. You kids out there in that shed, alone . . ."

"Really Daddy, honestly—"

"Just don't get carried away, kiddo," his face buried in nappy cotton. "It's a good thing we're leaving," she heard faintly. "It's high time you kids took a break."

Stunned, she swung her cast up in a mock threat. "One break is quite enough, dear Father!"

But she couldn't complain. If it hadn't been for the broken arm, where would she be with Theo? If riding her horse hadn't brought his mom over, the trip to One Oak might never have happened. And then she wouldn't have realized how little she knew about riding horses. One thing nagged. What little she did know could have faded away by the time she was back in the saddle. Good the cast was coming off as soon as they got back from Illinois.

THEO HAD CLOVER TRAVELING with her neck arched, back rounded, and haunches engaged—channeling power through to the bit as she raised from a slow, collected trot to a slow, collected canter. These weeks of ground work had her mind tuned; the clipped grass, her gaits even smoother. Bailey's father had brought in his high-tech mower and turned some 200 x 300 feet of stubble and weeds into a silvery-green park. The straight lines and tight corners gave Theo an advantage, applying his aids. And now ground rails would be visible. Six spindly old fence posts lay decaying in the woods behind his house, a readymade set of cavalletti.

Bailey and Glenna helped lug over the rails. He put Clover through a short warm-up, then brought his upper body forward. Cappy deemed half-seat safest for cavalletti, in case something went wrong. And it did, when he faced the horse with three rails. They'd been set properly, four feet apart, the length of a trotting stride, but the horse had no idea whatever for.

Glenna dragged one rail off by itself. Two made no more difference to the horse than toothpicks, so back to three. Clover didn't stop this time but broke into a canter, and her hit-and-miss attempt sent the rails clattering.

The girls dragged everything back into place. Clover hadn't chickened out, but a rigid back indicated misgivings. Theo trotted back and forth near the grid to allow her time to puzzle things out. She'd acted crazy with the music at first, too. He should have introduced the cavalletti one at a time.

He sat deep, pushed into the bit with his hips, and got an immediate transition to halt. Alert, attentive—she was primed. They'd made progress with the music, hadn't they, and that had been weirder than this. Her keen ears twitched as he steered out of a broad swoop.

Each foot planted with confidence, the horse popped straight through. *Magnifico!*

Then four rails, without one tick. The girls whooped, and went for another. Even with the cast, Bailey handled the unwieldy posts as well as Glenna. Faced with a set of six, the horse checked a moment, then took herself through with enthusiasm. He wasn't the only one enjoying himself.

"Let's try some music," Bailey cried.

He winced. The lesson had gone well; now she wanted more? They needed to end on a good note. He had meant to breeze and then leave Clover to rest on her laurels.

They were cruising in the lower pasture when the horse suddenly sped up. Theo's ears caught fire. Bailey was insane. What was she thinking? The bright melody accompanied their audacious trot back up the slope. Hocks sprung to the beat as the volume increased. Clover was tuned both into the music and him. The six rails awaited, perfectly arranged. He began legging toward them diagonally. Kinda reckless, crossed his mind, but it felt right. He fixed his eyes to a point straight ahead, and Clover paraded through like a drum-majorette.

"*Excelente*," he shouted, flashing a thumbs-up.

"Just as good as Tannenbaum," Bailey shot back.

But when he undid the girth, his bubbles of joy burst. A raw spot the size of a fifty-cent piece glared from the soft skin behind Clover's elbow. A muttered curse alerted the girls. Glenna peered over Bailey's shoulder. The abrasion glistened red.

"My gawd," Glenna cried, "a girth gall. You didn't tighten it!? There should only be enough room to slide your finger in, you know."

The bitch. He knew that. He couldn't believe he hadn't checked.

Bailey touched it with her finger, which came away bloody. Theo slapped his forehead. *He* had caused this.

"Let's take her out and wash her down," suggested Bailey. "That'll be soothing."

Amazingly levelheaded of her. He wanted to sink into a hole.

Glenna lingered with a scowl on her face. "That near fore is really noticeable when she comes through cavalletti."

"She'll be okay, Theo," Bailey said softly.

He stalled with the steaming trappings draped over his arm. "She worked harder today than she ever has," he said mournfully.

"So," Glenna said, "anyone knows hard work consumes fluids."

"That makes sense," Bailey chirped, as if the raw spot wasn't anything to worry about. "You get thinner when you perspire. Don't feel guilty, Theo. I should have noticed the girth was hanging."

He picked over the stall again and added another layer of shavings and swept the floor while the girls bathed the horse, mentally kicking himself all the while—the girth was the rider's responsibility. How could he have forgotten? Awesome, how well Bailey took it. He shrunk into himself, embarrassed by how she had come to the rescue of his wounded ego. He wiped down Clover's bridle and rubbed the old nickel bit till it shone. He put in an inordinate amount of time rubbing layers of grime off the stirrups. But it'd never be enough to make up for his carelessness. He thought of Spirit

Lake. No chance of getting that horse again. One Oak's best school horse had stepped in broken glass and been carried home in a trailer. Spirit Lake was a BMW compared to that blunderbuss Barrister. And Dakota Clover was a Porsche. He sighed heavily. Quality was no guarantee—even the top models went in for repair.

How long would they have to wait to tack up again? No way could Clover be ridden now. He rubbed hard at the girth, obliterating the congealed dirt. It'd be ages before it got buckled back on. His chest ached as he slid the supple length of folded leather through the neatly hiked stirrups and arranged it to lie flat across the saddle, just so.

27

Bareback

CLOVER'S BRISK, CLICK-CLOCKS nicked the air, and chipped away at the heavy plank in Theo's chest. It had been four days now, and he'd kept a close watch. The girth gall didn't seem to bother Clover, but it haunted him—not so much for the hold it put on riding, as for the burden of being at fault. Already it had shrunk to the size of a nickel, and Bailey had proposed lungeing. He hadn't watched the horse in motion for weeks. The trot was smooth, the hinds tracking even farther ahead than the fronts. *Muy elegante*, like floating.

Of course, watching didn't beat riding. Those shiny stirrups beckoned.

He was reaching for the lunge-line again the next day when Glenna's hand intruded.

"Why dontcha get on bareback?" She'd made it sound like a dare. Glenna was such a pain, even if she was Bailey's friend. Bailey lifted a cagey eyebrow and grinned. He sure didn't want any more trouble. His old jeans and sneakers would have him sliding all over the place.

"Okay, affirmative. But you better not laugh if I get dumped." Why not? Indians rode bareback on broader-backed horses than this one.

He slipped up from the tire-rim. The sheer warmth against his body gave him a sense of oneness with the horse, like they'd morphed into a centaur. His slightest move provoked an eager response, which he would have appreciated if not for the prominent withers. Urgent hip re-angling improved that issue. Relax, he reminded himself, and Clover swung into an easy walk. The effort to soften his legs found a groove behind the horse's elbows offering them a snug fit. Balanced now, he ventured farther out.

"What the heck?" His six rails, along with two brooms and four trimmed saplings were neatly arranged into an elaborate pattern of switchbacks.

"Ride her through," Bailey cried. "You'll be impressed. Glen already had her in there. It took some cajoling, but she caught on and followed right along." The girls had gone to a lot of work: these hairpin curves were a darn sight more complicated than cavalletti. He hated to disappoint Bailey. For all he cared, know-it-all-Munro could take a long walk off a short pier. "She takes to stuff like this!" Bailey's hands waved excitedly. "She'd adore a gymkhana."

Geez, she wasn't thinking about Playday!

"Let me get used to this wiggly seat, first!" They couldn't expect him to trot right through. He wasn't too sure about Playday, either. He'd had a look at the Pony Club flyer, and the races listed would drive this mare insane. The grand march sounded kinda neat, though, like a military drill.

He eased into a jog, and found further adjustments necessary. Geez, an education every time you got on. He had his doubts how Ms. Porsche would take to bareback. He was listing to one side, and bumped himself back over her spine, while trying to rein in. Clover snorted and tossed her head—full of herself after her four days' off. He braced, then realized she'd be aware of the tension, and concentrated on softening again. He began working the small of his back and no longer felt such jolts. Gaining confidence, he steered out of the mowed area. Leafy weeds and long grass swished against Clover's legs. A mere twist of his torso altered their course, and he steered long, loopy serpentines. He had forgotten the girls, simply grooving on the intimacy. His heel, pressed gently back from the tender spot, produced an awesome canter. Rolling along in his own cosmos, he weighed the possibilities of Playday. It wasn't till Labor Day weekend, some five weeks away—plenty of time to heal the girth gall and practice the finer points, like collection and extension. Since it was just up the road they'd be nuts to pass it up.

He suffered a few off-balance bumps as Clover yielded to his request for a trot. Once he'd softened again, he tried a leg-yield. Her right legs nimbly crossed over her lefts, turning his insides to warm butter. Those switchbacks didn't appear so terribly intimidating now. But Playday might be a different story. What the heck was a champagne ride? The strange sights and mob of horses there will send this greenie high as a kite. Clover hasn't seen another horse all summer. She's supposed to keep her head in a relay race?

He dawdled in the shed, intoxicated with the sense of accomplishment. Simply soft pressure from his leg, thigh, or seat, or light heel taps, or the least trip of a rein, had been enough to navigate through the convoluted grid. Afterwards, operating by visualization while walking out, he'd realized what Cappy meant by *Think Walk*.

Duker rested under the sawhorse with his nose on the ground, his big eyes blinking at Clover. The horse looked half-asleep on her crossties as Glenna ran a comb through the mane. Theo was camped on a hay bale with Bailey, her leg pressing on his, *muy simpatico*. A warm mist rose from Clover. Sun streaming into the barn rippled light through the comb-sifted mane. He gazed at the horse dreamily.

"Those silver strands have her mane shining like pin-striped satin."

"How poetic, Theo." Glenna went on combing. "Like it's been shampooed, and streaked by a salon. So sublimely silky."

"Special," Bailey peeped, then stared into space—probably searching for more good *S* words. The kitten climbing over his chest rubbed its furry back against his chin. "Especially smart," Bailey blurted. "Ahh . . . Really saintly."

"A saintly stepper, stately, and sprightly!" Glenna swung her comb like a baton.

"Affirmative," Theo growled, "that's a good one." Admittedly, Glenna's brains could work in her favor. "Strong. Steady. Surefooted. Sane," he proclaimed in the same deep voice. Bailey was wide-eyed, clearly stupefied as he rapped on: "Skillful, *absolutamente* swift sharp-sighted and safe!"

"Safe is questionable," Bailey said. "But I like it when she snorts, that short, soft kind of snorting she does."

"Oh, Bailey, for cute!" Glenna scrutinized the brush in her hand. Her forehead criss-crossed in concentration for another good one while she still had the floor. Her face lit up. "Satisfyingly sleek. Supple. Spirited!"

Bailey jumped to her feet proclaiming that Clover's streaked hair was totally stylish. Then, "A salute to the one who makes us smile!" She snapped her hand to her brow and collapsed in a gale of giggles, falling on Theo, who rolled back with a yelp. Glenna was doubled over, cackling uproariously. Duker cocked his head from side-to-side.

"Sassy!" Theo shouted. "Snazzy! Seductive! Ah, sensuous?"

The girls shrieked. Then, "S-ss-simulating a ss-ylph," Glenna sputtered.

"A sylph? What's that?"

"A fairy, stupid."

Laughter exploded into Theo's syncopated yelps, Bailey's trilling scales, and Glenna's donkey brays, which drowned out the other two.

"She's my super strawberry," sang Bailey with her head swinging like a metronome. "Like, real-ly spring-y. Real-ly spry!"

Glenna spoke through her teeth with her chin jutting out. "I say statuesque . . . Serene . . . Sedate." Then in her normal lilt, "Just look at her now." They looked. Looking back, like an imperious queen Clover angled her head and peered with both eyes.

"There's my sterling sweetheart," Bailey crowed.

"Affirmative, Bee!" His congratulatory pat triggered a playful push that caught him off guard. Suddenly he was being bombarded with prickly hay.

"Say uncle," Bailey cried as she pummeled his chest. *Caramba*, she sure was strong. "You're not getting up, Theo, until you agree to riding lessons!"

28

Hasta la Vista

"'UP!' CRIED MOTHER BECKER," her father cried from the foot of the stairs. "Up my children one and all! There's a storm upon the seas, and I hear the sailors' ca-allll . . . " Bailey snuggled deeper, not about to move until the last verse. She had packed last night, and showered with a two-gallon Baggie protecting the cast. Just a few last things to tuck into her suitcase, and she could run out to Theo. The rumble of Clover's sliding door had let her know he was here.

She tweaked a gauzy curtain and gazed out to her happy barn and thriving pasture. Lavender shadows cloaked the rolling grounds. Off to the east, an orange glow spread into the sky. Just the idea of saying goodbye had her homesick already. She was anxious to talk to Gammie and encourage her to get well. Still, leaving now was a major sacrifice. She doubted Dakota Clover and Duker and Hasty Pudding and Heather and loyal, supportive Glen and awesomely agreeable Theo were going to miss her as much as she was going to miss them. She would even miss the barn smells. She ran the zipper around her suitcase, taking care not to snag the sack of caramel corn she'd stuffed inside. The sun had climbed the horizon, and her curtains appeared on fire. A glorious sunrise, but now extra work for Theo. It was a scientific fact that a red sky in the morning indicated rain.

She grabbed her horse books and flew downstairs, past the sink's stack of plates and sticky silverware. She'd grab a bite later. She was halfway out the door when her mother asked nicely if she wouldn't mind packing up the cooler. Caught. She cast her mother a desperate, pleading look. She was expected to help in the kitchen, but—.

"Get to it, Bee! You're part of this family, no exemptions."

A frustrated kick slammed the empty container against the freezer. An impatient jab at its automatic dispenser sent ice-cubes skating across the floor. Ten landed in the cooler. The kitchen suddenly felt like a prison. Furiously, she began scooping wayward cubes into the cooler. Her mother grabbed her arm.

"Dump that out! No one wants a soggy sandwich! Get zip-lock bags. I've got everything ready here. Your father won't want to wait, Bee, and there're still dishes to do." Bailey huffed through her clenched teeth. She pressed down on the ice dispenser, gently this time, cursing under her breath while she waited the long minutes it took for two large zip-lock bags to fill.

The birds were tuning up for their morning overture when she at last went outside. A ridge of clouds had billowed in from the west—ominously purple clouds, rimmed in flaming red. She hurried down the path with the horse books heaped against her breast.

The shed looked bathed in a lavender mist. In the stillness, she heard her heart thumping. A kitten curled against her ankle. She set the books down in order to pick up the wriggly ball of fluff. No sign of Theo. "Books from Glen to me to you," she sung out, cradling Heather in her arms. Her heart jumped when the familiar head popped up. He'd been behind Clover, putting the halter on.

She walked along to the tire, while stroking the ridge of muscling beneath the flopped-over mane. If Theo hadn't been too far on the other side, she might even have reached out to him. After all their time talking and working and playing with Clover together, saying good-bye needed to be eventful. Like, at least a hug.

He fiddled with the halter snap. His eyes caught her doting gaze: surprisingly he dropped the rope. She snatched it up and began to grope for appropriate words. She hated leave-takings. Whatever happened now needed to last a whole week. He reached out on their way back to the barn, saying, "I'll take it." Her heart jumped at the sight of his hand, huge, reaching out. In her excitement she gave a hoot and swung the rope like a lasso. If he wanted it, let him come and get it.

He scowled, then caught hold of the tail in one quick move. She shrieked when he pulled, and did not let go. Swallows twittered, but she scarcely heard them, caught between resisting and giving in to the sparks in Theo's eyes. He towed her through the shadowed doorway. Her knees trembled as she let him reel her in. She felt his lips brush hers, then press eagerly. Her heart fluttered, and she began kissing him back. She was up on her toes leaning into him when a horn-blast brought her to her senses.

"Bailey Elizabeth!" Her father was storming down the path. She hadn't heard the gate latch. Just a little more—

"Come on, kids—" Her father's voice was gruff.

Theo let his arms drop. "*Hasta la vista*, Bailey," he whispered.

"Oh, Theo," she whimpered, "*hasta la vista*."

29
New Friends

THE RAIN STARTED FALLING Sunday afternoon, and it did not stop for three long days. Clover entertained herself by keeping track of the kittens, who entertained themselves by swatting at disoriented earthworms. The horse showed an uncanny awareness of Theo's approach. He'd push the poplar branches out of his face to find her staring into her waterlogged world with the rain running down her nose. Welcoming bops from the imperious nodder immediately dispersed any of the open shed's gloominess. A nudge from a cold, wet nose dropped Theo's able hands to mangling Duker's droopy ears, while two tiny bundles of warmth wound themselves between his legs. Urgent meowing seared his eardrums until kibbles appeared. Clover snatched hay out of the air as it flew over her bars. Theo ran the hose into her bucket and then, accompanied by munching noises and the rice-crispy-rhythm of the rain, swung into sanitation duty. A focused whisk of the Swiss Army knife split open shavings bags. And before long, arms wielding the manure fork reached unconsciously for the girl with unruly curls.

"Only too wicked." He sighed, then laughed out loud to find himself thinking so much about Bailey. A wayward lump sent him back over the section he had just raked; deeper thoughts surfaced, about protecting and providing. It must be love, the way he enjoyed taking care of things here.

The sun came out on Wednesday. Theo tacked up eagerly, brought the reins over Clover's head, and led her out. She needed exercise but not in the platter of steamed pudding her field had become. Better footing was on the driveway's light coat of gravel. Duker ran ahead and scrambled through the hollow under the gate. Theo shortened his hold on the reins before raising the latch, the passage between the posts particularly slippery. The horse pulled and snorted as the spaniel bounded off toward the bushes. Three days of pent-up energy burst into exaggerated high-steps as Clover was led across the new grass.

The rutted driveway traveled in a semicircle between towering evergreens and hardy shrubbery. Clover jerked against the bit as Theo jogged her onto the center crown's comparatively solid footing. As far as he knew, the horse had never been anywhere beyond her own fence. He pulled up short at the road. The sun glared off the mailbox. Clover's big orbs rolled up and down the blacktop's canopy of trees. Small rocks scattered as she danced in place.

Theo laid a reassuring hand and spoke soothingly, allowing a good, long look. "Take it easy, now," he said quietly as he led onto the tar. As her hooves clapped on pavement he suddenly needed to brace his shoulders and pull back. All the way down to the driveway's south entrance, then up past the laurel bushes and around again, he struggled to keep her in hand. Then, feigning nonchalance, he paused once more at the road. There was a fresh dewy smell in the air; the laurel leaves glistened. Clover assumed a pose of extreme attention, her neck arched toward a distant spot . . . which Theo saw morph gradually into a grotesque, four-legged creature topped by an oddly radiant globe.

Hoof beats. Louder. A tall person riding a tall horse with its ears pointed at Clover.

A trilled "Hello-oo," carried down the road. Marian Joyner?! The radiant globe nothing but her fuchsia hunt cap! His eyes slid off her pointy nose, down to one outrageous riding habit. Nobody at One Oak Stables wore skimpy tank tops and tights. Vibrations traveled up his arm as Clover sent all her might into a melodious snort. His own delight went into a deep-throated "Yo . . . ."

As Marian's handsome, ebony-brown bay came to a majestic halt, Clover advanced a mottled foreleg and stretched her neck for a polite snuffle.

"She sure is glad to see you," Theo said.

"What a pretty horse." Marian had a toothy smile. "Ree-boy seems to like her."

"The first horse she's seen in over a month, and it turns out to be your renowned Researcher!"

"This is incredible," Marian said with a sweep of her arm. "I never knew a horse lived here!" A stripe of hot pink zigzagging up the black tights wiggled wildly. Theo felt a rush of heat to his face. He got busy re-tightening the girth, needing time to compose himself. He'd never spoken to this girl, except in dreams, where she was "Maid Marian" and he was her golden knight. Coming together like this was huge.

"Meet Dakota Clover," he said when he could breathe properly. "Bailey Mason's horse, but I'm looking after her while they're on vacation." The urge to jump up and down with joy went into a hearty slap to Clover's neck. "I saw your picture in the paper, Marian. From the spring horse show? When you won the championship? Man, that is some horse!"

"Oh, I lo-ove this guy." Marian stretched over to pat her gelding's broad chest. Then she sat up and made a quirky face. "It's too wet to work today, so I'm walking the roads."

"Yeah, I know what you mean. This girl's been in for three days, and does she ever want to go! I'd kinda like to ride her out. Probably I shouldn't stray from the reservation, though."

Marian's thick eyebrows closed formation. "Come along with me," she said. "The mare'll be fine with Ree-boy."

He wanted to. Marian was an excellent rider. It should be all right. He'd probably never get another chance.

Clover had every muscle cocked when he mounted. "Easy," he murmured while settling himself on what felt like a keg of dynamite. "Say, wait a sec, Marian." Indicating the way with his chin, he suggested they walk up to the house and back a few times. "Kinda let them get acquainted?"

Maid Marian shrugged agreeably, then let her horse step out.

His dynamite sizzled, requiring too darn much attention.

"Wow Theo, is she high! Better move her out and let off some steam. This gravel's okay for trotting."

"Ah, yeah," he managed to say while dealing with the aerobics. "I was thinking the same thing."

Researcher surged ahead, with Clover on his tail. Theo fastened his eyes on the tiny waist undulating up front and the sleek legs straddling the big bay's girth. His tightly wound springboard twisted sideways and scraped him through some prickers. Give-and-take did him little good. Taking more than giving set up a chain of rough jolts warming him up for a high-dive. Marian's bright pink and black buttocks bounded directly in front of him. He was trying to concentrate, trying to hold back from Researcher, when a sudden rear whacked him in the chin. He shot his arms forward to bring the front down—which worked but, when Clover took off again, his leg side-swiped Marian's.

"This gravel's as good as any bush-league racetrack," she said as her well-mannered horse trotted on next to Clover, who stiffened her back and pumped her knees and hocks. A high, center crown offered the best footing but not nearly enough room for both of the horses, and Marian generously sidled into a rut. Theo accepted the favor humbly, feeling very ungallant. That he was no equestrian was only too obvious. They passed over the tar at a fast-clipped walk, and he worked at pulling his act together. Back on gravel, Marian suggested that they trade off the lead.

The blood drained from his face. Pass each other? Maid Marian did not know this mare.

Clover did seem happier in front. But she ballooned up when Researcher began his advance, and Theo saw himself hanging from a tree. He was ready when another rear exploded, and worked his legs and freed her head.

Down came the front end, and three days of pent-up energy burst into a hard gallop. The shutters converged into a greenish blur as they flew past the house. The air seethed with the sucking sounds of eight hooves pounding into stone encrusted mud. Theo rode crouched over Clover's neck with his reins so short the buckle kept hitting his ankle.

Researcher nosed up again.

"Easy girl, eeasy," Theo begged as the gelding steadily trotted on by. Fortunately, Marian pulled up at the road, making it easier for him to stop.

"That was great," she exclaimed, hardly out of breath. "Ree-boy needs this kind of work. Summer's incredible around here, what with shows and Pony Club and all. You guys ought to bring that horse to our gymkhana."

30

A Visit from Andy

THE POPLAR BRANCHES SHIFTED as Andy wriggled through. He was tired of throwing basketball hoops and had run out of things to do. Beads of water collected on his unlaced sneakers as his stumpy bare legs trudged through the saturated pasture, and then he wandered into the barn.

No Theo, nothing interesting.

He'd plopped down on a bale, when the Masons' dog ran in and dropped a tennis ball at his feet. The saliva-lathered offering got an indifferent toss. The dog scooted after it, and brought it back even wetter. Andy's grip slipped, leaving the dog victorious with the slimy ball tight in its teeth.

"S-stupid sonuvabitch." Andy pulled the brim of his new Indiana Jones hat over his eyes. He was slumped against the wall like a derelict in front of a saloon when the dog's nose got friendly. He kept fending it off. In this heat he didn't need some animal slobbering all over him. He tipped his prize hat back and looked around.

Some setup, just for a horse. What was so great about horses, anyway? Stupid horses were all people talked about lately. His dad talked to his brother and his mom about One Oak, about some horse Sheri might buy that was supposed to be the greatest thing on earth. His brother went on nonstop about which horse he'd been assigned, about the quirks of that one and every other horse at One Oak. Shit. No one was interested in anything *he* had to say.

The gate clicked. "Hey, f-fart-face," he yelled at Theo. He was safe, with his brother's hands full. "Wh-where you been?"

"Swallow it, kid. This mare had to get out. I just rode around the driveway."

"D-driveways are f-for assholes. Wh-what's wrong with the p-pasture?"

"Hey, I was having a nice day, until you crawled out from under a rock. Marian Joyner had her horse out there, too. Do you think anybody wants their pasture torn up?"

"B-betcha B-Bailey's horse misses e-e-eating out there." Andy waved his arm, indicating the whole outdoors. "All it ever does," he added under his breath. He endured a penetrating look, then was surprised to hear, "You want to graze her?" He went blank. With a shrug then, he heaved himself up.

"Just go where there's plenty of grass and she'll be good. She had a huge workout."

Andy didn't know if he felt like taking the horse anywhere or not. He thought about it while Theo slipped the bridle over the ears. His brother waited a whole darn minute for the bit to drop out. What a lackey! And now a thick blue rope was on that yucky colored halter, and the halter was on the horse. Up close, the creature looked awful big.

"Here."

The rope took up his whole fist. He stood up straight and tucked his chin, impressed with himself—his brother actually needed help from him. He took to whistling through his teeth, as if this was no big deal, and shifted from one foot to the other while Theo wiped off both sides of the girth, like it was gonna rot if he didn't do it right.

As soon as the saddle was off, Andy tugged the rope, ready to go.

"Hey!" His brother had blocked the way. "I've gotta sponge her first. Wait till I rub her down and do her hooves."

Andy rolled his eyes. "Come o-on, I haven't g-got all d-day."

He fiddled with the rope while the horse got fussed over. He was about to head off, when his brother laid his arm across the high back and said, "Good to go, bro."

"About time, too!" Andy reset his broad-brimmed hat, holding it by the crown. His legs moved stiffly as he led the animal out. It was a relief to have it stop at the first green patch. Eating kept it occupied for what seemed like a long time. The sun beat down. Andy shifted his feet. Horses were kind of boring, he thought. Stupid, too. He didn't know why he should have to be nice to Bailey's horse, anyway, when she'd gone and wrecked his jacket. Mr. Mason had given him money for a new one, but then the store was sold out. He stamped his foot to shake off whatever was stinging his leg. A toad hopped lazily across the horse's path, just in time to miss getting stepped on. Shit, if he didn't have to hold onto this critter, he could go after that creepy toad.

It was moving over, taking up on the rope. Two more steps scratched the rope through his fist. Three more popped the end-knot free. Wishing he'd never taken on this job, Andy stumbled after the slithering blue snake. Woody stalks slapped his bare legs. A terrific effort to stomp the slinky tail nearly got it. He took a flying leap, which sent his hat sailing—not into horse-crap, he hoped.

He'd caught the end knot, and was up on his knees when the rope jerked. Knocked flat again, he shut his eyes and tried not to think he might be dragged into a stinky clump of flies.

Finally, the stupid beast found something good enough to stop for. As it tore into this patch, he scrambled back to his feet. He snuck a glance toward the shed, hoping his brother hadn't seen anything. Loud chewing nearly drowned out the far off scraping sounds. He snickered at the idea of Theo shoveling crap. He wouldn't do it if they paid him a million dollars. He gathered up the rope, then wound it tightly around his wrist, just to be safe. Now he could look for his hat. This assignment sucked—though he'd never admit it. He slapped his stinging leg with his free hand, then fired off a string of cuss-words. His leg had picked up horse-crap, and it was all over his hand.

31
Theo in Charge

PLUMES OF CHEMICAL FOG permeated the air. The dung basket swarmed with flies, but Theo hadn't dared spray with Clover in here. Sending her out with Andy was a brilliant idea. Mighty decent for the kid to finally show an interest in horses. He took shallow breaths while he sprayed the wide aisle and then gradually worked into the stall. A diligent spider occupied a back corner; the filaments of its silky snare made him think of the rings a thrown stone made skimming over a lake. He would bypass that corner—spiders killed flies, too. He waved the rod back and forth, and his mind wandered for the umpteenth time to, "*Hasta la vista*, Bailey." He'd lost track where he'd sprayed—thinking about kissing her turned him to jelly all over again.

    The canister was empty. He waved off a survivor, heaved up the stinky tub, and headed around back. Three blackbirds pecked nonchalantly at the smoldering mound, which had multiplied unbelievably now that Clover spent more time in. He could see her now, happy with her head down and feeding. He dumped his mess and the birds scattered, cawing noisily. He pulled up his shirt and wiped the sweat off his face. He stood gazing through heat waves at Andy, absently wondering what had happened to the Indiana Jones hat. The kid was a brick to chip in and help.

He had started back with the tub at arm's length, when he noticed the furiously swishing tail. He paused. Andy'd better watch it. A fly burrowed into the sweat sticking to Theo's neck. A rare cloud hid the sun, and the day paled. He slapped his neck. A faint outline of the prized hat lay some thirty feet away from the kid. There was something blue around the kid's wrist.

Holy shit! If Andy had gone and tied himself—

"You're doing a dangerous thing, Andy!" Adrenalin coursed through Theo's veins. "Andrew, listen to me! Do naa-hot move." He tried for a stern, steady tone, afraid to display any emotion. "I will be right there," he yelled in all seriousness and started out, already breathing hard. The unsuspecting recruit squinted back with his mouth screwed into a question-mark. Please God, protect my kid brother. Any whim, a little fly, even a minor gust of wind could set Clover off. That kid thinks he can hold her?

His speed-walk took a circuitous route. No way was he about to come up by surprise. Clover had eyes in the back of her head, but he wasn't taking any chances. His throat was tight, and he fought for air while angling warily in the direction of her shoulder. Andrew Norton North would be hamburger if the horse decided to take off.

"Untie the rope, Andy." His voice sounded too darn shaky. Walk naturally, he told himself. Act calm. "Get that rope off your wrist right now, Andy. And be quiet about it."

"Not t-tied!" Andy yelled back and raised his arm for proof. Clover jerked her head up.

"No . . . " Theo prayed. "Stay . . . "

A short stride, then a long one, toward *him,* with Andy stumbling in her wake. His heart in his mouth, Theo caught himself from running up. The kid could still get close enough to—

Andy's foot slipped. His knees hit the ground—practically yanking his arm out of its socket. A longer, determined arm shot out. In one smooth move, Theo unsnapped the leadshank, then shoved off the horse. He yanked the leadshank so hard, Andy yelped.

"It could have been worse, you cretin! You think you're stronger than a horse? If she took off, you'd be dragged to hell and back." The rope was all tangled up. "Never," he shouted in the stunned boy's face as he tried to work it free, "Never wrap anything attached to a horse around any part of you!" To think what could have happened. With him responsible. Good God!

Andy slunk off to retrieve his hat. While he fiddled with the brim, Theo caught Clover and brought her up.

"Here!" He grabbed the boy by the shoulder and set him in place. "Just do what I say and you might learn something."

"I don't want to," Andy said in a pout, looking down at his hat.

"Oh yes you will!" Theo dug his fingers into the reluctant boy's forearm. This kid needed to learn a lesson! "Now stand by her left shoulder. You listening?" Andy grunted indifferently, slapped at a fly camped on his leg. Five or six flies clung to Clover's socks. Her tail whipped furiously, catching Andy, and he yelped.

"Pay attention, here." Theo grabbed the hat and flung it aside. He seized his little brother's right hand and positioned it on the rope. By the book this time, he told himself. "When you're leading a horse," he began, straining for a level tone, "hold about a foot down from the snap. The tail-end gets gathered up in your left hand, and don't you ever wind it! If the horse gets going fast, you can play some out. But, if everything gets out of whack and the horse gets out of control, you've gotta let go." Theo looked around, as if to make sure of the fence. "Don't worry, Andy, Clover can't go far here." He began guiding the irresolute paw to show how to work the leadshank. "See? Make the rope talk. Then when she waits for you, take up the slack. Here, signal like this." With his hand over Andy's, he jiggled the rope. "Don't try to muscle her—you never win!"

"Okay," said Andy in a feeble voice.

"You know this horse weighs a thousand pounds?" Theo ducked his sweaty brow to his sleeve, wiped his hands off on his jeans. Then he yanked the rope away. "Use psychology, kid. Your brain is bigger than a horse's, you know. At least, most people's is." He passed a sly look, but Andy was staring down at his messy sneakers.

"Now watch!" As expected, when he tweaked the rope, the horse's head came up. "See, there's a technique to it. Keep watching me!" He led Clover a few steps ahead, then turned and walked back with her still at his side. "See that? Just keep her next to you."

He stuck the rope in Andy's sweaty hands and began backing off.

Clover began tearing at some leafy weeds.

Andy held himself erect.

"When I call you, bring her in," Theo called out. "I'm almost done in there. Just stay by her shoulder. Only let go in an emergency."

THE HEAT HUNG ON, ninety degrees predicted again on Thursday. Theo snapped up Joshua Shapiro's invitation to spend the day on the water, sailing. After their huge workout yesterday, Clover shouldn't mind standing in. On Friday, he crossed to the barn just as the sun climbed over the low stretch of woodland that backed the stone wall. Clover got doled a fraction of her usual feed so he could saddle right away. Once through the gate, she hurried along to the driveway, and hardly stood still long enough for him to mount.

They had a brilliant trot going when, fifteen minutes later, Marian rode over with the same idea. They would beat the humidity and heat, and get in some work before the flies attacked. Clover turned hyper during follow-the-leader but, today, her rider was able to concentrate.

"She's going good, Theo. Nice job."

"Thanks, we needed this. Researcher sure makes a good role model."

The exertion and the excitement of traveling together got the horses' blood up, making them easy marks for the ravenous insects. Clover unleashed a full-body shake that left Theo limp. Researcher kicked up at his belly. The tossed heads jangling the bits continuously made further efforts at schooling useless. It came as a relief when Marion suggested that they quit.

He rinsed the sweat off and used up three towels before drier patches appeared. Back home in her stall, Clover took a few sips of water, then nosed around, plainly happy to be in the shade on fresh shavings with her hay. Safe, sound, in top form for Bailey. He was still kicking himself for leaving the horse alone with Andy. When he went back out, she was tracking a tight circle around the kid, thrashing her tail as if being eaten alive. Thank God, aside from some nasty bites, they had both survived.

A BARRAGE OF HEART-TWANGING trumpets accompanied Theo's tramp back through the spongy field. His whistled response carried over, slightly off-key, while he went about tending to his menagerie. Clover plunged her head into the bucket when he began running the hose, and came up dripping, to bathe his sweaty arm with a sloppy kiss. An impatient nose-thrust greeted the two arms full of hay, an approving snort the ice-cream-bucket full of molasses-laced grain. Nothing wrong with appetites here, even in this heat. Duker mouthed up his dinner in big chunks. Hasty and Heather steadied their platter with their paws for every last lick. Theo worked quietly in the stall, then froze. A tine of the fork had caught Clover's tail.

Coolly she swung aside to disengage herself, as he looked on in awe.

Having everything in order gave him a huge sense of satisfaction. He lingered in the airy doorway. Duker was back from his nightly recon, panting at his side. This was his last night in charge and he intended to savor every minute. Naturally, Bailey would want to take over. He'd be glad to see her, could not wait to see her, but he'd sure miss the *KP* duty. These critters liked him, their trust in him incredible. Clover let him reach under her neck, and would keep chewing while the flat of his hand latched onto the plane of that huge, working jaw. How cool to have her simply stand quietly and commune. Sometimes she'd blow and prickle her whiskers into his palm. And whinny. He loved it when she whinnied to him. He sniggered, figuring the whinnies were mostly mess calls.

He tuned into the crickets' twilight symphony, its cadenced creaking a counterpoint to the whispers of shifted hay. A high cry raised the image of a swallow making one last mosquito swoop. Here and there, tiny lights filled in the dots of meandering fireflies' flights. With his natural world at peace, Theo headed into the night.

32

Another Visit From Andy

THAT SATURDAY, ANDY NORTH ran out of things to do again. Nobody was home at his house except Theo—a total poop, conking out on the couch in the middle of the day. Andy shut his eyes, crouched side-wise, and wriggled between two scratchy poplar branches. On guard for the horse, he wandered into the pasture. He had his rubber field-boots on today, and went out of his way to stamp through an enduring mud-puddle. No sign of the horse here, just some old blackbirds noising off. A mound of petrified manure took a swift boot as he headed for the shed.

Guardedly, he sniffed. It didn't smell so bad, even though the horse was in here. Most of the field was dry now, so he didn't see why the horse wasn't outside. It looked half asleep, standing still and square with all of the mane falling on the same side. The broom hung next to the picker, along with the shovel, on brackets fixed to the wall. Nothing interesting, and Andy was about to leave when one ear flicked. He shuffled down the aisle, idly handling the rake, the railing, the stubbly bales, then thinking the horse probably wanted out of that cage.

"H-here, horsey," he coaxed, and rapped his knuckles against the door. He stretched his arm through the bars, but the long nose swung off to the side. Heck, didn't it know he was just trying to be friendly?

Duker ran in, jumped up, and muddied Andy's protesting arms. The horse looked a whole lot cleaner than the pushy dog. He stretched for another pat, but now the long nose went up. His eye lit on the blue rope dangling from the yucky-pink halter. What a contraption, he thought as he swooped the whole thing off its hook.

The bolt's metal slider scratched, and then clunked into place. The massive door rumbled across its track. Andy fussed with the halter-straps as he shuffled in. He wasn't sure how halters were supposed to work, only that they were SOP with horses. The slobbery dog stood in the partway opened door, wiggling excitedly and wagging its tail. "You stupid thing," Andy said to the halter. He got the long strap over the horse's ears, then strained his arms to fasten the snap.

It'd gone on kind of crooked, but now the head was too high again to fix anything. Anyway, he wasn't sure how. Outside, the sun beat down. The only thing moving was a pheasant pecking in the tire, which honked and scooted off when he led the horse out. He got pulled over to the tire, then a chance to reset his lucky Indiana Jones hat when the horse stopped and stretched its neck down to investigate. The new grass outside the fence looked better than anything in that tire. It hadn't been mowed for over a week. There was so much, nobody would mind if the horse took a little.

Andy made the rope talk, like his brother had showed him, and the horse came right along. Cool, it was minding. He unlatched the gate and, even before it got all the way open, the stupid creature sideswiped him. Then it wheeled at the end of the rope, firing up a hunk of sod.

"Hey, you!" Okay, it stopped. The ears were cocked, the eyes riveted on *him*. The hip bone seemed to be missing a whole lot of hair.

"See what you got, stupid bully!?" Clumsily Andy rearranged the rope. The scrape wasn't his fault, the darn thing better watch where it was going. The halter had slipped, he noticed just as the dog ran yipping by. Before he could position himself next to the shoulder, like Theo'd said, the horse started off. His rubber boots hissed through the grass. He had the end-knot tight in his fist, and was gaining, when an abrupt snatch in the finest section of grass slammed him into the beast's rear-end. He jumped back. At least this one didn't kick. But now it was stomping the lawn and tossing its head, flinging yucky green snot. A big glob got him in the nose. He swiped it away and peered back through the hot, wavy air, trying to ignore the mosquito ringing in his ear.

It was a long way back to the fence. He had lost his hat. Suddenly, he felt like he might barf. He saw it now, stuck at an angle in a hoof-crater, this side of the gate. He had a sinking feeling he was in trouble. His hand was supposed to be higher on the rope. His feet were supposed to be keeping up.

"Hey!" A mighty kick at its own belly nearly got *him*. Then the rear end swung and before he knew it he was down with the breath knocked out of him. He lay in a heap, gaping at the thick wad of grass hanging out of the darn thing's mouth. Mr. Mason wasn't going to like this. Shit, his brother was going to kill him. He could see the dog under a tree, watching with its tongue hanging out. He fingered the spot on his neck where the tail got him, and tried to think how the stupid rope was supposed to work. He could fix everything if this horse would only mind him. It shifted its feet now, and pointed one toward the panting dog. Then another. Then another, and now it seemed to be gliding. But the rope was still in his hand. A flash of color caught his eye, some yucky pink thing over in the grass.

33
Homecoming

BAILEY WIDENED HER EYES as the car swung off the Connecticut Thruway. Then, Custer Lane at last, what a relief. Not that the vacation hadn't been any fun. Pigging out and singing the night away at Britty's slumber party was just like old times. Sure, this visit had been fun—who wouldn't be happy to catch up on gossip and see all the cute guys at the park? But by the end of the week, it was clear her priorities lay in Greenham. Her animals and Theo came first. Even when she couldn't ride, she was happiest hanging out here. Home at last, and the ache in her stomach soon gone—gone along with the haunting feeling that something was wrong.

Her grandmother might have taken a turn for the worse. Immobile in the elevated hospital bed, dear Gammie had seemed a shrunken image of her former self. The frail woman had always been full of energy and cheer, had faithfully been her pal. These few days they had together were the most meaningful part of the trip. She'd spilled out her feelings about Clover and Theo. "So wonderful, really a super horse, Gammie," she confided when they were alone. "Clover and I belong to each other. We kind of commune—you know, like in the same spirit?"

"The horse is a noble beast," Gammie replied, her voice intense but thin. It was an effort to speak, yet she made herself clear. "Always give yours the benefit of the doubt, dearie. You'll get back an honest day's work."

"I do, Gammie. Really, so does Theo. He's very good with Clover. With me, too," she added bashfully. She rested her grandmother's thin, bluish hand in her square, pinkish palm, aware this might be the last time they could really talk. "Just being near Theo gets me sort of nervous, though . . . Happy-nervous, *you* know, Gammie, sort of giddy? He kissed me goodbye."

"Your first kiss?" Gammie whispered with a fresh shine to her eyes.

"Uh huh." She warmed the weightless hand in both of hers. "The first one that counts, anyway."

"That makes sense to me, my love,"—the voice stronger now. "You, and Theo, and Clover doing things together. You're like a golden triangle, reflecting glory on our Maker."

The memory of their private talk warmed Bailey's heart. A glimpse of yellow through the trees now had it beating faster. How she loved this place, everything about it. If only summer wasn't already half over. A golden triangle connecting her and Theo and Clover, oh let it shine! Let it shine even after school starts again.

The car emerged from the trees. Bailey's hungry, swooping gaze spotted Duker. Ears flapping, tongue hanging out, the spaniel bounded happily alongside the car. Bailey's gaze leapt past the tall yellow house to the small weathered shed. The late-afternoon light made the old boards look translucent. Her heart beat like a jack-hammer. Theo would be feeding about now, she could almost see him in there with Clover.

She took off running as soon as the car stopped, into what felt like an oven.

"Hi, you guys,""she called out, and slipped under the mass of wet towels strung across the chain. The splashing hose had drowned her voice, she thought, when Theo didn't turn around. She held back, delighting in the distinctive barn smell, and waited for Clover to finish drinking. Theo's mouth was set in a grim line. Peering up at his face, she thought his eyes looked like hers did when she'd been crying. Clover raised her head, and let out a deep throaty noise.

Bailey's heart lurched. There *was* something wrong. The horse's nose looked like a rotten apple. Instead of a cute little snip, it had a big, oozy booboo.

"Whaaat haaappened?" She burst into tears.

It seemed to take Theo forever to rewind the hose. "It's my fault and I apologize," he said, sounding strangely like a robot. "Your mare got loose and got creamed by Mom's fence."

She scrubbed her fists into her eyes. It was mortifying to be crying in front of Theo, he'd think she was such a baby. "It's just that," she blubbered weakly, "I was looking forward . . . Oh, this is awful!"

Theo seemed to shrink, and then he ducked under the towels and left.

She was stunned. She drew a shaky breath. Some homecoming. She had overreacted, but he could've at least explained what happened here. Should she run after him? Not to panic, there'd be a rational explanation. She shuddered, suddenly thinking there could be more than one booboo. Clover did seem restless now, trampling through her hay.

She needed to be in there.

"Hi sweetie, I missed you so awfully!" She bypassed the glaring wound to throw her arms around the sturdy neck. At last, this warmth and strength was back in her arms. She marched her fingers up to the roots of the mane and stroked there, kneading the deep muscles. "Not to worry," she was able to say after a while, "your nose won't hurt forever." She leaned in, against the solid shoulder, pondering. The guy who'd wanted to kiss and hug her wasn't even glad to see her.

"Let me look at your booboo, sweetie." She fetched her torch from the filing cabinet.

The wound looked worse in the light. What must be the biggest zit ever had Clover's nose swollen past the noseband line. Bailey gulped, gulped again, unable to take her eyes off the right nostril, which gaped open. She touched it, meaning to remove the mass of hay pasted into the ooze. Then she thought back to Clover's yucky nose during her sickness, and changed her mind. Hay was fairly clean, probably not so irritating as fussy picking would be. This oozy red stuff wasn't as scary as pus. "Did you just do this?" Her relief after the initial fright came out in a shout. "How come you got loose?" All the way over to the North's! Theo was always so careful, this was unreal. "You better not have wrecked Mrs. North's garden, Miss Dakota Clover."

No way would this horse wear a bridle. A stream of light cast down each leg showed nothing wrong there, but she ran her hands over them anyway. One flank had lost a ten-inch strip of hide, but the horse seemed fine, otherwise. She pressed the flat of her hand down on the backbone. "This hurt? Not like your poor nose, huh?" The back muscles had not flinched. "When your nose gets better, we're going to have fun! Two more days, and I get my cast off."

"I PAID OFF OUR caretaker," her father announced. He was back in his favorite spot at the kitchen table, waiting for somebody to hand him something to eat. "I caught him heading home already, obviously exhausted. Not a good day, especially in all this heat."

"Did he say anything about Clover's nose?"

"He did. Is it bad?"

"Pretty gruesome, Daddy. Theo feels so bad."

"He did the right thing and called his father. To make a long story short, all it needed was a thorough cleaning. That's all you can do for places you can't bandage. No stitches, either, Doc North said. She'd just rub them out."

"Oh." She hadn't even thought about stitches. With that swelling, you couldn't see how deep it was.

"You let me know how's she's doing, Bee. I hope we won't need the vet."

The bacon spattered, and she turned it down a notch. Her mother was making toast. She didn't turn the heat down very far, wanting to hurry back out. What a crummy welcome, nothing like she'd dreamed of. Clover hurt, Theo acting weird.

"Mom, I'll clean up later, okay?" She headed for the door.

"But you haven't eaten!"

"Later, okay? I've got to check Clover."

"You're excused," came back sweetly. Her mother could be so understanding.

The last rays of daylight had the swallows swooping in fervent pursuit with their beaks open. Bailey entered the stall and ran her hand between Clover's bulging chest muscles. The air was still, the heat hanging in.

"Let's get you out of here." Her hand came up dripping sweat. Most carefully, she slipped the halter over the bulbous nose. She really didn't need one, the horse coming along like a foal after its mommy. She hitched one crosstie and stood back to see all she'd been aching to see practically every minute she was gone. She dabbed a towel at her watery eyes. She dabbed at Clover's watery eyes. She bunched the towel in her good hand and scrubbed down the sweltering neck. Theo had done the mane, she discovered when the comb slid right through. Insane, how he'd hurried off. If he was the same friendly guy she used to know, couldn't he put up with a few tears?

She fiddled with her shelf, positioning the bristly brush over to the left of the soft brush. He wasn't as particular as she was about little things. Still, aside from this laundry draped over the chain, he had the barn in shape. Nuts, she hadn't even had a chance to ask what riding he'd done. He hadn't even stayed long enough to get his present.

The hide was drier now, the horse more at ease. Bailey fussed with her tools some more and rummaged through her drawers. Handling the familiar objects helped her feel grounded. Back with Clover in the stall, she spread her fingers over the sturdy backbone and felt even better. As she slipped off the halter she heard a clink, and then a harsh grating noise.

Her heart jumped. Theo was over by the grain can.

"Hi, I knew you'd come back!" She came out of the stall, crowing, "The barn looks great, you must have worked really hard. What did you do with all that rain this week? Did you get to ride much?"

"Yeah, sort of. Look, I just had—"

"Wait, you're getting a present. Stay right where you are." She made a dash for the gate and breathlessly flew up to her room, where the best thing relating to Clover she'd been able to find dangled from Ellie's nose.

Theo was slouched against the door frame. He stood very still while she pointed out the reddish horse printed across the front of the red-billed cap. "Supposed to be Clover," she said with a laugh and, her voice lifting each word, "It's from Arlington Race Track?" In this light she couldn't see any white between his lips. She could hardly see his eyes, the way his head was bent.

She reached up with the cap, and discovered the strap needed adjusting. He stood like a shop window dummy while she fixed it. The visor made a tight curve across his brow.

"Don't you like it?"

"Thank you very much," he replied in that moody monotone she despised. A swallow screeched and glanced off a thermal. Theo hollowed his chest to edge past her, mumbling, "I don't deserve anything." And with that, he walked away and faded into the gloom.

34

Neighborhood Upheaval

AFTER THE CONSTANT HUM of Parkwood, the quiet that night seemed unearthly. Bailey kept waking up, and making a conscious effort to release her rigid muscles. She'd stop breathing, lie still, and listen for strange noises. A strawberry roan with large, knowing eyes and a stripe running down to a cute little snip on the upper lip was right outside. The way the horse looked now, though, you wouldn't even know about that cute little snip. Heal, Clover. Even if it itches, leave your nose alone and let it heal. That Theo. He sure was abrupt. Daddy got more out of the guy than I did. How brilliant of him to phone his father.

She passed up a chance to sleep in and headed out just as the first rays of light slanted through the trees. No large, knowing eyes appeared, not even when the gate creaked. Two doves took off from the high edge of the roof. Bailey peeked into the dimness. A kitten raised its head, yawned, and arched its furry back. Clover was a large unfathomable figure, her wound in shadow. Bailey tiptoed in. Those eyes she loved were still undercover. Then, one ear flicked. Now both eyes opened wide. Hers did, too. The swelling was down, no longer an angry red but a testy pink.

She didn't think twice before slipping two flakes of hay into the tire well. She slid open the door, and Clover trotted out, stuck her nose in the tire, and began gingerly mouthing small portions of hay. Bailey sat down with her feet planted in the well. The rubber had retained its warmth, and felt good on her bottom. The steady chomping was reassuring, and for a dreamy while she simply let herself float in the horse's aura. Here was her same wonderful horse, acting normal. The booboo hadn't stopped her from flopping this hay apart. Bailey inhaled deeply. She was home.

After awhile, she left her balmy spot to fetch some grain. Sunlight glared off the hulking can. The galvanized lid was stuck tight and needed a tough yank. Then she froze with the lid midair. Right on top of the golden mixture lay a neat wad of dollar bills. Her eyes narrowed. Seven twenties, the same amount Daddy paid Theo. She sifted through the pebbly mix, thinking hard. Why couldn't Theo be straight with her? She looked back to Clover. If only this horse could talk!

Her father had his baggy, khaki shorts on and was devouring the sport section, bent on enjoying every last minute of his vacation. The kitchen's cheery Swedish designs paled while he studied her face. Without meaning to, she'd slapped the wad of bills on the table. Shit, she hated ruining his last day.

"Where'd that come from?"

"Outside. Hiding in the grain."

"What!?" He sat up, clearly disturbed. Now she felt even worse.

"I guess he feels real bad about Clover," she said weakly. "He was acting funny last night. He must only have come back to return his pay." More positively, hoping to cheer things up, "He should have looked at her! The swelling's way down. It's going to all heal up!"

"Naturally it will, Bee," her mother said, waving her coffee scoop in the air. "This isn't the end of the world. Everyone gets a little scrape now and then."

"That kid did a helluva good job for us!" Her father gripped the arms of his chair, his knuckles blanched white. "That's the gods-honest truth! Of all the unmitigated gall, sneaking his pay back!" Bailey slumped into the opposite chair. Daddy had been in a good mood all week. Now he'd hunched forward and was tugging his ear. She hated it when he tensed up.

"He must be miserable," she choked out, oblivious of the glass of cranberry juice her mother set in front of her, along with a multivitamin pill.

"That boy has no proper idea of what he's worth. He handled things quite well here. Literally, I'm not exaggerating the slightest. One isolated incident doesn't cancel that out. Fair statement?" Her fist burrowing into her cheek, Bailey nodded at the table. Her juice hadn't been touched, her stomach in a turmoil. "I suppose he needs time to reflect," her father went on, drumming his fingers on the table. "That makes sense to me!" He looked up, darting his eyes between her and her mother. "Huh!?" he barked.

Her mother brought the carafe over. "It might be more respectful," she volunteered, "if, instead of cash, we'd give Theo a nice present."

"Really?" Bailey jumped out of her chair. She flung her arms, crying, "Would chaps and work boots cost about the same?"

"Now just a darn minute!" Her father glowered, and pinched his ear. "No clothes, and that is final!"

"But Daddy, Mom's idea is awesome." Her hands sprung to life. "Check this out. I could come along and get a pair of chaps, too. We could do it together, so the focus wouldn't be on Theo, and he'd get feeling better about everything. It'd all get smoothed over and be okay, wouldn't it? Please?" This solved everything. It'd give her and Theo a chance to talk. Daddy had been such a pal on vacation, surely he'd see it her way.

"Pure and unadulterated fiction!" His fist pounded the table. "You don't know diddly about finance, young miss." The captain's chair made a sharp noise. He stood up and shook his finger. "I'll handle this. I took care of Andy's jacket, didn't I? And I'll handle this—unless you want to pay the bills?" His head loomed menacingly. "Do you have a problem with that, little girl?"

The back door slammed, and Michael burst in.

Bailey sunk into her chair, expecting a few minutes of relief.

"Hey, you know what?" cried Michael. Those glaring eyes shot from her to her little brother. "Andy can hardly move. His nose is broke and he's got two big shiners! Basically," Michael added, puffed with importance, "what's caused by hematomas, to be scientific."

"I bet he fell off his bike." Bailey peered into her cranberry juice.

Michael let out a gruff laugh. "The poor guy's a Rocky Raccoon clone!"

"Oh, poor Andy," Beth Mason said. The steaming carafe rattled back onto its stand.

"Now what's he been up to?" their father asked.

Bailey raised the cool juice to her lips.

"It was Theo! Theo pulverized him. Holy cripes, he drilled a basketball square in the poor guy's face!" The red liquid splashed. Bailey's glass jiggled as she listened to her little brother go on about the humongous mess next door. "The lawn's all torn up over there. Mrs. North's garden is totally, and I mean totally, totaled. His father's out there and, man, is he mad! Andy's got a concussion, too. Basically, he's on endless ice packs. Talk about black and blue! And is Theo ever in trouble, grounded for a whole week!"

THE MASONS SHOULDERED GARDEN tools and marched to the other side of the poplar trees. Clearly, their horse had caused all the damage. No one at the North's was talkative. Various uprooted vegetables lay scattered about, the cores of red and green peppers and tomatoes and eggplants exposed. A tangled mass of whitish wire littered one side of the unsightly plot. Leaning this way and that, three rows of sweet corn just into its vulnerable tasseling stage was bent in tatters. Mrs. North had gone off to the garden center. Theo worked on the far side of the property, digging up topsoil. Bailey couldn't catch his eye. She hovered close to her mother, knowing an apology would be required when the woman got back. A rake appeared in her hands. She couldn't see where to start. She was horrible at gardening.

The tomato patch lay waiting, so she squished through that mess and dug in, fuming inside. Daddy could use some anger management, he didn't have to get so mad. All she'd done was suggest a convenient way to settle up with Theo. The total situation must have him pissed, after spending so much money on Clover and everything. He was probably thinking if they didn't *have* a horse they wouldn't *be* in this fix. After all he'd done for her, after all the chumminess during their trip—now this!

The sound of a motor grew louder. It cut off, and then a car door slammed. Mrs. North came stomping around to the van's sliding door. Michael and Bailey were drafted to carry the fiery-eyed woman's purchases: bags of grass seed, young plants, and a new fence for her beloved plot. Not flimsy wire this time, but sharp sturdy pickets. The apology stuck in Bailey's throat. The woman appeared to be ignoring her. She snuck a look at Theo, who was off in the other direction, wrestling a wheelbarrow.

"Well don't just stand there, you two." Beth Mason straightened up and pressed her hands into her spine. "Bailey. Michael. How about neatening up that trail of divots over there?"

She passed her mother a muffled, "thank you"—anything to get away—and threw herself into stomping the clods of sod back into place. When she ran out of divots to stomp, she awkwardly stood by with Mikey while the two mothers fussed over a mutilated plant. Dr. North was hassling Theo, telling him to "step on it." She threw a sympathetic look, then waited. But to him, she no longer existed.

"Bailey, I know you want to check on the horse," her mother mercifully said. "You kids can run along home now."

"Okay, thanks," she answered meekly. But she couldn't go before she apologized.

She determinedly threw her shoulders back and approached. Then she stood waiting for the distraught woman to look up. "I'm really sorry about your garden," came out in one forced breath. Mrs. North nodded and went on digging with her trowel. A glance for Theo caught no more than long legs and the seat of his pants.

ON MONDAY A PLASTIC splint replaced the annoying cast. She still hadn't heard from Theo, but Glenna Munro had called.

"Can't she be ridden, Bailey?"

"The swelling's down to sort of a lump. It mustn't hurt much, seeing how she demolishes her bucket. We'll have to see how she takes the bit. My arm is good to go, as long as I don't overdo, and Clover should be great, considering all her schooling from Theo." She didn't mention their friend's weird attitude. It would be too hard to describe when *she* didn't have a clue.

The next morning, Bailey found Glenna ensconced on a hay bale, rubbing the kittens' tummies. An early appointment had put her mother available for taxi service at 7:15, or not at all.

"Environmental Engineer, huh?" Glenna stared at Bailey's chest.

"I'm making a statement, Glen." Her new tee displayed a rake and a manure cart.

Back on the job, she tried not to inhale the fumes rising from the wet-spot under attack—a disgusting job she wouldn't do for any other horse. She'd just think about riding. Clover was a real buddy compared to a certain boy she used to know. With a horse, at least, affection and effort were appreciated and given back.

Glenna seemed uncommonly gabby, rambling on about clothes and her mother's new boyfriend, which Bailey took in about half of. The prospect of riding had her too keyed up to think of anything else. An unexpected invasion of stomach prickles persuaded her to let Ms. Talkative ride first. With the lunge line strung through the shiny bit-rings, Glenna was soon trotting, and joyfully exclaiming that she still knew how to post. Just like old times, back together again.

The worry-pins had waned by Bailey's turn but, after all this time off, the old helmet felt like an iron pot. Ready to mount, she looked toward the poplar trees. She'd been counting on sharing this moment with Theo.

Her plastic arm was no help. Clover stood quietly while, rather awkwardly, Bailey pulled herself up. Both feet knew where to go, and having her legs around the horse again felt wonderful. Starting out, her body remembered what to do. But the legs screamed when she stood in the stirrups and pushed down on her heels. So she sat and swung her hips into motion. Glorying in a sense of oneness, she let Clover trot, relying on the lunge line for steering because her arm had started to ache.

"Phew, do I stink, Glen. Am I not pathetic?" Clover must think so, too.

"Gawd, now that you mention it, you do look out of it, Bee. Your leg is swinging!"

"I kno-ow." Probably just as well Theo was *not* here. "I'm slowly but surely regressing!"

She put in twice-a-day work-outs and pushed herself hard. She hadn't forgotten about Playday. There was a mountain of training to climb before they'd be ready for those games. She was counting heavily on Theo—if the mystery man ever showed up. He'd better come through with riding lessons. And he'd better explain how Clover got loose. Andy might have been involved. Dr. North had remarked to her mother that his younger son had trouble respecting other people's property. Including horses, obviously. Yet how Clover's nose figured in Andy's concussion, she hadn't a clue. If only she could talk to Theo. True, he was grounded, but couldn't he at least sneak in a call? Her babyish tears had turned him off. Or maybe he'd found somebody else while she was gone.

Bailey was sad. Bailey was mad. In her desperation, she decided to trust her little brother with a message.

"You tell Theo that Clover's nose is healing really well."

"No way," Michael shot back. "The dude keeps to his room. Andy says he's pissed at the world." Then Michael came back with more information. While they were away, Theo had gone riding with Marian Joyner.

That clinched it, he didn't like *her* anymore. She got Glenna on the phone. She jammed the receiver against her ear and savagely buffed her fingernails with a scratchy emery board. A decent rim of white showed at the tips. No more gnawing, she vowed, even in the face of revolting news. She planted herself in front of her *Sylvester* tape and played it twice, all the way through. Finally, she hauled herself off to bed and nuzzled old Ellie, salting the fake fur with more tears. Her legs ached, her arm ached, and now her heart ached, too.

That night Marian Joyner tied her up with baling twine and drove off with Theo in a blindingly pink convertible. The dream haunted, and Bailey didn't fall back to sleep until well past 4:30. And it was nearly nine when she crawled out of bed. Glen wouldn't be coming today, but she didn't feel much like riding, anyway. Downstairs, she found her mother hovered over the counter, making out a grocery list—something they'd often do together.

"Don't look at me that way, Mother!" She'd meant to slip through the kitchen without exposing her puffy eyes. "So I've been crying. Well, I'm mad!"

"Tell me about it."

She struggled for words weightier than cottage cheese and yogurt. "It's not fair," burst out. "I'm gone one week, and everything goes up in smoke? I'm totally burnt."

"Very *punny*," her mother said, and then delivered the clenched fist pressed against the counter a loving pat. "No, seriously, Bee, not everything?"

"Theo's not speaking to me."

"Because he's grounded! Maybe they took his cell phone away."

"He's been acting weird ever since I got back. He won't even look at me."

"That was right after the accident. He wouldn't have been his normal self."

"Exactly!" She leaned over the counter, moaning, "It's like he turned into some weird zombie while I was gone."

"Give him a break, girl. It has nothing to do with you. All the responsibility here was on his shoulders. Just be glad he took it seriously." Bailey tried to consider it from the other side. Maybe Clover's booboo and the mess in his mother's garden had shocked Theo senseless. But he should've at least sent a text message and let her know he hadn't fallen off the face of the earth. If he still had his phone. When, if ever, was he coming back? And what about Marian Joyner?

"He used to be so nice," she whimpered. "He was going to give me riding lessons."

"Hmm. No more riding for you until you get a proper helmet."

"Really?" One that wouldn't fall off.

"On our way today, we could stop at The Saddlery. Say, it's nearly a week since Theo's incarceration. Why don't you go over there?"

"Mother, it's not that simple. I can't go over there!" Her fiery eyes took on a glow. "But I will most gladly go to The Saddlery."

"See how sweet you can be? Go over and tell Theo how much you miss him. Remember, it takes two. You need to hold up your end. Be pleasant and give him the benefit of the doubt."

"But what if he's so disgusted he doesn't want to come back?"

"Oh, I imagine he will . . . If only to see Clover."

35

Strawberry Shortcake

SHE HIKED OVER THE long way and came in through the North's curlicued iron gates. It was noon, on the dot—according to Mikey, the end of Theo's house arrest. The massive front door loomed as she strode up to the tall brick house. Sunshine glinted off the brass-shield knocker. Her hands shook as she set the platter against the back of the step one down from the stoop. Safely nestled beneath a sheet of see-through wrap, on her mother's prettiest, flowered platter, rested her peace-offering for Mrs. North. The sugary, perfectly browned biscuit was slathered in layers of whipped cream, with juicy berries dotting the pearly peaks.

One crack on the knocker, and Bailey's knees joined in. Mrs. North would come to the door, accept her apology and ooh and ah over her masterpiece. And that would be it. Unless—

The door opened, half way.

"Is this okay?" she whispered to the lanky frame behind the shadowy screen. "I mean, can you talk?" Five heartbeats of silence, then her blood resumed pounding. "Clover's missed you, Theo," she blurted, afraid he would disappear again.

"She's got you to take care of her now."

"Don't be silly." Her knees gave way, and she sat down, inches clear of the platter. "*I* missed you, too," she said into the air.

"How's her nose?"

"It's practically all healed up." Faint strands of music came through as the door opened wider.

"I see you got your cast off." Theo let himself down on the third step below hers. His shoulders were hunched, so tense he looked ready to run away. From what she could see of his face, his lips were narrowed, as were his eyes, which gazed off into the distance. Downed branches lay every which way beneath a stand of gnarled fruit trees. The North's front grounds weren't the park she had expected to find behind those imposing gates. Clusters of wild roses cluttered the brick path, poppies poked from the untended grass—all a natural cover for wildlife. Mrs. North had to fence in her garden against the rabbits, raccoons, and hedgehogs—and horses now, too. Bailey rested her elbows on her knees and sunk her cheeks into her clasped hands. She'd had enough of this coolness. Theo ought to clear up the money issue and get on with life. He deserved a scolding for bringing back his pay.

"You have a good trip?"

"Fine," she answered, with a cheerless laugh. "I saw the kids who weren't off at camp or someplace. Really, visiting my grandmother was the best part." She thought of Gammie's golden triangle. Might not be a good time for sharing that, even though Theo had cocked his head slightly, as if wanting to hear more.

"Brittany Belso had a party." If she was willing to talk maybe he would open up. "Brittany lives out near the forest preserve, and there's a riding trail by her house? Theo, it was so good to see horses again. Of course, it just made me miss Clover even more. I felt so lucky, knowing she was with you." No reaction; she went on. "You know, being back with my friends was cool. Still, I kept wondering what you guys were doing."

"Clover's got a friend now. You should have seen her with Researcher."

So, he really did go riding with Marian Joyner. She leaned forward, directing an inquiring eyebrow.

"It got too wet to ride anywhere except around your driveway. Standing in three days had that mare edgy. She's pulling on her crossties, pawing while I tack her up. Out the gate, and she's even higher. Then at the road she stops and arches her neck."

"Oooh, she saw the other horse." Bailey's hands flew up. She could just see Clover doing a double take.

"Yeah. Researcher stops, and she sticks one leg out and stretches for a polite snuffle. Ha, she's not so polite after that!"

"She went nicely in company at the sale." Too defensive sounding, maybe. Theo was coming around. Mustn't break the spell.

"Well, I just about had it with her. She nearly dumped me. She sideswipes bushes and then rears when I pull, and like I'm bouncing on a diving board. We never did all-out canter. That Researcher is incredibly cool, talk about manners. Even when she runs up on him, he's steady as a rock. No way was I taking your mare up the road, though, so we just went around on gravel."

"How come you didn't lunge her?"

"How could I? She could have slipped in all that mud. All there was, was that narrow driveway to work on."

"I guess. Good judgment. You did a good job, Theo. Daddy went nutso, thinking you thought you hadn't. You sure caused a ruckus at my house, bringing back your pay. You definitely earned that money, Theo. Giving it back was totally wrong."

"There's lots I did wrong." His face went dark. He turned away and wrung his hands.

"Ah . . . What really happened?" she asked quietly, and reached out to touch his hunched shoulder.

"See, I let Andy hold her one day." He ran his hands through his hair, shook his head in disgust. "I never thought that little cretin would take her out by himself. Here I was cooling it at home on the couch, and she was out running loose. When I saw that nose, I lost it." He pulled in a jagged breath. She prodded his shoulder encouragingly. "I didn't see anything wrong, at first," he went on. "I was just glad to catch up after calling and whistling and running all over the place." He dropped his head between his knees, mumbling, "You can't expect a horse to come like a dog." He turned, grabbed Bailey's hand and looked her square in the eye. "We had this great thing going. She'd look out and whinny whenever I came. I'd whistle back, and most times she'd whinny again, so cool, like we actually talked. I don't know, I guess that's why I thought she'd come."

"I can just see your mad dash after her. I would absolutely have panicked about the road."

"I thought of that right off. In case she turned back, I sent Andy to make sure the gate was wide open. And to collar Duker. What a good dog. Nothing was Duker's fault, I found out later. See, Duker was keeping his distance, just waiting in the shade. She pulled away to get over there. Andy says she got him in the face with her tail. Good, he deserved it. But *I* shouldn't have hit him."

"Huh?"

He dropped her hand, sent her a sidelong look. "Why do you think I was grounded, Bailey? Andy's concussion was from me."

"The ball—"

"I saw red and jumped in and stole it. After I left you that night? I was out of it, in a total funk. He was shooting baskets, bam-bam-bam! Totally unconcerned about the turmoil he'd caused, and playing! All those slam-dunks got to me. I was miserable enough about Clover's nose and Mom's garden. Then he starts whining, 'Give it here, give it here,' and I lost it big time. The little shit. I gave it there, but good. Drilled it straight up his nose." Theo jammed his fists into his cheeks. "This week at home," he said mournfully, "was supposed to teach me to control my temper."

"After all you'd been through that day—"

"I took it out on my little brother, that's my major problem. Geez, I still think all the time about chasing after her. He'd seen her in your yard, so I ran over there. Can you believe that moron took her out on your dad's new grass?! I guess you saw where it got torn up. Your dad must have had a fit."

"Actually, bringing your pay back made him madder, and—"

"There were tracks in the gravel so I raced to the road. Nothing there. I figured in the soft tar they'd have to show. Halfway back, I see some bushes that look crushed. It's like a marker leaps out, pointing over here. She would end up in a wild life habitat! I was insane. See, I kept thinking about you and what you'd do if something ever happened."

Bailey tipped back her head to bank her tears. A smear of clouds made the sky look gray. She spread her hands across the cool bricks, and her fingernail ticked the china platter. Oh. Well, Mrs. North could wait.

"I nearly died, tailing her to Mom's garden." Theo's eyes were narrow slits, as if searching for those tracks. "Then all I could see was . . . Well, you saw the mess."

"I felt so sorry for you. I was pretty sure her nose would be okay, but all your mom's work was done for."

"Yeah, and the fence got totally screwed. I saw where she went through but I didn't see her. I slunk along the edge, not to set her off in case she was in there." Theo kneaded the tops of his legs as though desperate for something to hold on to. "Some foreign shape off in the cornstalks"—voice cracking—"turns out to be her. No halter. I had that and the rope with me. I was shaking all over, scared she wouldn't stay for me. The way she sees sideways, even behind, is unreal."

"I know what you mean," Bailey said in a low hush. The dreadful scene swam before her eyes.

"I guess I started praying then. I was half-scared and half-mad, but I made myself keep going."

"Oh, Theo, I—"

"You should've seen the blood. She swung her head and sprayed it all over. Geez, I thought it was tomato pulp, tomatoes smashed all over the place. Man, did I ever scold her after I got the halter on. Naturally, I'd be the one who'd have to clean everything up. I'm leading her through the wrecked stalks and we're crunching what's left of everything and red stuff is gooing up the rope." He paused, eyelids lowered as if screening it all again. Bailey's knuckles tightened over the bricks.

"When I discovered it was blood, I almost threw up. I just told myself to keep walking and get her home. The flies were biting, and my head buzzed like they'd got in there." The brick's sharp edges cut into the backs of Bailey's legs. "I'd only spent all morning getting ready for you! Of course she had to run straight to her rolling spot when I let her out, so she needed a bath. Those pasterns sure don't clean up easy, either."

"Laundry soap works pretty good on the socks."

"Sounds logical, I should've thought of that. Then I still had to go over the tack and muck the paddock and all."

"Mud in her mane makes obnoxious dreadlocks."

"Yeah, I put the hose on her before the gunk got hard."

"What a bummer. She looked fine when we got home, though. Except for that booboo. It's lucky you got your dad on the phone."

"I thought she was gonna need stitches, but he said just wash it with a little salt in the water. Probably stitches would just rip out. You had those towels in the file cabinet, and I filled the ice-cream pail. Dad said to make sure it was completely clean, and that was a problem. Her nose looked worse every minute, like growing some gruesome fungus. I couldn't believe how she put up with everything I went through to clean her up."

Bailey shook her head in wonder, giving him a long, sympathetic look.

"That must have been scary. It's horrible having someone really precious in a fix, especially when the solution's up to you." She shut her eyes, recalling her misery when Clover was sick. She opened them, and saw the platter.

"Hey, you want a strawberry?" She swung the platter into her lap and crinkled back a corner of the see-through wrap. His amazement made her laugh. "It's for your mother, Theo. I guess one bite would be okay. After all you've been through, you need nourishment." He seemed to be in shock, so she lifted the plastic higher and plucked a tiny berry. Resisting the impulse to eat it herself, she popped it into his mouth.

He hitched up to her step.

She rotated the opening and nodded encouragingly.

He crooked his pointer daintily to his thumb and hollowed out a man-sized taste. The whipped cream shifted but didn't quite fill in the gap. Bailey opened the wrap a little farther and painstakingly extricated a little taste for herself. Sweet juice spurted onto the roof of her mouth. The biscuit showed now, and Theo's next sample included a smidgen of the delicate crust. He licked his lips and stretched his legs out across the steps.

"Geez, I'd already had her cleaned up once that day."

Bailey groaned understandingly. She idly picked at the platter to neaten the cavity. Maybe Mrs. North wouldn't notice. Ignoring a sharp click, she asked what Marian had to say about Clover.

"She says Ree-boy likes Clover." Theo had a Swiss army knife in his hand. To Bailey's astonishment, he sliced into the shortcake. He sent her a funny look with his hand hovering over two sizeable wedges.

"I guess we *could* each have a piece. Just one."

"'What a pretty mare,' she says, but that was before she saw what a witch your horse can be."

Bailey laughed with crumbs in her mouth. Giddy with relief, she couldn't stop laughing. Her cheeks ached, and she tried to swallow, then nearly choked when she saw Theo's creamy clown-mouth. "Probably Marian had on boots and breeches," she got out. He gulped, and his adam's apple jumped. His face was so red, she already knew the answer. "She had on that hot-pink, zigzaggy-stripey thing?"

He hooted. "Talk about distracting! There was this wiggling—"

"Oh, you . . . " She was laughing with her mouth full again and her cheeks were in pain.

"She's nice, though, Bee. There wasn't enough room in the middle to ride abreast—"

"Abreast?!"

Another high hoot. Then he explained how generously Marian had sidled into a rut to leave Clover on level ground. Also, she had told him about Pony Club. "We're supposed to bring Clover to Playday, since it's at her place this year."

"I don't know . . . Do you think we should? Your mother did mention it . . . A gymkhana, right?"

"Affirmative. That's games."

"I know that!" Whenever she thought of Playday, she imagined Clover racing to win. "Games on horseback does sound fun." She set the platter down and looked Theo in the eye. "You're still giving me and Glen lessons, aren't you?"

"Do you think it'd matter if I had another piece of your cake?"

36

Good Hands

TODAY WAS THE DAY. He hadn't said, but after yesterday's good talk, surely Theo would come. She had the snaffle-bit tee on he liked and her new, state-of-the-art helmet—a white micro-shell, with completely washable, adjustable padding and a quick-release buckle. It weighed hardly an ounce and had cost less than any of The Saddlery's other regulation helmets. "Cool," Glenna'd called it. Their eyes kept straying to the path, watching for Theo.

Clover's nose was in the tire, and Glenna was out there with the curry-comb, when Bailey went to check on the water-bucket. Still full. Not sick?! Brownish globs floated in the murky water. "Eeuw, gross," she exclaimed and rushed outside, gasping huge breaths.

But she had to face it, had to empty the bucket and wash it out.

She planted her feet and flexed her arms. This was a job for both hands. She pressed her lips tight and braced her back. The bucket was off the hook, being warily lugged across the aisle when her left wrist gave out.

Her panic-stricken shriek brought Glenna on the run, only to erupt in hee-haws when she saw the revolting mess on the floor, and down the front of the snaffle-bit tee.

"It's not funny!" Bailey wrestled with her shirt. She yanked it over her head and tossed it in the direction of the partly loaded manure tub.

"Your bra is absolutely soaked!" Glenna's hands dangled helplessly. "I can see straight through to your nipples! Theo would freak if he saw you now."

"That is the most insensitive thing I ever heard!" She started wiping down with a towel. The early morning air made her shiver. Luckily, her hair had escaped. But she didn't appreciate the smell coming off her. She turned her back to slither out of the slime-gooped exercise bra and, arms folded across her bare chest, glanced back at Glenna. The teasing expression on Glenna's face had contorted into one of horror.

Here came Theo through the dip on the path, the leering logo on his sweatshirt growing larger.

"Run, get me clothes!" She thrust the polluted bra at her dumbstruck friend. "Please, you've got to! And don't say a word!" She pressed the hopelessly inadequate towel to her chest and scooted for the hay. "Oh, hi there," she heard Glenna say, as if Theo were an everyday visitor. Sounding darnright cheery. Glenna hadn't a care in the world and *she* was crammed into the narrow opening between the back wall and the stacked bales.

She heard faint, measured sounds. Footsteps? Defenseless in her spider-hole, she held still, despite the sharp hay-shoots digging into her back. Definitely human, those steps. Clover had the run of the shed but would still be outside enjoying her breakfast. They were growing louder. Bailey squirmed further down and attempted to crush her springy hair. With luck, the hay stuck in it would serve as camouflage. She focused on some other obscure sounds, trying to detect what was happening. Her heart pounded so hard she could hear it. Had Theo come over to start her riding lessons? Something clunked—maybe he'd picked up the bucket. The chance of hyperventilating had her afraid to breathe. The bucket clomped down. Now some knocking noises. Her knees were severely cramped. She wished he would go outside. Why didn't he go outside and talk to Clover? A swishy, gurgling sound. He could be sweeping. No, scraping. It was the shovel!

Eeuw, a slushy plop. She squeezed her eyes shut, took shallow breaths, and squelched her urge to peek.

"Watch out there, Hasty." More muted, "Com'ere, Heather." Oh, good, he was moving away. She didn't dare look. She would die if he found her basically naked. An image rose of herself stripped bare, suddenly standing up. Theo without a stitch on, too. How absurd—the stress had her hallucinating. Standing up would be insane, even though both of her legs had cramps. She forced herself to play dead.

The footsteps stopped. She held very still, praying he couldn't hear her heart beating.

"You little dickens, did you miss me?" He wasn't speaking to her?! She had wanted him to come, and now she wanted him to go. If he discovered her sneaking around like some foreign spy it would be most unromantic.

More sweeping. She drew a cautious breath and stretched for a peek. He was wiping crud off the wall with their best towel. She ducked back down. She heard nothing for awhile and started extricating herself. Suddenly louder footsteps. She squeezed into a tight ball clamped in goose-bumped arms.

"Hi there, girl." It hit like a stun gun, right behind her!

"*Como está, mi querida Clover?*" He was right out back! Clover must be trimming the base of the wall again. "Let me see your nose. Let me see, *mi querida caballita.*" Dear little horse? She giggled at the baby talk. He let out a whistle. He'd heard? Her nose itched, threatening a sneeze. If only she could vacate this cave. What in heck was keeping Glen?

"You naughty little thing, running off and getting hurt. You made me very sad. *Si, muy triste.*" The way Theo broke into Spanish was fantastic. She held one finger under her nose, and made an effort to translate. "You made *mi querida amiga muy triste*, you made her cry." He was talking about her! The sneeze came with a rush.

"Bailey? You in there?" She froze.

A patter of footsteps came from the other direction. Just in time, she snatched her butterfly tee from Glenna and dropped it over her head. This would have to do until she found an excuse to go in and clean up. "Just a sec," she sang back through the wall. "Is it time for our riding lessons?"

"YOU'RE DOING FINE, BEE." Clover kept to an even pace at the end of the lunge line. Bailey felt like she was doing fine, until Theo had her drop her stirrups. Then she felt brave. Then totally pitiful when she tried to post. Already he had put her through *Propeller* and *Touch-your-Toe*, which felt peculiar on a horse but didn't loosen her up very much, she was so excited. She had thought the lunge-line would only apply to Glen. But her legs were Jell-O today—a little help here was just as well. She curled her fingers under the pommel and gave up on trying to post. "Just let your legs hang straight down," Theo'd said. Usually she sat on a horse like on a chair with her feet braced forward but, without stirrups, this worked better. Already she'd learned something. "Lighten up," she told herself, willing her bone connections to give.

"How's this, Theo?" The stirrups tapped at her ankles; Clover trotted serenely.

"Much better, Bee. Keep it up."

"Hey, I knew you'd be a good teacher."

"Well, it's kinda fun." He doffed his barely broken-in Arlington cap. "I'm like riding by remote-control. I get in a mind-set of being up there myself." He was quiet for a while. Bailey rocked to Clover's rhythm, pondering Theo's mind-set. He sure could be analytical. Her buttocks had softened into the saddle, and she was waiting for more approval.

"I was just thinking, if my dad *had* bought me a horse, lessons wouldn't have been an option. With you and Clover right next door, I've got the best of both worlds."

"*We* have the best of both worlds. You and me and Clover, in a golden triangle."

"Yeah, you could say that, I guess."

"The good things we do are golden, the way God wants us to be."

"Right."

She waited for additional feedback, expecting more enthusiasm for the golden triangle concept. Really, the three of them working so well together reflected glory to their Maker. Maybe he considered it a given. Going to church would make him more of a believer. She didn't go, but she had faith. She trusted God to watch over her. And Theo. And Clover. And her family. And Glen. Gammie's golden triangle concept was huge.

Muscle strain pulled her mind back on riding. With permission to retrieve her stirrups, she'd been introduced to the half-seat. Balancing with no saddle support required serious concentration. Precarious attempts at holding the forward position had her hovering, clinging to the mane for two, three, five unendurable minutes. After that, it actually came as a relief to turn the horse over to Glen.

The instructor went easier on the rookie, even when Glenna stopped two, three, four times a session to fiddle with her stirrup irons. Bailey kept the tread under the ball of her foot, like Theo said, but Glenna felt safer with it under her arch. Glenna's abundant hair never all fit under the old helmet, so she got a new one, covered with real velvet. For her third lesson she appeared in English paddock boots, buttery custom-made chaps, and little leather-palmed riding gloves. Theo's paycheck arrived in the mail, and went towards leather-thonged work boots and roughout chaps. He was awesomely patient, even with nit-picky Glenna.

"Not to worry," he'd say when Glenna fussed over her insecurities. "It'll come easier once you've logged some mileage."

Bailey's hips hitched forward automatically; Clover's legs trotted forward mechanically. Four sessions on the lunge line was quite enough, she thought.

"When am I getting off this dorky leash? These circles are boring, Theo. Clover must be dizzy by now. Shouldn't she be practicing straight lines, too?"

"We'll see," he said, with a meaningful glance at Glenna.

He looked so attractively authoritative with his gangly legs encased in those handsome chaps, she nearly gave in. But, "Come on, Theo."

"I'll tell you when you're ready there, Ms. Mason. Just keep your shoulders back. Eyes up. Heels down. You can't say you didn't ask for this."

The hours spent stretching calves and strengthening thighs built up the girls' endurance as well as the horse's. Theo came over whenever he could, and began bringing along Joshua Shapiro—the best rider in their class, Bailey recalled from her visit to One Oak.

"Hi, cool shirt, Joshua," she said. Big enough for someone twice his size, the tee had a school of fish on the front evolving into a flight of birds.

"Cool horse," he replied, sounding as if he really meant it. He climbed up on the fence after she was settled on Clover. With his dark mop and Glen's streaky twine, they could have been a pair of pepper and salt shakers perched on a shelf. It wasn't long before Bailey sensed that, behind that black curtain of hair, beady eyes followed her every move.

"Take it easy on that mouth," Joshua growled when she had Clover trotting. She'd been posting quite well, she thought, in her normal way letting her hands go up along with her torso. Now his remark had her bouncing like a beginner. Next minute, she jerked to a halt. Defiance glared off her face when she spun Clover around. Joshua flung back his hair and jumped off the fence.

"Basically, North," he called out, "she's agitating the bit. I could hear it jingling from here."

Her imploring eyes shot to Theo. But he seemed to have mutated into a zombie. In a moment, though, he came to, lolling his head and acting ridiculously silly to cover his embarrassment. He'd want to do everything right in front of Joshua.

"I suspected something funny was going on," he said, forcing a laugh. "Good hands are basic, Bee, and Josh has a point. She'll go better, like soften and flex into the bit, if you can keep your hands still. Get'er trotting again and try it."

Her spine had gone rigid; her arms bobbed like unlocked oars. A veiled peek confirmed those dark eyes pinned on her still, that back-and-forth swishing hair masking disapproval. Joshua must think she was hopeless. Oh help, he was saying something more.

"Try poking your fingers, Bailey-wailey," Joshua said kindly—lots calmer, compared to his outburst. "We've got to equitate those elbow joints of yours. Theo's been telling me about this lovely mare. She doesn't much like having her mouth fussed at, now does she?"

She smiled timidly. He was probably right. But how—

"Let's see you take just your pinkies off the reins," Joshua went on. "Jam those cute little pinkies right into Deekotie Clovie's pretty neck."

She laughed. He wasn't as conceited as she thought. But how was she supposed to steer with her hands jumping around on Clover's neck? She shot a glance at Theo. Oh. The lunge line would take care of that.

"Check it out, Bee," Theo said. "It could help."

Her pinkies hopped helplessly. Joshua was right. She wasn't doing as well as she had thought. She'd take his medicine, study equitation. Having jumpy pinkies was better than nagging a sensitive mouth.

What seemed like miles later, her elbows flexed naturally, her forearms virtually floated—at last her hands were following.

Progress was slower with Glenna, who needed major technical support. Anything new had the greenhorn tripping to a halt and wanting to talk. Theo never objected when Joshua came up to deal with the deep thinker. Besides, Glenna seemed to work harder for Joshua.

"Relax, Glen-friend," Josh would say when her forehead wrinkled with tension. His silly word-play helped to cut through her nervousness.

"You're thinking too much. Basically, Cappy says to ride like your seat is a half-inflated balloon."

"Gawd, it feels more like a sack of potatoes."

"Wrong!" Theo threw in. "With all this attention, you ought to feel like a princess!"

"Come on, Glenishness," cajoled Josh. "Loosen the reins and shrug your shoulders."

"I'm trying!" She gave a tinny laugh and began shrugging her shoulders and flopping her elbows and cackling like a chicken.

"Constant, quiet contact," Josh reminded, no longer kidding around. Just then Clover tossed her head and took a few choppy steps. Two squirrels were staging a boxing match in the tire. "Raise your hands when she raises her head, Glenny-wren." Minutes later, squirrels gone and Clover calm, "Put your hands down!"

"First up, then down. Give me a break, that's oxymoronic! Gawd, I feel like a moron up here."

"Nooo," Josh drawled. "Basically, it just depends on how your horse is going. At the trot, she normally holds her head still. But when she raises it, you raise your hands, too. You gotta keep *with* her. Make your forearm an extension of the rein."

"All it is," Theo volunteered, "is keeping a straight line from your elbow to the bit."

Glenna slowed to a walk with her eyes cast to heaven. "You boys are being intolerably picky."

"You think they pick on you?" Bailey hollered. "On me, they're relentless!" Glenna stuck out her tongue, and then she pressed Clover into a trot, a big fast one.

Josh looked startled. Swiftly he let the line out. As Glenna trotted on, he cocked a hip, swirled his hair. "Bitch, bitch, bitch," he shrieked dramatically, which worked, for the pupil exploded in braying laughter.

"You prick, Joshua Shapiro, I'm supposed to be a princess!"

"Thatta-girl, Glenny-friend. Your hands are following now." All the silliness had helped her relax. "You look quite decent!"

"How neat," she cried, "like holding hands!"

"Hey, Theo," Bailey yelled, "she's going so good can't we ride off the line now?" She had been riding off the line whenever the boys were not here, without mentioning it.

"Pretty soon, pilgrim. Safety's the bottom line, remember. No runaways, thank you. We're not making a horse that'll end up traded in, like some of those weekend riders. Besides, I like you right here in front of me."

37

Contact at Last

"JUST A SUGGESTION, TEACH. You don't need to stand out in the rain, you know." She'd mounted up in a warm drizzle, and was sitting Clover's even-paced, energetic trot so well, Theo had to see she no longer needed the lunge line. Their pals hadn't come today, making a perfect time for him to give in. She dropped her stirrups—this would convince him. Even with her legs dangling, the miles of practice had her weight evenly distributed through her seat and thighs, her hands asking and answering independently. The vulnerable wrist, released from its protective shell, along with the wet, slippery reins, had her using her back more than usual.

The drizzle had advanced to a soft rain. A thin stream of water ran off the beak of Theo's cap. "You're getting wet, Theo. Can't you just watch from inside the door?" He didn't need to be such a control freak.

"Not about to disturb a spider's progress." He cocked his chin toward the doorway's dew-beaded web they'd been careful to duck. "Anyway, it's not raining that much." He shrugged, and she imagined trickles down his neck. Ha, now he'd give in. "You do look good, Bee, at least from what I can tell in this cloud. Your hands aren't messing with her mouth."

"Josh says her mouth is really soft. I sure don't want to spoil it." The clouds were on the move, a patch of blue in the western sky now. Bailey sat easy, breathing deeply. From under the white peak of her helmet, her green eyes leveled serenely at Theo.

"How ya' doin', pilgrim?"

"She is so good today!" They were in the golden triangle, even without any sunshine. Her happiness bubbled. He was stepping forward, reeling in the line. The click of the snap jumped her heart a beat.

"Not to worry, we won't run away," she told his furrowed forehead. "I've still got a lot to learn. You know, like, when do I get to canter?"

Two days later, Joshua succumbed and let Glenna off the line. Now he'd trail after her, strutting about like Cappy with his elbows cocked and his hands jammed into his hip pockets. Theo didn't hover when it was Bailey's turn. He'd lounge on the tire or fool around with Josh and Glen, who'd position themselves cross-legged on the grass, face-to-face. Fiddling with his wiry hair, Josh hung on Glenna's every word. Just when Bailey thought Theo was talking to them and paying no attention to her, he'd be back on the case.

"Look up, Ms. Mason, not at your horse's neck! Nobody stares at the hood driving a car." She kept to the mowed area, and could be working on serpentines or cavalletti some fifty feet away when, out of nowhere, "Use your eyes!" Then, steering straight on, "Eyes between the ears!" She'd been a stiff stick-figure when they started out, but now her head moved as though it wasn't attached to an iron rod. The tips concerning good posture—shoulders back, tuck in your butt—hardly disturbed her, so preoccupied with the horse. Still, having Theo's eyes on her was pretty exciting.

One morning she was trotting her gazillionth circle for him when he flung his arm and shouted, "Take a trip around the pasture!"

In her excitement she took off without considering pace. The boys were yelling, but nothing registered. She was on her own, balanced precariously as the horse stretched into a mighty trot that accelerated going downhill. A branch loomed: she ducked that, and then veered off from the trees. She'd show them! She dug in her heels and braced her back against the mighty thrusts to rebalance for a turn. The trot turned even rougher, as if Clover had caught her excitement. Bailey was vacillating between sitting, posting, and two-point when the fast clip brought her forward, and suddenly they were cantering.

She was balanced over the horse's center of gravity when they crested the rise.

"Trot!" Theo yelled and kept bellowing as they surged up the fence line. "I never said to canter!"

She braced her back, twitched a rein, and the three beats converted to two. A big trot carried her the length of the fence and on behind the barn. Then, certain she was out of sight, she used her heel and let Clover canter again. The freedom had her feeling like a tiger sprung from its cage. She flexed her back to the rolling lifts, relished the power in her hands. Theo had started running in her direction and was waving his arms wildly. His outlandish panic only made her braver, and she opted for two-point. Clover launched into a hard gallop as she leaned forward. Her hands dove into the mane. The horse had taken over and was headed straight for the tire. What a disaster if she got dumped! The ground fell away as they took it in one stupendous leap.

"You idiot!" Theo thundered. He ripped off his cap and slapped it against his leg. "She's a turkey, riding forward. No cantering!"

"Or galloping, or jumping," Bailey muttered, as Clover carried her back up the fence line in a rollicking canter That jump was fun—well worth the near whiplash, and she'd stuck with the landing. She caught the exuberant rhythm and rocked in time. Approaching the spooky place in the bushes, she checked, but the horse kept on rolling, all the way down to the stone wall. Instinctive leg nudges tacked them away from protruding branches as they coursed back up past the line of poplars. Out of the corner of her eye she saw Theo fling down his cap.

"Sit!" he barked as they shot past him. "Ask and release! Pull and release!"

She could stop if she really wanted to, but the speed was all too awesome. Theo was running now. His face was purple.

"Hop off," he ordered the instant she had Clover settled. "Like now! I'm getting on."

"Tune her up, teacher," Josh hollered, earning a dirty look.

Bailey squinted at her irate instructor through suddenly stinging eyes. An abrupt, "Hmpf," erupted from deep in her chest when her feet hit the ground.

"She needs more schooling," Theo said in a strained voice. He hurried to reset the stirrups. "You gotta be tactful about that half-seat or she goes screwy."

"We were having a ball, and you had to go and spoil it!"

"Listen, I'm trying to keep you out of trouble!" The weight of their squabble charged the air. "Now watch!" he barked as he climbed up.

Bailey turned on her heel.

Glenna ran over. "What happened?" she cried.

"That bully thinks he knows everything!"

A WHITE SAILBOAT CURTSIED to the wind. Bailey wiggled her toes in the sand and gazed across the Long Island Sound to the opposite shore. She thought of Clover lazing in her stall, licking her salt block. Lifting her arms, she examined her new batch of molasses-colored freckles. "We oughta do this more often," she said, "and even-out our goofy tans." Her legs were white, also the tips of her fingers where they curled under the reins.

"Cool idea to take off for the beach, Glenny-wren." Josh smoothed back his mass of sand-speckled hair. "No question we can use the water-therapy."

Bailey grunted agreeably. She'd been so mad yesterday, she couldn't imagine ever wanting to be kissed by Theodore North. He sure acted stupid when Clover took off with her, like it scared him. Speed definitely was not his thing. But she knew what she was doing. And that jump Clover threw in was awesome. Bailey swished her arms through the grainy sand as though making a snow-angel. Basking in her triumph, she decided to be extra nice today and try to sugar Theo past the cold shoulder stage.

"Mom'll be at Collector's Item till four-thirty," she directed at the sky. "If she's not too tired, she'll take us over to see their new paintings."

"Cool, we get to stay here all day," Josh said. "Not that I want to lose my rider's tan." He shook his head like Duker did, spraying clingy sand on everyone in range. "Basically," he went on, "I count a rider's tan a badge of honor."

"Dittos, Shapiro," Theo was looking down at his flat, pink stomach. Bailey wished she could read his mind. Her stomach had a hollow feeling. His, too? "Hey, is anybody hungry?" he asked. She smiled to herself. Basic instincts would land them back on the same wavelength.

SHE STEADIED HER HORSE and sat quietly as her instructor painstakingly spelled out the proper way to cue up a canter. According to him, if Clover learned there'd be certain times for cantering, she wouldn't take off on her own so much. "Now would she?" he added with a sharp laugh. He was trying to make this no big deal, but the tightness in his voice told her that for him it was. Back to his normal self now. It had taken a whole day of water-therapy. At the art shop, he'd edged over in front of her mother's nasturtium splash and nudged her arm. "*Que talento*," he said, and she knew he'd recovered. The Spanish got aired only when he was in the zone.

Now he high-fived Clover's neck and stepped back, saying, "Try a little one, okay? Just around the tire here."

She sat deep and tweaked the reins. Her heart stuck in her throat, even though she'd cantered dozens of times when he wasn't around.

"*Muy bien!*" Right on cue, Clover had rolled into three buoyant beats, rhythmic as a metronome. "*Muy bien*, Bailey!"

"*Muy gracias, Theodore*," she answered sweetly, and cantered a broad circle around him. Then she propped to a halt at his feet. "Thanks to you, and the practices we've been sneaking in."

His glare was outrageous.

"Come down from there! Oh, man, I'm gonna wipe that shit-eating grin off your face!"

She laughed and clapped Clover's arched neck. Shrieking, "Oh no you don't!" she wheeled and cantered off. With her arms pumping and knees absorbing jolts, she let Clover take the rise in a hand-gallop. The wind in her face felt glorious. Glen and Josh applauded from the top rail. Theo stood with his arms spread, staring wide-eyed.

Ten minutes later, she was walking out with her stirrups dangling. Clover carried her head low, stretching her back and chewing the reins out of Bailey's hands. Theo was busy sweeping when she brought the horse in. He couldn't be mad, she told herself. There'd been a touch of pride in that wide-eyed look.

The husky, "Hi, hotshot," gave her a start. Her fingers shook unbuckling her helmet. It came off leaving her hair pressed into a shiny cap. She was acutely aware of how close he stood as he took the bridle out of her trembly hands.

She was wiping the reins down when he extended his arm to the wall, practically in contact with her shoulder. She could feel the heat coming off him.

"This is a good day for some more sun and sand," he said, leaning on his hand.

"Can't. Hay today, 'member?" She couldn't believe the trouble it gave her to complete a decent sentence.

"Oh, yeah." His eyes were deep purple pools. He stationed his other arm on her other side. Shoulder-blades pressed to the wall, she was drowning in his pupils. "You call me when the truck comes," he murmured, bringing his face closer.

She forgot to breathe. She waited, but just then Glenna burst through the door.

"That was an incredible canter, some pro you are, Bailey Mason! Right, Theo?"

One hand went to his cocked hip. "Unnn-believable," he groaned through clenched teeth. His face was red. Hers, too—fired by more than exercise. Her father had interrupted their first kiss and now, of all people, Glenna!

A horn tooted. Two minutes too late, Mrs. Shapiro had arrived.

Theo went back to sweeping after Glenna and Josh left. Bailey finished cleaning the bridle, then lingered to fiddle with the reins to make them dry straight. The spell must be broken, she thought, and fought to quiet her wildly beating heart.

"Guess I'll take off, too," Theo said, with what seemed like a question in his eyes. Suddenly shy, she could only nod. Then stood there feeling like a dummy as she watched him go. She had wanted the kiss. Sometimes she'd pat his arm or take his hand, when what she really wanted to do was give him a hug. Okay to kiss and hug Clover but not each other? Plainly, he'd wanted it, too. All it'd take was the right opportunity.

The right opportunity came up by surprise, before she even knew what was happening. They'd worked putting up hay through that afternoon's hottest hours. The driver slung the heavy bales to the edge of the flatbed, and left the rest up to them. Theo made it look easy, hoisting two at a time like suitcases. The twine strings cut into Bailey's fingers. Perspiration dripped from her nose. Why ever had she bothered to shower and change into her good shorts!? One unusually heavy bale would not budge until, on the count of three, they hoisted it between them and hauled it into the barn. Then the monster turned on them and morphed into a musty accordion in all directions.

"Geez!" Theo wheeled, gagging. He made a face and spit.

"Yuck!" Bailey coughed up dust into her hand. Clover wouldn't get this crud. She chucked the moldy slabs aside. Her wrist throbbed, but she went back for another bale, a tight one this time, neatly tied. Just to check, she dug in her fingers, and sniffed. This lot felt completely dry yet smelled like new-mown grass.

The flatbed was bare at last, and the barn stacked to the roof. Bailey paid the driver and came back carrying two paper cups and a cold jug of sweetened tea. In a patch of shade behind the shed, she set everything down in front of Theo. He had his shirt off and was using it to wipe his head and neck like he wiped down Clover after sponging her off.

He drained a cupful, resting his eyes on Bailey's face. Those blue irises, so intense.

She gulped hers down and filled his cup to the brim again. Settling next to him, she watched how he ducked his mouth and slurped. He gave her a look, those usually soft eyes blazing.

"You've got hay all over you," he said, and reached over to flick a stem caught in her hair.

"Thee-O!" The jug fell away as she popped to her knees and pulled her shirt out. The cup in his other hand had tipped. He was gaping at her chest. Distract him, came her first thought—wet, clingy fabric shows everything. "And so do you!" she squealed, and slid her hand down his arm. "See?" Her cupped palm presented a mishmash of hay scraps.

He took a colossal swig, the liquid dribbling from his lips. They were sitting very close.

"Save me a little sip?" she asked tenderly.

A funny smile spread across his face. He pitched the paper cup over his shoulder. All at once her back was pressed to the ground and that smile was closing in. Her heart raced to meet his kiss. It was surprisingly cold and wet.

Muffled screams bubbled up through the sweetness dribbling between her lips. He had her pinned so tightly, she started squirming. She kicked her legs, but then his legs trapped hers in a scissors lock. He was stronger; she couldn't move. This bright idea must have been building till he was about to burst. His lips pressed so hard, hers couldn't kiss him back. She managed to wrench one hand free, and then pushed hard against his shoulder.

Giving a frustrated groan Theo pulled back to let her sit up. While the revolving tree-line regained its natural space, Bailey wiped her hand across her drippy chin. Theo had a broad grin, clearly pleased with his ingenuity. He had seized the opportunity . . . but did he have to turn it into a wrestling match?

She sprang to her feet. Tightly gripped his hand in both of hers. Tugged. Kisses were supposed to be romantic. Those eyes sparkled with expectancy as he let her pull him up. That broad grin fell apart as she wound her arms around his neck and came in for his kisses.

38

The Lucky Clovers On Their Way

NEARLY EVERY DAY THROUGH the heat of August, one or another, and sometimes two of Clover's disciples, dedicated all morning to improving their riding skills. Bailey often saved her time until the cool of the evening. Clover would be keen to go again after her break from the morning's work, ready for the reasonable facsimile of musical chairs concocted out of Theo's rails. Bailey could cue an alert with a half-halt, then weight her inside hipbone while pressing her outside leg, and the horse would turn on a dime. Her father would often be seeing to his lawn then. Once, with Clover in a full gallop along the fence, she caught sight of him crouched on the other side, trimming grass from the base of a post. She cringed as hooves thundered inches from his head.

He jumped to his feet. She braced for an outburst.

When she looked back, he was watching her with his hands on his hips. That spurred her on and she kept up the speed. Then sent her horse into a sharp skid topped by a pirouette that popped them into their practice-stall.

Pleased with herself, she dropped her stirrups and jogged over to him.

"Nice going, Bee," with a high-five to Clover's neck. Indicating the dangling feet, he asked if she didn't want her stirrups.

"Not really. I can't use them in the relay race. Our stirrups need to be long then, Daddy, so everybody can jump on fast. My legs don't reach once I'm up, so I'm practicing without." She pulled on the straps and crossed her irons over the withers. Exulting in his look of astonishment, she trotted off without bouncing.

A few of her mother's paintings at Collector's Item had sold, one netting more than enough for Bailey to get a snazzy helmet-cover and some fine schooling chaps. Tan, top grain leather, piped in black. Then her mother purchased four white polo-shirts and embroidered four-looped shamrocks on them, tagged "Lucky Clover."

"Fabulous, Mom!" The logo was the same color as the watermelon-print helmet cover. "Cool," Josh said, fingering the curlicued letters. "*Ingenioso*," from Theo, "*muy professional!*" "Incredible," from Glenna. "At least I'll look like a pro."

A relay race. Apple-dunking. Upside-Down race—cantering in this one, the flyer said, but it shouldn't get too raucous because whoever came in last would win. A champagne ride; musical stalls; bareback dollar; a Grand March. With so many options, who should enter what? They had a readymade team for the relay race, and probably should each go in that. Plus maybe one other—not to make it too hard on Clover. Or them. Musical stalls sounded hilarious to Bailey. Indecision plagued Glenna. The idea of coming in last, still cantering, intrigued Josh.

"Basically, I go for a challenge," he confided to Bailey. She could identify with that; musical stalls sounded challenging. Still, maybe not as hard as convincing Clover to canter slower than everybody else.

"What about the Grand March?" Theo said.

"You go," chirped Bailey, "be our representative."

He sucked air with his teeth clenched, smiling. "It'd be an honor."

They had one more week. Summer was slipping away, and all too soon Clover would be left idling her mornings away while they were in school.

The mare was in top shape. A solid flank of muscle bridged her ribs to her hips; an inch of top-line muscle kept the saddle off her spine. Her grain had been upped to six quarts a day, shoes nailed to her hooves, and another component added to her tack.

Bailey smelled new leather when Josh presented The Saddlery sack. Her eyes lit up at the shiny halter at the top, then narrowed dubiously at the unfathomable collection of straps curled underneath it. The makings of a standing martingale, Josh explained. "Mr. Sebastian insists on martingales. The only exception, if you're showing in a fancy flat class. Some woman at One Oak got knocked cold when her dingbat threw its head. She was leaning forward, and whammo!"

The new halter was cool, but Bailey wasn't sure about the martingale. Theo had doubts, too.

"Shapiro, Cappy says a martingale is rarely, if ever, required."

Josh scratched his head, making the owl on his T-shirt nod sagely. "I thought, you know, in case she goes ballistic. This is a standing martingale, the simplest kind. She won't even know it's there, unless her head gets too high."

Bailey ran her thumb over the narrower strap. It had a buckle on one end, and the thick strap had loops on both ends. "We can try her with it," she said.

Josh made the necessary adjustments. "The nose needs leeway, to come up high as the withers," he explained when they tacked up. He raised Clover's muzzle to gauge how long to set the main strap. Even though her gash from the garden fiasco had disappeared into a tiny dimple, he handled her muzzle gently. Making little fussing noises, he ran the sturdier strap down from the back of the noseband, between the front legs, and anchored it with the girth. The narrow strap went around the neck to fix the main one in place with a keeper. Bailey could see how a martingale might lower the chances of anybody getting hurt. Clover was so agreeable, though, they didn't really need one.

When everyone arrived that Thursday, Theo called for a conference. Glenna was allowed forty minutes on Clover, and then they all flopped down with their water bottles. The lawn was thick and lush. Theo stretched his long legs into the grass, appropriated Bailey's lap for a pillow, and began.

"There's the logistics of getting there. Huh, just up the road? There's bound to be traffic and we can't screw up."

"Oh, let Bailey ride her," Glenna said with a yawn. "She's getting so good." Glenna massaged the small of her back against the ground. Sitting the trot helped loosen her up, but now she ached. Her head was propped on Josh's lap, and Bailey's head on her lap.

Bailey gazed up and watched the clouds waft. She'd only ridden Clover in the pasture. Riding in traffic would hardly be a good way to start out. She'd need to stay focused on musical stalls, if only for Clover's sake. It might be better to lead the horse. That'd be easier on everybody, and Clover wouldn't need to be tacked up all day. Trickling sounds shifted her gaze. Clover had come up to drink and stood gaping over the fence. Water dripped back into the tub from the corners of her mouth, as she focused in on the curious square with legs sticking out at each corner.

"She knows something's up," Theo said. He dug the rumpled flyer out of his pocket and smoothed it against his thigh. Then, "See this Clover? You'll get to meet some other horses!"

"All dressed up in your new tack," added Josh.

"Yeah, it'd be insanity to ride her bareback."

Fluffy clouds tracked the sky; the sun drifted in and out. Glenna shut her eyes against the glare. "A champagne ride sounds cool," she said. "I just might go in that."

"They might even let you drink some!" Josh's quip earned him a poke in the ribs from Theo.

"Don't count on it, Marian Joyner says those kids are really serious about horses. Pony Club introduces them to fox hunting, polo, dressage—hey!"

Theo swatted his ear, which Bailey was tickling with a piece of grass. "Also, jumping. Do you want to hear about it or not?"

"Sure," Bailey said. "I guess we should."

"They work on both riding and training, you know."

"Like us!" Glenna crowed. "We're a mini pony club."

"They're real fussy about stable management," he added.

"No more than we are," insisted Josh.

"They are, though. They have written tests." He spit out the grass Bailey'd tossed like confetti, then declared that the kids got rated. "They compete on their own level, beginner to advanced."

Josh covered a yawn. "It didn't say anything about ratings on the flyer."

"Maybe anybody can enter anything," Glenna moaned. "Gawd, I don't know if I should."

Glenna's voice reverberated in Bailey's ear. Would *her* echoes sound gross to Theo? No matter, he knew her so well now, knew how she'd all but melt whenever they kissed. Kissing Theo was magical. "I played musical chairs in Brownies," she said, watching his head wiggle with her every syllable. She swallowed a giggle. "It'll be cool on horses."

Theo pushed himself up. The girls' hands flew to their faces. Josh pinched his nose, whining, "Blow it out the other end, willya, North?"

"But listen, we've got it made!" Theo flailed his arm through the tainted air. "For the relay! I'll bet not one of those other horses will know all four of its riders as well as ours does."

"Clover will be great in that relay," Bailey said supportively. "She has a big fart." There were two beats of silence before the square exploded. Josh jumped up in a crazy dance. Theo clutched his side while crawling drunkenly. Glenna hee-hawed outrageously. "Heart, heart," Bailey wailed with her face buried in the grass. "Clover has a big heart!"

Her face was redder than her watermelon cap when she sat up. She rubbed the heels of her hands into her streaming eyes. Half laughing, half crying, she swatted at Theo, who'd begun wiping his eyes with her shirt tail. "You're no help, Theo, laughing at me!"

Josh blew hair off his face. The singular noise threw them back into hysterics.

"Quit it," Glenna sputtered. "I'll wet my panties."

"Why can't we just walk her over," Bailey blubbered, "like they do at the racetrack?"

"I don't know." Theo sobered. "Those huge vans—"

"The groom leads the horse, and all the people walk along, trainers and handlers . . . you know."

"That'd be good," Glenna said. "What about all our stuff?"

"Get her ready here," Josh proposed. "She carries the saddle. I carry towels and combs and stuff in the water pail, no problem. I hope you take that crappy-looking twine off, Bailey."

She picked at the blades of grass stuck to her shirt. No way would she let on how demanding the whole prospect sounded. She hated to change anything she and Clover were used to. That twine hadn't come off since Mrs. Knott tied it on.

"WATCH IT, CRETIN," SNAPPED Theo. They'd just started out when peculiar clickings came up from behind. Now Andy stood up from his banana seat and waved back his broad-brimmed hat. Dakota Clover carried on in her distinguished new halter with her nose bopping at Theo's shoulder. He spit in disgust. Okay, the kid deserved credit for leaving the dirt-bike home.

Bailey had taken the lead, a stack of towels clutched to her chest. Theo's work boots marched after her. The red bill of his Arlington cap pointed straight ahead, yet his eyes swung between attention to the footing and to the nicely rounded butt wagging in front of him. Bailey's legs operated like an old cowboy's. In the few days she'd worn her new chaps, the leather had broken in for riding but not for walking, and they refused to bend. He wouldn't kid her, though—today anything could set her off. Anyway, those clunky PVCs he used to wear weren't so great for walking either.

The little troop sidled over to hug the shoulder. Sunlight filtered through quivering leaves. Custer Lane had never seen such traffic, all headed in the same direction—mercifully, at a considerate crawl. These people knew something about horses. Glenna trudged along in her designer-jeans with her knees propelling a bulging, striped beach-bag. Shapiro carried his riding boots and a couple of helmets slung over his shoulder in a shopping bag. The white pail loaded with Clover's stuff must be pulling his arm out.

"Nice nag, there," someone called out. Clover tossed her crème-rinsed mane and showed the whites of her eyes. The continuous stream of traffic had elevated her walk into an energetic jig. Quite decent, considering. But now she stopped short with her legs braced at odd angles, and peered into the field of horses across the road as though longing to be over there. Memories of running with her herd had her ready to bolt.

A mindful tug and "Easy, there," helped the moment pass. No more jigging as Theo moved her along, but now a lofty jog. Joining the throng streaming onto the Joyners' estate gave him the sense of piloting a canoe through surging rapids. Clover's shod hooves clattered up the driveway, scattering flights of crushed rock. He muscled her away from a row of red geraniums, circumvented three long tables manned by adults. A number of horses were already warming up. A generation ago, they'd be dodging whipping mallets here, dashing after small willow-wood balls. Now blotchy shadows cast by the puffy clouds raced across the former polo field. More Greenham kids had horses than Theo would have thought: all kinds—Appaloosa; red roan; blue roan; bay roan; light chestnut; liver chestnut; dun; piebald; skewbald; black; bay; gray; palomino. Rope strung along a line of stumpy posts marked out the playing field. Clover strained her neck and humped her back as Theo navigated between the mass of scattered base camps. An awning-striped chair blowing end over end nearly clipped them and made her shy. *Once that bit's in her mouth*, he told himself, *she'll handle easier.*

"There's a good place," Glenna called out. She hobbled on ahead, weighed down even more now by the unwieldy pail.

"Hey, Shapiro. Register for me? The relay, and the Grand March!" Theo slipped his pal ten dollars, muttering, "I've got to get on before she explodes." Then, "Who's got the bridle?"

"Not me," Josh called back.

Bailey had run on ahead with Glenna. Clover jogged with her nose at Theo's shoulder, as he peered past the mounds of gear. Kids in breeches, jodhpurs, and jeans; horses in ankle boots and leg-wraps. He didn't see the girls. The striped beach-bag, at least, would stand out. Geez, they'd never thought of wrapping Clover's legs. She could get kicked, even by her own foot. They should at least have brought a first aid kit. Where was Bailey? He needed that bridle.

HER UNZIPPED CHAPS WENT flopping over to the big white water pail. Clover shifted about under her saddle and its fleecy pad, eyeing the strange horses and the even stranger goings' on. Theo needed the bridle. She was trying to focus on one thing at a time and push her own problems aside. Once he was up, Clover'd get to work off some tension, and maybe *she'd* feel better. She began pawing through the pail. The clean, buffed to gleaming leather, along with the meticulously polished hardware, ought to make the bridle stand out. She dug deeper and tossed out the soft body-brush, then the body sponge and the tack sponge, the black-bristled brush, the oval, rubber-pronged curry-comb, the unbreakable stainless-steel comb, and her mother's old hair-brush. No bit. No bridle. She couldn't believe it. She couldn't bear to look at Theo. She fished between the bottles of bug-spray and fly-spray, down to the pink hoof-pick stuck in a bar of saddle-soap at the very bottom.

She sent Glenna a desperate look. Glenna flung up her empty arms. Bailey stared into the vacant pail, then back at Glenna, who'd buried her head in the beach-bag. Helmets, sun-block, combs, brushes, water bottles, and a Ziploc® bag stuffed with moistened washcloths came flying out of the beach-bag. The corners of Glenna's mouth drooped as she rested back on her heels. Bailey stamped her foot. They wouldn't have packed the bridle in the beach-bag!. Why didn't someone hang it over their shoulder?

"Hand it over, Glen," she yelled on impulse. "Theo wants to get going."

"I believe that the bridle and the new martingale are hanging on their special hook in *your* barn, where *you* put them." The beach-bag took Glenna's irritated kick with a whomp.

"Not!!?"

"Oh, Gawd."

Bailey's eyelids dropped like the curtain after the last act. Never should she have sacrificed her lucky twine. She glanced at Theo, who was engaged in keeping Clover away from their and everybody else's gear. The mare had built up a light sheen of sweat, even in this breeze. Her ears were pointed antennas, her eyes bulging binoculars. A sharp gust interrupted a staring fit, and she started digging with her right fore.

"She's as eager as any polo pony to play," Theo called out. "Get a move on!" He swung the horse around and headed back over. Then his look of disbelief broke off a piece of Bailey's heart. The idea of running back home had her nauseous.

She began unbuckling her chaps. It struck her then that if Andy was here, Mikey probably was, too.

"Say, Mikey should be here! We can get him to ride your old bike back."

"No!" Theo's jaw was set. "Andy can do it."

Bailey stalled. No way could you rely on Andy. She searched for a sight of Michael and surprisingly found herself staring at something headed her way that looked like the Indiana Jones hat. "Andy," she yelled in a rankling tone. "Where is Michael?"

"H-how should I know?" Andy rolled to a stop and set one foot down.

"Hey, dude," Theo said, controlling his voice. "How 'bout doing a favor?"

"Why should I?"

Bailey sucked air. Her eyes strained for her little brother. But Andy was better than nothing, she supposed. And if she got in the way now, it'd totally humiliate Theo.

She took a deep breath, and began explaining about the bridle, pouring the words like syrup. "We can't ride her without it, Andy." The wide hat brim dipped sideways as the wary boy eyed his big brother. It tipped the other way, and he eyed *her*. "Please?" It practically killed her to beg this measly kid for help. "You'll see it as soon as you get there, right inside the barn."

"How about it, Andy?" Theo urged. "Ride back on your bike? It won't take you long."

"Give me a break, you guys. I just got here!" Andy juggled his handlebars back-and-forth.

"C'mon, bro, don't be a weenie."

Andy fidgeted with his hat. "Where?" he said offhand.

"On the far wall." Theo delivered Andy's shoulders an encouraging whack. "On the hook above the sawhorse, where we keep the saddle and stuff. Right to the left of Clover's stall when you go in. You'll see it. Hang it around your neck and come right back, *comprende*?"

Andy gripped the crown of his prized hat between his thumb and two fingers, then reset it perfectly horizontal. Bailey's lips were drawn back in a fake smile; she stared at the boy imploringly. If he didn't do this for them, he'd really be a shit.

"Can you go right now?" Theo asked. Andy had turned his head to gaze off into the distance. Bailey moved into his line of sight and shot him a thumbs-up.

"Huh, it's no big deal." Andy's tongue dropped in a fake puke. Then he stomped on the pedal.

"Oh, thank you," Glenna sang. "What a cute little guy!"

Bailey's troubled eyes chased after their make-shift savior.

"C'mon, Glen. We might as well register."

39
Nerves

A THOUGHTFUL LOOK AT some of the other kids in line drained the color from Bailey's face. Leather boots softly creased at the ankles; leather chaps softly creased at the knees; no tan beyond the knuckles. These kids were totally experienced. Maybe she shouldn't have come. *Their* team had riders' tans, too, but Josh was the only one with more than a few months' worth of experience. Are we having fun yet!? She wished she wouldn't feel so grumpy. This was supposed to be a *PLAY* day. Where was Andy *now*? For once, the sight of the #2 North son wouldn't make her see red.

"Check out these trophies," Glenna muttered in her ear. Sunlight glinted off the silver parade marching across the top step of the veranda. "About as close as I'll ever get to one of those."

"Who cares? We've got a real silver horse right here!" Clover would win a trophy like that someday. Someday when no one was out of sorts.

"You mean *you've* got." Glenna heaved a sigh. "Don't think I'm ungrateful. My entry fee's going down a rat hole, that's all."

Bailey gave a sharp laugh. "Lighten up, huh? Consider it a worthwhile donation, why dontcha!" On top of everything else, she didn't need grouching. A woman fighting stacks of flapping papers looked over and called her name. From under the brim of a floppy white hat, smiled Mrs. Knott. The qualms floated away as Bailey placed her ten dollar bill in the warm hand of her benefactor. Everything would be fine, with the guardian angel here.

On the way back to Clover and Theo, she bumped into another familiar face.

"Hey there, Red." She'd last seen Billy Calderone when they'd first turned Clover loose. How clueless she'd been back then, absolutely no idea of what to expect.

"Hi, Billy, how ya doing?" She wished they could sit down here and just talk.

"Good enough, how's that mare of yours?"

"Stupendous!" Bailey shot back, and took a few light-hearted steps.

CLOVER STOOD AT RIGID attention, her mane streaming out like a chiffon scarf, and the glossy new halter still on her head. She whinnied inquiringly at a horse on its way to the warm-up area, and Theo began walking her around again—likely as much to release his own tension, Bailey suspected. What a let-down, Andy not back. The little creep better not catch those reins in his chain. She stared hard toward the driveway, as if to conjure Andy up. The tables there were deserted. Her arms hung like lead as she huddled with Glen and Josh while the mainstay of their team tramped around their island of despair. The games would begin any minute.

A wide-brimmed hat and a little bicycle came weaving between the abandoned stations of gear.

"Hip, hip, hooray!" hollered Glenna and Josh as Andy pedaled up. He had the brow band over his shoulder, the reins and the martingale lashed across his chest like a Sam Browne belt. Bailey flung all her pent-up anxiety into the next hurrah. The kid had redeemed himself—Andy a hero! "Hip, hop, horse-shit!" Theo boomed ridiculously in time with the last salvo, and Bailey whooped. Good, *he* was riding high, in top shape to deal with whatever their star-player might pull. She got busy extricating their good

Samaritan from the precious bridle. Theo had his chaps zipped down and had changed hats, handing his prized cap off to Glenna. Now he checked the girth for the umpteenth time and pulled out his stirrups. Ready to mount, he reached out to give Andy's arm a solid punch.

"Good work, bro!"

TWO HORSES CAME OUT just when Theo was about to go in, and he veered off. Clover needed acclimating time within the ropes, but no way should she feel rushed. A ghostly white gray coming by missed them by a hair, and he cursed under his breath. Not a good start.

Her trot was choppy at first, down the long side. Theo darted his eyes defensively through the crush of dashing, spinning, and frustratingly slow-moving horseflesh. Clover pointed her nose against the martingale. Soften. Relax. Help Clover relax. Congestion wasn't exactly foreign territory to *him*—rainy Saturdays at One Oak could be just as bad. His eyes wheeled like a horse's, alert for trouble. Clover's prominent eyes picked up far too much. Peripheral vision was supposed to be protective, not distractive; this mare was all over the place, as volatile as a volcano.

"Chill, girl," he muttered, yet talking with his hands more than his voice. "Let me do the looking. Easy . . . eeeasy," he chanted into the alarmingly active ears. They shot past a grim-faced guy attempting to cramp his wired horse into a tight circle. Another horse, which appeared to be walking calmly, suddenly reared as Clover charged past. The rider went down, reins tight in her hand, and got dragged into the rope.

Theo kept up the sweet-talk. His own volcano could erupt any minute. He coaxed and crooned to hold her attention but, when a horse whooshed through his peripheral vision, up she went.

"Trot on," he barked as her crown bumped his chin, hard. He braced while her hooves pawed air, and whacked her neck. She remained vertical so he kicked, and got pitched into a bucking canter. *If Cappy could see me* now, flashed through his mind. *Just keep riding!* He kept checking behind, beside, all about. What horse was *this*? Not the one he'd been riding all summer. Even sawing the reins wasn't enough to soften this stubborn jaw.

Marian Joyner's father was watching from the sidelines. No sight of Marian, though—was Researcher entered? That horse was a made hunter-jumper, a pro at measuring strides—but at quick spins and sprints? Clover could do it all; Bailey had her sharp for musical stalls. This mare would be fine as soon as he worked the edge off.

"Hang in there, boy," Mr. Joyner hollered as they passed him in the weirdest, hoppy canter ever.

Theodore North and Dakota Clover were the last ones through the exit, dismissed from warm-up before they had time for a decent trot.

On solid ground again, his legs felt weak. He stripped off the saddle and the steaming pad. Glen and Josh toweled briskly, while Bailey wiped flecks of foam from Clover's lips. Galvanized water tubs were being hauled to the far end of the playing field. The announcer called horses in for the first heat of apple-dunking.

"I'm taking her out of here," Bailey announced. "Somewhere quiet. Thank goodness nobody signed up for apple-dunking."

"Be careful, she's a total nut today," Theo called after her. No answer, so he turned to scrubbing coagulated sweat off the girth. He or Shapiro should be handling the horse right now. But what could he say?

Standing about ten feet away, a boy even smaller than Andy held onto the reins of a handsome white pony with caramel-colored patches. A Pinto, or a Paint? The classification had something to do with coloring. When *he* was that age, all he knew about ponies was to sit in a big old saddle while the creature traipsed around a beaten track. The kid had on pressed jodhpurs and polished paddock boots. The pony's turn-out was just as sharp: a spiffy little saddle and full-cheek snaffle bridle. The kid yanked at his pony's head whenever it came anywhere near something to nibble. Then he'd rub his arm, like it ached. No doubt he had orders to keep himself and his pony clean, and out of trouble.

A whistle blast and then thundering hooves made Theo look up. Clover was hopping around like a tap-dancer, even though Bailey had her far off from the playing field. He tensed, dying to run over and help. He squeezed his eyes shut to squelch the urge. Better not go there, Bailey was sure to take offence.

The pony seemed to have given up. It stood quietly now, swishing away flies with its tail. The muzzle looked clean. Someone should have run up those stirrups. There was a big fly on its flank. Theo was trying to see past the colorful patches to analyze the little horse's conformation, when suddenly it jerked its head around.

The reins whipped through the air. The terror-stricken boy fell back.

"Whoa," Theo cried, along with everybody else, as they scrambled to get out of the way. The pony was leaping and kicking with its neck bent double. Theo stared, his fingernails digging into the tacky girth, as the possessed creature whirled. The stirrup-leather ran horizontal now, tight to the pony's impossibly angled head. Caught? Holy shit, the iron was hooked on the bit's jutting cheek-bar! The poor thing would have a heart attack if somebody didn't get in there fast.

"Heads up!" A tall woman ran up. Theo cringed, sure she was going to get hurt. Her hat went flying when she reached out and snatched the reins. Surprisingly spry for her age, the woman hopped and skipped up close to the whirler's shoulder. Her free hand groped back to work the cheek-bar free.

The tempest died down as quickly as it blew up. "Well done, there, Julia," someone called out as the woman smoothed her skirt. The courage and quick thinking had Theo awestruck. This old gal would be a match for that old goat, Sebastian. He picked at a resistant spot on Clover's girth, going over the course of events. Just a simple thing like running up your stirrups . . .

BAILEY DETOURED PAST TWO horses behaving like juvenile delinquents and didn't pull up till she had Clover nearly as far back as Brownie's little barn. Up close, it looked even prettier, the white paint showing through its shutters' silhouetted horse heads. Off by themselves, while Clover ogled the bewildering change in her world, Bailey gripped the solid withers and leaned her chest into the welcoming shoulder. This supposedly fun day was starting out wrong. She'd taken great pains to clean and polish the bridle—and then forgotten to bring it! And what was Glen doing with Theo's cap on her head?

Clover had her head in the grass when a rumble of hooves put her on alert. "Cool it," Bailey snapped, as much to herself, as the horse hopped around. It would probably be fun to watch the game, but she needed a time-out, they both did. The smell of fresh droppings drew her closer to the barn. Clover lowered her head again, leaving Bailey at ease. But then Brownie poked his head over the Dutch door, and her heart jumped. He looked so distinguished with his mane done up in braids—"Researcher," now.

The horse let out a tentative whinny, and up popped Clover's head.

Now Glenna came running. "How is she?" Glenna called out.

"Don't worry about her," Bailey shouted, suddenly tense again. "How come you're wearing Theo's hat?"

"Oh." Glenna looked bewildered. "I just kept it on so it wouldn't blow away while he was riding."

"Well, he's not riding now!" Incredible, upset over a simple hat.

"Do you want it?"

"No, of course not!" She jerked the shank and took Clover off again, not stopping until she'd distanced herself from everybody, including Glenna Munro. She fixed her eyes on Clover, who was staring back at Researcher. She'd begun to compose herself again when the mare gave a start. Out of nowhere, a camera.

"Don't take her picture!"

"Oh, Bee, she is so gorgeous."

"Watch it, Mother, you'll scare her."

Her father sauntered up. Clover remained vigilant while he pummeled her neck. "You'll be fine," he said. His hand was on the horse, but his words touched *her*. "Just a few games, girl. You're in for more fun than you've ever imagined." She got caught scowling at him, and managed a fragile smile. So, Clover had an imagination!? Cool, how Daddy smoothed things over.

She trailed along as her parents gravitated toward the excitement.

No equitation in apple-dunking—these kids played rough, jumping off *before* their horses stopped. One vaulted to the ground and sunk her teeth into an apple and sprang back up, all in one bounce. Her father laughed at a puny pony's gangly rider bracing her feet like airplane wings so they wouldn't drag. Bailey didn't see anything funny. That girl's expression was tight with stress.

"Loose horse, heads up!" A pony with its stirrups jingling and its saddle vacant came trotting through the crowd. Hands reached, but missed until the little palomino pulled up next to the taller strawberry roan.

"Good work, Daddy!" Her father had grabbed the reins as the two equines blew into each other's nostrils. A little girl dolled up in jodhpurs and paddock boots ran over and hopped aboard. "Well done," someone called out when the reins were presented. Bailey's father tipped his conspicuous hat and smoothed his carrot top. She looked around, wishing Theo were there. Clover was quiet now, nearly cool and ready to go again. With no idea of where she'd be going—which might be best, actually. "Ignorance is bliss," it was said. Her parents had moved on and met up with some people. Bailey fell back on her breathing exercises: deep inhales through the nose, gradual exhales through the mouth. Five times. Just a few pestering pinpricks now, probably normal for a day like this. There wasn't *that* much to worry about. Theo'd be riding first, and Clover always minded him.

40

In the Race

THE WIND RUFFLED THE saddle pad, whipped the mane in their faces, and it took all four of them to tack up again. Theo swung his leg over just as the rules came rattling out of the loud speaker. Clover's eagerness blocked out the details, but he did hear that intermediates were to run first. That didn't leave much time for a warm-up. But relay races were his thing, so there shouldn't be a problem. He'd run plenty—on foot, anyway, and intermediate here would just be trotting. The other horses doing their warm-ups were cantering, and he let Clover canter, too. She moved out beautifully, and tuned in even to the point of helping when he got pitched to one stirrup. A split-second after a chunk of turf snagged her hoof, she hopped a half-step to switch back under him.

"Good girrrl!"

The organizers were pulling wads of fabric out of an enormous box. Not clothing!? He hadn't heard anything about changing clothes. He scanned the crowd for a sign of Bailey. The pink polka-dotted helmet cover was easy to spot, if she had it on.

She did; he could see her buckling her chaps on, too. Circling back, he shouted, "What's with those humongous rags?"

"We've got to wear that!" she called back as her unzipped leathers came flapping towards him.

299

"No way. She'll go nuts!"

"I kno-ow. They should have told us there'd be costumes! But it's only trotting, Theo. She'll be good." Bailey forced a sturdy zipper-tab over her muscular thigh, then looked up, saying, "If she breaks into a canter, remember, you have to go back and start over. Don't let her get too wild."

"Yeah? In your dreams." This could turn out worse than riding in back of Researcher. He hadn't seen Marian and wondered why. After all, it was her place.

He was ready when the five, four-man teams were directed how to line up: mounted horse on the starting line, two team members behind, and one on the other side of the field, who'd be hanging on to the costume. The horse would take one run with its rider out of the costume and five more runs in the costume. Theo's face sagged into a grotesque scowl. All that changing in and out of clothes? Clover would never put up with that.

Before the announcer had finished the horses began jostling for places. Theo tried for the outside track but ended up one over. He took a firm hold, to indicate *no cantering*. Or *galloping*. At least they'd get one run for Clover to see what the deal was. Bailey stood a few feet back, then the team's light-weight, Shapiro, who'd ride last and make up for any lost time. If things went according to plan, they had a chance to win. Clover looked as fast as anybody else in the line-up. Glenna waited on the far side with a scarf and something blue rippling like a flag. A dress? Shit.

Clover was high at the whistle but minding well enough. Theo vaulted off as they trotted across the end line.

"Don't pull the skirt down, Glen, I need my legs!" The dress was so baggy it slipped right over his head.

"Hold the skirt up!" She flipped a scarf around his neck as he jumped back on. The scarf surprised him as much as Clover, who wheeled and took off at a run with her back as rigid as a surf-board. Even severe, one-sided rein-jerks couldn't convince her to trot. Bailey held her arms open as if welcoming home a soldier from the battlefield. The flapping scarf was getting to Clover, and now a nervous buck twisted Theo off balance. The stiff-legged landing whacked him with the saddle. Then three high-flying bucks turned the scarf into a whip, the skirt into an unpegged tent in a windstorm. He could hardly see through the gauze clinging to his face. A horde of hooves pounded past with an unearthly roar, and Clover dipped her shoulder.

The whiney whistle sounded miles away. Blurred shapes; running feet; far-off voices. Dimly, a wavery watermelon. He would have raised up if the rock on his chest didn't have him pinned.

"Just had the wind knocked out," he heard as he gulped for oxygen. "Six more like that qualifies him for the Prince of Wales Club!" He hazarded a deep, jagged breath and tried to push himself erect. It was embarrassing to lie crumpled while everybody else stood up.

With Bailey on one arm, Shapiro on the other, he made it back to their spot. A woman ensconced on a camp chair looked up from her knitting to ask if he was alright. A few swigs from the water bottle would fix him up. He lowered himself to the ground shakily, let Bailey press a moist washcloth to his forehead. Clover was coming with Glenna. The mare had stood for Glenna to walk up and take the reins! He would have thought Bailey'd want to catch her. Awesome, she'd run to him instead.

"That's enough racing today," declared Shapiro. "I had my doubts, but at least nobody got hurt. You all right, North?"

"Affirmative. See if Clover's okay and get back on for me?" Mainly, only his feelings were hurt. He tried to ignore the emotions swimming in his gut. Bailey understood: her small hand had slipped into his hand's inviting cave. He leaned back on his elbows and, swiveling his head between the excitement on the field and the performance Shapiro was cajoling out of Clover, began to unwind. Someone near them mentioned *musical stalls*. A paunchy woman in a floppy red shirt strutted in front of the camp chairs, raving about her daughter's horse.

"Musical stalls will be a breeze for my Darlene and Midnight, didn't they win at Hartford? Against better horses than this!"

Bailey rolled her eyes. "Thank goodness that's not like most easterners," she said into his ear. Clover was cantering sedately now. This was good. After the control required by the best-in-slow-cantering event, she'd be keyed in for Glenna. That girl needed all the help she could get.

"Too bad musical stalls doesn't come right after the upside-down cantering thing," Bailey said gloomily, staring at her polished work boots. "She'll be going good then. Glen'll probably just louse her up."

"Shapiro's got her looking at things, getting acclimated. By the time you get on, Bee, she'll be settled. You'll do great!"

"I hate waiting. My stomach's in knots." She patted her tummy as if to console it. His had settled, but his head still ached. "I might as well take off my chaps," she said forlornly. Theo had a lump in his throat. It wasn't like this girl to be so glum. He took her hand again and didn't let go while she used her other one to unbuckle and extricate herself from the tight-fitting leathers. She needed to know he was there for her. She needed to think positively—for the horse's sake, as well as her own. He wasn't going to let this spill trouble *him*. Even experienced riders bit the dust. He wasn't sure if he wanted to qualify for the Prince of Wales Club, though, whatever that was. He could ask Cappy. Anyhow, the Grand March would be orderly. He and Clover would get a chance to shine.

"Are you going to be okay to ride again?" He started in surprise. This girl was right inside his head!

"That's affirmative, Bee! Hey, check out Shapiro."

Clover was traveling in a rounded frame. Josh sat erect with his shoulders level and ears, hips, and heels aligned, his seat lightly brushing the saddle. Quite a pro in his trim white shirt, rust-colored breeches, high black boots, and the hunt cap hiding his hair. Walk-to-halt, then trot-to-halt. The small crowd gathered there was getting a show as his patient, methodical, imperceptible aids gained ever sharper transitions. Clover's quiet snort came with her precise canter depart. Josh took back briefly, released some, then legged a surge and allowed the vigorous stretch for a round or two before he collected again. He slowed the pace for a longer spell, prolonging the studied lifts with a firm seat and leg. Clover's white pasterns angled so low her tail nearly dragged on the grass.

"Awesome, right Theo? Practically sitting on her hocks!"

"*Muy affirmative.*" He'd recovered, and Bailey was happy now. She shouldn't object if he put his arm around her waist. Aah, *muy simpatico.* Their mutual arrows of strength and faith shot to Clover. If the mare behaved this well in the implausible test to come, she'd beat any horse here.

The crowd regrouped when the horses were called in. Bailey grabbed Glenna's hand as the three of them ran to the rope. Clover stood poised at the far side of the fourteen-horse lineup, set to spring. Theo clenched his teeth. In this mob, she might be too much even for Shapiro. Radical—a race awarding the last one in.

The scuffle at the start was so confusing, he lost sight of her.

"Collection is not exactly her strong point," Bailey groaned as the hooves drummed up the field. She bounced up to her toes. "Do you see her, Theo?"

"Now I do, way back." That reddish-hued horse couldn't be anybody else. "Man, those haunches get a work-out! Cantering this slow is probably the hardest thing she's ever had to do." He counted six horses trotting; three already across the finish line; five still in the running.

"Gawd, with a rump higher than her withers, that back-wise balancing is too damn—"

"Shush, Glen!" Bailey hissed. Theo felt fingernails digging into his arm. Their know-it-all should know to zip her trap.

The end was close. All they knew was that Clover had still been cantering. Shapiro had her headed their way now, sitting easy with the reins looped over two fingers at the buckle. From his other hand fluttered a blue ribbon.

"That was sooo good," Glenna crooned, running up. "You are unbelievable!" Josh's eyes sparkled like black diamonds.

"Awesome," Bailey exclaimed. Theo shot up a high-sign. Bailey had let go of his arm, and he figured she'd be running to Clover. Instead, she stepped to one side, away from the horse. She stood with her hands gripped behind her back while the stirrups got reset. Glenna was frowning, no doubt worrying about the trouble people got into with champagne.

"Mount up and just walk around, here," Shapiro said off-hand, plainly doing his best to help his Glenny-wren relax. "*Ne quid nimis*, Magic Munro, nothing in excess."

Still frowning, Glenna pulled on her gloves. "Confidence-wise," she moaned, "I suck."

"Not to worry," Theo volunteered. "Nothing'll wipe out that win she's got under her belt." Glenna's tanned face had turned a pasty white. Buckling her chin-strap was taking forever.

"You guys pray for me. Pray whatever I do doesn't end up with Clover in disgrace."

"Take heart, fair Glenna," boomed Shapiro. "Less is more, remember? *Multum in parvo*. You'll stay out of trouble if you just sit quietly."

GLENNA WAS SITTING QUIETLY all right, her back ramrod straight. Bailey scowled; no, she wouldn't look. *She* might even turn out worse. She picked up her chaps and buckled them on, experiencing today's standard amount of worry-pins when she tacked *herself* up. Put them on, take them off; she'd been doing it all day. Enough already. Soon she'd be able to focus on her horse and not think about herself.

A muffled buzz came from the loudspeaker. Barely inside the gate, Glenna reined in, curled over Clover's neck like a banana. The horse stood still while an official handed up a brimming plastic goblet. Glenna switched the reins to her right hand and reached out with her left.

"Too bad that isn't real champagne," Theo remarked. Bailey gave a short laugh. So far, so good. She'd be glad when this was over.

"Move along, everybody walking now," called the announcer. Rounds of encouragement rose from the people gathered along the ropes, many parents among the helpers. Clover stepped out, and precious liquid spattered down Glenna's pretty chaps. Stage-fright had wiped out every ounce of practice: she could not sit up. Bailey heard a plop, then more plops as goblets started to drop. Glenna still had hers in hand.

Josh pushed hair back from his face with both hands. "Look where you're going," he hollered, with his lips pulled back from his teeth. Clover wandered toward their section of the rope as Glenna stared into her sloshing goblet. A few horses meandered around the ringmaster. Horses' rumps got bumped, yet their low-keyed reactions showed them merely bemused by the muddle. Glenna wasn't the only one spilling; they had never practiced neck-reining.

Eight goblets were history, eight horses halted in the center and out of the way. A "Trot, please!" sent the disorganized herd into a hesitant pitta-pat. Nobody wanted a fast trot. Clover had sashayed sideways, clearly eager to move out. Glenna's lips were set in a grim line. She yanked the reins, and more champagne spilled. The shallow party glass wobbled. Bailey had turned to ice. Josh hopped up and down as if on a leash. If only he *could* run out there.

"Turn your cup hand into a gyroplane," Josh shouted. Clover trotted past two other horses with her passenger crouched in the half-seat, the reins in her stomach. "Heads up," growled a guy intending to pass. The ringmaster threw his arm at a contestant still walking and Clover sprang as if a whip had snapped.

41

Priorities

CLOVER STOOD QUIETLY IN the middle of the ring. Glenna slumped with both hands on the pummel while the survivors went through what seemed like miles of cantering rounds. At last, all the champagne was gone and the horses filed out.

"Gawd, I'm sorry," wailed Glenna, as Bailey ran up and snatched the reins. Her dismount was more of a slide, still clinging to the saddle. Her face looked blotchy, on the brink of tears. "I rode so rotten. Really, Bee, I lost it and couldn't do zilch! She started getting frisky—"

"Yeah, you screwed her up," snapped Bailey, half under her breath.

"Gaa-awd—" Glenna quit stripping her gloves off and reached—

"Look out!" Bailey ducked, thrusting herself between the woeful girl and the instantly wary horse. Josh stepped up to drape his arm across the shrinking wren's shoulders. Bailey caught Theo sending *them* a sympathetic look, not even looking at *her*. Okay, so she was a bitch—that didn't matter now. She muscled Clover's rump aside and aimed for the stirrup. No way was she pulling out.

The chaps wouldn't bend. An *Oomph* erupted when her foot missed the tread. The horse's tentative backing made the next awkward aim hit air. She gripped her reins tight to the pummel and hopped after the moving

306

target. When her toe did hit iron, it poked Clover in the ribs and made her jump.

"Thee-o!" She was so rattled now, she needed a leg-up.

In two giant steps, he'd snatched the reins. His steely blue eyes leveled to her visor.

"Chill out, girl!"

She froze, smarting like his words were a slap. The whirling tops in her helmet whined to a stop, even though he was shaking her shoulders back-and-forth.

"Come on, Bee." Incredibly, he didn't sound mad. Blindly she let her forehead find its way to his staunch chest.

"I'm so nervous, Theo."

"Hey, musical stalls will be a blast." He turned Clover by the bridle. "You'll be okay once you're up there, trust me. C'mon, I'll give you a leg-up."

Her knees wobbled. She gathered her reins and forced the left one to bend. For a moment she was afraid he had backed off.

The lift was exulting. The horse's warmth came through as her seat and legs settled in. Clover got a "Hi-there," cuff to the neck as she rearranged her reins. The solid boost had been Theo's best leg-up ever. And now he was singing!

"BEE . . . what you wanna BEE . . . " She pulled in a deep breath, and then let her hands go forward. She never knew Theo could sing.

THEY MOVED OFF SMOOTHLY. She rolled her shoulders, rotated her neck, caught the rhythm and posted. Clover was tuned in, clearly happy to be moving out. Theo was right—the planet looked so much better from a horse. Here she was, part of an equine world she never even knew existed. The familiar smells and noises—one saddle squeaking, four hooves thumping—were all about, multiplied. The kids called back-and-forth and laughed as they patted their horses' necks. Musical stalls on horseback might not be totally scary. After all her hard work in that weird cantering race, and then the champagne fiasco, it was time for Dakota Clover to have fun.

Cantering with the other kids was awesome. Bailey hummed along blissfully and let her head bob with the downbeats. The organizers had begun dragging fence poles from behind the ropes, and arranging them like straight stalls—two long rows set back to back. She navigated toward the ropes, and now Clover strained against her martingale. She talked and stroked to ease the tension, trying to transmit confidence. The layout was a lot like they'd practiced.

The contestants were directed to enter at a walk, traveling clockwise. Bailey kept her eye on the petite woman wearing flowered cut-offs, who held the whistle. She twitched her reins for a priming tweak. They'd be ready when that whistle blew.

The shrill blast threw everybody into a muddle that made riding in single file impossible. Bailey maneuvered to the inside, straining through all the rumble for the next whistle. She would simply die if they were the first ones out.

She was traveling so close to the ends of the poles, Clover began treating them like cavalletti. They had rounded the end cone, and were one speckled pony away from a stall when the woman in flowered cut-offs got inspired to blow. The speckled pony wheeled, just as Clover snuck in. The speckled pony reversed again and beat out a horse twice its size farther up the line. A sudden wave of panic seized Bailey, it'd been so close. Then they were off again. The whistle caught them hustling between stalls. She kicked, and a desperate plunge landed Clover in the far one. Her blood pumping with victory, Bailey sat tight as another pole was dragged off the course. Clover craned her neck to peer over the field. Bailey did a quick search for the intrepid speckled pony but didn't see it. Clover chewed her bit, ever as keyed up as she was.

They made it through the next round, and again the next. A few hairy experiences as the mob got ruthlessly thinned convinced Bailey that rushing ahead at the whistle worked better than reversing. They hugged the grid, and Clover switched between hunching her haunches and stretching her neck against the martingale. Bailey switched between hastily slithering in her reins and throwing them loose. The horse's quick response sent thrills. Clover could dash, weave, slide like a stock horse, or stop on a dime.

"Go Clover—Go Clover!" echoed in Bailey's ears. The crowd was roaring, her helmet about to explode.

The next break lasted long enough for her to catch her breath. The field had narrowed to four, all four sweat-darkened flanks heaving like bellows. Clover was up against a rangy, chalky bay; a husky black with an enormous head; and the speckled pony. The tall boy on the rangy bay had on loose coveralls and rode swinging his legs out front, letting his reins droop, and grinning. His horse must really like games, she thought. Well, guess what? Hers did, too. And her father would be so proud—

The whistle sent the four survivors into a vital glide with their eyes on each other. There were three stalls now, ten feet apart, with the bright yellow end cones set farther out. Two stalls opened to the west, one to the east. No whistle, but suddenly the horses were tearing through whirls of dust again—all together, as if on cue. Anyone closing in on an opening throttled down until they practically had their horse trotting in place. No whistle, so onward the flying hooves. Bailey leaned forward from her knees and worked her elbows like a turkey taking wing. The broad-shouldered girl on the black grimaced as if in pain. The pony's pudgy rider brandished a crop that wouldn't quit. The tall boy on the bay rode leaning back, slapping his flapping legs along his horse's shoulders. The husky black was terribly close, right on Clover's tail. Coming down the other side, the harassed pony nosed out the bay. Clover pulled away from the black and, as they rounded the north cone, Bailey chanced a look. The black's short ruff stuck up in the wind like a mohawk. The pony's little legs churned like egg-beaters. She surged with outrage—those red streaks on the pony's flank were blood!

"Come on, Bailey," her father cried at the top of his lungs. "Come on, Clover!"

A hard gallop carried them up and down the grid and around one cone after another for five circuits while listening for the whistle. Clearly, that woman in the flowered cutoffs wanted them worn out—only a truly fit horse should win. Bailey reexamined her tactics. She was trailing the pack—a lucky position, or not? Her horse had speed. Height and a lean frame gave Clover an edge over the chunky black and the quick-footed pony. Maybe even over the rangy bay.

She dug her knuckles into the withers. "Go for it, girl," she growled. Pure momentum was the key. Clover sprang and, leaning in, swept past the yellow cone at the north end. Headed south with her ears on pivot, she swiftly passed the bay. She rounded the south cone and passed the pony. No whistle, not until, heading north again, her tail whisked past the last pole.

"Hurry!" "Right behind you!" "Go around, go around, the other side!"

The black got caught heading south, unopposed. Now, unless Clover reversed in a flash, the pony and the bay coming up behind her had it made. A quick weight-shift and a fierce leg produced an instantaneous spin, just as a splash of red shot under her nose. Tears sprang to Bailey's eyes. The crowd was screaming. She squeezed them shut to keep them from running over. The crowd was hysterical. She gulped a sob. They were yelling for Clover! She opened her eyes, and gasped. The hounded pony was on the far side of the pole. Those little legs had never stopped!

Another set of poles got dragged away. While two stalls were being set fifteen feet apart, midpoint between the distant end cones, Bailey shot a triumphant look across to the girl on the stocky black. That girl sent back a furious scowl. Bailey patted her valiant partner's sweat-soaked neck. They had made it into the ribbons, and could actually walk home with two blues!

She scrubbed the seat of her pants not hidden by her chaps to wipe the sweat off her hands. She ran her eyes over the crowd for Theo. He was with her parents, their eyes beaming back faith and hope. The petite woman with the whistle had turned her back. Bailey shuddered. Her destiny depended on a mere whim.

The horses were directed to reverse, and sent to separate corners. Clover sauntered to her designated spot exuberantly. A little cloud slid under the sun, casting a shadow. The whistle caught Bailey off guard, but Clover jumped even before her cue to sprint right past the bay. The crowd went wild as she drew closer to the black. "Come on, Darlene, get your ass in gear," broke through the din. "Go for it, Bailey, Go for it, Bailey!" Then four more runaway, agonizing rounds before the whistle caught all three bunched within feet of an opening. Bailey felt Clover check yet kicked her on. A stall in the clear waited on the other side. As they scrambled around the end cone, a jolt shot up her spine. The next stride was even worse. Something was wrong.

"Hang in there, sweetie," she gasped. They still had a chance to win. But the tossing head and dipped shoulder were calls for help. She vaulted off on the run. The last two contestants looked on with stunned expressions as she dug in her heels and tugged hard on the reins.

"HOLD IT THERE, RED!" Billy Calderone ran up as the valiant mare staggered to a halt. Now Theo and Glen and Josh were here, with her father right behind them. He turned her roughly by the shoulder.

"You threw it," he croaked. "You were winning!" Bailey reeled; her head was hot and light. Didn't Daddy know—

Billy's hand went up like a stop sign. "Hold on, we've got trouble." Clover wheezed, radiating heat with her weight supported on three legs. Billy grabbed the suspended near fore.

"We're screwed," Bailey heard, and her heart dropped. The near fore's shoe was mangled, bent into a horrifying "S." Her father still had hold of her shoulder, squeezing it now as if to shore her up. Her eyes burned; she tried not to cry.

Theo slapped the side of his head. "Geez, she must have grabbed it taking that last cone."

Glenna sobbed into her cupped hands. "That p-poor leg," she hiccupped.

"Grabbed it with a hind," Billy said in a tone of wonder. "Coulda ripped the whole hoof off."

Bailey's forehead pressed into the horse's sweltering cheek. They deserved to win—Clover had done everything right, more than anyone asked for. "Isn't there anything we can do?" she wailed. Her wild eyes stared around. The bay and the black stood by, pouring sweat and breathing as hard as the mare. The stewards had their heads together. For a moment, hope soared. If a time-out was called while they got that shoe off . . .

"Better get her out of here," Billy said. Clover had started hopping about on three legs and thrusting the disabled hoof against his hand. Billy released it, and she started pawing up turf.

"Oh don't do that," moaned Bailey. Theo stood close with a sympathetic hold on *her* neck. Her hands shook so much she surrendered the reins.

THE MUCH-LOVED MARE LIMPED off the field with Theo. Joshua moved in to loosen the girth. Glenna came bearing towels. Billy tested the twisted shoe. Bailey's hands itched to get in there and work it loose.

"Is there anything I can do to help?" Julia Knott inquired. Her face paled when she saw the mangled shoe. "Won't it loosen, Billy? I'd like to see this mare in the Grand March." Bailey sent Theo a hopeful look. He looked so glum, his heart aching as much as hers. He had been counting on getting back on again, if only to erase that spill.

"When we get this stupid shoe off," Bailey was saying when Billy broke in.

"'Fraid this needs tools, ma'm."

"Righto. Fortunately, we have Elmer Klachner here on standby." She had last seen the farrier easing into a lounge-chair up by the house, she added, with a look at Theo.

Bailey took back the reins, and Theo took off to round up the farrier. She managed an appreciative smile for Julia Knott, whose face drooped with sympathy. "Elmer Klachner will fix you up, dear girl," the woman directed at Clover. The crowd was cheering for Darlene and her invincible Midnight, when Julia Knott left Bailey with a supportive grip on her arm.

Bareback Dollar got underway. Jeers and jolly hoots went out to riders struggling to anchor slips of paper by their various body parts. A horse totally bareback milled about like it'd lost its best friend. Stray slips fluttered about like butterflies, but a white corner of Chuck Calderone's poked out from under his thigh. Billy came to life.

"The dude's riding his tail off!" Chuck had to lean back with his legs extended so his high-heel boots wouldn't catch. "That's Copper Penny he's on, the pony your poppa caught for Sissy Ludlow?"

"Really?"

"She headed straight for your mare when she got loose."

"Funny, but right after that Clover settled down." Bailey sighed. Clover had been so happy to find a friend.

"Penny's been-there-done-that, she'd know what to tell a greenie—much too much horse when I first saw her. You made out good, though. You gave Darlene Bond and her gamer a hard time. It's not where you place but who you beat that counts. You got mighty close to beating the famed Midnight, our regional games champion."

There was a rowdy cheer, surprisingly for Chuck Calderone.

"We're rich!" Billy exclaimed, and took off at a run.

Josh glanced up from swabbing Clover's flank. "Obviously you would have won if she hadn't grabbed that shoe. Give me the reins till the farrier comes? I need to tell her how great she was for me."

Bailey's head buzzed with burning sensations. She was trying not to fret, at least not until Elmer Klachner had a look. She scanned the crowd for a familiar loping walk. She couldn't look at Glenna—not up to a decent apology just yet. She felt weak now, and needed to sit down.

A butterfly touched her toe and fluttered on by. She leaned back, transmitting the kiss to Clover's hoof, and sighed. Her spot of ground felt welcoming. She loosened her collar and shook her shirt loose from her back. Her helmet popped, coming off like a suction cup. She ran her fingers through her hair, opening paths to refreshing air, then dragged the beach bag into her lap. She had Glenna's packet of lilac towelettes open when her parents came up.

"Don't feel too bad about not winning," her father said, clearly trying to hide his disappointment. "Your horse brings home a blue today, quite a feat for her maiden flight."

"Here comes Theo," her mother said. "Oh, I hope Clover will be all right."

Bailey jumped up. Her heart called out to the gnarly old guy trudging after Theo.

"What's the problem?" The farrier's piercing gaze fixed on *her*, even though Josh was still holding Clover. Surprisingly unable to speak, she pointed to the horse's near fore, propped on its toe. While Elmer Klachner's educated hand ran down that leg Theo and Bailey stared with their shoulders hunched. Grunting with the effort, Klachner turned the hoof over and set it on his knee. His low whistle broke the silence. Bailey held her breath while his knobby fingers prodded the sole of Clover's foot. Those last jerky steps were critical. If only she had pulled out immediately.

"Is she going to be okay?" her father inquired quietly.

"Might be. All 'pends on what weight put down. Might be strained lig'ments. Get this bridle out of the way." Glenna had the leadshank fastened to the shiny new halter. Taking it from her, Bailey got a lump in her throat.

She owed her friend an apology. She didn't deserve to win anyway, she had been so mean. And she had put her horse through lots worse than anything Glen ever did.

"Lotta fight in that mare," Klachner said. Clover wouldn't let go of the bit. Normally it dropped when the crownpiece pressed her ears, but now her teeth held on tight. Bailey moved in and coaxed a disconnect with her thumb, feeling rather like a traitor. The horse's whole body was still fighting to win.

Klachner took up his pincers and nipped out the remaining nails. Firm pressure eased off the deformed shoe. The team hovered supportively while he leaned the heels of his hands and thumbs into the exposed sole, as though his sinewy arms channeled critical data. "Some heat in there," he said, and set the hoof back down, muttering, "Might be common, all she done today." Straightening back up, he locked his eyes on Bailey. "Good you pulled up, girl. No blue's worth going lame for."

She stole herself for what more he might say, then was surprised to hear her father inquire if it wouldn't hurt to take their horse in the Grand March. "They're not planning on anything more than a trot in there."

Bailey raised her eyebrows to Theo. He so needed to ride again.

Elmer Klachner paused with the weighty tool caddy at his knees. He set it back down, took a few steps off, and turned around. As if the mare was asking for consent, she swung her head his way. "You got plenty hoof there," Klachner said slowly. "Jog 'er out fer me."

42

A Grand March

"SHE WORKED SO HARD for me, Glen." Bailey wriggled her shoulders, burrowing her head into the lumpy beach bag.

"I guess! It takes true spirit to beat out a seasoned game horse, which she absolutely would have!" Glenna had her hair down and was combing vigorously. The boys had taken Clover off to eat grass. Once Elmer Klachner watched her jog, he'd set to rummaging into his caddy. Then a bit of rasping, hammering, and he had a new shoe on. It hadn't taken long, but every crack of the hammer stabbed Bailey in the stomach. Today's stress had her exhausted, yet she couldn't rest. Not until she apologized. She lay back, and sought to blot out the thought.

"She's amazing, Glen. Her hoof caught a divot or something and knocked me sideways. But she threw in a hop then—awesome, like on purpose, just to save me."

"Because she loves you. You must feel in a sort of purple, velvet-lined ecstasy."

"Uh huh." Glen always understood. True friends considered your feelings, but here she'd let her best friend down horribly. "Li-isten," she got out, and sat up to grip Glenna's knee. "I am totally sorry. Believe me, Glen, I'd never want to hurt your feelings. I was a total wreck and didn't even know what I was saying. Oh, I am really, truly sorry."

"Gawd, I forgave you ages ago."

"It kills me to think I'd be so rude to my best friend. All your coaching . . . Daddy would never have believed I knew enough to take care of a horse if it hadn't been for you. And, your little lectures at the sale about lameness and economy of motion really impressed him. If it hadn't been for you, we might not even have Clover!"

"Gawd, but you can lay it on. Thank you, though." Glenna dropped her comb. "Those guys have picked up some girl, look! She's got on dove-gray breeches and a windowpaned riding jacket with a collar the same color as her hunt cap, outrageously purple, and—"

"C'mon, Glen!" Bailey lumbered to her feet. "I think I know that horse." That big brown horse with the girl was Researcher! The girl had to be Marian Joyner.

"Here comes our Bailey now," she heard her father tell a stout man who wore his hair combed over his bald spot. "Honey, say hi to Mr. Joyner, the head honcho here."

The man's crooked smile and teasing chastising for tearing up his field put Bailey at ease. She liked Mr. Joyner immediately. But his daughter? With that fancy outfit and conceited smirk? Whose painted nails were scratching Clover's shoulder as though she owned her!

A glance at Theo found him leaning on one foot and gazing at Marian as if he'd discovered a longlost friend. Josh eyed Marian quizzically. Even though she had two years on him at Sage Hall, he probably knew who she was. Josh cockily flipped his hair, remarking this hunt cap must be the only "fee-yeeuu-shia" one in Greenham.

"I feel good in fuchsia," the fashion-plate declared, batting her mascaraed lashes. "Off-beat colors are taboo in showing, but you can wear anything today." She whisked a bit of chaff off her sleeve, and volunteered she would be leading the Grand March. "That's why I'm dressed up and Ree-boy's in braids." Josh rounded his mouth, rolling his eyes from Glen over to Bailey, who wasn't sure what to think. Marian did sound kind of snotty.

Mr. Joyner was rocking back and forth on the balls of his feet, and talking to her father about Pony Club. "You ought to look into it, Phil. The membership fee includes insurance, a first-rate deal. We backyarders stick together, right?" His pocketed hands stretched his pants across a protruding middle as he ran his eyes over Clover, who appeared ever as beautifully composed as Researcher.

Marian's thick eyebrows perked at Bailey. "Philip's your father's name?" The question floored Bailey. She checked for Theo's reaction, but he was busy with Clover, straightening the bridle's noseband, sliding strap-ends into their keepers. "Philip means 'lover of horses,'" Marian explained. "I was just wondering—"

"He sure loves our horse."

"Your mare's a natural for Pony Club. Does she jump?"

Bailey's face lit up. Clover was a jumper, alright. "Uh huh, we've done a little," she replied, surprised to hear herself sound shy. She'd heard about this girl all summer; meeting her at last had her a bit undone. She grabbed at Glenna, now intent on adjusting her dark glasses. "Glenna Munro rides, too," she blurted.

"Oh, yes. Wasn't that you on Dakota Clover in the champagne, ah, party?"

Glenna quit fussing with her shades. "I can't do zilch one-handed," she said, pulling on a stray hank of her hair. "Unbelievable, my boo-boos out there." All three laughed a little. "That's a cool outfit, Marian," Glenna got out, clinging senselessly to her hair.

"Utter turmoil, that's games for you. Pop wouldn't let me take Ree-boy in anything today." The expressive eyes turned on Bailey's father. "Parents get involved in Pony Club, too," she said. "You're a horse-lover, Mr. Mason?"

"As far as this one goes, Marian. People say horses are stupid. Certainly not. This little lady kept me from looking like a fool after I lost my head at that sale, that's a fact!"

"That was far from foolish, Daddy."

"You picked that mare up at a sale?" exclaimed Mr. Joyner.

"God's-honest truth." Mason swept off his hat and fanned his face. "Hate to admit it, Jake, but I had no idea back then what I was letting myself in for."

Mr. Joyner laughed like he knew all about it, and then they all laughed.

"Let me shake your hand, sir." Theo reached out from holding Clover. "Thanks for letting us all come here today," he said with sincerity as they shook.

"Here we go, Ree-boy!" Marian tweaked a rein and flashed her Joyner smile.

Bailey ran over and hugged Clover. "Good luck, Theo, have fun," she called out as they rode off.

Her father was still talking to Mr. Joyner when Julia Knott strode out to the center of the field. The tail of the robust woman's blouse flapped loose from her skirt as she waved the horses in. Researcher came first, his proudly arched neck outlined by a row of tiny white dots. Another big horse with a ripple of fringe along its neck followed a few paces behind, and then ponies and all the rest, gradually increasing in size, back up to the taller ones. Marian sat Researcher's exuberant trot with elegance. Clover's conspicuous coloring made her easy to spot. Traveling strung out, she carried her head unusually low, nearly touching the turf. Just needs to stretch, Bailey told herself, still floating from her pleasant encounter with Marian. It seemed like they might be friends. Seeing her horse in the same event as Researcher and what must be Greenham's entire equine population made her feel blessed.

"Evens to the left, odds to the right," shouted Julia Knott, swinging her arms like a traffic cop. An earthy fragrance wafted across the field. Bailey peered through the line streaming back and spotted Clover on the far side. Her heart caught. Clover was carrying herself nicely. Right—she simply needed time to warm up.

Julia Knott motioned to a steward, who ran in with a megaphone. "Spacing," rolled out . . . . "Four feet behind . . . And up the center in pairs!" Stirrups clinked as the horses squared off. Clover traveled in a rounded frame, her neck arched ever so handsomely as Researcher's. Bailey trained her eyes on the bobbing dappled rump; on Theo's upright shoulders and the redder-than-tan nape of his neck. She wrapped one arm around her mother and the other around Glenna, who wrapped one arm around her and the other around Joshua.

"I feel like I did watching you in your first school play," her mother whispered in her ear. "Think how far you and this horse have come." Bailey grinned. And how far her preconceived notions had come. Five months ago she had arrived in Greenham, never expecting to like it so much. Never expecting all the attention to detail and hard work and mutual understanding it took to bond with a horse. Not unlike making a new friend. She let her face go silly.

"Inch by inch, right, Mom?"

"Exactly," Glenna chortled. "We just kept chugging along like *The Little Engine That Could*."

"Chugga, chugga, chugga, Glenny-wren. We are the four parts of a smooth-running engine."

"Totally with horse-power, Josh," amended Bailey.

"And, waaalk," Julia Knott intoned. She adjusted her hat and hastily tucked in her blouse.

Researcher's lofty trot leveled into a neck-rolling stroll. Clover's frame rounded even more; the way she practically piaffed, lifting and trotting in place, raised a lump in Bailey's throat. The mare had surpassed herself, had come through unscathed, even willing to carry on. If only Theo . . .

She was off picturing them riding together, each on their own horse, when she caught a bit of the conversation going on behind her. Mr. Joyner was saying that Marian would be off for Switzerland soon, to take her fifth-form year abroad. Arrangements for their horse were up in the air. Bailey slumped, gazing out at Marian and Researcher. Now that she'd finally met the girl, she might have had someone to ride with.

"We're looking for a hand with transportation, Phil, plus a goodly amount of experience. Researcher deserves to stay home in his own barn." Bailey's forehead wrinkled. Billy or Chuck might want the job. They had transportation, if their truck held up. What about *her*? She certainly lived close enough to make it work. But where would she find the time? She'd never take anything away from Clover, even for Marian's horse.

"Jake, we were in the same boat. Luckily, the neighbor-boy knows our menagerie pretty well. He snapped up my offer. You met him, Jake—that kid jockeying our mare now, Theodore North?" Bailey stopped breathing. Her father was brilliant.

"Marian will be back in time for the spring shows," Mr. Joyner said slowly, as though thinking hard. "She'll want Researcher in top shape. It'd be a plus to find somebody who rides."

Bailey's mind raced. Theo would be perfect! They could ride out together! Greenham had miles of trails. Even if they landed in a tight spot, like needing to detour around a downed tree or cross a rocky stream, they'd have each other to help make it through. Riding out together would be so romantic. She slapped her forehead. Had Mr. Joyner seen Theo fall off?

"As it happens, Phil, I noticed the kid right off. He had a lot of horse under him, but he knew what to do. Too bad about that spill, however." Bailey bristled. That spill was totally Clover's fault, and you couldn't blame her either, sent into such a crazy game. What? She couldn't believe her ears. "I'll have a talk with that kid," Mr. Joyner was saying. "See if we can work something out."

Julia Knott had her troop trotting again. The late afternoon's long shadows formed surreal silhouettes marching along in step. The two lines came together to sweep into one wavy stripe that stretched the entire length of the field. Bailey welled with quiet excitement. A reverential hush had settled over the crowd, and a cadenced thumping came through. Now the leaders swung around again. Researcher's ears were cocked, and Marian was smiling at her.

Polly Thompson was married with two children before she was a horse owner. Besides participating in suburban New York and Connecticut horse shows and Pony Club events, she furthered her Cornell University-Nursing School education with courses in horsemanship and stable management. Thompson coached young and adult riders and school groups in dressage, jumping, and hunt seat equitation. After she and her family moved from the East Coast to the farm her husband, Peter, bought in southwest Minnesota, she broke and trained the offspring of her sport horse breeding program, conducted clinics, and judged horse shows. Polly Thompson lives with her husband in Mountain Lake, Minnesota, and Palm Desert, California.

www.horsesandheartbeats.com